Operation Silver Star

Jennifer Haynie

ISBN:
978-1-943398-26-3

Other Books by Jennifer Haynie

Last Chance Series

Operation Shadow Box
Operation Peacemaker
Operation Music Man
Operation Javelin

Unit 28 Series

Panama Deception
Loose Ends
Uncommon Vengeance
Orb Web (short story)

The Athena Trilogy

The Athena File
No Options

Other Books

Exiled Heart
Hunter Hunted

To those who are able to rise above false accusations and forgive.

Blessed are those who are persecuted because of righteousness, for theirs is the kingdom of heaven.
—Matthew 5:10 (NIV)

THE TEAM

Victor Chavez (call sign One) – Team leader, former Special Forces captain and Secret Service agent, owner of Sentry Securities, Flagstaff, AZ

Suleiman al-Ibrahim (call sign Two) – Sniper/observer, former Hezbollah sniper, Chief Financial Officer of Sentry Securities, Flagstaff, AZ

Sana Jain al-Ibrahim (call sign Three) – Breaking-and-entering specialist, former Olympic gymnast and cat burglar, owner of Pause Café, Flagstaff, AZ

Shelly Wise (call sign Four) – Computer and security system specialist, independent computer contractor, Flagstaff, AZ

Butch Addison (call sign Five) – Mechanic/escape-and-evasion expert, former Special Forces soldier, currently owner of an auto mechanic shop, Flagstaff, AZ

Diana Kasem (call sign Six) – Doctor, former Army cardiothoracic surgeon, currently practicing cardiothoracic surgery, Flagstaff, AZ

Fiona Mercedes (call sign Seven) – Pilot, former Army helicopter pilot and CIA contract pilot, owner of Kitchen Sink Air Cargo, Flagstaff, AZ

Skylar James (call sign Eight) – Procurement officer and disguise specialist, former CIA agent, currently owner of Regions Café, Flagstaff, AZ

THE SUPPORTING TEAM

Deborah Chavez – Wife of Victor Chavez

Anna Fields Chavez (19) – Oldest daughter of Deborah

DJ Fields Chavez (17) – Only son of Deborah

Gracie Fields Chavez (11) – Second daughter of Deborah

Marie Fields Chavez (10) – Youngest daughter of Deborah

Jace Choi (39) – Physician assistant in Amal, Iraq

Libby Holt Mansour (39) – Teacher in Amal, Iraq

Northern Iraq

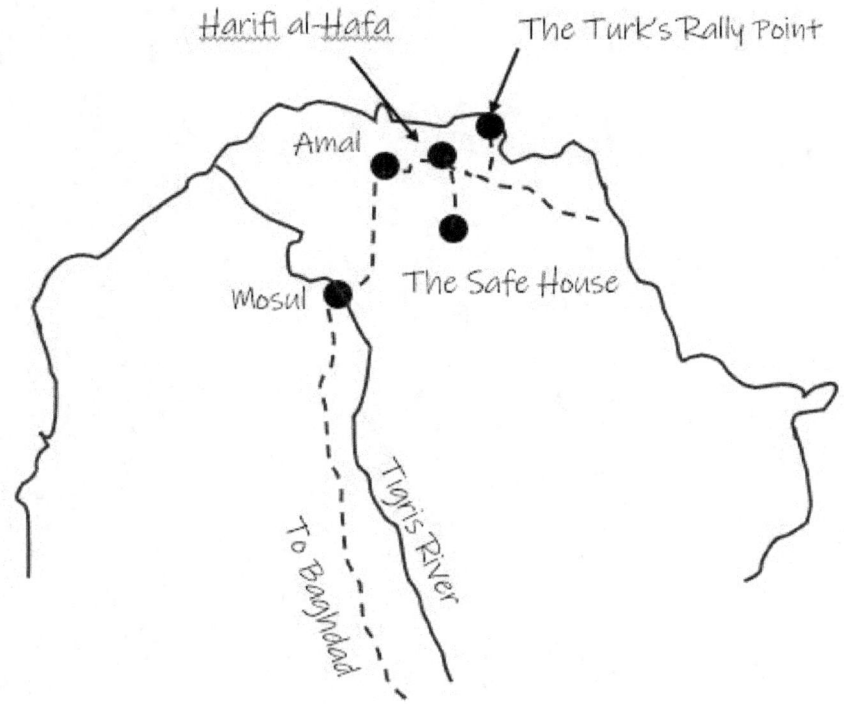

Harifi al-Hafa

The Turk's Rally Point

Amal

The Safe House

Mosul

Tigris River

To Baghdad

1

Wednesday, July 3, 2019, 0300 hours local time, Amal, northern Iraq

A small noise awakened Libby Holt Mansour. Moisture dampened her cheeks. She'd cried again in her sleep. With an impatient thrust of her hand, she brushed the tears aside. Wouldn't be the first time or the last. Over the past five years, she'd lost count of the number of times that had happened. After one last sniffle, she took a deep breath. Lifting her head from the pillow, she listened. The sound didn't repeat itself.

Nothing moved in her small house. No hum from the fridge. No glowing numbers on the clock. No power. So typical in the Zagros Mountains of northern Iraq.

Libby slipped from the warmth of her quilt. Summer nights at altitude got chilly, and she was grateful for the long-sleeved T-shirt and leggings she'd worn to bed. She slid open the drawer of her nightstand. Her fingers found a mug holding pens. Charger cords. A couple of books. Then a cylindrical object. She pulled out the heavy-duty flashlight Jace had recommended she buy shortly after her arrival eighteen months ago.

She flicked it on, and its strong beam guided her to the bathroom. One flip of the switch confirmed what she already knew. If she were lucky, the local power company would restore the electricity by this time tomorrow.

Libby stepped from the bathroom. Angling the flashlight toward the floor, she shuffled down the short hallway to the front room of the house where the kitchen lay to the left and the living room to the right.

The edge of the light caught a flash of movement. Her breath hitched. She angled the beam higher.

The walls rippled like living creatures.

A man knocked the scream from her throat. The flashlight spun end over end, and she skidded across the top of her kitchen table. A chair clattered to the floor, and her oven door cracked as she crashed into it. She slumped to the floor.

No one would take her. She hadn't nearly died five years ago to face death again.

Libby screamed and could only pray her cries made it through the windows she'd opened to the night air. She scurried toward the other side of the kitchen and wrenched open a drawer. It fell to the tile. Silverware clanked and scattered. She snatched up a knife and threw it. And another. Anything she could grab, she sent sailing toward her attackers.

A man yelped.

Another raced toward her. She hurled the drawer last.

He knocked it aside. Wood splintered against the wall, and his hand brushed the sleeve of her T-shirt as she ducked under his arm.

If she could make it to the back staircase leading to the flat roof, she could jump to safety.

"Libby!"

Jace. He'd heard her.

She hesitated.

Another man shoved her into shelving, and her back hit the boards. They gave way. Pictures crashed to the tile. Books pelted her, and a heavy ceramic jug cracked against her skull. Stars sparked.

She sagged to the floor.

Get moving!

Her limbs refused to obey the frantic orders sent by her brain. The sound of flesh on flesh barely registered.

White-blue light seared her vision. A man cried out.

"Jace!"

One of her attackers took hold of her ankles. Her T-shirt rode up as he dragged her into the living room. The coarse weave of her area rug scraped against her back.

Another electric arc. Another scream. Jace moaned.

"Don't hurt him!" Libby kicked at her captor. She reared up to bite him, only to have her wrists caught by another and pressed to the rug.

The man who'd caught her ankles landed across her hips, effectively trapping her to the floor. "None of that, Libby Mansour."

His finely accented English flowed across her ears like honey. *He knows my name?* She tried to bite the man who had her wrists.

The man across her hips barked something at his comrades in another language. A meaty hand pressed down on her forehead. The sour stench of sweat brought bile to her throat. "Let me go!"

Her cry sounded so weak.

More groans from Jace across the room.

Another electric streak. His cry chilled her.

She squirmed. "Don't hurt him anymore."

The man on her hips leaned forward. "The more you fight, the more he will suffer."

She gagged at the garlic, onions, and whatever else he'd had for supper. He yanked up her sleeve, and alcohol flashed cool across the hot skin on her forearm. A needle pricked.

She moaned at its sting.

He issued another command, then rose.

Her wrists came free, and the pressure on her forehead released. She rolled onto her stomach and stared.

Her neighbor and friend lay still. Too still for her.

"Jace." That came out in a ragged whisper. Libby crawled toward him. The floor began tipping as she reached for his hand.

No reaction. No nothing.

Please don't be dead. Please! Her limbs didn't seem to work. Whatever they'd injected had already impacted her brain. Her head swam.

Jace didn't move.

As she completely collapsed, she curled her fingers around his.

3

"Jace." His name died on her lips. The room spun out of control. Her fingers relaxed, and her hand slipped to the floor.

Strong arms lifted her. More words surrounded her. Not English, her native tongue. Not Arabic and Kurdish, her adopted languages. Foreign words that sounded vaguely familiar. Within seconds, it didn't matter.

Thursday, July 4, 2019, 0600 local time, outside Amal, Iraq

High in the Zagros Mountains of northern Iraq, Makmoud Hidari crouched with his back against the outside wall of a sprawling villa that served as a safe house. As he contemplated the events of the past twenty-four hours, he tapped his phone against the palm of his hand.

Granted, kidnapping Libby Mansour had held its own twist when her friend unexpectedly rushed to her rescue. His men handled it most excellently. They took him down but didn't kill him, per Makmoud's direction to avoid collateral damage. Libby had fought, but from the information he'd collected on her, he'd warned his men she was a fighter. If she got a little banged up, no worries. It happened. Just don't assault her in any way. Anyone who did would face his wrath. His men knew better than to cross him.

Makmoud's lip curled as he straightened. His knees creaked, and he winced from that and the cement wall scraping his back. Once again, he found himself serving more as an errand boy for someone else rather than the person who gave the commands. Perhaps after this job, he would re-establish his status among the *Quds* force, all by helping Paul LaRue achieve his supposed dream.

Which, of course, required a few problems to go away.

Makmoud muttered in Farsi under his breath as he contemplated his next move.

Everything hinged on how Butch Addison would react. A smile curled Makmoud's lips. Butch was tight with Victor Chavez, and he counted on him building a case to rescue Libby. Victor generally listened to his deputy.

If he didn't? He still had the five million he'd requested from Paul LaRue. Right now, that money resided in a Geneva bank account, ready to transfer to the Iranian *Quds* force after he accomplished his mission.

Thing was, he'd promised General Soleimani that this time, he would indeed deliver. Makmoud shivered as he considered the general's response. "I am counting on you to achieve your objective, Colonel Hidari. This is your last chance to prove yourself."

He wouldn't fail. Not this time. Not like he had in 2014.

The gate leading from the villa's courtyard squeaked. Jibril, his younger brother by two years, yawned loudly and carried two steaming mugs of coffee. He extended one and, in Farsi, said, "I know you've barely slept, so I thought I'd bring you this."

The mug warmed Makmoud's chilly hands. "I'll take a siesta today." He blinked, and his eyes burned from too much concentration and too little sleep. He sipped the strong Turkish coffee and sighed in delight. This would keep him going for a few more hours. "I believe we are ready for the next step in our plan."

Jibril held the mug in his beefy hands as Makmoud caught him up on the phone call. He didn't react, just raised an eyebrow. He'd worked with Makmoud long enough to know when something ruffled rather than rattled him. "Do you want me to get her ready?"

"Is she up?"

"Hassan reported she was able to take in some broth this morning."

"Excellent. I'll take care of her. Be ready in half an hour."

Without a word, Jibril retreated. The call of their imam filtered over the rocky walls. The bleats of goats in a pen in the courtyard punctuated the eerie sound. Makmoud didn't budge. His whispers sheened white in the morning light as he automatically mouthed words he'd known since childhood but had ceased believing. No, his patriotism for Iran drove him, not some higher calling to Allah.

Makmoud's thoughts shifted to their hostage. The more he'd studied her in preparation for the mission, the more she reminded him of Susanna, his wife. Susanna had come to him via kidnapping as well. She fought hard before he'd broken her. Like his wife, Libby was beautiful, except a brunette instead of a blonde, and every bit as much of a fighter.

One who had gotten his attention. The day before, after she'd regained consciousness, Hassan, his medic, had begged off for some sleep. Rather than call one of the other two medics, Makmoud sat by her side. It quickly became clear the heavy sedative impacted her with side effects. He barely got her to the bathroom before she retched into the toilet. As he held back her hair, he sent a guard to fetch Ali, another medic, who injected her with some anti-nausea medication. She quieted and slept some more.

Makmoud cat-napped through the afternoon. When he awoke, he found her curled on her side, the blankets pulled over her as she shivered from a fever and chills, another byproduct of the drug. Then she slept some more in the late-day heat, as did he on a thin mat. A quiet sigh roused him.

Libby sat upright and gazed at him with intriguing sherry-colored eyes that adapted a golden hue in the light of a nearby desk lamp. Per protocol, she covered her hair with a scarf they'd left for her. A blanket draped her shoulders. In Arabic with a Kurdish accent, she said, "I know you. You're not ISIS."

"Oh?" Makmoud sat up and smiled at her. "What makes you think I'm not ISIS?"

"I'm alive. I've not been raped. And just maybe, because I still have my limbs attached."

He chuckled and ran his hand down his beard. "Ah, perhaps ISIS has grown a conscience."

"And when does ISIS speak Farsi?"

He stilled at her discovery.

"You were here three years ago, weren't you?"

He couldn't lie to her. He'd seen her before. When his *Quds* contingent fought hard against ISIS, they'd been stationed in Amal with some of the American Special Forces. Back then, she'd fought with the men of her Kurdish militia. She'd been too thin, a shadow of her current self who suffered from amnesia, thanks to a head injury. "I'm surprised you remember."

"Getting proper treatment has helped restore much of my memory."

Libby shifted. "Why did you kidnap me?"

Makmoud rose and left without answering her. He spent the rest of the night lying on his bed with his hands behind his head as he contemplated the task ahead of him and what it would do to the woman next door.

Now his eyes snapped open. He'd dozed off standing during the recitation of prayer. Libby still had that spirit he remembered from three years before. He'd have to watch his step, lest he err due to his fatigue.

He pushed through the gate and found the courtyard empty save for the goats. Chatter and laughter filtered from the covered veranda where several of his men gathered to partake of breakfast. His mouth watered at the smell of eggs and bread cooking. Later.

He strode to where the villa became two stories. Jibril had done well in transforming the main room into a studio. ISIS flags draped over and between the windows. One man set up a small video camera on a tripod. Two others, with their heads covered in black shemaghs, chatted. Rifles hung across their shoulders. Jibril finished scrawling a message on butcher block paper. A newspaper sat on the floor beside a stool. Perfect.

Makmoud climbed the stairs along the wall. They turned right, and he arrived at the landing. At the top were the rooms he and Jibril had, plus another for the men guarding Libby. And the room where she stayed.

He puffed out his chest, then shoved open the door as if he owned her soul.

She curled into a ball under her blankets on the single bed. No headscarf. Not surprising seeing that dawn had just arrived. Her eyes snapped open. She raised her head from the pillow.

"Get up." Those two words in a low voice conveyed strong, terrifying command.

With a gasp, she sat up. "Wh—"

"You're coming with me!" He dragged her from the bed. She still wore that same T-shirt and leggings from when they'd kidnapped her. He shoved her, and she staggered into a dresser.

Libby whipped around. "Why are you doing this? You were so kind earlier—"

"Shut up!"

She darted toward the door.

Makmoud grabbed her. He popped her across the face.

She yelped and stumbled, but she steadied.

Defiance at every turn. Normally, he admired strength in a woman, had ever since being raised by his mother, who'd overcome a man who'd repeatedly abused her. Not now when Libby would play a crucial role.

That of a beaten hostage.

With a growl, he pushed her hard. She crashed into the wall next to the window. Her head snapped back against the plaster, leaving cracks behind. Her knees folded, and she moaned as she slid to the floor. He kicked her in her side. Another cry escaped her, and he slapped her. His wedding band opened up a cut across her cheekbone.

Tears trickled from her eyes and created shiny paths down her tawny skin. They mingled with the blood oozing from the cut. Chest heaving, she whimpered. "Why are you doing this? What have I done to you?"

He grabbed her hair and forced her to look at him. "Are you ready to comply?"

"Y-yes." That came out as a whisper.

"Then on your feet." He lifted her until she stood.

Once on the landing, she broke loose from his grip. With fury blazing in her eyes, she screeched and clawed him. Her sharp nails opened up hot lines across his cheek. He spun her and pushed her face first into the wall. Makmoud twisted her arm behind her until she yelped. "You both impress me with your courage and annoy me with your impetuousness, Libby Mansour. But enough is enough. If you come at me again, I will kill you. Understand?"

She still struggled, so he yanked upward again. Only then she did she nod.

Into her ear, he hissed, "Downstairs, there are guards. You go against any one of them, you may not make it to noon."

He released the pressure. Like a cat gone mad, she tried to bite him.

In a smooth motion, Makmoud wrapped one arm around her chest and the other around her neck. She struggled, but in a few seconds, she sagged. He swung her into his arms, then carried her down the staircase.

He dumped her at Jibril's feet. "We start as soon as she wakes up."

He chuckled. "Seems she got the best of you."

The cuts on Makmoud's cheek flared. He raised his fingers, and they came away scarlet. He shrugged. He'd attend to the cuts later, after they were finished with Libby. He nudged her still form with his foot.

Libby moaned, and her eyes flickered open.

"Get up and go sit on that stool."

On all fours, she crawled to it and hunched on it. He'd beaten the fight from her, at least temporarily. She now knew to respect them and the sorry position she was in. She fit the role of the hostage perfectly with her mussed hair, bloody cheek from her cut, and dirt on her face. Her dark hair clung to tearstains.

Makmoud smirked. With arms folded across his chest, he stepped in front of her. "Are you ready to comply?"

Small mews escaped her, and she nodded.

"Hold this so we can see it." He handed her the newspaper, then retreated behind the camera before nodding at the butcher block paper his comrade held up. "Read it verbatim. Do you understand? Mess it up, and you'll receive more of what you got."

Libby hung her head.

The two guards stood just off her shoulders.

Something must have broken in her. Exhaustion, fear, who knew? Her hair hung in front of her face.

Jibril hit the record button. When the red light glowed, one of the guards nudged her. She read the message, even did it in a trembling voice with more tears. The red light turned off. Her head drooped, and the newspaper fluttered downward. Makmoud caught her as she fainted. He lowered her to the floor.

Jibril slid the SD card from the camera and asked, "Do you really think they'll believe we're ISIS?"

Makmoud shrugged. "Perhaps. It adds a sense of urgency, but that isn't the point. The point is they will see she is alive and actually come to investigate. And then we can move with our own plan. He nodded at the SD card. "Process that while I take her to her room."

He lifted Libby to her feet. With his hands under her elbows, he led her to her room. She trembled against him, then lay down and curled onto her side. When he reached to pull the blanket over her, she flinched. She probably feared he'd strike her again. It tore at his heart, but he shoved it aside. He'd done what was needed. She could deal.

Makmoud left without a word and called for her guard to bring her something to eat later. Then he took another staircase leading to a trapdoor that opened onto the flat roof of the villa's second story.

One of his men stood guard. Makmoud had posted him there due to the rumors he'd heard while casing Amal. They demanded the precaution. Disappearances. Graffiti. Words eerily reminiscent of ISIS. If the vermin had returned, accomplishing his plans would be the least of his worries. He released a breath into the rapidly warming air. He only had hearsay related to ISIS, not proof. For now, taking down Victor Chavez and his team remained his top priority.

He swiveled and studied the terrain. They sat at the top of a draw. Steep mountain ridges surrounded them on all sides. A road led down the draw and curved at a pinch point that was barely ten meters wide. Trees dotted the arid landscape, and slightly above the villa, a small gap in the valley walls contained a narrow road that ducked between the ridges and connected with a road along a river. Their escape route, something he always worked with.

After chatting a few minutes with his man, Makmoud clapped him on the shoulder and retreated downward. He really did need to catch some sleep before exhaustion completely muddled his brain.

Jibril leaned against the open doorway to Libby's room. He gazed at her with an intensity that caught Makmoud's attention. Then his brother softly shut the door and led the way into his room. The video glowed on the laptop. Without a word, he played it.

Perfect. "A most excellent job, brother."

"What are your plans for her?" Jibril asked as he removed a thumb drive and shut down the computer.

Makmoud considered that. Paul LaRue had been specific. She had to die, and he wanted proof. Makmoud disagreed. "She'll come to Iran with us. We'll come up with convincing proof that we executed her."

As if he could see right through it, Jibril stared at the wall separating his room from hers. "I want her."

The man had never married and only occasionally indulged, so it wasn't surprising that he viewed a woman as beautiful as Libby as desirable. "And you shall have her when this is all over. Until then, you are not to touch her. Understand?"

Jibril briefly bowed his head in submission. "Of course."

"We'll continue with our plan tomorrow morning. For now, get some sleep. I'll be doing the same." With that, he retreated to his own room. A hot shower in the villa's western-style bathroom eased his tense muscles. He stared at the tile floor as scarlet water briefly flowed down the drain before running clear again. By the time he tended to the scratches and yanked the curtains closed, his yawns came every few seconds. He had one more task, one that he would accomplish in the wee hours of the following morning. And after that, it would only be a matter of time before Victor Chavez and his team would be in his hands.

Thursday, July 4, 2019, 1930 hours CDT (0330 hours local time, Iraq), Destin, FL

What a perfect ending to a perfect day. Paul "Roo" LaRue patted his stomach, then dabbed his lips with a cloth napkin. He folded it, first into a triangle, then into another, smaller triangle that he laid across his dessert plate, where only crumbs remained from the chocolate chess pie his wife, Tina, had made.

"Daddy, can we go down to the beach and watch the fireworks?" Six-year-old Lucy beseeched him with her blue eyes and blond curls, a gift from her mother.

Roo smiled at her. "It's too light outside. Give it another hour." He shot a sly look at his friend, Tank Russell, who sat to his daughter's left with Josette, his wife, on the other side. "And if you're patient, maybe

Uncle Tank will shoot off some fireworks as well." His gaze drifted to his cell phone. He'd laid it on the table when they sat down to eat despite Tina's subtle scowl.

"Will you, Uncle Tank?" Four-year-old Paul LaRue, III, better known as Tripp, widened his eyes. He fairly bounced in his seat at the anticipation of bright lights and big booms.

Tank took Josette's hand and shot Roo a look that bespoke of many years of raising three boys who'd thrived on big booms and bright lights. "Only if you promise to go to bed right after that."

Tina grinned. "Fat chance of that, Tank. They're going to be too jazzed by the time they're finished. Then they won't want to go to bed. I'll simply hand them off to you." She chuckled at her own joke, but her laughter faded when Roo glanced at his phone again.

The kids clambered down from their chairs and darted toward the doors leading to the deck and walkway to the beautiful white sand beach. Tina jumped up. "Hey, hey! Wait on your mama, would you? Gentlemen, if you could clean up, we'll keep an eye on these rug rats."

Roo carried some plates to the kitchen, as did Tank. Just as he returned for another batch, his phone pinged with a text notification. He snatched it up.

Hopefully it was Barry Marstein, his manager for his gubernatorial campaign that year. Barry was also known as "the Swamp Rat" thanks to his Louisiana roots and work in Washington, DC. That call would be easy to handle. The man had wanted him to campaign all the way through the Fourth of July weekend. Roo had protested, done one appearance in New Orleans earlier the day before, then retreated to his vacation home in Destin for a long weekend. He'd maintain his position to hit the campaign trail hard after that, starting with a dinner Saturday night.

The other call? Not easy to handle at all.

The message came from a six-digit alias. He sucked in a breath.

Call me. Now.

Goose bumps popped up along his arms. He rubbed them.

Tank began rinsing the dishes. "You okay?"

"AC got me for some reason. I'll be right back. Nature's calling."

Tank snorted at his obvious lie.

Roo slipped into the master bedroom and shut the door, then drew in a deep breath to calm his racing pulse. He crouched in front of his travel suitcase, which sat in the closet, and loosened a bit of stiff siding to reveal a compartment where he'd stashed the burner phone he'd bought a couple of weeks ago. With shaking fingers, he powered it on, then called up the one number he'd entered into the contacts menu. This one contained a whole lot more digits than needed for a domestic call.

His heart thumped as several beeps blared into his ear. It rang on the other end. Before the other person could even speak, he blurted, "You have her?"

A few seconds' delay, then, "She is secure, Paul LaRue."

Roo listened carefully. Nothing except for the occasional bleat from a goat and someone laughing. "Is she okay?"

The man chuckled. "A bit banged up, perhaps, but she will live. We made the video yesterday morning, and it is scheduled to be sent within a few hours. A copy is now in your inbox. You know what to do, yes?"

Roo smiled. "Most excellent. I'll make plans to head out to Flagstaff tomorrow."

"Take careful care, Paul LaRue. This mission is at a sensitive juncture. If you err, then you may wreck all of it."

Roo ground his teeth at the needless reminder. "I know what I'm doing."

"I would hope so. That is my advice. I suggest you follow it." The man's thinly veiled threat rang in his ears. "If you do not, it may not go well for you. Understand?"

"I do. Um, I'll be in touch." Man, that sounded lame. So not like a man who knew he was in control. His phone pinged, and he pulled up an email from the account he'd created per Makmoud's direction. He played the video, cringing at the brutal images. Then he smiled. Libby would play her part, and then she would vanish, just another lost soul in that part of the world.

Roo returned the phone to its hiding place and retreated to the bathroom. He swiped a hand down his jaw and winced at the sandpaper feel.

He'd definitely need to shave tomorrow. With a deep breath to quiet his racing pulse, he opened the bedroom door.

Tank wiped down the table to free it of the crumbs Lucy and Tripp had generated. Roo crossed to the kitchen.

His enforcer rinsed the washcloth. "I took some wine to the ladies on the beach. They're with the children." He stretched the cloth along its rack. "You got anything good to drink here?"

"Some Johnny Walker." Roo opened a high cabinet and reached for the bottle. "Glasses are above the dishwasher."

"Got it." Tank pulled down two and loaded them with ice. "I assume on the rocks."

"Sounds good to me." Roo dimmed the can lights in the kitchen and living room.

After adding the amber liquid, Tank handed Roo a tumbler, picked up his own, and strolled toward the living room. As he passed Roo, he gripped his bicep so tightly his skin burned.

Roo nearly dropped his drink. "Hey! What's that about?"

"Are you crazy?" Tank hissed. His gaze shifted to the dunes, where the two women laughed and sipped their wine as they stood on the deck and kept an eye on the kids.

Roo shook loose. "I'm not sure what you're talking about."

"Tina noticed you constantly looking at your phone. You keep doing that, and she'll think you're having an affair."

"I was waiting on the call."

"I realize that. But you weren't acting natural. I'd thought you knew better by now."

The remark stung. Over the years, especially during his time in the Army, Roo had learned the need to play a role, be it when dealing with chieftains in the field or as chief operating officer of LaRue International Transport, better known as LIT. "If it makes you feel any better, they got Libby and made the video. I got a copy. I'm taking the next step in a few days."

Tank continued to a recliner near the open floor-to-ceiling windows and sank into the plush fabric. "Very good."

"Why couldn't they go ahead and send it to Libby's parents? Instead, it's going out early tomorrow morning." Impatience tugged at Roo. "Maybe I should send it to—"

"And you would be a fool to do so." Tank lifted the tumbler. He took a sip and smacked his lips in satisfaction. "Makmoud has his reasons, understand? He's the ground commander." Glass clinked against glass as he set the tumbler on a side table. "You've got to trust him because he knows what he's doing. Remember that."

Roo paced. How could his campaign security chief and enforcer look so unruffled?

"He's a man of his word, Roo. Remember, he's eight hours ahead of us. It'll show up while we're all sleeping."

"But I only have until Saturday morning. Then I've got to be at an event in Baton Rouge that night. The Swamp Rat says this is a can't-miss event."

"It will happen." Tank's sharp tone froze him. "We're at a precarious point right now. You act rashly, it could complicate things."

"I'm *not* going to act rashly. You know me better than that." Roo blew out a breath. Low and slow. Like he'd learned when deployed to the sandbox called Iraq so many years before. Things were precarious, all right. If he didn't show at supper Saturday night, The Swamp Rat would have his hide. Not to mention, he'd tick off over five hundred supporters—voters—each who'd shelled out two thousand bucks to hear him speak at a formal banquet. "Okay. You're right."

Tank only raised an eyebrow, as if he doubted his words. Then he shrugged and shoved his feet into some flip-flops. "I'm headed out to join the ladies and the kids. You coming?"

"Yeah, in just a few. Let me make a call." Roo lifted his phone. "The Swamp Rat texted as well. Let me call him, and I'll be out."

Tank cast him another long look, then headed onto the deck walkway.

Roo released another slow breath to calm a heart suddenly racing with the news he'd anticipated for so long. The process of eliminating his last skeleton in the closet had finally begun.

He continued wearing a trench in the floor, this time extending his reach onto the porch. His pulse hammered like it always had when he'd headed out on a mission in the sandbox. And in this one, he had a part to play to kick things off.

Like now.

Roo did the math in his head. If he left early the next morning, he'd be in New Orleans by noon, in time to catch a flight out to Arizona. An overnight stay, and he'd be in Baton Rouge by early afternoon Saturday. It'd work. And he had to admit Tank had been right. Makmoud knew his stuff.

He picked up his cell phone and dialed the number for his favorite pilot in the LIT fleet of three private jets. "Hey, Jake. Question for you. Can you get me to Flagstaff tomorrow by three-thirty?"

2

Thursday, July 4, 2019, 1745 hours MST (1945 hours CDT), Flagstaff, AZ

"You sure you know what you're doing?" Thanks to the blindfold he wore, Butch Addison stood in darkness.

"You've done this weekly for how long? Like, since January?" Sana Jain al-Ibrahim's melodic voice floated to him from his right. "Learning to fight blindfolded or in the dark is really, really good for you."

"Hah. It's been really, really good for getting beat up," he groused. "You remember right before I got married? I was lucky I didn't have a black eye for the wedding."

She chuckled. "Yep. You wound up with Paw Patrol Band-Aids on your face right before the rehearsal dinner because Marie insisted that Diana put them in her medical kit. Now focus. Take some breaths. Calm yourself. Let your senses expand."

"Okay, Ninja Girl. You gonna tell me to feel the force next?"

A bell-like laugh rewarded him. "Where am I?"

He took a deep breath and slowly released it, taking longer on the exhale than the inhale. His shoulder muscles relaxed, as did those in his neck. "Mars?"

"Butch!"

"No, I meant Venus."

"Keep laughing it up," Skylar James, his friend and the intelligence and procurement specialist on the former Shadow Box team, said. His opponent for the day shuffled.

Ah. Ten o'clock position. Butch's hearing sharpened. So did his sense of smell since Skylar had arrived dripping wet from a run. Nothing like good stink to reveal someone's presence.

"No, I just feel like Luke Skywalker." Butch shifted so Skylar was at his twelve, directly in front of him. "You know that scene. Where he was learning to fight with a light saber on the *Millennium Falcon*. And if I remember right, that little ball of a droid got him good."

"Keep talking, and your senses won't open up," Sana warned.

"You're at my four o'clock."

"Precisely. Now keep Skylar in front of you."

Butch fell silent.

He became acutely aware of the spongy feel of the mat beneath his bare feet. And the whisper of the wind outside the roll-up doors at the gym on Last Chance Ranch. Not to mention the tangy scent of the ponderosa pines so common outside of Flagstaff.

Feet shuffled, picking up in frequency. He rotated like a radar dish honing in on a signal.

A small puff of breath. Butch jerked back, and he blocked a right hook. He jabbed out in a side kick.

Skylar grunted. "Good job, dude."

"You got it. Keep going," Sana called.

Butch barely heard her as he began bouncing on his toes like a boxer. "Do it again."

More breeze whispered toward him down low. He jumped. The sweat smell grew sharper. Breath puffed out.

Butch ducked to one side and aimed a punch that Skylar blocked.

"Jedi Butch." Skylar's shuffling decreased over so slightly as he backed away.

Butch grinned. He could do this. Fight like a Jedi, that is. Easier than—

Another punch grazed his jaw.

"Aw, man!"

"Okay. Enough," Sana announced. "Bow to each other."

Butch took off the blindfold.

In front of him, Skylar smirked as he performed the perfunctory bow Sana, the ninja of their group, always required. They bumped fists. "Good job, dude. My turn?"

"Not today." She joined the two men. "Anna's party is at seven, and it's already five forty-five."

Butch gasped. "Girl, I've got to get home, clean up, and get the wife."

"Yeah, I hear you," Skylar said. "Fi told me not to be late."

"Hah." Butch tossed the blindfold into his gym bag and grabbed his cell phone. With a "See y'all later." he headed to his silver F-250, tossed his bag inside, and cranked the big engine. He lowered the window, turned up the radio so country music blasted, and headed toward the outskirts of Flagstaff.

Man, what a great way to spend a day off. Sleeping in, which meant 0700 hours for him rather than his normal 0400. Hanging out with Shelly, his bride of seven weeks. Then a good lifting session and sparring match with Skylar, one of his buds. Now, it was home to get cleaned up before coming back for Anna Chavez's nineteenth birthday party. Fancy a teen-ager would consider hanging out with her family and parents' friends. Showed just how mature that young lady was compared to her peers.

He swung into the walk-up apartment complex where he and Shelly lived until they could get their house built on land Victor Chavez, his best guy friend and owner of Last Chance Ranch, had deeded the two of them as a wedding gift. Shoving his phone into a front pocket of his workout shorts, he climbed the steps to the second floor, undid the screened door to the two-bedroom apartment, and grinned when he stepped into the combination kitchen and living room. Shelly's back was to him as she worked on the dessert they'd volunteered to bring. "Babe, that looks so totally delicious."

Shelly Wise Addison screeched and jumped. "Butch! You scared me!"

"Sorry." He peered at the concoction. "Looks good."

She carefully arranged blueberries and strawberries along the top of what looked like a mixture of vanilla pudding and whipped cream with layers of cake, strawberries, and blueberries intertwined.

She completed the American flag. "Festive, patriotic, and absolutely yummy. I need to take a pic for Facebook and Instagram. And I get to use one of the glass bowls we got as a wedding present."

"Mmmm. Hmmm." He nuzzled her hair, tipped her chin, and kissed her. Behind her, he reached a finger toward the dessert.

"Oh, no you don't." She pulled away and swatted his hand. "Nice try, Butch Addison." She shoved a metal bowl toward him. "Here's the leftovers. Have at it while I put this in the fridge."

Oh, yeah, baby. He sighed in contentment. The mix of vanilla pudding and whipped cream was heavenly. She closed the refrigerator door. Pulling her into his arms, he kissed her again. "Sweet, babe, but not as sweet as you."

"Keep talking."

He preferred action over talk. Backing her against the fridge, he cupped her cheek in his hand. She sighed against his mouth. "Butch, it's past six. Anna's party—"

"Starts at seven." He nibbled on her ear, then pulled loose the tie holding her dark blond curls in a twist. Her hair tumbled around her shoulders. "I love days off like this."

She entwined her arms around his neck. Praise God he'd waited for a woman like her. He came up for air, and that little smile crossing those full lips of hers told him everything he needed to know. Taking her hand, he led her toward the bedroom. As he kissed her again and again, his phone began chiming. He tossed it onto his nightstand. It hit the edge and clunked to the carpeted floor.

She groaned. "Maybe you should answer that."

"Nope. Not happening now."

She giggled.

Thirty minutes later, he stepped from the bathroom and pulled on his jeans and a T-shirt. Shelly curled up on her side with the sheet up to her chin. His heart skipped at the sleepy grin on her face. She stretched. "You know we're going to be late."

"Hah. We're newlyweds. I think Vic'll understand." He added his belt and checked his beard in the dresser mirror. No trimming needed for to-night.

"Maybe?"

"Yup. Maybe. Go ahead and get ready while I see who had the audacity to call me while I was romancing my bride." Now where had his phone gone? Not on the floor in front of the nightstand or beside it. He got onto his knees. There. He retrieved it from under the bed and cued up voice mail as he strolled into the living room. Roo had called. His message was succinct. Mysterious. "Cajun Man, hey. Roo here. Something's come up that's urgent. Call me ASAP."

That was it. A grand total of ten seconds.

Okay. He'd seen his former commanding officer just seven weeks be-fore, when the man had stood as a groomsman in the wedding. What could be so urgent now? Well, he had one way to find out. He dialed and lifted the phone to his ear.

"Cajun Man, hey," Roo said after the first ring, almost like he'd been waiting on Butch to call. "Sorry if I'm interrupting anything."

Not that Butch was going to tell him. "You're good. What's up?"

"I just found out some disturbing news."

"What's that?"

"Libby Holt Mansour's been kidnapped."

Those words sucker-punched him like he'd taken one in the gut. Butch stilled and stared out the balcony doors to the woods beyond. "Say what? When?"

"Just a few hours ago."

"How did you find out?"

"I've got a buddy at the State Department. On the Middle East desk."

Questions swirled in Butch's mind. "What else do you know?"

"Not much right now. He just got the call from the embassy in Bagh-dad. Hey, listen. I'm coming your way tomorrow to ask you for a favor regarding the kidnapping. Are you and Ghost going to be around?"

Butch struggled to remember Victor's Special Forces moniker. "Yeah. I'm headed to the ranch in a few. I'll mention it to him."

"See if we can meet about this. I'll be getting in around three-thirty or so. Maybe you and I can grab supper before we meet."

A little early, but that was okay. His manager could handle closing the auto and body repair shop he owned in downtown Flagstaff. "Sounds like a plan. Meet me at the shop?"

"Will do. Thanks, man, and I'll see you tomorrow."

"Uh, yeah." Stunned, Butch wandered onto their balcony and leaned with his forearms against the wrought-iron railing. His mind whirled as he tried to digest the news Roo had dumped on his plate. Then memories of Libby superseded those.

"I know you can do it, Alfie," she liked to say as he'd struggled through homework. Back then, she'd always used his given nickname. But for her and her family, he would have dropped out of school a long time before, thanks to an undiagnosed learning disability. First, he and Libby had been playmates, then study buddies, which coalesced into a hot, passionate romance the summer before their senior year in high school.

God had moved them in different directions after that. She headed to Wheaton to obtain a degree in education, then to teach school in northern Iraq. He wound up in the Army, where he'd found both a calling and Jesus, though the second one took a few years.

Like when he'd been sparring with Skylar, Butch drew in a deep breath and released it, which loosened more memories of the way the Holts had become his surrogate family. Gerald and Joyce Holt had modeled what normal parents looked like. He'd grieved with them—

"Butch?"

Shelly's soft voice from the open sliding glass door pulled him from his brooding.

He glanced over his shoulder.

She, who swore she was a thinker rather than a feeler, instantly interpreted his change in mood. She pressed into his side. "What is it? Who called?"

"Roo. He's coming out."

"Paul LaRue? But we saw him only seven weeks ago."

He shrugged. "I know." He returned his attention to the woods. No other way to say this. "He called to say Libby's been kidnapped."

She drew in a sharp breath, then began shoveling questions his way like dirt.

He held up his hands. "I don't know anything else. Just that he wants to talk with Vic and me."

"Oh, wow." She rested her head on his shoulder and wrapped her hand around his arm.

Thanks to the memories of those long-ago days when he and Libby had dated, he barely heard her. He pushed away from the railing. "We need to get going."

"I already texted Deb and said we'd be late."

He failed at his attempt to smile. "Though not too late."

Once she lifted the dessert from the fridge, he led the way down to the ground floor and his pickup. As he helped her inside, then handed her the dish, he banished thoughts of Libby from his mind. He'd take them down and dust them off later. Like way later. After tonight.

3

Thursday, July 4, 2019, 2200 hours MST, Flagstaff, AZ

Butch slouched on a rocking chair on the balcony of the apartment. His second favorite place in their lair. His first was beside Shelly in bed. Classical music wafted from the second bedroom. Shelly worked on one of her many jobs as a cybersecurity contractor.

Bracing his feet on the railing, he hunkered down in his fleece jacket and shook a cigarette from its pack. After he lit it, he gazed at the lighter in his hand. Black with silver trim and a silver skull.

Cowboy's old lighter. One that now belonged to him.

Oh, man. Here came the memories Roo's call had dredged up. 2009. Butch's jaw tightened, and he took a drag to calm himself. Once more, gunshots and shouts from that fateful night, the early hours of April Fool's Day, peppered his mind like buckshot. That dark, dark night, he'd played the fool. He'd awakened in a stupor to find himself slumped behind some pallets next to the small warehouse that held their ordnance and ammo. Adrenaline spiked. He heaved himself to his feet. His head swam, and he stumbled. He charged into the fight, battling with courage to make up for mysteriously falling asleep on the job. He tripped and fell to his knees. Butch gaped wide-eyed at the object that had caused him to fall.

Throat slit in a jagged cut, Cowboy stared at him with sightless eyes. Anguish fueled Butch's courage. He leapt to his feet. As he staggered upright, he barely noticed the doors hanging wide open at the warehouse he'd been guarding.

Tires crunching on asphalt brought him back to the present. A truck pulled into the parking lot and into a spot right out front. Its headlights shut off, and a door shut. In the dim glow of the parking lot's lights, he barely recognized Victor Chavez. The truck chirped. He climbed the steps to the second floor. The music fell silent. A few seconds later, Shelly's cheery greeting floated through the apartment. Victor tapped on the door frame.

Butch kept his foot on the railing as he rocked. "Hey, boss. Saw you pull up."

Victor gestured to the other rocking chair. "May I?"

"Of course." Butch lifted the cigarette to his lips, then blew the smoke out. "Sorry I didn't get up." *Didn't feel like it after you turned down the notion of helping Libby.*

"No worries. Shelly said to help myself." He held up a can of Coke before plopping onto the wood. "I did."

"You're going to stay up all night."

"No biggie since I'm taking the day off tomorrow." He nodded toward the fleece. "Your smoking jacket?"

Butch hated these pleasantries. He touched the fabric. "Hah, something like that. Shel makes me keep it out here so I don't stink up the apartment. She's been after me to quit for months."

"But no success yet."

"'Cause every time I try, something comes up." Part of him wanted to growl out his angst. He couldn't. Not when Victor had been right on every point. Too little evidence. Just Roo's hearsay. They'd have to wait on the meeting tomorrow. Of course, Victor didn't have the emotional tug that came with Butch's relationship with Libby.

"Butch!"

"Huh?" Suddenly, he realized he'd tuned his friend out.

Victor didn't seem fazed. "I said I'm sorry about earlier tonight."

"I just wish you'd not shut me down."

"I'm sorry, but I'm not going to consider mobilizing until we hear

Roo out."

Butch hated when his friend was right. He fell silent and rocked some more before jabbing his cigarette out in an ashtray the shape of a truck tire. "We go way back, Libby and me."

Victor raised an eyebrow. "How far?"

He rested his head against the chair. "Since kindergarten. Her mama, daddy, brothers, and her became my surrogate family after Daddy and Mama essentially kicked me out. Even before then. But for them, I wouldn't know what a normal family looks like." He shifted his gaze to his friend. "You remember when we went to Amal, right? In the late summer of 2003."

"Yeah. Rebuilding schools, medical work. Training the Kurdish militia."

"Restoring trust." Butch smiled at those heady memories. Too bad they hadn't lasted. "Then for those six months in 2005, right before you and Old Man got out."

"Yeah." Victor chuckled. "Probably our best mission ever."

"The Silver Star mission." Butch uncapped his water and took a swig. "Libby and Samir were newlyweds then. Samir was a brave one."

"You were too. You and Old Man."

"Well, you didn't get the name Ghost for nothing, boss." Butch set his water aside. "We flitted in and out of that camp like we were shadows. Didn't take no rocket scientist to take the insurgents' command post. Just us getting in there, taking out who we needed, and calling Samir and his boys to come and clean up so the people of Amal could be secure. I still can't believe you recommended me for a Silver Star. If anything, you should have gotten it."

"Nah. Not me. You were the one who singlehandedly took out five guys without a shot being fired." Victor took a swig of Coke, then rested his can on the arm of the rocker. "Those were the days."

Butch rocked in silence. "I think Libby, Samir, and their friends always helped us stay sane when we were there."

The wind puffed, bringing with it the pine scent that reminded him of those spring days in the Zagros mountains. Those mountains had always come alive in the spring, much like they did in Flagstaff.

Victor cleared his throat. "What happened over there? I mean, after I got out. The file I got when you joined Shadow Box didn't have much in it."

"In 2009?"

"Yeah."

Butch stilled. He feared judgment from his friend. "This doesn't get to anyone else?"

"No. I assume Shelly knows."

"She does." Butch rubbed his bald head. "Maybe my first question is what do you know?"

"You got out of the Army, said you were done with it. And you were only ten years into a career that was onward and upward. The file said you were investigated after an attack in Amal, but it didn't have many details."

Thankfully, details in the file were sparse. The questions from that interrogation so long ago cracked through Butch's mind like rifle shots. "Were you drunk, Sergeant Addison? Why were you sleeping on the job? Who did you conspire with among the insurgents so they could steal arms and ordnance?" His answers? "No! No! What? Why would I do that?"

"It was… awful." Butch didn't want to discuss this with Victor. With anyone, for that matter. He stared into the forest of ponderosa pine that ringed the complex. "You know, Shel and I have seen all sorts of wildlife out there. Bear. Deer. Coyote, if you're patient enough."

"Butch…"

He so didn't want to talk about this. "Sorry. I guess I'm stalling, huh?"

Victor shrugged.

Butch sighed and stared at the cigarette smoke wending its way upward from the ashtray. "Sorry. I'm just not ready to talk about it." He thought about the fallout from that terrible night. Everyone on his team had run from sticking up for him. Everyone except for Roo and one of their medics. "You remember Jace?"

"Jason Choi? Korean-American guy, right?"

"One and the same. JC went through Q course with me and wound up transferring to our team when Roo did. I had to laugh because he said that when everyone else was swearing and taking the Lord's name in vain, he wouldn't. And thanks to his initials and his vow, he got the nickname JC. He was there when everything went down. Saw symptoms in me that bothered him and conveyed that to the docs who were taking care of me after I was shot. They did the needed blood work and passed it on to the investigator. JC had my back and saved my skin. But for him, I might have wound up at Leavenworth."

Victor crumpled his empty Coke can. "Jace was never wrong when I knew him, and he's a man with good instincts. I'm glad he sensed something wasn't right and stood up for you."

Butch got to his feet. "Thanks. I needed to hear that."

Some vertebrae popped in Victor's back as he rose.

"I heard that, boss."

"Yeah, getting old sucks. Darned if I almost forgot the most important thing I came here to tell you."

"Another symptom of getting old."

Victor chuckled. "Just you wait, Butch. You're turning forty in a few months. I wanted to tell you that if Roo has more than just hearsay, I'll consider mobilizing the team."

Butch bumped fists with him. "I know. Thanks, boss. Libby means the world to me."

Victor paused. "Well, let me get back. The wife is waiting on me."

"Will do." Butch rose and strolled inside. "I know it's the weekend, but at least I can walk you out."

"Hah. Thanks, brother." Victor followed him to the front door. "Keep me posted."

Butch nodded. He returned to the balcony and watched his friend drive away. His traitorous thoughts immediately turned to Libby. If she were indeed in trouble, he'd move heaven and earth to return her to safety.

4

Butch and Libby strolled along a stream near where they'd grown up in Bayou, Louisiana. She wore a caftan, and he wore ACU pants, a T-shirt, and hiking boots. Since when had they both been in Bayou as adults? Since never. They chatted like the best friends they'd been in high school. She took his hand and tugged him to a stop along the banks. Before them, the stream tumbled over fallen logs, and leaves rode along with the current. "Do you remember this stream?"

"Huh? Can't say I do."

She giggled. He'd never forget that cheerful sound. It brought back so many memories of their time growing up together. "We looked for tadpoles here." With that, she crouched and gazed at the sunlight dappling the water. "There, do you see them?"

He knelt beside her. "Nope. But then again, you were always the science person, not me."

She gazed at him, and the sunlight streaking her face made the sherry color in her eyes almost glow. It also caught the red highlights in hair so dark brown it was almost black. "No, I think *you're* the science person. Years ago you helped catch a bunch of creepy crawlies, right?"

"When?"

"When you helped Deborah Chavez."

"You know her?"

"A sister in Christ."

Butch stared. This was getting weird. Then he shrugged. Maybe Deborah and Libby had talked when his childhood friend had visited them two years before. "Yeah, I did. Except the spider. You know how much I hate spiders."

She gently swirled her hand in a still patch of water. A bunch of specks shot around. "Alfie, look. There are probably hundreds here."

Butch winced at the sound of his given nickname. "Libby, you know I legally changed my first name to Butch when I was eighteen and joined the Army."

"So you say." Straightening, she cut her eyes toward him, and a little grin crossed her full lips. "But I still see you as Alfie."

No, she'd called him Butch when he'd seen her as an adult. He mirrored her. Her gaze spoke volumes and enchanted him.

But hadn't she married? And hadn't he? What was going on? Her smile sent shivers down his spine. He stepped closer. She kissed him, drew him down onto the ground.

A stick snapped.

Her father loomed over them. "Leave her alone!"

Before he realized it, Butch leapt to his feet and jumped him. The two men fought, and Libby screamed.

Butch's eyes flew open. He wasn't in Louisiana, and he certainly wasn't with Libby. Instead, he lay on his side. The glowing-blue numbers of the clock on the nightstand told him all he needed to know. 0430 hours. On a Friday. Curse this early rising routine he had during the week that sometimes made him wake up way before any sane human would on a day off.

He eased onto his back and angled his head toward Shelly.

She curled on her side and faced him, her knees up, her hand tucked under her cheek. A stray curl spilled across that beautiful skin of hers. Ever so gently, he lifted it and sifted those silky strands through his fingers before laying it on the rest of her hair. She, the heavy sleeper, only sighed and snuggled farther under the covers that protected them against the chill.

Butch pushed himself upright. Grumbling under his breath, he pulled on some sweats and a sweatshirt before shambling from the bedroom. He shut the door behind him, got the coffee going, and stretched his body. His muscles lengthened, then relaxed. Maybe he'd do a run today. Maybe one of the other guys would join him. He certainly wasn't going to ride like his friend, Diana Kasem, did. On her days off, one could find her toodling down the highway on her road bike as she trained for her next triathlon. Not him. He joked that he looked like a circus elephant riding a bike. Funny how no one disagreed with him.

The coffeemaker coughed out the last few drops of Arabian-blend caffeinated goodness one of his Iraqi buds had introduced to him. He always kept a stash at the apartment. That and Kona coffee in honor of Old Man, one of his buddies from the Army who lived on the Big Island. He poured himself a stout mug, then took a sip. Ahhh. So nice.

At least he could put his early rising to good use. Butch eased onto the couch and swiped his Bible from a side table. He'd been reading 1 Corinthians, and he came to the verses about temptation. God would always provide a way out. The Lord had always guided his reading, and each day, he found some nugget to apply. But he wasn't sure about those verses or how they pertained to him. He shrugged and finished before setting the book aside. Then, with elbows on knees and mug in his hands, he began praying.

The topics ranged widely. Libby. The shop. His marriage to Shelly. Victor's kids, especially Morgan, who was in her second year in the Army serving Uncle Sam as an MP in Texas. He swung back around to Joyce and Gerald Holt, Libby's parents. Strange that he'd not heard a peep from them. If the kidnapping had been for real, the State Department would have contacted them. Or they would have received some sort of a ransom video. Maybe Roo had gotten his facts mixed up.

His phone began vibrating and dancing across the coffee table where he'd accidentally left it. Caller ID flashed up a number. Gerald Holt. Almost like the man was psychic. "Gerald, hi."

"Butch, I'm so glad you're up."

He struggled to calculate the time difference between Arizona and Alabama. His mentor was two hours ahead, meaning Gerald had probably risen and gotten a cup of coffee, maybe checked his phone. Butch kept his voice quiet to avoid waking Shelly. "Yeah. Getting up at four during the week has its disadvantages on a long weekend. What's going on?"

"Libby's been kidnapped."

The statement sucked the air from the room, and Butch struggled to take a breath. His skin tingled, and cold flashed over him. "How do you know?"

"Ransom video." Gerald clipped his words. "It came to my email three hours ago while we slept. They say they're ISIS and want five million from us. Who are these people, Butch? We're not rich. We don't have one million, let alone five."

Pain in Butch's knee distracted him. His hand gripped it like prey in talons. "Darned if I know."

"They have Libby." The older man's voice caught on a sob. "She's been through so much. I told her not to go back. I told her! A couple of nights ago, she emailed us and said she was coming home to stay at the beginning of August. So close…"

"I'm sorry, sir." Butch's mind darted in all directions. "Listen. Can you forward me that message? With the attachment? Shel can take a look at it."

"Yeah. I'll… I'll do that. Butch, I haven't told Joyce." Gerald drew in a shaky breath. "I'm terrified."

"Contact the Feds, okay? Start with the Middle East desk at the State Department. See what they have to say." Maybe Roo's guy there could help them.

"I will. And Butch?"

"Yes, sir?"

"Pray."

"Absolutely. Always." Butch signed off. Heart heavy, he tossed the phone on top of his Bible. Low words escaped him as he scrubbed his hands across his bald head, then down his beard. Sounded like Roo had been right after all. Someone had indeed kidnapped Libby.

His phone vibrated again. An email icon glowed on his screen. Without hesitation, he opened the message from Gerald. It came from one of his friends, supposedly. Butch knew better. The alias had teased Libby's dad into opening it. And that's when he saw the video. He clicked on it.

Thanks to his forgetting to lower the volume after watching some silly video on YouTube, the sound played at full tilt. Libby's words came across literally loud and clear.

They seared his soul.

ISIS wanted money from the Holts. Five million. No payment in ten days meant they'd never see her again.

Crap. Well, he could think of a dozen other words that fit that. None of them nice and all of them ones he'd vowed to stop using.

"Butch?"

Clad only in a nightshirt and with her curls standing on end, Shelly leaned against the wall next to the hallway. Normally, such a sight would have made him salivate, and he would have immediately begun kissing her.

Not today.

He stared at the video he'd paused. "Hey, babe. I didn't mean to wake you."

She shrugged and curled up beside him. "What's going on?" She came more awake as she stared at the frozen image of Libby's battered face. "Oh, no."

He fixed her in his gaze. "Libby's in trouble. I think we need to call Vic."

Friday, July 5, 2019, 0530 hours MST, Flagstaff, AZ

"Looks like ISIS got Libby," Butch reported as he marched into the studio of glass and stone that served as Victor's home office at Last Chance Ranch just outside of Flagstaff.

Victor headed toward the coffeemaker. "Coffee first. Then we talk."

Butch held up a travel mug containing his second brew of the day. "I got me some."

"But *I* need some." Victor picked up a hefty mug with the Secret Service seal on it. "Sorry, but you got me out of bed."

"No, my bad." Butch huffed out a breath and plopped into a chair in the conversation area. It groaned under his six-four, two-forty frame. He nodded toward the large monitor on Victor's worktable at the other end of the studio. "Can Shel connect to your screen?"

"Sure. Skylar's on his way. Let's wait for him."

"Where are the others?"

"I wanted to wait until we were sure what we're dealing with is genuine."

"Of course it's genuine."

"Butch." Warning edged Victor's voice. Or was it the annoyance of being pulled from a sound sleep by bad news?

"Sorry."

"Let's watch. Then we'll decide."

Skylar joined them. He filled a mug bearing the logo for Regions Café, the restaurant he owned. What with his khakis, golf shirt, and fleece and with every strand of blond hair in place, he looked like he'd just stepped off the cover of GQ rather than getting four hours of sleep at best. "Did I miss anything?"

"We just got here." Butch rose and paced to the other side of the studio to the worktables. Shelly sat on one of the lab chairs, hit a few buttons on her laptop, and mirrored her screen to the monitor.

Only the sounds of Libby's message penetrated the studio's still air.

Victor handed her a thumb drive. "I can see you're itching to do work on the email. Copy the video to here."

She did and returned to the couch in the conversation area.

Victor took control. He played it again.

"Again, Vic," Skylar said.

The process repeated itself a few more times.

Butch couldn't take it anymore. He retreated to the other side of the studio and rubbed the back of his neck as he stared at the dormant fireplace. He glanced at Shelly. With her hair pulled up in a messy twist and her eyes intent on the computer screen, she tapped furiously on her laptop.

He eyed the crystal clock on the mantel. 0630 hours.

"It's genuine," Skylar finally said.

Butch whipped around and rejoined them.

Skylar, chin resting on hand, brow furrowed, nodded at the screen. "It's genuine, not something cobbled together. She's scared. I'm pretty darned sure it's her. You say it's her voice, Butch?"

He'd never forget that lilting Louisiana drawl that years of living in the Kurdish autonomous region in Iraq hadn't taken away. "Very much so."

"Dang. Vic, play it again."

"Do we have to?" Butch asked. Irritation and the lack of sleep had taken over.

Skylar shot him a look. "Dude, I'm playing it until I'm sure of one thing."

"What's that?"

"I don't think it's ISIS."

Butch stared. "You say what?"

"She's alive. She's got her arms and legs. I don't think she's been sexually assaulted."

"You can tell that?"

Skylar shrugged. "As a fact, no, but while she's traumatized, it doesn't look to that level."

Victor shut the video off. His fingers flew across the keyboard, and a few moments later the State Department's Internet site popped up. He located a list of numbers and pointed to the screen. "Butch, call this number."

Butch did. The emergency number. They routed him to a woman named Xenia Frances. Gerald must have already spoken to her because his name opened all sorts of doors. Her reaction? "We're handling it," she told him with a clipped New York accent. "Representatives from the embassy were on-site this morning. Let us do our work."

Point taken.

Butch checked the clock. 0700 hours. 1700 hours in Iraq.

"Hey, guys," Shelly said.

Butch settled beside her on the couch. "What did you find?"

"Zilch." She sighed. "I ran the IP address down. It's to an Internet café in Amal in northern Iraq. And nothing on the email address except that it was scheduled to release fifteen hours after whoever sent it logged into

37

the system."

Butch ground his teeth. A dead end.

His phone began chiming. "Hey, Roo. You hear?"

"Libby's daddy called me," Roo said. "I'm headed out to Flagstaff by noon. I should be there by three-thirty. I'll join you guys at the ranch. Is Ghost there?"

Butch glanced toward where Victor now stood, his arms folded across his chest, his feet shoulder-width apart. A tired frown marred his olive features. "Yeah, he's right here. Hold on."

Victor took the phone, and Butch eavesdropped on the conversation. Sounded like his friend might now be taking this more seriously. Butch shook his head. That wasn't fair. They had the solid evidence they needed to act. Good enough in his book.

Victor handed him his phone. "Okay. We're going to talk some more when he gets here. Let me call Ms. Frances back." That conversation seemed shorter, more intense. He sighed as he hung up. "State doesn't want us to mess in it."

"We need to mess in it," Butch muttered.

Victor just gave him that look, the one warning him he treaded in dangerous waters.

"I offered. Their stance is we don't negotiate with terrorists."

"But we ain't the government," Butch reasoned.

"That's what I told her."

"Can we go to jail if we go?" Shelly asked. Her hazel eyes had widened. "I mean—"

"Does it matter?" Butch blurted.

Another stermer look from Victor sailed his way.

"Sorry, boss." He rubbed his hands together and clamped his jaw shut, lest he say something boneheaded that would set his friend off.

"No, no. Shelly's got a point, but you do too. We won't go to jail, but if something happens, we're on our own. So get ready for a long day and night. We've got lots to do once we get the rest of the team together and when Roo gets here."

5

"That so went to plan," Roo chortled after his meeting with the team. In his rented Land Rover Discovery, he barreled down desert roads between the buttes and mesas sprinkled south of Flagstaff. An open can of beer sat in the center console's cup holder. He was too keyed up to return to his hotel in Flagstaff. Now the heavy metal blaring from the stereo's speakers amped his mood as he drove down Sedona way.

So perfect! He laughed and laughed. So easy. All he'd had to do was play on Cajun Man's childhood loyalty to Libby. Then it was a matter of portraying that he had so much concern for her he was willing to shell out the big bucks to get her back.

"The video is enough evidence to show she's been kidnapped." He mimicked Ghost's reply to his desire to hire Sentry Securities to rescue Libby for a cool five mil, plus expenses.

Makmoud had been right. Just like that, Ghost had fallen for it.

Now he could clean up a loose end. Drugging Cajun Mans' coffee ten years before when they'd served together in northern Iraq could end his run for governor faster than anything. Or worse. His desire to control things, to control the outcome, hadn't marred anything. He slapped the steering wheel and cackled.

He'd better slow down. Driving aimlessly and recklessly with an open beer in his SUV wouldn't work. If he weren't careful, he'd either get lost or into a wreck.

Roo twisted the wheel hard to the right and followed a road to the top of a ridge. From there, buttes scattered across the desert stretched before him. So what he needed. A scenic vista. He rolled down the windows and cut the engine. Silence prevailed. All around him, the last vestiges of the day cast golden rays on the red rock to where it almost glowed. His heart rate slowed. His mind loosened.

It wandered toward a scene in Louisiana almost a year ago on the campaign trail. They were canvassing small towns down in the bayous of the southern part of the state. Crowds of Cajuns and other locals came out in droves to hear how one of the sons of New Orleans planned to help them if elected governor. Oh, he remembered that speech so well. Promises to provide these mostly poor people with adequate health care. Access to broadband. And other things to make their lives, which were a daily struggle, better. He glad-handed many of them. Tank's security team kept a tight eye on them and pushed the crowds back as he shifted toward the Chevy Suburban that would whisk him away to his next stop. As if he sensed something could happen, Tank didn't stray from his side.

"I know who you are, Paul LaRue!" a woman's crackly voice stopped him in his tracks. "I know who you are!"

She shoved past everyone and stopped three feet from him. Time had etched its lines into her face and patched it with age spots. Gaps in her mouth revealed the lack of dental care and nutrition over the years. But her eyes scared him. Deep, dark pools that almost gleamed with evil. He automatically stepped back.

She pointed a gnarled, bony finger at him. "I know what your family did. And a curse be upon you. You will pay for your sins and the sins of your family."

Tank stepped between them and hissed, "Get in the Suburban, Roo. Now."

He didn't hesitate. He slid behind the darkened glass.

The hag's cries still penetrated. "You will pay! You will pay! A curse be upon you!"

The SUV pulled away, and he shoved it out of his mind as the Swamp Rat handed him the agenda for his next stop.

"And why am I thinking of that now?" Roo's voice split the still air of the Land Rover. It's not like he'd had control almost a hundred years before when his ancestors had needlessly blown the levy south of New Orleans during the Great Flood of 1927. He hadn't had a hand in the way they'd promised compensation to trappers and other poor people, then refused to pay hardly a cent to them. He wasn't the one who'd left thousands of people completely destitute with no way to earn a living.

But he *was* responsible for his own sins.

He shoved that aside.

Roo shook himself. Outside, the red rock now glowed a scarlet so deep it looked like blood. The sky above softened toward orange. He shivered and chalked it up to the cooling breeze flowing through the open windows.

His secret phone, which he'd powered on in a vain hope he'd hear about the video, chimed. His tense shoulders relaxed. "Finally!" He lifted it to his ear. "Makmoud."

A string of words in another language answered him. Probably cuss words. "I *told* you to not to use my name, did I not?"

"Whatever." Boy, Roo's high from a day of working with Cajun Man's team had made him mouthy. "They fell for it and will be leaving out on Tuesday. I've got to be back in Baton Rouge for this big supper tomorrow night. I have no time to spare now."

Another breath, an audible exhale. "Most excellent. But it is not certain, no?"

Roo did a silent snarl. "It is. He's sending me the contract tomorrow. I imagine Cajun Man will make sure it gets done because he's known Libby since childhood."

Makmoud sighed. "Very well, then. You let me know the second you hear that they've left the country. Understand?"

"Absolutely. I just worry the Feds are going to get involved." *And start asking too many questions.*

"It's inevitable. The second you hear from Victor Chavez that they are leaving, we'll take it from there, and your worries will be over."

One could hope. "Tank or I will be in touch."

Silence. The man had hung up on him.

Roo sat there grinning for a moment. Things were now seriously in motion. He dialed Tank's number and reported out.

"Excellent. I'm glad Victor's been convinced."

Roo wanted to shout out his victory for everyone to hear. "I'll be leaving first thing in the morning." Should he mention he'd thought of the old hag and her threat? No. Tank would laugh it off, say he was superstitious that the woman could put a curse on him. Well, Tank didn't know those in the bayous who openly practiced voodoo.

"And I'll meet you in Baton Rouge tomorrow at the airport," Tank was saying, "and make sure security is tight. I've also requested they bring your LookingGlass fitness mirror so you can get your workout in."

"Excellent. I'll see you then." Roo signed off. Another exhale swept the incident from his mind. He had to get ready for tomorrow night, after all. Things were moving, with just a little kink. With one last glance at the clock in the dash, he put the SUV into gear and headed toward his hotel in Flagstaff.

6

Sweat poured off Roo. On the LookingGlass fitness mirror in front of him that connected him to others in the class across the country, a shapely CrossFit instructor hollered at her virtual class to "Get down on the floor and do those burpees!"

Roo dropped and pounded out a dozen.

More sweat beaded on his nose and splattered onto the polished floor of the workout room at the hotel where he was staying.

"Good job, crew," she said. "Time to slow it down. Side step now. One, two, three…"

Roo gazed at her. But for her full figure barely cloaked in a sports bra and biker shorts, he would have quit a long time ago. He refused to miss a week, even when on the road. His crew had commandeered the fitness studio and set up the LookingGlass for his use. The workouts kept him in shape and burned off the extra calories he'd consume that night. At least now he'd sleep good after the banquet. More pressing of the flesh. More chatting it up with people as shallow as some of the swamps in his home state.

He thought about his wife. Tina hadn't appreciated the way he'd rushed away from Destin on Friday. Tank had been the one to soothe her, had told her something had come up related to the campaign and not to worry. He and Josette stayed and helped with the kids until they all returned to New Orleans Saturday morning. Then Tank escorted her to Baton Rouge where she met up with Roo. Not a warm greeting, meaning she was still upset with him.

His heart rate began dropping, thank goodness.

"Onto the floor, everyone," his instructor ordered.

He eased onto the yoga mat he'd spread. Ahhh. Much better. Except they went right into a series of planks that made his muscles scream even more.

Finally, they stretched. Then, with a cheery wave, the instructor said, "I'll see you all next weekend. Remember to do your Workouts of the Day because I'm going to push you hard."

I'll bet. With a grimace, he hit a remote, and the LookingGlass fell silent.

For a moment, he lay on the mat and stared at the ceiling. His gaze drifted to the smoked glass door. The light from the hallway outlined the bulk of one of Tank's security guys who kept other hotel patrons away from the candidate.

Roo's cheeks puffed out, and he sat up. His cell buzzed with a text.

Ghost. Just sent the estimate as we discussed. Let me know if you have any questions.

He tapped out his reply, then climbed to his feet, rolled up the mat, and left his sweat for others to wipe off the floor. He opened the door. "I'm finished, so you can take the LookingGlass away. I'm headed up to get ready." *And to look at that estimate.*

Two other men closed ranks behind him. They rode the elevator up to the penthouse.

Tina sang in the bathroom, probably putting the finishing touches on her outfit for the evening. Roo pulled out his computer, settled at the worktable in a corner, and called up his email. There it was. The estimate from Ghost. A hefty price tag, especially with the five mil in fee he'd impulsively promised, along with hourly rates for the team and the expenses to travel to and from Iraq. If things went to plan, Roo would make it back along with the five mil he'd already paid Makmoud to kidnap Libby and take care of the team. Ghost had asked for questions and noted he was open to negotiation. None needed for this one. Roo signed the document online and ordered the entire first payment to be sent from various accounts that filtered from the illegitimate side to the legitimate side of LIT. An email later, and things were set into motion.

"Honey, you need to get cleaned up," Tina said from the doorway.

With her blond hair up, body shimmering in a light blue, sequined evening gown, and diamonds dripping from her ears and neck, Tina hustled into the main room of the suite. She froze. "Don't you ever stop?"

"I just had to send one email. Promise." Roo stepped in for a kiss.

She wrinkled her nose. "Man stink. Get ready, and I'll kiss you."

She returned to the bedroom.

Since when had a little sweat stopped her? In their dating days and early marriage, she'd kissed him no matter what his condition.

He'd have to fix that tonight after their banquet.

His tuxedo hung on the open closet door. "Give me half an hour."

Roo enjoyed the feeling of the dual-jet stream and the rainfall feature. The warm water sluiced away the stress from his initial blunder as well as the sweat from his workout. He took his time shaving and moussing his hair so it would stay in place. Once dressed in his tux, he looked the part of a governor. When Tina joined him and finally kissed him, he gazed at their images in the mirror. Yes, the perfect couple. The perfect family. The perfect man for the job.

Tina walked ahead of him into the main room to meet the Swamp Rat. He paused, then called the concierge for some champagne for later that night so he could love on his wife.

Soon, his loose end in the form of Libby Mansour and Cajun Man and his friends would vanish, leaving him a clear path to the governor's mansion and maybe the White House.

7

Butch grabbed a T-shirt from his ruck and pulled it on. He located his trusty Beretta in his backpack, loaded a magazine into it, and chambered a round. He slid it into a holster and placed that at the small of his back. His overshirt hid the gun, and he pronounced himself ready to go.

Shelly sat cross-legged on the queen-sized bed of their quarters. She'd twisted her curls into a messy bun, and her eyes remained half-closed from the nap they'd all grabbed after arriving in Amal earlier that afternoon. She reached out and took his hand. "I can go with you if you want me to."

"I'm good." Butch stared out the window at the landscape of the warehouse complex where they stayed. It shimmered as the metal, rock, and asphalt released the heat of the day.

She wrapped her arm around his waist. "You sure?"

"I'll be fine, babe." He hated the small edge in his voice. His shoulders remained tight like they'd been since the wheels of *The Kitchen Sink*, their C-130, touched the tarmac in Mosul. "I need to walk the town some. I'll meet y'all at 2000 hours at Colonel Farhad's house." He tried a smile and failed. "Kurdish hospitality is the best."

Though doubt filled her hazel eyes, she stood on tiptoes and kissed him.

He released her and headed onto the metal walkway of the massive warehouse that was their quarters. So ironic that ten years before, he and his Special Forces team had constructed the complex, which the town now used for some of their facilities until permanent structures could be built. His SF team had made this warehouse their temporary lair. They'd taken their meals at the big, cafeteria-style tables. They'd done calisthenics, held their briefings, and cleaned their weapons in the open space. If he closed his eyes and let his mind settle for a moment, he almost could hear the low murmur of their voices as they planned a mission or their laughter as they shared a meal.

His footsteps echoed across the common area. He headed toward a pedestrian door and pushed it open. Dusk softened the sky from a pale blue to yellow headed toward orange. He deeply inhaled the scents of dry earth, animal dung, and unwashed bodies. So strange and familiar all at once. Strange since they weren't common scents in Flagstaff and familiar since he'd lived with it to the point of tuning it out when he deployed. This time, no one walked guard duty along the chain-link fence that surrounded the complex.

Ahead of him stretched a wide-open space. To his right lay a long, low building painted white. A red cross hung over the door. The hospital, just like he remembered. To his left lay another building. The school. At least that's what Colonel Farhad had told them, during their brief meeting upon their arrival shortly after noon. Behind their lodging lay the warehouse that had been his undoing. No way would he pay it a visit.

Butch let himself through the gate and made sure the combination lock's bolt shot into the plate. As it had earlier that afternoon, his heart sank as he stared at the rubble across the street. ISIS had left a path of destruction in its wake, including the three churches that served the Christian population of the Kurdish town. The churches had once held two thousand souls. Now, only five hundred remained. Precious few. Even fewer children. Libby taught fifteen primary school kids ranging from five to nine.

The jumble of stone and concrete across from him used to be the church where he and some of his comrades once worshiped alongside

Libby and her family. Back then, children played football—the non-American name for soccer—in the dusty street. Some of his buddies always joined in for the sheer fun of it.

Butch began walking toward downtown where the team had stopped briefly upon their arrival, just long enough to meet Colonel Farhad and obtain the combination to the compound. An administration building remained. Some enterprising citizens had built a couple of stores and one restaurant. Maybe one day, more people would mean more commerce.

As he neared the core of the town, houses began rising among the rubble. A row of ten led all the way to the town square. He paused and gazed northward. The spire of the town's only mosque, the one Islamic place of worship, was clearly visible. Though from what he remembered, ISIS had done a fine job of killing not just the Christians in Amal but also the Muslims, simply because they refused to prescribe to the radical brand of Islam spread by the group. So much suffering. So much loss. He blew out a hard breath and rotated his shoulders to work loose some of the tension.

Butch's steps slowed as he came to the first house made of mud brick and stone. His mind recalled the aerial photo the guy from the consulate had included in the report the team had received from the State Department. Libby's house lay next to him. No crime scene tape, no nothing, though her kidnapping occurred just nine days ago. The gate remained ajar.

Butch froze. Had someone freely helped themselves to her possessions? Darned if he was going to let that continue. He slipped into the courtyard and ensured the gate clicked shut. A bench and a couple of cheap plastic chairs sat underneath an awning she must have erected to keep out the strong sun. On the other side of the courtyard, a scrawny pine rose above a concrete table and benches. *Libby, do you like to spend much of your time out here? You always were someone who loved fresh air.*

What about the rest of the house? The report had at least mentioned someone had cut the power. The grate over the doorway hung open, and he tried the front door. It creaked inward at his touch. Once inside, he shut the grate behind him and flipped the light switch. Nothing. No power. Still.

Despite the light remaining outside, darkness permeated the house. He detected a faint scent of rosemary and basil as well as a slightly iron scent that seemed out of place. Shivering in the cooler temperature, he let his eyes adjust to the gloom.

He drew a sharp breath. Chaos everywhere in the form of upended furniture, broken dishes, and blood splatters, hence the iron smell. From Libby or her would-be rescuer? He yanked a small flashlight from his cargo pants and clicked it on.

He took a step farther inside. A scraping sound rewarded him. A shard from what might have been a vase. Books lay spread-eagled. He shifted the light to the kitchen. Silverware everywhere. A shattered chair and over-turned table. A crack in the oven door.

Oh, Libby, what happened? It looks like you fought. Or someone fought for you.

His fingers tightened around the flashlight, and he made his way down the hallway. Bathroom first. Then what appeared to be a small closet and laundry room. Then a bedroom on the left. Too small for someone to comfortably sleep in. Libby had converted it to a study.

Her laptop and printer sat on an old desk, their sleek outlines in stark contrast to the scarred front. A photo caught his attention. His heart caught as he gazed at Libby and her husband, Samir, with their three children. Had he seen any photos in the living room? Not that he could remember, but then again, the place had been such a mess he could have missed them.

Three sheets of paper lay on the printer tray. He studied the first one. It seemed to be confirmation of an airline ticket for the second of August, a one-way ticket to Birmingham, Alabama, where her parents now lived. Also a letter signed by her that looked like a resignation letter. And the third one—

The front door's grate squeaked. Immediately, he shut off his light. Did he have a way out? He had no idea.

He stepped into the hall and found a ladder to a trapdoor at the end and a door across from him that led to the other bedroom. He could go onto the roof if needed.

The grate clanked shut.

Butch drew his gun and snapped on his light. "You'd best identify yourself now," he growled in Arabic that wasn't too rusty.

"Hey, I come in peace," a vaguely familiar voice replied in the same language, though flawless, unlike his own Arabic—and without the Cajun accent that had always made Butch's Kurdish and Iraqi comrades laugh.

Butch shone the light in his face. What on earth? "Jace Choi? JC? I-I don't believe it!"

Jace squinted in the glare of Butch's flashlight. "Cajun Man?"

"Yeah." Butch snapped off his beam.

"Let's get where we don't have to blind one another," Jace said. "C'mon out to the courtyard."

Stunned, Butch followed his old teammate to the awning. Sure enough, Jace Choi, one of the medics from his old SF team, stood before him in the deepening dusk. "Jace, it's good to see you, man."

"Same here." The two men shared a brief embrace and three slaps on the back. Butch studied him. "You're looking a little rough right now."

The Korean-American touched a shiner at his left eye that remained red with tinges of yellow around the edges. Other bruises created a rainbow of colors across his face. Come to think of it, his friend moved slowly, carefully, as if recovering from a beating. Could it be—

"I've been watching her house ever since she was kidnapped. I heard you arrive and came to check what was going on."

The mystery friend from the report. Wow. Did God work in strange ways or what? Stunned, Butch eased onto a plastic chair, which creaked under his weight. "You're the doctor in the report."

"Physician's assistant, actually. People think I'm a doctor. I'm one of two PAs, and one of the missionary docs from my organization comes up from Mosul a couple of times a week to see the more serious cases. Libby and I have been next-door neighbors since she arrived eighteen months ago." With a small groan, he lowered himself onto the bench. His features twisted in a grimace as he leaned back. He stared at the ground, then met his friend's gaze. "I tried to save her, Butch. Truly, I did."

"What happened?"

"You saw the damage inside."

"What I could see. The power's still out."

"Good luck on getting it fixed any time soon. You know how things operate around here."

"Slowly."

That earned a wan laugh, which turned to a wince. "That's one way of putting it. I couldn't sleep that night and wound up waking up around two-thirty or so and going into my courtyard to think and pray." He paused and stared off in the distance. "I heard a cry. I did the first thing that popped into mind and charged over here. They got me the second I rushed through the door."

"Hence your black eye."

"Yeah." With a sigh, Jace shook his head. "I don't know how many of them there were." He heaved himself to his feet and shoved his hands into the pockets of his jeans as he meandered to the table. "Probably four. Maybe more. They beat me really good. Then got me with a taser more times than I care to think. When my brain finally started firing in the right direction, they were gone, Libby with them. Somehow, I made it to the police station. They were out here within minutes, but it was too late. Colonel Farhad called the consulate in Mosul."

"How long did it take them to get up here?"

"Not long. They showed up shortly after dawn." Jace fell silent for a moment. "Colonel Farhad did a pretty thorough investigation, but their forensics investigations aren't near what we have back in the States." He resumed contemplation of the mountain peaks. "You talk to him yet?"

"Just long enough to meet each other. He's invited us to his house tonight for supper and a deeper discussion."

Jace swiveled. "So that's why he invited me. The colonel's a good guy. Better than his weaselly captain, who was the one to talk to the guy from the consulate."

"Yeah, the report we got was kind of thin."

"I know. Do I ever know." A smile crossed Jace's lips and faded. "You know, when Libby showed up here in January 2018, I was so shocked."

Butch thought about the traumatic brain injury she'd suffered in 2014. "You know what happened to her, right?"

"Yeah. TBI. She told me, and I've been providing follow-up care to her." He shuffled to the bench and resumed his seat. "She told me all that happened, what with ISIS invading and Samir's murder. That her children are missing." He winced and bit his lip. "I have to say we're good friends now. Well, I want more than that. I think she's slowly coming around. Except for…"

He didn't elaborate, and Butch didn't push. Maybe later, he would. He glanced at his watch. "Why did the colonel invite you?"

"He said Victor Chavez wants to talk to me. It's like old home week all of the sudden, just in the wrong part of the world. When was the last time you, Vic, and I were together?"

Butch chuckled. "Try 2005. It *is* good to see you." He sobered as his mind returned to 2009 like a dog did to its vomit. His mood, which had lifted when he'd met Jace, nose-dived again. "You don't know what it meant to me when you stood up for me ten years ago."

"You were the reason I got out of the Army."

Butch stared. "What?"

"Yeah. I couldn't stand the way they treated you like a criminal. It galled me to no end. And I knew I'd come to a crossroads. Get out, go to college, and do physician assistant school or stay with an organization that shot first and then asked questions. I knew if I didn't start college at thirty, I'd never go."

Butch extended his hand. "You're a good man, Jace Choi. C'mon. I'll help you up since I guess we need to get going."

Jace struggled to his feet. He grunted and braced his hands on his knees as he hung his head. "Sorry. It's been over a week, but man, I still hurt sometimes. Thankfully, nothing was broken. The chief's house isn't far from here." He nodded to the gun Butch stashed in its holster. "It's good to carry. I think everyone does here." His shoulders sagged, and he sighed. "I wish this had never happened."

They began walking, and Butch slowed his pace to accommodate Jace's injuries.

At the town square, his friend turned and faced Libby's house. He shook his head and began shuffling down the street again. "You ever been tased? I mean, beyond training?"

Butch winced as he remembered his close encounter of the taser kind a year and a half before. "Oh, yeah. I'm convinced my brain didn't function well for a few days after that."

"Mine too." Jace cast him a long look. "And after they got me, I was in and out of consciousness, but I don't think they realized it. I heard two strange things. I think they had Libby secured by that point."

"What were they?"

"First, one of them spoke immaculate English, almost like you and me. Second, they were talking to each other in another language. I couldn't tell at first, but then I think I did." He stopped and faced Butch square on. "They were speaking in Farsi."

Thursday, July 11, 2019, 2045 hours local time, Amal, Iraq

"Farsi?" An hour later, Victor stared at Jace. "You sure about that?"

Butch stroked his beard as he studied the former medic in the dim light of the elegant brass chandelier hanging above a large, circular dining-room table. He had no doubt about his friend's words, but it seemed strange to him.

"Like I said, I can't be sure. I was in and out of consciousness, and I'm only proficient in Arabic and Kurdish." Jace raked his hands through his hair. "I've picked up some Farsi since I've been here, but in no way am I fluent."

Victor turned his gaze toward their host. "Colonel, is Farsi spoken here?"

"The Turkish border is barely ten kilometers from here, and we are just over a hundred kilometers west of the border with Iran," Colonel Amar Farhad replied in his precise English. "So yes, we do have some Farsi and Turkish speakers, though Arabic and Kurdish are by far the most common languages."

Butch did the conversion in his head. Around sixty or so miles away. Slightly over an hour in a car going sixty. That was close. Too close for his comfort in some respects.

Colonel Farhad poured some water from a brass pitcher into a crystal goblet before he handed the pitcher to his wife, who had appeared by his side. "That is why in 2016 and 2017 when we were fighting against ISIS, the Iranians participated along with your Special Forces. Strange bedfellows, eh?"

Oh, yeah. Butch still marveled about the bizarre alliance that had been formed, even for a short time. What had the powers-that-be been thinking? Survival. Eradication of a force that had brought darkness to this area and threatened the surrounding nations—and potentially US interests. He leaned back in his chair, stretched his legs straight, and crossed them at the ankles. "Jace, maybe you know since you and Libby are friends. Why was she headed home in August? To hear her talk when she visited us in 2017, she felt like she was more Kurdish than American since she'd lived overseas for thirteen years until 2016."

Jace shifted in his chair, glanced at Butch, and looked away. Strange. Had Libby told him something in confidence? Could be. Well, if he'd gotten sweet on her, Butch could understand. "Things started happening around here."

Skylar and Victor both leaned forward, and Victor asked, "What kinds of things?"

Butch cast a long look at Colonel Farhad.

The colonel's voice came across as a low rumble. "At first graffiti on the sides of courtyard walls and buildings. Death to Americans. Death to Kurds. Nothing too out of the ordinary that we have not seen before. Then small animals were killed."

Colonel Farhad glanced to his left at his deputy, a Captain Alkana if Butch remembered the last name correctly. Weasel. A perfect description of a small man with almost bulging eyes and two large front teeth that seemed to stick out of his mouth.

The colonel returned his gaze to their mission commander. "A couple of weeks ago, two young boys went exploring. They wandered far enough away to go over a mountain ridge to the north. Not too far away in terms of distance, but enough for them to be isolated. We," the colonel's gesture encompassed the deputy, "initiated a search party after they did not return when they should have. Jace joined us as well since he has familiarity with these mountains and in case the boys needed medical assistance."

Butch closed his eyes. Part of him didn't want to know what they'd found.

Victor asked the question for him. "Did you find them?"

"Yes. Both were dead."

Fiona gasped, as did Shelly. Diana flinched, and a muscle twitched in Victor's jaw. Skylar, the only other team member besides Butch who could keep a complete poker face during news like this, remained expressionless. Butch's gut tightened. "Who do you suspect, Colonel Farhad?"

"There is a new force arising north of here in the far eastern stretches of Turkey led by a man who calls himself the Turk. And he is just as radical as the members of ISIS were. I have been talking with my Iraqi comrades, who are scared. They fear he was part of ISIS and has begun to resurrect the same. And I have discussed this with those in Turkey as well. Their attitude is that if it doesn't impact farther west, they don't care." He clucked his tongue. "As for those boys, we did find them. You see, my friends," he rested his elbows on the table, "it is not just that we found them. They were cut open, gutted for lack of a better term."

Shelly moaned, and Butch took her hand.

"The killers used their blood to write on the side of a cliff the Arabic phrase that was found on the flag ISIS carried during their sweep across this land."

"Dang," Skylar muttered. "You think the Turk wants Amal?"

The colonel's thickly accented English rested easy on Butch's ears and reminded him of years ago when he and his team trained with the Kurdish militia on a regular basis. "It is difficult to say. I do not think his army is large enough to face even our militia. But that is not certain. I can say the Iraqi army is scared. They seem to think if they ignore the threat, it's not there."

"That's what got them into trouble the last time," Skylar muttered.

"I do not disagree, Mr. James." Colonel Farhad lifted the proffered water pitcher from his wife and handed it to Butch. "We do have a militia of a few thousand men here in the autonomous region. We are aware of the situation. We are certainly here to keep order and protect, but we do not have the manpower or funds to hunt them down. And we've seen no signs as of now that they are amassing anywhere."

"What about you all here?"

"We are readying, though I do worry. We are small here, as you know. Just five hundred souls and a militia force of ten, though I daresay that every adult here is a fighter. Even the women like Libby Mansour."

Butch stroked his beard as he mulled Amal's precarious position. He glanced at Skylar, whose brow remained knit in thought. "Skylar, you look like you have something there."

"Naw, it's just that it's weird. From what I remember, ISIS was routed all the way back to Syria, with the leadership getting destroyed fairly recently."

Butch glanced at the chief and his deputy. "One would think. But the presence of those killers being potentially from the Turk does lend some credence that the kidnappers who took Libby could be ISIS leftovers. Would you agree, Colonel?"

"I cannot deny it." Colonel Farhad nudged Captain Alkana, who'd remained silent throughout the meal. "Your thoughts, Captain?"

"I have none." His words came out nasally.

"That doesn't leave a lot for us to go on," Victor said. "Would you approve of us asking questions around town?"

"People are generally not willing to talk with foreigners. But we are willing to go with you. We did check already with those around town during our investigation. No one saw or heard anything. And yes, there is an Internet café here where you say the video originated. I'll not deny that, but no one has mentioned seeing any strangers."

"Shelly, any luck with anything else related to the email?" Victor asked.

She shook her head. "Nothing. It dead-ends at the café. Nor are there any cameras anywhere, so unless we get a lead on a visual from an employee, we're out of luck."

Victor focused on the colonel. "Colonel Farhad, may we go to the café ourselves?"

"I will be glad to go with you. But I can tell you that there is also fear. People definitely do not trust foreigners, even ones concerned for their friend."

Dang it. Butch shook his head. "What's next, boss?"

"I'm thinking." Victor tapped his fingers on the table, then glanced up. "We're stuck for tonight and running out of time. Tomorrow at first light, I want to do a thorough search of Libby's house. Maybe then we can discover a clue or something that will lead us in the right direction."

The smallest of noises distracted Butch. He glanced at Captain Alkana. The man shifted in his seat, almost squirmed like he had to go to the restroom. He lifted his phone from its face-down position on the table and put it to his ear. He spoke softly in Kurdish. Butch doubted anyone was on the other end.

The captain rose. "I am sorry, but I must go now. Something has come up at the station."

Colonel Farhad frowned. "Do you need me?"

"No, no. One of our officers has something he wants to discuss in person. Until tomorrow." He bowed stiffly toward the team. "It is a pleasure to meet you, and please know we will do anything we can to help you find Ms. Mansour. She is a favorite among those of us who live in Amal."

One of mine too, Butch almost blurted. The captain's actions bothered him. Once the man had slipped from the room, he rose. "I'll be back in a few."

"What's going on?" Shelly asked.

"Not sure yet." Butch ignored the other questions from the team. Instead, he pushed through the door into the quiet foyer of the house, then into the cooling evening air. The courtyard's gate opened without a sound, and he stood in the shadows of the wall.

Captain Alkana wandered toward the station a few blocks away. Not at all like a man who'd been summoned. He punched a number into his phone.

Butch stilled and buried himself in the darkness. So long as he didn't move, the captain shouldn't see him.

The man spoke in low tones in Arabic. Not loud enough to be able to discern any conversation. But he nodded as if he agreed with whatever was being said. He lowered the phone and swiveled as he surveyed the area.

Butch barely drew a breath. Thank goodness for no streetlights. No way could Captain Alkana know he was being observed unless he sensed a presence nearby. At last, he continued on his way to the station.

Who had Captain Alkana called? Sure, it could have been legit, but the way he moved bothered Butch. Time would tell. Reluctantly, he returned to the dining room and slid onto his chair at the table. Out of sight, Shelly took his hand. All he knew was one thing. Time was indeed running out, and if they didn't get a move on it, Libby could very well die.

8

Makmoud smiled as he slid his phone into his shirt pocket. His quarry lay not too many kilometers west of their hideout. Where he stood in the courtyard, smoke wafted across his face. His stomach growled at the delicious scent of goats roasting. He approached the dining area where one of the men on kitchen duty that night set out plates and silverware for their supper. Another lit the heat lamps that would stave off the chill settling over the mountains. "Has anyone seen Jibril?"

The man at the grill flipped the meat. "I think he was headed to the roof. If you're going that way, food's up in ten minutes."

Makmoud's mouth watered. Supper would indeed be good when coupled with the potatoes and greens he'd seen on the stove inside. He headed up the three flights of stairs to the second floor's rooftop. A chilly breeze teased his cheeks. The waxing gibbous moon coated the surrounding mountain peaks in a soft, silvery light. The better to spot anyone trying to sneak up the road.

Facing northwest, Jibril stood next to one of the guards and held a pair of binoculars to his eyes. As he lowered them, the taut set of his shoulders signaled trouble.

Makmoud came to stand beside him. "Brother, something has

you vexed."

"I'm concerned about what we discovered in Amal last week as we were preparing to kidnap Libby."

"About the boys dying."

"More about what the police found when they searched for them. They were gutted, their blood used to paint ISIS words on a cliff. The local militia suspects the Turk." Jibril almost spat the words. "He's just as dangerous as ISIS was. You know we are not many."

"Twenty-four. A fairly robust team, I must add." Makmoud paced back and forth as he peered into the darkness. His *Quds* comrades in Iran had been tracking the Turk since he'd come onto the scene late the year before. All rhetoric is what they'd initially assumed when the man had begun preaching a virulent brand of Islam in the town squares of small communities in eastern Turkey. But not now. The Turk had begun gaining a following from all over Turkey, Syria, Iraq, and Iran, and he hid out in the wildlands of eastern Turkey. He definitely warranted careful watching. "They are north of the border, yes?"

"We're not sure." Jibril cradled the binoculars in his hands. "I'm concerned a small force of the Turk's may have moved south."

"Show me."

His brother led the way down to the main room, where a topographic map lay on a large pool table. He jabbed a beefy finger at a valley. "Here. Not forty kilometers northeast of our location. Just inside Iraq. Too close for my comfort."

Makmoud's eyes narrowed. "Mine too. But we are close now. Calling for reinforcements will blow our cover with the Iraqis. So far as they think, we are simply a hunting party going after wild boar. Little do they know who we're really hunting."

Jibril cocked his head. "You have news?"

"Our contact called. They arrived this afternoon, and it is time to start leading them in the direction we want them to go." He reached into a pocket and pulled out a cigarette lighter of light blue plastic with gaudy gold Arabic writing on it. He pressed it into his brother's hand. "This will be like a ring in the bull's nose. They'll bite, and we can lead them wherever we want them to go. You know what to do now."

"I do." Jibril's next question came out as a low rumble. "And what of the situation to our north?"

"We'll place them under surveillance. Go on, and I will dispatch two of our men as scouts."

Jibril clapped him on the shoulder and headed outside. Makmoud traced a route from the valley Jibril had pointed out to their location. Northward to the east-west highway they'd used to enter Iraq. Not even a kilometer away lay a sharp turnoff northward to where Iraq jutted into Turkey. There lay the valley in question. Just as hidden as their own and too close for comfort. Though the valley was small, it could hold a fair number of men completely out of sight. He couldn't ignore this threat. Doing so might cost him his quarry, his unit, and even his life. How had the roving patrols he'd dispatched missed them? Isolation. The Zagros Mountains were rugged. Inaccessible, even. It would be easy to miss someone in them. Not anymore.

Makmoud summoned two of his men and gave his orders: At daybreak, head to the valley—probably a half a day's hike away thanks to the terrain. Keep a twenty-four hour watch and report in every hour. They understood and promised to move out on foot at first light. They'd be in position by noon.

Makmoud peered around him. Those not on kitchen or guard duty tuned in to one of the television programs beamed out of Baghdad. An action movie. One the mullahs in Iran would have frowned upon and forbidden, thanks to the clothing the leading lady wore. He shrugged. No worries for him. He'd long since ceased to obey the mullahs.

Too noisy. He needed more privacy for his thoughts, time away from the noise and any prying eyes. He returned to the roof where his sentry kept watch over the landscape.

Makmoud leaned against the parapet and folded his arms across his chest as his thoughts turned inward. Soon, very soon, Paul LaRue's troubles would go away, and the man would drop another five million into the account Makmoud had set up on behalf of *Quds*. Once he had Victor Chavez and his team in his hands, he would transmit the full ten million into the bank accounts of *Quds*. He'd regain his status by bringing Victor and his team to Iran and breaking them, just as he'd promised General Soleimani five years before. No longer would he have to buy girls for sale on the black market for senior government officials. No longer would he serve as a high-ranking errand boy for *Quds*. Instead, he'd be back to having the latitude he'd had years before when he'd first come in contact with Victor.

A low growl like that of a wolf escaped him as he contemplated the man. A grudge match if there ever was one. Victor was the man who'd destroyed any future he'd had. He was the man who'd caused Makmoud to lose face with the general. Of course, hubris had played a role in that. He'd been so sure, so confident five years before with his surprise attack on Last Chance Ranch. Back then, he'd planned to capture the Shadow Box team, take them to the *Quds* facility in Venezuela, and break them before turning them into moles for his government.

He just hadn't considered the ingenuity of the part of the Shadow Box team that had escaped. Butch. Shelly. Sana. Diana. And Suleiman. The cuss word came as he remembered his half brother, who'd ditched the name of Ibrahim Hidari out of shame and was now known as Suleiman al-Ibrahim. Twenty years his junior, Suleiman had been a loyal follower until he had an attack of conscience and betrayed his older half brothers. His actions cast Makmoud in a bad light, one the failed mission completed, and destined him for scut work.

The time to change that had come.

Makmoud pushed away from the parapet and drew the knife he wore on his belt. Moonlight reflected off the blade. A nice, sharp edge on one side. A serrated edge on the other, with teeth just as sharp. He imagined Suleiman in his hands. When that time came, he would do the honors of making his half brother suffer before ending his miserable life. Then the rest of the team would be his to break and re-form into moles he'd be able to use in the future.

He shook himself. Time to call his client and let him know that soon, very soon, his troubles would vanish. Returning the knife to its sheath, he unclipped the SAT phone he used for overseas calls and dialed.

Thursday, July 11, 2019, 1300 hours CDT, New Orleans, LA

"Gentlemen, it seems as if we're ready for the home stretch of this campaign," Roo announced as he gazed at every person around the table. The Swamp Rat sat to his right. Then came the representatives of his campaign who worked across the state, from the very southwestern parishes to the northern parishes to New Orleans and parishes south of the city. He shoved any thoughts of the old hag he'd encountered into the darkest recesses of his brain.

Time to focus rather than catch some badly needed sleep, which was what he wanted. He folded his cloth napkin into a triangle, then a smaller one, and laid it on his plate. "I want to commend you for the groundwork we've laid. Thanks for your hard work and reporting on it here today. Have a safe trip home."

As they rose, people began talking. He smiled at the saucy brunette who handled the parishes south of New Orleans. Part of him wanted to ask her about the old hag, but he brushed it off. Like she'd know her. The woman's smile widened. Look, but don't touch. His mantra ever since things between him and Tina had cooled.

He cast a glance at Tank, who stood by the door in the role of head of security for the campaign.

As he exchanged parting handshakes with his staff, his phone vibrated inside his pants pocket. He pulled it out and glanced at it. Makmoud's six-digit code. He awaited his client's call. Fair enough. He was done with this lunch meeting. "If you'll excuse me, I need to take a call."

Everyone filtered from the room, and the Swamp Rat lingered. "Anything I can help with, Roo?"

"Negative. Just something I need to take care of." *The second skeleton in the closet you told me to get rid of,* he wanted to add. He led his campaign manager to the door and saw him out. The less the Swamp Rat knew, the better. Plausible deniability and all that.

He wandered to the windows overlooking the city as he remembered his first skeleton. When he'd been in the Army and engaged to Tina, he cheated on her with a fellow officer. Thanks to Tank's work, the woman died in an auto wreck in Arizona. And now Tank would help him take care of Libby, Cajun Man, and his pals. His enforcer had known Makmoud, thanks to his connections in the gunrunning world. He'd been the one to set up the plan.

Once they were alone, Tank locked the door to the private dining room and faced Roo. "Makmoud?"

"He needs me to call."

Tank reached into the black denim jacket he always wore and handed him the phone he used for communications with the *Quds* man. "Go ahead. We swept this room before lunch started. No bugs anywhere."

"I have good news for you," Makmoud said after initial greetings. "Victor Chavez and his team arrived in Amal this afternoon. By tomorrow evening, they will be in my custody."

"I want evidence they're dead," Roo hissed.

"And you will have it. That, I promise."

"I'll be sending my man there to ensure that."

"To Iran?" Amusement tinged Makmoud's words. "You are more foolish than I thought."

Roo's hand tightened on the back of the chair he stood behind. "No, to Mosul. I want photographic evidence of that when he arrives. You understand?"

"Ah, Paul LaRue, you surprise me." Makmoud's smooth voice washed over him and sent shivers down his spine. "You doubt me."

"The deal was they die."

"The deal was I will *take care* of them. Do you understand me?"

"*Taking care of* means many things."

"That, it does. Know I have your best interests at heart."

He could play hardball just as well as his ally could. "Bring him evidence, or you don't get the remaining five mil in your fee. Them and Libby Mansour."

"Trust me to take care of things." Makmoud cleared his throat. "Send

Tank to Mosul, and we will go from there."

With that, the call ended.

Tank had drifted closer and listened in on the conversation as best he could.

Roo handed the phone back to him and blew out a hard breath. Who knew that a simple favor to his father, who was president of LIT and heavily involved in gunrunning, would have made life so complicated? "What do you think? Will he kill them?"

His security head studied him with narrowed eyes. "I think he's going to take your problem off your hands and make it go away. How that looks isn't up to you. You're not over there."

"He promised he'd kill them," Roo growled as he headed to the window and stared over the Mississippi. "His promise for ten million was the death of Victor Chavez and Butch Addison, not to mention Libby. She knows too much about what happened in 2009. She's a smart one. She easily connected what I did that night when insurgents stole a bunch of arms from our camp in Amal."

"Roo, Makmoud and his men will make the problem go away. He's one of the most pragmatic men I've ever met. He's good for his word, even if his word looks different than what you think it should be."

"They can't come back and finger me for what happened. Not at all. Not when—"

"I think Makmoud has plans for them that he doesn't want you to know about. Trust him, why don't you?"

"Easy for you to say." Roo picked up the suit coat he'd hung on the back of his chair. "Look. Go to Mosul, okay? Let him know when you arrive."

"Will do." Tank pulled out his phone and checked it. "I'll set up a ticket, then."

Roo's lips curled as he thought about the outstanding reward offered by the feds for the capture or death of one Makmoud Hidari. Twenty million. Too big to pass up. Tank would carry out his bidding, and when he finished, Roo would have earned back the money he'd forked over to

Makmoud and Victor and then some. "When you get there, you know what to do."

Tank's brow furrowed.

Roo lowered his voice. "I want you to kill him."

9

Butch yawned and stretched in his rack as he came fully awake. 0300 hours. He lay beneath a blanket and quilt. Shelly curled up with her back against his arm, almost to the edge of the queen-sized bed thanks to his bulk. Cool air sifted through the cracked window.

No way could he go back to sleep, no matter how badly he needed it. Not when his mind immediately snapped into gear. Wide awake, he stared at the ceiling. Dang time change. He sat up, the blanket and quilt falling to his lap. After tucking it around his wife, he dressed in a pair of cargo pants, a T-shirt and fleece, and his hiking boots.

No one else roamed the warehouse at that hour. Not surprising. He'd managed on five hours of sleep plenty of times in the past, and he'd get through the day, albeit with a huge need for rest the next night. After creeping down the stairs, he headed toward the kitchen, his footsteps echoed off the corrugated metal walls and roof. Same everything, like the massive industrial stove where Libby and her Kurdish women friends would cook up the best meals to the huge mixer and deep sinks. Laughter. That's what he remembered the most. If he listened closely enough, he could still hear it. Faintly, like the distant sound of church bells pealing. Libby and her Kurdish friends had been close, even to the point of calling each other "soul sisters." How many of them had ISIS permanently silenced? The town had lost three-quarters of its population. Women had returned, but the area remained devoid of the cheer and joy he'd remembered. To hear the colonel speak, the number of children was gradually increasing. Smiles too. And giggles. Hopefully, it would continue.

Butch eased onto the top of one of the tables and rested his feet on the bench. With his elbows on his knees, he rubbed the back of his tense neck. The memories came unbidden.

A good sleep in his rack that fateful day in 2009. Ten hours, which would help him stay alert during his third-shift stint on guard duty. As the non-commissioned officer in charge, he took his responsibility seriously. He briefed Cowboy and the two Kurdish militiamen who would walk the four sides of the compound from 2300 hours to 0700 hours. As he talked, Libby shooed the other women away and finished her own version of KP duty. Samir, her husband, joined her. After a brief conversation, he touched her cheek and headed out, most likely to prepare for class the next day.

Butch joined her in the kitchen. "You got any coffee left?"

"For you, always. Grab it, and I'm dumping the rest."

He handed her his thermos, and she filled it to the top from an urn on the counter. He carried it to the table closest to the pass-through window. Time to hit the latrine, a must-do before walking guard duty for eight hours straight. When he returned, Roo sat on the same table where the thermos resided. Typical. He always made sure his NCOs were ready to go. Libby slowly wiped down the counter and wouldn't look at them. Strange. Then she mumbled a goodbye and something about being wiped out from a busy day of teaching and parenting.

Roo clambered to his feet and clapped his gunny on the shoulder. "You good to go, Cajun Man?"

"Good as I'll ever be."

"Stay warm out there. Good thing you prepped some coffee 'cause it's cold. Brief me when you get off duty."

Butch capped his thermos. "Wilco, sir. Until then."

Once gunned up, he stepped into the cold and began his patrol near the warehouse closest to the perimeter. This particular one was a smaller cousin to the one where they stayed and held all of their ordnance, so if something blew up, no one would go boom. All of the doors to the windowless building were padlocked.

Butch set his thermos on an upended crate and kept his gun at relaxed ready as he did a circuit around the building and then walked his side of the compound. He continually scanned the area beyond the fence. Nothing moved. Not even an animal. They were all smart and stayed warm inside their burrows or wherever they lived. He was the dumb one, walking around in subfreezing temps. At least he had his coffee. After another circuit, he took a large gulp. The hot brew warmed him, and the caffeine gave him the jolt he wanted. Just two more weeks. Then he'd be back home in North Carolina. So it went for the next couple of clicks around the clock.

Why was he feeling sleepy? His rack time had been significant. Was he coming down with something? He didn't feel bad. He shook his head, and his world spun. Whoa. The dizzies. Maybe he was indeed getting sick. Wouldn't be the first time that had happened in the field.

He slugged up another round of coffee.

Man. He was so sleepy now.

Butch did something he never did when on sentry duty. He leaned against the side of the warehouse as he muffled a massive yawn that would have made a bear proud. He finished off the coffee, then began another circuit. He got three sides in and stood next to a pile of pallets stacked as high as his chest near the wall of the warehouse.

Oh, man. The dizzies returned in full force, and the ground tilted around him. Keeping his eyes open became a major battle he was losing. He stumbled into the metal side, then began sliding, not just to the ground but into darkness.

Only gunfire—

"Butch?"

His eyes snapped open. He sat on a table in warmth, not on the ground in the cold.

Clad in leggings and a long-sleeved T-shirt, her standard sleeping gear on cold nights, Shelly stood before him with her curls sticking out in all directions in a way that always made him smile. Not tonight. Her brow puckered. "Are you okay?"

"How okay should I be?"

At his harsh question, she stepped back.

He sighed. "Sorry. That didn't come out right."

She tucked an errant strand of hair behind her ear. "I-I was wondering what happened to you. Vic said to meet up at six, not three-thirty."

"I couldn't sleep." Suddenly, Butch realized he sat on the very same table where his thermos had rested ten years before.

"Why?"

"Jet lag? Honestly, I have no idea." He stared at his wrists resting on his knees. His hands trembled. He clenched them into fists so she wouldn't notice.

She swung onto the table beside him. "Your hands were shaking."

Best to be honest with her. "You remember when I told you about everything that happened here in 2009?"

"Yeah."

"This is where we stayed. When I got into trouble for sleeping on duty."

"You were drugged. I mean, the doc found Ketamine in your system, right?"

"It doesn't matter. One of our guys died, and I spent a day in the brig. And the rest of my comrades except Jace treated me like a pariah after that. They accused Libby—Libby!—of drugging my coffee." He clamped his jaw shut. He shouldn't be mouthing off at someone who was totally innocent in what had happened.

Thankfully, she didn't shrink away from his outburst. Instead, she looped her arm through his and pried loose his left hand from his knee. She fingered the silicone wedding band he wore when at the shop or on a job like this one when he could accidentally get his finger caught on equipment. When she laid her head on his shoulder, her hair brushed his cheek. "It wasn't your fault."

"So you say."

She lifted her head. "It wasn't. Not that I can attest to it, but someone had nefarious intentions that involved you. And it wasn't Libby. From what you told me and what little I know of her, she wouldn't hurt a fly."

Her words affirming his vindication didn't help. He'd been betrayed, and he couldn't forgive those who'd jumped to conclusions before even asking questions.

He couldn't.

Not when insurgents had made off with most of the arms and ammo from the warehouse he was supposed to guard. Not when two militia members were found with bullets in their heads. And not when Cowboy died because someone slit his throat. Knowing he'd failed his comrades still hurt. Big time.

Nothing could ever erase the shame the incident induced.

"Go back to bed, Shel. You can sleep for a couple of more hours."

"You need to sleep too."

"I'll be fine," he lied.

She pulled back and gazed at him. Nope, she didn't believe him. Not one bit. That wasn't right. Two years ago, when he'd told her the unvarnished truth, she'd believed him and held him close as once more, he grieved his friend's death. Now Shelly leaned over and pecked him on the cheek. "I love you, my big man. Don't ever forget that."

With that, she retreated upstairs.

Butch watched her go.

Sadness for all that had happened sucker-punched him in the gut.

With a low growl, he hopped off the table and pushed through the outer door into the night.

Nothing but stars in a clear sky. Not even the first vestiges of light showed at that point. Just moonlight casting its ethereal glow all over the place.

He slipped a cigarette between his lips, then felt around in his pocket and touched the long, slim shape of his lighter. He drew it out and stared at it. More than ever, he missed Cowboy.

When Butch had visited his widow in Wyoming shortly after his return to the States, she'd given the lighter to him and, through tears, told him what her husband had said. Cowboy had wanted him to have that lighter, that it showed a bond between brothers. Now, he cupped his hands around his cigarette and lit it.

Old home week.

Jace had used that term.

How strange that here, he, Victor, and Jace had reunited. And at the behest of another man who'd known this place as well. What was it that drew them to Amal?

Hope. That's what Amal meant in Arabic.

Jace had found it here in the form of a woman he loved.

Victor had found hope after losing it over five years before.

What about him? Hah. He'd lost hope here. Lost faith in an institution he'd sworn to serve for the entire length of his career. That same institution had persecuted him for a crime he'd not committed. He'd lost his purpose, at least for a while.

Lord, why'd You bring me back here? It's caused nothing but pain for me? And why did Libby return here when she had nothing but bad memories?

As he smoked and paced, those questions ran through his mind like a song stuck on repeat.

Problem was, he doubted he'd ever get his answers.

10

"What's the plan, boss?" For the second time in less than twenty-four hours, Butch stood outside the wall surrounding Libby's house. His glance skated to Skylar, Shelly, and Victor, who had joined him for this morning's venture.

Victor gazed at the metal pedestrian gate. "We go in and do a detailed search. Find anything and everything that you think offers a clue as to what happened. She wasn't a random target. Someone probably had an eye on her long before they took her. If you see something, bring it out to the awning in the courtyard, and we'll go from there."

From next door, metal scraped on metal. A moment later, Jace joined them. "Hey, you guys need some help?"

"Can you provide additional info if we need it?" Victor asked.

"I'll do my best."

"Then hang with me. Skylar, you, Shelly, and Butch go on in."

Butch wanted to take a deeper dive into what lay in the study. Besides, he had no desire to violate Libby's privacy by going through her very personal things. "Shel, you take the bedroom and bathroom. I'll take the study."

"I've got the kitchen and living area," Skylar added. "Give us an hour, and hopefully we'll know a lot more than we do now."

They could only hope. Their teamwork had previously proven successful when it came to thorough searches.

As he headed with Shelly down the hallway, Butch briefly touched her on the shoulder. This earned him a small smile before she drifted into the bedroom.

He paused in the doorway of the study. The power remained off, but the sunlight streaming through the small window made it seem a little bigger than the ten-by-ten room it was. Her computer sat where it had been, along with the photo of Samir and the children. Only now did he notice the smooth glass over the desk and some children's drawings creating a collage underneath it. Were these from her kids or her students? Probably her students since Joyce and Gerald had told him ISIS razed the Mansour home during their destructive tidal wave through Amal. *Why, Lord? Why her? Why did she suffer so much?* Pointless questions. He let out a heavy sigh.

He studied the picture of the Mansour family. How old were the kids at that point? An infant, three, and five. Upon closely examining the background, he recognized the living room of her parents' house in Birmingham. He should, since he'd spent several Christmases with his surrogate parents.

He turned to a trunk that held a dormant digital clock as well as several frames. These seemed to be more recent, like just in the past two years. Pictures of Libby with some of her students. With friends. Even though she wore a smile in every one, the solemnity in her expression jerked at his heart. Grief could do that to a person. He knew about it all too well. One of her with Jace caught his attention. They seemed to be on one of the many hiking trails in the surrounding mountains. This time, her eyes crinkled at the corners and sparkled, all sadness erased for that one moment. Did she care about him as much as he did her?

Maybe the trunk held some clues about her life and what might have made kidnappers target her. After moving the frames, he opened it. Nothing, really. Just towels and sheets. Probably a makeshift linen closet in a two-bedroom house that topped off at maybe five hundred square feet.

He sorted through her desk drawers. Office supplies. Lots of pens in different colors, none of them red. She probably used them to grade papers since she'd often joked to him that she hated sacrificing small animals when grading. No, they bled purple. Or green. Even orange or hot pink. Anything but red. He didn't find any schoolwork, probably because the colonel said school had ended in June to make way for the hottest months of the year, to pick up again at the beginning of September.

Another drawer held random computer equipment. The third drawer was locked. A barrier, but an easy one to overcome. He straightened and called down the hall, "Skylar, buddy. You have some lock picks?"

"Just a sec," his friend replied.

Butch focused on the top of the desk, just like he had the night before. Her laptop. A potential treasure trove of information. He unplugged it and set the power cord and mouse on top. Shelly could check it in more depth later. He turned his attention to the pages sitting on the printer.

The email confirmation for the one-way ticket to Birmingham for the second of August. Another the copy of her resignation letter to her principal, effective the end of July since she'd decided to return to Alabama in early August. And another email.

As he scanned the subject line, chills rippled across his shoulders. What...

Last Mass Grave Found.

Man, if there ever was a subject line, that was it. The email came from a Felipe Letre, a United Nations representative stationed in Mosul who worked on something called Project Peace.

He continued reading. Last mass grave site found. Samples taken in mid June in a grid, as per testing protocol for DNA analysis. Results of said DNA analysis due back in late July, with a meeting scheduled for the afternoon of Thursday, July 25, eight days before she was scheduled to fly home. Each fact from the brief email slapped him upside the head.

He needed into that drawer. Now.

"Sky—"

"Right here, dude," Skylar replied. "What do you have?"

"That drawer." Butch pointed to it. "Something tells me this has a lot of info in it."

"Gotcha." Skylar wielded his picks, and within a minute, the bolt clicked back.

Butch slid the drawer open. Oh, man. Totally full of files.

Skylar pulled a bunch.

"Shouldn't you be searching the living area?"

"This is more interesting," his friend replied. He dumped a load into Butch's arms. "Check these while I go through the rest."

Butch opened the first one. Bill stubs, all very organized. He ran across a folder full of sweet notes from her students printed in blocky Arabic, English, and Kurdish. She loved teaching elementary kids, especially in the subjects of math and science. Heck, she'd met her husband, a secondary-school math teacher, while teaching at the international school in Mosul. Only when Gulf II had begun did they retreat to Samir Mansour's hometown of Amal. Here, they'd wed and taught together as they started their family. A lump formed in his throat as he remembered the heinous way in which Samir had died.

Focus, Butch ordered himself. He set that folder aside, then picked up another one. Pay stubs. Teaching in Kurdish Iraq didn't pay a lot. She did it for the love of the job rather than the money. All teachers did, no matter where they were. These pay stubs only went back to the beginning of 2018.

Then he came across a thick accordion folder. It didn't have a tab like the rest of them, but it certainly contained information that mattered to Libby since the papers strained the sides. The team would have to examine it later.

"From what I can tell, she had her finances in order," Skylar said. "Her bank statements show she didn't make a lot, but then again, she didn't spend a lot. She didn't use her credit card hardly at all, just to send gifts to her parents, siblings, and their families at certain times of the year, probably birthdays and Christmas."

"Until a few days ago." Butch handed him the email he'd seen the night before. "A one-way ticket to Birmingham ain't exactly cheap."

Skylar took it and gestured to the folder Butch held. "What'd you find?"

He hefted it. "We need to take a look at this somewhere else. I think it has something to do with this second email." He held up the one he'd begun reading. "Let me stick this into that folder." He slid it inside. "Nothing else?"

"Nope. Evals from her school showed she was a great teacher. She received some follow-up to a TBI she had."

"That happened when ISIS showed up. Jace was seeing her about it." Butch frowned at the thought of all she'd suffered from 2014 to 2016.

"You know the details?"

"Nope. She never talked about it."

"Hmmm. That's it. Seems you got the golden egg with that thick one."

Butch rose, wincing as his knees creaked. He'd turn forty in November, and he already felt like an old man. "You mind taking this out to the boss?"

"Sure. I can do that. You sure you don't want to?"

Shelly stepped from the master bedroom.

What with the hallway so crowded, Butch remained in the doorway. "You find anything?"

She shook her head and ran her fingers down one of her curls. "Nothing. She lived simply. Dressed modestly, of course. Didn't use makeup, it seems."

"She didn't need it," Butch said, then realized he'd uttered words with such admiration about his childhood friend, Shelly would think he was still in love with her. His cheeks heated.

Skylar gave him a quizzical look before telling Shelly, "We found a bunch of files."

"And her laptop." Unable to meet her eyes, Butch shoved the computer into Shelly's arms and added the power cord and mouse. "Surely there's something on here."

She met his gaze, then bit her lip as she looked down at her reward for her search. "I'll take a look at it when we get back."

"Y'all go ahead out. I'll finish up the living room," Butch said in a desperate attempt to move past the awkwardness.

Skylar paused. "I can finish it since—"

"Nah. I got it." Butch tried to cast a jovial tone into his voice, as if he relished searching the crushed remains of Libby's possessions.

Shelly cast him another long look, then began chewing the nails of her free hand as she followed Skylar into the brightening morning.

Now with more light, Butch had his first good look at the living area. Like he'd seen last night, splinters of a chair covered part of the floor in the kitchen. Silverware lay scattered from the drawer missing from its slot in the counter. He found pieces of it in the living room. How on earth had that happened? He didn't want to know. By the door were rust-colored splatters as if an abstract artist had visited. Blood. Libby's? Maybe. Probably more like Jace's. He'd fought and fought hard, apparently. All to no avail. A coffee table was shoved out of the way. He made his way to it and gazed at the stairway leading to the trapdoor, which opened onto the roof.

Colonel Farhad had supplied a whole lot more detail than the report they'd gotten a few days ago. The kidnappers used a ladder to climb up the wall and another to cross from the wall to the roof. They gained access to the living area by that very trapdoor. Otherwise, if they'd gone through the rear one, they would have seized her while she slept. Jace reported at least four men. One who knew English very well. All Farsi speakers. Why Farsi? Butch shrugged at that one since he couldn't quite figure it out.

He turned to the remains of a shelving unit next to the kitchen cabinets. Jace reported one of the kidnappers had shoved Libby into it, which stunned her enough for them to grab her. The shelves lay in shambles on the tile. What a mess. Glass. Shards of pottery. Some more pictures. Books face down, their spines broken.

Kneeling, Butch began sifting through the remains. He only learned from the pictures what he already knew. She treasured family and friends. She loved her parents, her brothers and their wives, and her nieces and nephews. He found some dried roses, probably from Jace.

Since Colonel Farhad had released the crime scene, Butch began a feeble attempt at cleanup. He closed the books, most of them classics, and stacked them. He gathered the photos. Maybe Libby could take them with her when she left. With his hand, he began shoving the potsherds into a pile to be swept up and disposed of later.

A piece of baby blue plastic caught his eye. Strange. So out of place in the muted colors of the living area. Shifting aside some of the ceramic bits, he held it up. A cigarette lighter. Say what? He studied the gold Arabic writing. The Falafel Restaurant in Harifi al-Hafa. He had no idea of where that was.

As he rose, his knees once more popped. He winced. Hopefully, surgery wasn't in his future.

He marched into the bright morning sunlight.

Victor glanced up as he and Jace sorted through several photos from the file folder. "What do you have?"

"You go first." Butch gestured to the folder. "What's this Project Peace?"

Jace's head drooped.

Victor leaned against the bench. Shelly, seated in the plastic chair across from Skylar's, kept her gaze down as she ran her fingers over the edges of the laptop. Victor said, "Jace has been telling us about it."

Butch shifted his attention to his friend. "What is it?"

"A tragedy," the PA mumbled. When he met Butch's gaze, the pain in his eyes startled him. "ISIS invaded in 2014. It was awful. The people here put up a huge fight, but by June when Mosul fell, ISIS began its march on Amal. By that point, the militia was strong, but ISIS was too much. I'm not sure how much you know, but most of the women and children were either kidnapped or killed. And pretty much any man, young or old, who didn't escape, was killed like Samir. Libby fought with the militia, and it's a miracle she survived."

That much he did find out. Not from Libby, who refused to talk about those dark times, but from her parents.

"She sustained a TBI, and while she got treatment at home before she returned, she still requires occasional follow-up."

"And you see her about it."

"Every few months." Jace carefully took the folder from Victor. He gripped it as if he were afraid to let it out of his sight. "Project Peace is an attempt by the UN to bring closure to those who lost children either via kidnapping or killing. The team has been using using scientific means to locate mass graves. Once they find one, they do a very thorough grid search of the remains and pull DNA samples. If they get results from those relatives who volunteer their own DNA, then they let the parents, if any are remaining, know. If not, they try to let extended family know."

"And Libby hasn't found her children."

"No." Jace rubbed his temples. "I mean, I came back because I had a chance after finishing PA school to serve with a missions organization in a place where I was familiar with the people and the culture. In return, they paid off any educational loan expenses not covered by the GI Bill. After what Libby suffered, no one expected to see her again. She surprised everyone when she showed up here."

Butch leaned against one of the posts holding up the awning. "Did she ever wonder what would happen if she never found them?"

Jace met his gaze with a sad one of his own. "You don't think I ever asked her that? She told me she wouldn't leave until she got closure, even though it would be perfectly acceptable for her to be in Alabama while waiting on confirmation. It's not like she needed to be on-site."

"Did you know she bought a one-way ticket back to Birmingham?"

Jace's gaze didn't waver. "Is that an issue?"

"No. I'm just asking."

"I helped her search for it. We talked about what was going on here, about the kids disappearing and being murdered. About who the Turk is and what his army is capable of. I think that put a scare into her. I think I finally convinced her of just that, of returning to Birmingham to wait for answers if she got none at the end of July. We were flying back together."

Butch put his hands on his hips and paced in a small circle as he considered that one.

Skylar, who'd stayed silent as he sifted through the folder, held up a stapled copy of a report. "I'm not sure what this is, but one of the maps shows what looks like several mass graves and sites of other potential graves that were going to be examined with ground-penetrating radar. Not that I've dug into this, but I'm wondering if what's referenced in the email is one of those sites?"

Jace took the paper Skylar handed him. "She printed this right before she texted me the night she was kidnapped. Those are the last sites."

Butch paused in his pacing. "So, if they don't find any remains there, then most likely, ISIS carried away her kids?"

"Possibly. It doesn't sound like they have any hope of finding more mass graves, which means they may shut down the project in this part of the country."

Then Libby would never know. She'd never get the closure she so badly wanted and needed. *God, why is life so unfair? Why?* Butch paced a groove into the ground.

Shelly sat back in her chair and held the laptop to her chest, as if shielding herself from additional talk of death. "Vic, I can dig into this when we get back to our lodging."

Victor held his palm out, like a traffic officer signaling a car to stop. "Butch, it's okay. You can stop pacing. Did you find anything interesting?"

"This." He dug into a pocket of his cargo pants and produced the cigarette lighter. "Jace, you ever hear of The Falafel Restaurant?"

Jace's brow crinkled as if he'd sampled a pickle. "The awful Falafel? In Harifi al-Hafa?"

"One and the same." Butch tossed the lighter to him. "You see this before?"

"Yeah, at the restaurant. The one time I went. Think of the cantina scene from *Star Wars*, and that's what it is. Even the Iraqis won't touch the falafel. Worst ever."

"You ever pick up a lighter? Or did Libby ever visit it?"

"No. The translated name of the town is The Edge. It's literally within a mile of the border with Turkey. Kind of a wild-west type of town that services the nearby border station. Lots of traffickers, human and otherwise. It's a rough place, in other words."

Butch muttered under his breath at what his reply implied.

"Believe me, Libby would never go there. She hates cigarettes. Hookahs even more."

"A woman after my own heart," Victor muttered.

Skylar snickered and playfully shoved him. "The only thing you and Makmoud Hidari have in common, right? A shared hatred of hookah smoke?"

"Eh, something like that. So there's no reason why you'd bring one back to her? Or own one?"

"Nope. I went there like one time and said I'd never return."

"Where is it?" Butch asked.

"About twenty miles east of here."

"I'm wondering if it fell out of one of the kidnappers' pockets," Butch continued. "And if it's one of theirs, we've got to go and check it out. Like today."

Victor shifted. "Butch, it's just one clue."

"It's enough."

"Let's let Shelly—"

"Boss, this is a solid lead. It ain't Libby's. It ain't Jace's. Who else could it belong to?"

"I want to study to learn more about Harifi al-Hafa to know exactly what we're getting into."

Butch wanted to howl. "Analyzing ain't going to get Libby back."

Victor's look turned to a glare. "You're always the one to say let's do our homework."

"We've done it. Ain't much in Harifi al-Hafa, apparently. We go there. We ask questions, maybe knock some heads—"

"We're not going to knock any heads around," Victor countered. "Period. I think we should wait until we've had a chance to know more about this place."

Butch ground his teeth. "In the meantime, Libby could be tortured, raped, or—"

"I'll research this place, okay?" Shelly's voice broke into their brewing argument. "Give me the rest of the morning. If it's not twenty miles from here, we can be there in a half hour and go from there, okay? Can you do that, Butch?"

He stared at his wife.

She released a breath and lowered her gaze as she again ran her fingers along the laptop's edge.

What more could he say? He was upsetting her, and he didn't want to do that. "Okay, then. We go mid-afternoon."

Victor's gaze turned to flint, but he didn't object.

Butch turned to Jace. "You going with us?"

The PA shook his head. "I can't. My first patient arrives in forty-five minutes, and I've got a full dance card all day. Keep me posted?"

"Yep." Despite the warm sun beating down on him, a shiver rippled through Butch. "We'll check in when we get ready to leave. Later, then. Be in prayer for us."

'Cause we're going to need all the prayers we can get.

11

Friday, July 12, 2019 1400 hours local time, Amal, Iraq

Outside the warehouse, Butch tossed his backpack into the cargo area of one of the Humvees and checked the spare can of fuel. There, ready and waiting. The 50-cal machine gun lay disassembled in its carrying case underneath a tarp. Should he pull it out? Nah. Best not to scare those in Amal, and he doubted anyone in Harifi al-Hafa would be receptive to it either. Today wasn't a day to find out. He hefted three collapsible five-gallon water jugs to fill.

Once inside, voices caught his attention. Female voices. All four of them raised. Oh, crap. The ladies were going at it hard with Victor to the point where they'd backed him against the metal wall near the kitchen like a cornered dog.

Fiona Mercedes, their pilot, got right up in his face. "You know something? This entire time, you've had us either waiting around or doing scut work. What happened to us all being together?"

"You don't know what kind of condition Libby's going to be in. What in case she needs medical help? Or something happens to one of you guys?" Diana added, standing next to her friend with her fists jabbed onto her hips.

Victor spluttered, "I—"

"What if the search leads us away from Amal?" Sana hopped onto one of the table benches and glared at him. "If that happens, we'll need the whole team together because you wouldn't have time to come and get us."

He tried again. "Sana, I know, but—"

Shelly piled on. "She's right, Vic. We shouldn't split up. And I didn't find out anything more from her computer. You may need my computer skills, right?"

Victor's voice raised in exasperation. "I know that, okay?"

Lest he get sucked into the argument, Butch tiptoed past them to the kitchen. He set the jug on the counter, pulled out the sprayer, and began filling it. He eyed the group. They continued their bickering. He checked the range. Could he get all five of them with the sprayer? Negative.

Victor huffed out a breath. "Okay. We're *all* going. And you're right. We stick together on this."

Fiona and Diana slapped hands.

Butch fought a grin as the ladies dispersed to grab their packs. Victor turned and kicked the wall. The noise echoed through the warehouse.

"I heard that," Fiona called.

Victor entered the kitchen. "Women!"

Butch snickered. "You've got to admit they make life interesting."

"Hah. That's one way to put it. So guess what? We're taking two Humvees now."

"No worries, boss. I got the other one all fueled and ready to go save for filling the water jugs."

Skylar strolled through the door with them in hand. "And here they are."

Butch capped the first one and began filling the other one. In a low voice, he asked, "You sure it's a good idea for them to go?"

Victor stared through the service window. "They're right. We do need to stick together. From what Colonel Farhad told us, the women in Harifi al-Hafa are just as rough as the men."

"So our women should fit right in."

His friend snorted, then lifted the jug onto his shoulder. "Something like that."

In his head, Butch ticked through the time they needed for their quick trip. Half an hour out. Maybe an hour to chat. Half an hour back. They'd be back in time for supper. Easy peasy. And maybe they'd be one step closer to finding Libby before time ran out.

Once he finished with the other jug, Skylar took over. As he headed from the kitchen, Shelly caught his arm and pulled him aside. From behind her glasses, her eyes searched his face. "Are we good, Butch?"

His heart thumped an extra beat. "Why wouldn't we be?"

She fidgeted with the cross necklace she always wore. "Back there at Libby's house. You, um, seemed upset."

"I'm fine, babe. Seriously. Let me go and check with Vic one last time." With that, he pecked her on the lips and headed outside for one last check.

He barely listened as Victor gathered the group. Everyone was going. He asked the ladies to wear headscarves. At first, Fiona protested, at least until Diana nudged her hard in the ribs. They'd go in armed only with rifles and pistols. The mission was clear. Go to The Falafel. Talk with people there. Stick together. No one was to go wandering off by themselves. Butch's attention turned inward to Libby. They had until Sunday. Then, all bets were off. If they didn't find her, they might be looking for pieces of her.

"Butch!"

Oh, man. The sharp edge in Victor's voice meant his friend had said his name more than once. "Sorry, boss. What?"

"You ready to go?" The question came out as a frustrated statement.

"Uh, ready."

"Then let's go."

Clad in his white doctor's coat and a set of scrubs, Jace joined them. "What time do you think you'll be back?"

"Five at the latest," Victor told him. "Start worrying if we're not back by sunset."

Butch did the calculation in his head. Yeah, if they weren't back by 1900 hours, something was wrong.

"Will do." Jace glanced at Butch. "I hope you find her. Or at least another clue."

"You and me both." Butch put the Humvee into gear. "Later."

Friday, July 12, 2019, 1430 hours local time, Harifi al-Hafa, Iraq

"Looks like we're here," Butch announced.

The blacktop of Harifi al-Hafa's only road widened to four lanes but remained marked only for two. Trucks and cars with plenty of dents and dings lined the side of the road. As they went to and from various shops, people walked along dirt paths that must have passed for sidewalks. A mosque rose up on the far end of town. On their right, they rumbled by a small building with a cross on top. Even here, it seemed, Muslim and Christian lived together in harmony.

They slowed even further as they reached the middle of town. Men lounged at café tables over what was surely good, rich cups of Iraqi coffee. Smoke rose in gray-blue ribbons from the tips of numerous cigarettes. Glares smoldered from dark eyes in faces sporting beards or day-old stubble.

Most of the women wore a *shalwar kameez,* the pajama-like garment of rich jewel tones commonly found in that part of the world, along with headscarves. Butch found it hard to tell just how old a woman was because the harsh sun creased their faces with wrinkles even from a relatively young age. They shopped for the evening meal at open-air markets.

Nearby, Iraqi soldiers left a small building and climbed into pickups. Most likely, they headed for the border crossing barely a mile north of their location.

Butch's nose twitched at the smells of butchered animals hanging from some of the stalls. Vegetables brought in either by local farmers or from other parts of the country painted a rich portrait in reds, greens, yellows, and purples.

In the middle of it all sat a low building built of stone with a light blue backdrop proclaiming The Falafel in bright yellow neon. "And we've arrived."

"Looks that way." Victor nodded to an open spot several feet long in front of the restaurant. "Cruise on down. Hopefully we can squeeze in there rather than walk."

Very quickly, the buildings on the east side of town fell away to mud-and-brick hovels dotting the steep slopes of the mountains. Butch U-turned and snagged the spot with the other Humvee right behind them. Everyone climbed out.

Several of the townspeople paused and glared at them.

Diana's gaze pivoted. "Something tells me they don't like strangers."

"You got that right." Butch didn't like the way the men continued staring at them. Most likely, they kept guns close at hand. He pushed through the heavy wooden door into the dark interior, his eyes gradually adjusting to the low light.

Jace hadn't been too far from the truth about the awful Falafel, at least in the looks department. In front of him stood a circular bar with dim fluorescent lights running around the top edge and along the floor. Iraq might have been a dry country, but at least in the Kurdish autonomous zone, no one seemed to abide by it. Sitting on back-lit shelves, bottles of almost every liquor imaginable kind glowed blue, green, gold, and even red. Did he see a bottle of Jack Daniels? What did the local mullah think? He probably joined in the fun.

Aisles ran at right angles from the bar and divided the restaurant into four quadrants. Even at this hour, some patrons leaned on cushioned divans and smoked hookahs. Butch winced at the sharp stench filling the room. His nose watered, and he fought the urge to sneeze. Techno music and a woman whining in Arabic ground on his nerves and brought back even more memories of serving in Iraq. What conversation he'd been able to hear ceased as the patrons perused the newcomers.

To his right, a sign had a gun in a red circle with a bar through it. At least he could read the Arabic on this one. No guns. A detector flashed to show he indeed carried, but no one cared.

Victor grimaced. "I hate hookah smoke."

"You and me, boss."

The bartender set down a glass he was drying. In rapid-fire Arabic, he asked, "You come to visit? What can I get you? A drink? You look like Americans. Perhaps this Jack Daniels. And I have arak. For you and the ladies. Come. Come. Try it, my friends. Have a seat. Have a seat. I will bring it to you. I know you'll like it."

Butch glanced at Victor, who shrugged. In the deserted quadrant to their left, they settled on low divans in one corner. At least this one didn't have a hookah on the hammered brass table.

Shelly sat beside him. Out of sight of the other patrons, she curled her fingers around his. "What's our escape route?"

His gaze swiveling to the doorway, he released her hand and touched the butt of his Beretta stashed at the small of his back. Unlike the States, no Exit signs glowed over them. "Dunno. My guess is it's either out the front door or through the kitchen."

"And my bad feeling is that every other male in here has a gun," Skylar added softly. "And maybe every female."

Jace had been right about the women being as rough as the men. As they lifted cigarettes to their lips and blew out the smoke, a few of the women examined them with disdainful gazes. Did he see a bandoleer of bullets criss-crossing the chest of one of them? Butch couldn't be sure, but most likely everyone in the place sported either guns or knives. "Boss, I know how folks in these parts like to chitchat, but it might not be best this time."

"I agree." Victor kept his gaze on the bartender as he poured their drinks into small glasses over ice. The clear liquid turned a translucent color.

With a broad smile, the bartender brought their drinks over and set all eight on the table along with some falafel, figs, pita, and hummus. In heavily accented English, he said, "For you, my friends. Would you like anything else? Perhaps some dates? We are preparing our supper. Stay, please. We begin serving at six."

No way were they going to stay that late.

"Sir, much as we would like to stay, we must leave shortly, as we are passing through." Victor pulled out his phone and located a picture of Libby. "We are looking for this woman and wonder if you have seen her."

"No, no, my friend. We rarely get visitors here in Harifi al-Hafa. You are the first in many weeks."

Really? This was one of the main roads between Iran and Syria. The man most certainly lied.

"Where does she live?" the bartender asked.

"Amal," Butch replied.

"Ah, yes. Amal. A nice town." The bartender gestured. "Give me your phone. I can show others here."

Victor shook his head. Smart man, his team commander. He knew better than to relinquish his phone to a stranger. Victor nodded to Butch. "I'll come with you, as will my friend."

Butch joined him and their unanticipated tour guide.

"Come with me, then."

They made the rounds. As they did so, the glares of the other patrons scorched his back. No one knew anything. Hardly anyone ever stopped in town. Sure, people did come and go, but no one had seen Libby. Who had told them about Harifi al-Hafa?

As they returned to their seats, Butch muttered, "Any other ideas, boss?"

"I'm thinking." Victor coughed after he took a sip of his drink.

Butch did the same and almost gagged. Good thing he'd stayed hydrated. This would have put him under the table if he hadn't. And now, to save face, he had to drink it all. He nibbled on some falafel and tried to mask his wince. He now knew why the restaurant had gained its rep. People didn't come for the food, at least not for the falafel.

Skylar smacked his lips as he placed his empty glass on the table. "Best drink *ever*."

"Gag, you sound like a teenager," Sana muttered. "And for the record, I think it tastes disgusting. Thank goodness for hummus and pita."

"It's good?" Butch choked after downing the remainder of his arak. His cheeks flushed. No more for him, not when he had to drive

Their procurement and intelligence specialist leaned in and said in a low voice, "I think strangers have indeed visited. They just don't want to tell us."

Victor pulled out a wad of Iraqi dinars and left them on the table. They more than covered their bill. "I think it's time for us to head out. No one's going to tell us anything, and I prefer for us to get back to Amal in one piece."

Butch studied the other patrons. Several still stared at them, while others had gone back to their conversations. He had the bad feeling they were now the subject of discussion at the restaurant. "Boss, we need to question people in more detail."

"Even if they did know something, I think they'd rather run us through with a sword than tell us. I've got the safety—"

"Then you go back and I'll stay."

"Butch!"

Diana straightened. "Um, boys, we have company."

Two men approached them with a swagger that told Butch they had the advantage. No way could he go for his gun.

"We go now," Victor hissed and rose.

Just as they stepped around the table, the other patrons in restaurant jumped to their feet and drew their weapons, even the women.

So did the team.

A classic standoff. Several patrons slid their fingers from guard to trigger. Butch began praying in earnest because one twitchy finger could mean a whole bunch of people could wind up dead.

"No guns! No guns!" the bartender shouted. "Please, this is a—"

"Shut up, Daran!" One man strolled through the crowd like he owned the place. Maybe he was indeed the owner. Could be he owned the entire town. Butch took stock of this new player. A husky man. A good six or so inches shorter than Butch, but his bulk and the scars on his face spoke of going a round or few and coming out on top. Not someone he wanted to trifle with by any stretch of the imagination. One scar ran across his eye, and that eye had a milky translucence to it that indicated he didn't see out of it. "And you will not leave until you answer some questions."

"Team, weapons down," Victor ordered.

"Oh, no," Fiona lifted her Glock so she could sight down the barrel. "Not until they do the same. I'm nobody's fool on that one."

Eyes not leaving their group, the man barked a command in Kurdish. A woman growled in reply, and the man lowered his voice, hissing another firm command. Only then did the other patrons lower their weapons. Butch doubted they were far from reach. In heavily accented, deep-voiced English, the man continued, "Now, ladies and gentlemen, I ask that you do the same. No harm will come to you so long as you answer my questions."

Nausea touched Butch's stomach as he realized their error. They'd come to ask the questions. Not anymore. *Lord, get us through this. Protect us. Give us favor in this guy's eyes. Otherwise, we're not getting home tonight or maybe ever.*

"We will be glad to share what we know," Victor said. "But it would help if we knew your name."

"I am Yado. And who are you?"

Victor introduced them by first name only.

"Please, have a seat, and we will talk." Yado cut his eyes toward where the bartender poured another round of drinks. In a low voice, he added, "Though this restaurant is called The Falafel, we are not known for that food."

"So I hear," Skylar replied dryly.

"Why did you come here? To seek this young woman?" Yado asked as he gestured to the picture still glowing on Victor's phone. "Because it is true. We have not seen her. Or do you seek something else?" His eyes narrowed. "If so, you have stumbled into great trouble, my friends."

"We've come looking for her," Victor said. He shared an edited version of their investigation.

As he did so, Yado's shoulders relaxed. "You mean us no harm, then?"

"None. Look." Victor leaned forward. "From what we have heard and from the well-armed nature of your friends, the suspicion in this town and its location, you all run goods and services across the border to interested parties."

Read, Harifi al-Hafa was home to traffickers.

Yado's faint nod rewarded them.

"We're not here regarding that. We simply want to find our friend and safely return her to her parents."

Yado considered this. "Her parents must be wealthy if they hired you."

"A benefactor did."

Butch cleared his throat. "Sir, we suspect either ISIS or someone named the Turk might have taken her. What are your thoughts regarding him?"

Yado snorted. "ISIS is gone. The Turk and his army? Not so much. He is indeed over the border spewing out hate. His men have ambushed some of our people from here and taken all they carried. Even killed a few. Our routes do run through Amal, and we have heard about the two boys they lost in the wilderness. The Turk is real, and he is a threat to this part of Kurdistan. But why kidnap this woman? She is beautiful, yes, but why her, when there are plenty of beautiful women in this part of the country?"

Butch glanced at Victor.

His leader's brow furrowed, and he knew he considered this new twist. Butch studied those who had gathered in the archways, about a dozen or so men, probably part of Yado's trafficking ring. Everyone seemed to wear the same expression of wariness but now stood in a relaxed quarter circle around them. All save for one, whose leg jiggled as he lit another cigarette. A young man with shifty eyes and a scraggly beard. Probably not even out of his teens.

Butch placed him under watch.

"Then another question," Victor said. "Have you seen any strangers besides us recently?"

Mr. Fidget really began shuffling his feet. Why?

Victor set the lighter upright on the table. "I'm asking because we searched the woman's home this morning. This is what we found. It's a lighter that comes from this restaurant, correct?"

Yado didn't move. "It is."

"Our friend doesn't smoke. Neither does the man who tried to save her. Do people from Amal visit Harifi al-Hafa?"

Yado picked up the lighter and turned it over and over in his hand as if the motion helped him think. "Rarely. As you can probably tell, people know better than to stop and tend to pass through town. And people from here do not spend time in Amal."

"Which leads me to believe one of the kidnappers was probably here at some point, stopped in for a meal or a drink, and picked up the lighter."

Yado handed it back to Victor. "That is a very good question. And yes, I do think you are correct. Though it has been a few weeks, we did have visitors. Several. In early June. They rode into town much like you did. They are staying nearby."

"A family?"

"No. All men whose stated purpose was to hunt wild boar. They are a constant problem in this part of Iraq. Twenty-four men who all had a good time. Daran could tell you that."

By this point, Mr. Fidget edged into the aisle leading to the front door. With his dark eyes on Victor, he backed away. He knew something.

Butch refocused on the conversation. His talk with Jace crept into his mind. "Yado, I have a question for you." He kept one eye on Mr. Fidget. "Did these men happen to speak Farsi?"

The teenager bolted toward the front door.

Butch vaulted the table and nearly squashed Fiona in the process as he jabbed his foot onto the seat beside her.

"Hey!"

He barely heard her startled cry as he leapt over the half wall separating him from the aisle.

His fingers brushed the fabric of Mr. Fidget's shirt. The teenager slammed through the wooden door. It crashed against the outer wall and rebounded with such force that it nearly smacked Butch in the face.

The kid raced across the street and mounted a motorcycle.

Butch hollered, "Stop!"

The kid glanced back, revved the engine, and took off.

No way would he let him escape. Butch bolted toward the first Humvee.

Victor burst into the bright afternoon light. "Butch, slow down, okay? We can ask Yado—"

"I ain't losing this guy, boss." Butch jumped into the driver's seat. "He knows something about Libby's kidnappers, and with or without y'all, I'm going after him."

"We're coming!" Skylar cranked the engine of the second Humvee.

The remaining team barely had time to pile in before Butch did a hard U-turn and raced after the motorcycle.

Victor struggled to hook his seatbelt. "What on—"

"The kid knows something. When Yado started talking about strangers in town, he got really nervous. Then, when I asked if those strangers spoke Farsi, he took off." He focused on the road, which quickly narrowed. Were they on the way to the border? The compass on the dash said yes.

The kid hung a hard right.

Over the noise coming through the open windows, Victor shouted, "We've got to stop and—"

"I'm not losing him. I think he's key to all of this." He focused on driving and clenched his jaw. No more thinking. Time now to act.

The road curved to the right, and the teenager disappeared from view. It curved even further, then straightened. Dead ahead the road forked. The whine of the motorcycle's engine bounced off the rock walls of the canyon and faded. Impossible to tell which of the two strips of asphalt he'd taken.

"Boss?"

"I don't want to get us separated."

"We've got to." Butch gestured toward the split. "He could have gone either way."

"I'm thinking."

"Just. Stop. Thinking!"

Victor's cheeks puffed out with a breath. "I've got our crew to consider."

Butch wanted to howl. "We only go one way, we could be wrong and completely lose him."

Victor glared at him, then peered out the front. "Okay. I get it. We'll go right. I'll send the other team left. But we don't go far. Just five minutes up at twenty miles per hour. I'm deadly serious about that because something doesn't feel right. We're going operational now. Call signs from here on out." He hopped down and gave the other group directions. When he returned, he picked up his rifle. "And this time, we're going in fully armed."

12

"This is starting to creep me out." As they crawled up a road rutted with potholes and littered with small rocks, Butch kept his head on a swivel. Both sides of the narrow valley rose almost vertically. The mid-afternoon sun pounded down on them and beamed off the slopes. A hot wind moaned along the valley floor. His mouth went dry, and sweat broke out across his bald head. He slapped a bush hat on it to avoid the sun's burning rays.

Victor keyed his microphone. "One to Eight. Any sign of him?"

"Negative." Skylar's reply crackled a little, the steep rock walls interfering with the signal to their satellite. "You?"

"Negative. We go on for two more minutes. Then turn around and get out of there."

"Uh, it's so narrow we might be backing out."

Butch assessed the blacktop. Dang it, same thing on their road. The Humvee took up its width. They hadn't thought this one through. Okay, *he* hadn't thought it through. He'd been the one to push it. They could escape, but it'd be more like an eighteen-point turn, which would make them dead meat in case of an ambush. His palms moistened as he began mentally rehearsing what he'd been taught about driving backward at high rates of speed. Be fast but careful. He twisted in his seat.

Shelly stared at him with wide eyes. "Bu—Five?"

"We'll be fine, Four." With his heartpounding in his ears, he reached back and took her hand, which had turned cold and clammy. "Keep your rifles handy, ladies."

"No worries on that one," Diana replied.

Butch faced forward again and peered around him. Ragged trees dotted the landscape. So did boulders, some perched almost incomprehensibly on the valley walls. Did he detect movement? Or ropes leading downward from the ridge? Too hard to tell, but his internal alarms started blaring. They were isolated in an unknown location. If things went south, no one would even know where to look for them.

"Five, time to call it," Victor said.

A cold feeling, one he'd always known in combat, washed over him. Tangos lurked nearby, and they were split up.

"Eight, abandon ship. Now," Victor ordered.

Static.

"Eight? Do you read me?"

"Brace! We're getting out of here." As his pulse ramped up, Butch threw the transmission into reverse and stomped on the accelerator. The jolt slammed everyone against their belts as they shot backward.

"Oh, no!" Shelly cried.

The boulders turned to eight men rappelling down the slopes. Blips of light shone, followed by crackles. Bullets slapped into the front of the Humvee.

Two men shoved a large boulder into the road behind them.

Butch screeched to a halt. He released his seatbelt and grabbed his rifle.

"Out!" Victor shouted.

Butch tumbled from his seat and landed in a crouch. Using the door as a shield, he pumped some lead downrange while Shelly lined up back-to-back against him to cover their rear flank. Bullets pinged off the armored doors. Nothing else. Butch took aim and fired. No scores, but the barrage sent his attackers scurrying behind boulders.

Butch's gun clicked. Empty. He ejected the spent magazine, rammed home a new one, and turned the lever to triple shot.

Their attackers began advancing in perfect leap-frog formation as they kept their quarry pinned down with gunfire. Who were these guys?

Butch's breath came in faster and faster pants. Tunnel vision could be his undoing if he weren't careful. He sucked in a breath and released it to make his adrenaline abate.

One of them hurled a cannister toward him before ducking behind a rock. Gas spewed from it as it landed short of its target. More followed toward the other side of the Humvee.

"Tear gas!" Victor shouted as another it sailed their way.

Butch scrunched his eyes closed and yanked up his gaiter to cover his nose and mouth. He kicked the cannister, sending it out of their way. A close call.

Until another and still another landed right beside him and Shelly.

"Five…" Shelly began coughing.

The hot breeze blew it directly over Butch. Now no gaiter or closed eyes could save him. His eyes burned and watered. He hacked and struggled to clear his lungs. He sank to his knees as the fusillade ceased. Why? His fritzing brain couldn't make the connection. He staggered upright and bumped into his open door.

Over his pounding heart, Shelly's cries barely penetrated.

When he forced his eyes open, only haze and pain greeted him. His attempt to call her name degenerated into a coughing fit.

A rifle butt blazed toward his head. He snagged it with his hand and shoved as he kicked out. His world spinning, he jumped the guy.

Or thought he had.

He merely stumbled into him. His attacker side-stepped. Butch lost his rifle as he crashed to the ground. He stared at the other-worldly face peering at him. Gas mask on a guy. People shouting. Shelly? Diana? Victor? Their ambushers? He couldn't be sure. He swept out his foot and caught the guy at the ankles. He fell onto his side, and Butch ripped off his gas mask.

Hacking rewarded him.

The smoke began clearing.

A voice spoke, one he thought he'd never hear again.

"It's game over, Victor Chavez. I suggest you stop trying to fight. Now. Lest you force my hand."

Finally, nothing but clear air.

Butch rolled onto one knee and drew his pistol. His heart dropped to the soles of his hiking boots.

Makmoud Hidari wrapped his arm around Shelly's chest so she couldn't fight him. He pressed the muzzle of his gun against her temple. Another man had Diana, her braid caught in his hand, a pistol muzzle against the base of her neck.

The *Quds* agent spoke again. "Drop your weapons, gentlemen. Both of you. If you don't? Well, Mr. Addison, it might be a very short marriage for you."

"No," Shelly croaked. Tears from the gas streamed down her cheeks. She shook her head. "Don't. Don't."

She still believed in him. He wouldn't risk it. If he didn't obey their captor, he knew Makmoud would make good on his promise.

"Slowly," Makmoud advised.

Butch ejected the magazine from his Beretta. It clattered to the ground. Slowly, carefully, he crouched and set the pistol on the ground.

"Both of you, get onto your knees. Hands on your head."

Victor must have been out of sight on the other side of the Humvee.

Assume the position. Butch got it. He lowered to his knees and placed his hands on his head with his fingers interlaced.

"At least you know how to follow directions."

Diana's captor kicked the backs of her knees. When she collapsed, he pushed her onto her stomach.

Makmoud nodded in her direction. "Now all the way down, just like your comrade, Diana."

A blow between his shoulder blades caught Butch off guard. He barely got his hands underneath him to avoid a broken nose. Skin skidded away from his palms, which began burning. "Hey! You mind?"

"Hands on head!" Pain blossomed when his guard jabbed his rifle muzzle hard between his shoulder blades.

Butch eased completely onto his front. Pebbles ground into his cheek as he placed his hands on his head.

Shelly whimpered. She came down beside him. Her eyes so wide he could see the whites of them, she stared at him.

Babe, I'm sorry. Be brave. Please.

Makmoud's voice came from above. "Bind them."

His guard yanked his hands behind him, and a cable tie tightened over his wrists. No give whatsoever. These guys were pros, and no way would he be able to get the drop on them.

"To their knees."

His guard gripped him around the neck and forced his chin up. Butch had no choice but to rise to his knees. Once more, the rifle jabbed against his spine.

For the first time, Butch got a really good look at their old foe. Makmoud, his dark hair and beard now peppered with gray, stood in front of him, his arms folded across his chest. He stroked his beard, then hooked his thumbs in his belt. A smirk curled his lips, and he shifted his gaze to Butch's left. "You do not know how long I have been waiting for this opportunity, Victor Chavez."

Butch risked a glance at his friend.

Victor's jaw clenched. He struggled until his guard cuffed him across the head. He wasn't going to go down without a fight either.

Makmoud's smile widened. "Yes, I knew if I waited, bided my time, thought several moves ahead, that I would have you in my hands. And guess what? This time, you play in *my* territory. Bag them."

Butch's guard yanked a burlap bag over his head and secured it with duct tape. He kicked him between the shoulder blades. Butch careened forward and downward. He fell flat on his front. Stars sparked in his vision as pain exploded in his head. Moaning, he fought to stay conscious. Just before he slipped into blackness, Makmoud's words chilled him to the bone.

"Checkmate, Victor Chavez."

13

Creaking metal brought awareness to Butch. He lay on a hard surface. A motor hummed. Transport? From where? Memory returned with startling clarity. An ambush by Makmoud Hidari and his men that ended badly. They were now hostages of a man who wanted nothing more than revenge. The staccato pops of gunfire echoed in his ears. He still coughed a little from the tear gas. And man, oh, man, his head now pounded from falling flat on his face.

Rough burlap rubbed against his head. Stickiness pulled against his skin, and he had to breathe through his mouth. Broken nose, for sure. *Lord, what have we gotten into this time?* Had he been separated from his team? He listened. Nothing but a truck's engine. Wind blew over him. A body pressed against his back, and he felt boots against his legs. He opened his mouth. Gunk caked his vocal cords, and the engine noise ate up his croak.

They cruised over a deep rut. Butch briefly came off the truck bed. He slammed down and tumbled onto his front. His face met metal. Pain bloomed, and once more, he toppled into blackness.

Awareness slowly returned. Two men held him upright and dragged him somewhere. Try as he might, he couldn't get his feet underneath him, and they scraped across either dirt or pavement. The floor smoothed out.

Men spoke in Farsi, and their voices echoed a little, like they were in a large room with a high ceiling. Chains clinked as feet scuffled, and Victor protested. Flesh on flesh answered him. His friend groaned.

Butch couldn't fight, not in his condition.

His hands came free and his captors leaned him against a wall. His shirt rode up as he slid downward until he rested on the floor. Cold metal wrapped around his wrists, and chains clinked when he moved them. His head swam at their precarious situation. No one knew where they were, which meant no one to help, no one to rescue them. They were stuck in the worst way possible. One of their captors worked the duct tape loose, then snatched the bag from his head. He squinted in the mid-afternoon light blazing through the windows of the large room.

A bruise already forming on his cheek, Victor sat beside him in a space that could have passed for a large dining room. Seemed they'd put the men on one side of the room, and twenty feet away, on the other side, they'd chained up the ladies. Their packs lay at their feet. Strange, but then again, their captors had probably gone through them and removed anything remotely perceived as a weapon.

Across from him, Diana gasped. "Butch, what happened to you?"

"Guess I stuck my nose where I shouldn't have." His attempt at humor fell flat. His voice sounded peculiar, like when as a kid, he'd held his nose and talked while trying to be the resident comedian of his elementary school class.

Diana struggled to her knees as she peered at him. She shifted her gaze to a hulking man who strongly resembled Makmoud. Probably the man's brother. "Please. He's hurt. Please let me at least tend to him. I think he broke his nose."

Glaring at her, the man muttered something in Farsi, then switched to English. "No. We leave him as-is."

More chains clinked when she clasped her hands together as if pleading his case. Butch had to give her credit. She didn't flinch as she faced the man. "Please. Butch is hurt. He needs medical care. Let me help him, okay? That's all I want to do. I promise I'm not going to try and escape because I know you all hold the upper hand. Please let me help him."

Standing in the doorway, the man's gaze shifted to Butch. Did he see that blood all over his face? Feel bad about it? Probably not. Most likely, he didn't know the definition of compassion and didn't have an emotional bone in his body, at least when it came to his prisoners. He refocused on Diana.

She tried again. "Honestly, what could I do to you?"

His lips twisted in a smile. "Much. Fool is the man who turns his back on a woman like you." He gestured toward two of the four guards in the room. "Get him up and take him next door into the kitchen."

Man, if they ever got out of this mess, Butch would remember Diana when he needed to negotiate with someone. His captors undid the shackles on his wrists. Grasping him under the arms, they hefted him to his feet. He wobbled, but this time felt steady enough to walk under his own power. They pushed through a door and into a large kitchen far too modern for their remote location. One of them pulled out a chair at the kitchen table and pointed. "Sit there."

Butch's sigh escaped him before he realized it. His head pounded, and all he wanted to do was lay it down on the table's polished wood and take a nap. Instead, he focused on his surroundings. Nice fridge and stove. Even a microwave to boot. And a dishwasher. All way too sophisticated to be a hovel. And too big. A villa or something? A large window above the sink let in the afternoon sun and filled it with a warm light. Too bad he wasn't hanging out here with a gigantic mug of coffee and his best friends.

The other two guards escorted Diana inside, and Makmoud's brother followed with her pack, which he set on the kitchen table. He and two of the four guards stayed. Butch wanted to laugh. Like he could do anything. Maybe Diana could, but he was dead weight when it came to any escape.

The man leaned against the counter and folded his arms across his broad chest. "We will stay. Now do what you wanted to do, Dr. Kasem."

She stared him down. "Just who are you?"

The man's lips curled as he glared at her. "Jibril Hidari."

"Makmoud's brother, then." She unzipped her pack and pawed through the various compartments as if searching for her medical kit.

Butch knew better. She looked for anything she could use as a weapon. The smallest shake of her head confirmed his earlier suspicion. Could she use needles as a weapon? Doubtful. She wouldn't do anything that endangered the rest of the team.

She set her medical kit on the table. A frown marred her pretty features as she examined the light above the table. "That'll have to do. Butch, stay right where you are."

"I ain't moving. Promise." Butch grunted as his head throbbed in time to his pulse.

Diana sat in a chair so their knees almost touched. A professional doctor took over the friend he knew. She peppered him with questions. His zip code. Cell number. Address. The light from her penlight temporarily blinded him.

"What's the verdict, doc? Concussion?"

"Thankfully no. Just a knock on the head and most likely a busted nose. Let me get your face cleaned up, and I'll be able to tell you more." She rose.

The guards' guns came up. Jibril, who'd kept his arms folded across his chest, merely cocked an eyebrow. "And what do you think you're doing?"

"Finding a bowl for water." She began opening cabinets. One of the guards stepped aside. She pulled out a metal bowl from a cabinet beneath the counter and filled it before setting it on the table beside a wad of gauze she'd pulled from the kit. "Can you breathe through your nose?"

Like that would be happening any time soon. "Negative. And I've got a massive headache. Now I know what it feels like to fall flat on my face."

She didn't even smile at his lousy attempt at humor. "Let me clean you up a little. Then I can tell just how bad it is."

Her touch remained gentle as she washed the blood, tears, and snot from his face. At least the water added a modicum of comfort. "From the bruises I see forming, you'll look like abstract art for a few days."

He groaned. "Thanks, I think."

Her fingers moved closer to his injury. Tiny points of fire opened up as she dabbed at his cheekbones and nose. He avoided looking at the small pile of blood-soaked gauze forming on the table. She finally sat back with a furrowed brow.

"Bad, ain't it?"

Diana rummaged around in her kit and came up with a splint and a roll of tape. "It's broken, all right. Kind of twisted. I'm going to have to reset it." She stood and stepped so close to him that her shirt was inches from his face. She leaned closer and whispered, "Normally, I'd do this with you sedated, but you need to be alert."

Yeah, he'd figured that. "Do what you have to do."

She pulled back. Sweat sheened her face, and a few curls had fallen from her braid. "You're sure."

More of a statement than a question.

"I've faced worse. Please," he added as she lifted his chin. "I'm a big boy—"

Who shrieked like a girl as she swiftly realigned his nose.

The other men in the room snickered.

He moaned as more blood began spilling downward. "Oh, man, oh, man, oh, man, girl. What on earth?"

"You had less time to think about it." She once more cleaned around the area before taping the splint on. She blotted his mouth and chin, then took care of his palms. "It's going to heal. It may heal a little crooked, but you shouldn't have an issue breathing in the future. Time to healing is four to six weeks."

Jibril muttered something in Farsi, and his two goons laughed.

She glared at them, then turned her back and loaded a couple of needles. "To take the edge off the pain. A basic antibiotic too. You've got aspirin in your pack, right?"

"We all do if they didn't take it." He focused on Jibril. "And they wouldn't be that mean, right?"

Sarcasm and Butch were one at that moment.

Diana's lips twitched. "Take some."

Butch shifted in his chair and faced his captors. "I want to see Libby. I know you have her here."

Jibril studied him through narrowed eyes.

Diana joined her friend. "Is that such a difficult request? We just want to make sure she's okay, and I want to make sure she doesn't need medical attention."

Bless her. She knew what would ease his mind at that point.

Jibril murmured something to his men. One left. A minute later, a swinging door on the other side of the room flew open.

For a moment, Butch forgot about his raging headache or his lack of ability to breathe through his nose. "Libby!" He leapt to his feet and enfolded her in his embrace.

Finally, he pulled back and held her at arm's length.

She did indeed stand before him, all five-nine of her. Small wrinkles had gathered at the corners of her eyes. Faint bruising lay underneath a scabbed-over cut. Her eyes filled, and a tear trickled down her cheek. His name came out in a ragged whisper. "Butch."

He hugged her again, and the warmth that shot through him startled him. He pulled back and ran some of her dark, dark hair that had escaped her headscarf through his fingers. "You're... really alive."

She took his hand. "Praise God. I-I-I don't believe it."

"We came to find you." The words popped out of his mouth.

Her brow crinkled. "You what?"

"Came to find you. When your mama and daddy called, I wanted to find you, to rescue you. Even before that, when Roo—"

"Paul LaRue?" She stared at him and consternation. "What does he have to do with this?"

"He remembered you."

She flinched and stared at the ground.

"What?"

"Nothing. I never understood why I was kidnapped. Why I was targeted."

Butch hung his head. The reality of their very precarious situation settled over him like a lead blanket. Makmoud had used Libby to lure the team to Iraq. And they'd played perfectly into his hands. The scum. "I think I know why, regretfully."

"I believe you do," Makmoud said from the doorway.

Slowly, Butch swiveled. Their captor leaned against the door frame, his arms folded, one ankle crossed casually over the other. Makmoud knew who ruled the roost at the moment. He did, and Butch saw no way to even the odds, not when the rest of the team sat in chains next door.

"Guards, take Libby back to her room. Jibril, return Butch and Diana to the rest and bring me Victor. It's time he and I had a talk."

His brother bobbed his head in submission. Jibril yanked Libby away from Butch's embrace and shoved her toward her guard, who escorted her from the kitchen.

Butch gazed at the door, then at Diana.

His friend stared at him, those sea-green eyes of hers unreadable. What? That he'd hugged Libby? What was wrong with that? What should he have done? Shaken her hand? Bowed to her? Except holding her close unleashed too many memories from years before.

The doctor gathered the dirty gauze into a pile. Jibril brought over the trashcan, and she deposited them inside. He returned it to its spot, and with a small bow, gestured for her to precede him through the door. He snagged her pack and walked after her.

What a strange day. Butch heaved himself to his feet and shuffled after her.

Jibril had already shackled her to the wall beside Shelly.

Butch let the guards seat him and manacle his wrists. He couldn't look at his wife right then.

Jibril kicked Victor. "Get up."

He curled away from the assault. "Hey! Do you mind?"

"Get up, I say!" Jibril barked something at his men.

After unbinding him, they hauled the leader to his feet. He struggled, but one of his guards kicked him in the back of his knees. He staggered, and his guards used the opportunity to cuff his hands behind him.

As they led him from the room, Butch leaned his head against the wall with a small thump. Wrong move because it felt like his brain sloshed around in his skull. What kind of mess had he gotten everyone into? He didn't want to know. All he knew was they probably wouldn't escape this one alive.

14

Friday, July 12, 2019, 1645 hours local time, north-eastern Iraq

Fear uncoiled in Victor Chavez. He'd been Makmoud's captive before and suffered a beating so brutal it left him with a bruised kidney for weeks afterward. At least then, he'd come out on top and kept his freedom. Not this time because Makmoud had been right. Five years ago, they'd been on Victor's turf. Not today. No way could he escape, not with being separated from the rest of the team. He knew exactly what his foe would do. Kill the rest. He began praying. Fast prayers. Desperate prayers. *Lord, I need Your strength. I need to stand up to him. Somehow. Protect me. And the others. Please!*

One of the guards shoved open the swinging door leading to the kitchen. With a ominous grin, Makmoud leaned against the counter with his hands braced along the edge. "Well, well, well, at last you and I get to have some quality time together."

Victor's stomach hardened, and his legs locked. He tried to yank away from the guards, but as their grip tightened, spots of pain flared on his arms.

Makmoud pushed away from the counter. "No need to fight, Victor Chavez. You start now, and it will not go well for you." He pointed to a lone stool in the middle of the floor. "Seat him there."

They shoved him onto the hard wood.

Behind his back, Victor's fingers curled into fists. This was too much like five years ago, except back then, his prison had been the master bedroom at the Big House on Last Chance Ranch. It sank in. Makmoud intended to intimidate him. Victor's head swam, and he began taking and releasing deep breaths to stave off the panic threatening to swamp him.

Makmoud smirked. "Yes, remember the last time we had a bit of one-on-one? This time, Victor, it is you and me again, though I can't trust you alone. So, guess what? The guards will stay here to ensure you behave."

In. Out. Breathe slowly. Sweat broke out on Victor's forehead. The silence stretched long, and it unnerved him. Finally, he blurted, "What do you want?"

"What do I want?" Makmoud's chuckle came out low, almost like a growl. "Where shall I start?" He dragged over a chair from the kitchen table, turned it backward, and straddled it so he was within arm's length of his captive. His smile drained from his face, and his eyes hooded. "I want lots of things in this world. Some I have attained. Some I have been denied all these years."

"Like what? Respect?"

Makmoud slapped him across the face, popping Victor's head to the side. Burning erupted along his cheek.

"You have no standing to disrespect me," Makmoud snapped. "Remember your foolishness and what brought you here."

The slap rattled Victor. His head swam, and nausea roiled his stomach. *Breathe, man, breathe. Got to breathe.* "Why did you kidnap Libby?"

"Why should I tell you?" His foe rose. With his foot, he shoved the chair away. It skittered into a cabinet and banged against the wood. He put his hands on his hips as he began a slow walk around his captive. Makmoud toyed with him.

It was working because his actions brought back the fear from five years before. Victor kept his gaze pinned to the floor.

Makmoud's voice came from behind him. "You see, Victor, five years ago, you and your team escaped me. The humiliation!" He cuffed him across the head.

Victor fought for balance to stay on the stool and won. His shoulders stiffened.

"Yes, I see you remember. The part of your team that escaped had surprise on their side. And an intimate knowledge of Last Chance Ranch. I realize the foolishness of our ways. We erred in making too many assumptions. Had we succeeded, do you know what we had planned for you?"

Victor clenched his jaw. No way would he cater to his questions.

"Answer me!" Makmoud jabbed him hard in the back.

Victor gasped and struggled to stay on the stool. He ground out his answer. "What you did to Gary."

Returning to stand in front of him, Makmoud slowly clapped his hands together as if applauding a dim pupil. "Bravo. So you do remember. I was quite successful, yes? I would have done the same to you." His eyes narrowed. "And *will* do to all of you. Save for my half brother. Yes, don't think I didn't recognize that my half-breed brother had changed his name from Ibrahim Hidari to Suleiman al-Ibrahim. When he ran away nine years ago, he shamed the family name."

"You know he's married—"

"I don't care that Sana Jain is now his wife." Makmoud got in his face. "Not a bit. I vowed he would die by my hand, and once we reach Iran, he will. Slowly. And Sana will be broken like the rest of you. I know Jibril looks forward to the opportunity to do just that."

Victor winced at the foul odor of the man's breath. "You know we won't—"

"Everyone breaks, Victor. Your friend, *your best friend*, Gary Walton, was one of the strongest men out there. Even he, who withstood beyond what any human could or should endure, broke."

Sweat trickled down Victor's temple. His heartbeat increased as his mind darted to unpleasant places. He didn't have to think hard to imagine what his captor implied. *Lord. Lord. Jesus. Save me. Please!* Those desperate words sped up and blended into a mush he couldn't comprehend.

They were going to be tortured, die horrible deaths. At least Victor knew he would be with Jesus if that happened. Or in a living hell before that, depending on how fast his body and mind gave out.

Then, just as suddenly as panic had bound him, his thoughts cleared. A question popped into his head. He asked again, "Why take Libby?"

"Because from what I understand, and indeed what I have seen, Butch Addison would do anything to save her. Even make foolish decisions." Makmoud resumed his slow circling. "Right?" He jabbed him once more in the back. "Even you understand that."

I will not react. I will not react. Victor clenched his jaw. More breaths slowed his racing mind. "How did you know about her?"

Makmoud stopped at his side. "A client of mine."

Client. Client. What? That was weird. "You're so hard up you're having to hire yourselves out now? What are you? An errand boy or something?"

With a snarl, Makmoud swept his foot out.

The stool went flying, and Victor slammed onto his back. The wind knocked out of him, he wheezed as pain shot through his shoulders. His foe blurred above him. With a moan, he curled onto his side.

"You're a fool, Victor Chavez." A swift kick of Makmoud's boot jabbed him hard in the kidney.

Pain ignited in his back. He thrashed, but what with his head swimming, he couldn't regain his balance enough to sit up. "Please... let her go. She means nothing to you now, right? You just wanted us. She's an innocent pawn in all of this. Please. Her parents are worried—"

A harsh blow to his solar plexus silenced him.

Hot, burning agony spread throughout his abdomen. Victor curled into a ball and grunted to relieve the pain. He scrunched his eyes closed. Red flashed across his vision, and a roaring filled his ears. He struggled to draw in a breath.

Makmoud's voice came from far off. "I cannot do that because of my client's request. No, she will be Jibril's concubine. You see, he's already asked for her. And if she's lucky, she'll become his wife. Of course, I might have to break her, just as I broke Susanna years ago."

Finally, Victor drew oxygen into his lungs. "Su... Susanna Marina?"

"You remember her, eh? Yes, your dead fiancée's sister. She never was killed by lions all those years ago. We kidnapped her to make your now-dead lover do our bidding, which she did quite well."

I can't think about the distant past. Not now. Stay present. Stay present. He forced his eyes open.

Makmoud crouched in front of him. "Yes, Victor. I broke her, then married her five years ago." A brief, tender smile flickered across his face. It vanished, just as surely as a flash of lightning in a dark night. "If Libby will not cooperate, then she will follow the same path."

Victor rolled against his hands. "Who is this client? Why is he so interested in Libby?"

"Who is to say my client is a man?" Makmoud chuckled and straightened. "And why should I tell you?"

Victor sucked in a deep breath as his head finally cleared enough to draw a conclusion. "This client. Whatever his name is. He wanted her out of the way for some reason. And he knew enough to distinctly point her out to you. Let me take a guess. She knows something. What is so important that he paid you a bunch of money?"

Makmoud stilled. "You are a fool, Victor Chavez."

Victor steadied as he re-engaged his brain. "How much did he pay you?"

"You are worth ten million, apparently, five of which I've already collected."

The number stuck in Victor's mind. He couldn't figure out why. "You do realize our government is offering a twenty-million-dollar reward for your capture or death, right?"

Makmoud's nostrils flared, as he cracked his knuckles. "I'm well aware of that, Victor Chavez."

Victor dug in. "Only a fool would trust a man like your client. Something tells me this client of yours is very wealthy but very pragmatic. He's not going to give away a ton of money without any chance of getting it back. What if he wants to wipe you out? Then he wouldn't have to pay you. I mean, we could have taken you down. Or maybe that wasn't his intent. Maybe he wanted us and Libby out of the way. Maybe he's sending someone else to do the job. If so, he can collect that twenty mil. Earn back at least the five he's already paid you and make fifteen more."

Makmoud's face reddened. With a snarl, he drew a hunting knife. It flashed in the bright overhead lights.

"Makmoud!" Jibril's gravelly voice saved Victor from certain death or at least severe injury.

With his knife still cocked for a strike, Makmoud growled a reply in Farsi. At his brother's answer, he sheathed it.

As he watched them, Victor released a slow breath. Weakness surged over him, and gradually, his mind cleared as adrenaline dwindled. He flopped around like a fish as he struggled to a sitting position.

Jibril jabbered in rapid-fire Farsi. His gestures swung wide, and he pointed as if indicating a direction. Something had obviously happened because Makmoud tilted his head to one side as he asked several questions one right after the other. He barely glanced at Victor, as if tormenting him had taken second place to whatever was now going on.

Using the heels of his hiking boots, Victor scooted backward until he leaned against a corner where the cabinets met.

Makmoud's voice increased in pitch. Something rattled the normally unflappable man. His brow furrowed, and he peppered his brother with even more questions. What had him acting so worried all of the sudden?

Finally, Victor could stand it no more. He loudly cleared his throat, causing both men to pause their discussion. "Uh, gentlemen, something seems to be worrying you."

Jibril studied him for a long moment, then said something else in Farsi.

That launched the brothers into an argument that grew fiercer by the second. Finally, Makmoud stared out the window above the kitchen sink. Outside, the light began softening as evening approached. His gaze flicked to Victor. The leader drew in a breath. After a short comment in Farsi, he faced his captive. "Well, it seems as if you've earned a reprieve."

Victor's heart raced as more adrenaline poured into his system. "I'm all ears."

"It seems as if we have had a situation arise. Perhaps you have heard of the Turk."

"Our contacts in Amal told us about him."

"Fair enough. Our sources position his army in the very southeastern stretches of Turkey. But since we have maintained strict radio silence on this mission, we have not tracked their movements, except for what we found out when we scouted Amal a few days ago. Out of caution, I sent out two scouts to a valley where the man's army may be gathering. My best. With strict orders to report in every hour on the hour."

"Let me guess. They missed a check-in." Sudden, insane hope rose in Victor's chest.

"Two, to be exact. They reported they'd found something. Our man documented it while we were away. Then... nothing."

Victor didn't have to imagine what had happened. "Do you know anything else?"

Makmoud's brow knitted. "We are severely outnumbered, if the reports we received before our men went silent are correct."

"What were these reports about?"

Makmoud glanced at Jibril. "Troop numbers."

"How many?"

"At least five hundred."

Victor froze. "Your scouts are most likely captured or dead."

"I agree."

"And you want our help." Victor couldn't keep the sarcasm from his voice.

"No, we have a miss—"

Jibril butted in with more Farsi peppered like machine gun fire.

Makmoud didn't interrupt, only listened. Slowly, he nodded, then said in English, "Get him up." He switched his attention to Victor. "You will come with us."

Jibril hauled him upright and led him through a door opposite the one leading to their holding room.

Glad to be on his feet again, Victor let Makmoud's brother lead him into a large living area. A wall-mounted television hung between two windows. In a corner sat a pool table, complete with a rack of cue sticks and balls hanging from one wall. Makmoud flicked on the light over the table. On the green felt lay a topographic map that showed the mountain ridges surrounding them.

Makmoud pulled a pair of black-framed reading glasses from his shirt pocket and shoved them onto his face. Rubbing his bearded chin, he studied the map, then jabbed a finger at a red circle. "We are here."

"Where's here? I can't see anything without glasses." He nodded downward. "They're in my shirt pocket."

With a sigh, Jibril pulled them out. The earpieces fell to the floor, just another casualty of the ambush. With an eye roll, Makmoud handed his pair to his brother, who placed them on Victor's face. Now with his vision slightly blurry, Victor noted their location. In a narrow valley with mountain ridges surrounding them. And boy, it was altogether too close to Iran. He shuddered as Makmoud took the glasses back. "I get it. Where did your scouts go?"

"Here." Makmoud traced a path northward to a valley eclipsing the Iraq/Turkey border. "This is wild territory. Neither the Turks nor Iraqis mind the fence. Actually, there is no fence here."

"Last radio call?"

"1400 hours, as you would say." Makmoud took off his glasses and rubbed his hands over his face.

Victor hazarded a guess at his thoughts. Two men missing, presumed dead. He had a small squad of maybe twenty-four men. Against a force of five hundred massing not too far away. "You're worried."

"Very much so." With narrowed eyes, Makmoud studied him. "But, like you said earlier, perhaps you can help us."

Victor gave him a sardonic stare. "Let me remind you, we're your captives."

"But, if our reports are correct—"

"You're outgunned. Way outgunned."

A red-hot glare rewarded him. Then Makmoud broke his gaze. "You're very perceptive. And correct."

Victor's heart dropped to his feet as he realized the implications. Men like the Turk took no prisoners.

"That is the report. If it is true, then I do have many concerns that the Turk's army is preparing for an attack. On us or someone else, we don't know. I'm quite sure he now knows someone is nearby who knows about them. And I worry they may have interrogated our men and know our position. We need eyes on the target to truly understand what we face."

"You need us."

"We are twenty-two now, if my instinct is correct. So yes. Perhaps your team of eight would be beneficial." Makmoud studied the map. "I need to know for sure what numbers we face. And here is how it will go. Jibril, Parviz, Butch, and Diana will all go."

"I'm not sure I follow. Why Butch and Diana?"

"They will go." Makmoud traced a route on the map. "I need to know intelligence now." He met his brother's gaze. "Jibril is resourceful and will work with Butch on reconnaissance. Hope against hope, if my men are alive, Diana can provide medical assistance. Parviz as well since he is one of our medics. Then we go from there."

Had the pain raging in his middle made him hallucinate? Speech suddenly was impossible. Maybe they could escape, then come back and rescue the others.

Makmoud touched the butt of the pistol resting at his waist. "But, don't think there will be an opportunity for you to escape or free your comrades." He once more gazed at his brother. "Jibril will check in every half hour. And if he misses a check-in, guess what?"

Victor's optimism faded. "The rest of us die."

"Exactly. Jibril, go and get them ready." Makmoud switched his laser-like focus to the team's leader. "In the meantime, Victor, you and I have much to discuss related to planning our potential escape."

15

"You want us to do what?" With Diana beside him, Butch stared at Jibril, Makmoud, and Victor. They stood in the dusty courtyard of the villa for their semi-private discussion. "This is nuts!"

Makmoud hooked his thumbs in his belt. "We need to know what we face."

"Well, poor pity you 'cause I *know* what *we* face."

Makmoud's eyes narrowed in his reddening face.

Still bound, Victor stepped between the two men and turned his back on Makmoud. "Makmoud, give us a minute."

Their captor harumphed but stepped back.

Victor nudged his friend away from the group. He glanced at the others. "Butch, I know what you're saying, but the brutal reality is we've got a ton of radicals within twenty miles of here. And if they get their hooks into us, we all die."

Maybe they stood a fighting chance in the end. His friend was right. If the team banded with the *Quds* men, they might avoid a very brutal death and live to escape. The old adage rang in his ears. *The enemy of my enemy is my friend.*

Makmoud and his goons stood on opposite sides of the gun from his team. But right then, they both had a common goal. Survival. In no way did he want to die by beheading or being gutted, which was what these radicals seemed to like if they were the spawn of ISIS. "All right." Butch cut his eyes to Jibril and Makmoud waiting with Diana next to them. "But after all of this is said and done, I ain't going down without a fight."

Victor bobbed his head. "Agreed."

Butch approached the two *Quds* men. "What do you want us to do?"

"Come with me." Jibril undid the cuffs binding his wrists together before doing the same with Diana. "Parviz is going with us. We check in every half hour. And if we miss a call, the rest of your team dies."

"Fair enough." Butch's mind clicked into warrior mode. "We get arms?"

"You have what you brought. I trust you have plenty of ammunition."

"Enough if you didn't loot our stuff."

Parviz joined them with their packs. Another man handed them their tactical vests, guns, and boxes of ammunition.

Butch caught Victor's eye. Should they? His gut said no, and the smallest shake of Victor's head confirmed it. One gunshot, and the eighteen *Quds* men inside would execute the other five team members without hesitation.

Butch checked his pack. Still enough food and water to get them through the night and the next day if he was careful. At least they had plenty of other supplies, including Diana's larger medical kit, in their Humvees, which sat just outside the courtyard along with their captors' vehicles.

At least his mind had begun clearing. The aspirin he'd taken had done a fine job of chasing away the headache. He shrugged into his tactical vest. "Let's do it then. Which vehicle are we taking?"

Jibril led them to a four-door Jeep Wrangler. "Butch, get into the front. Diana, into the back with Parviz." Once everyone was aboard, he unfurled a map, crammed a pair of blocky reading glasses onto his nose, and pointed to a road winding down their valley to a main east-west highway. West led to Harifi al-Hafa, then to Amal. East ran to the Iranian border. No way did they want to go that direction. Except Jibril's finger traced a route eastward, then almost immediately turned north, into a wild area of Iraq that curved sharply northward toward the Turkish-Iraqi border. It stopped at a valley just south of it. "This is where we got the last radio call. Then their transponder flickered out."

"When was that?"

"1400 hours. We fear they are dead. If so, they died with a minimal report. Just troop numbers."

"How strong?"

"He said five hundred."

Butch whistled. Things began making more sense now. "How long to get there?"

"It took them a good half day to hike in. For us, an hour by road and on foot."

Butch peered into the evening sky. Sunset would be within a couple of hours. Good and bad at the same time. On the western horizon, clouds had begun massing. "What's the weather going to be like?"

"Clear for now, but a front moves in later tonight. We should be back before that."

One could hope. "Then let's go."

They began their journey. Butch kept his rifle pointed downward with his finger on the trigger guard. He didn't miss the headset Jibril wore and the way that every few minutes, he provided an update to his brother. A smart one. A good comrade if they'd been on the same side. Well, they were. At least for now.

In the back seat, Diana and Parviz chatted like old buddies. Thanks to the young man's good English, Butch caught some of the conversation. Seemed Parviz wanted to be a doctor, and he peppered her with questions about applying to medical school and what her training involved.

They arrived at the intersection with the highway and turned east. Suddenly, trepidation gripped Butch. Was Jibril going to drive them straight to Iran? Leave them no choice but to fight to the death? His mind began darting in all sorts of directions, all of them bad.

Until they made the turn northward. The road curved to the left, then to the right as it steepened and followed a draw up toward the ridges towering over them. "Did your men climb to the top of the ridge?"

"Yes. They stationed themselves there, said they were well hidden." They rode along in silence for several more minutes. Butch kept his eye out for any posted sentries. Nothing, but the good ones camouflaged themselves. If Jibril wasn't careful, their engine could alert any random patrols.

Jibril slowed and backed into a spot nearly hidden by large boulders resting beside the road. "We go on foot from here. Up to the ridge." He nodded toward a trail that resembled a goat path. "Let's go. You go first, then I. Then Diana and Parviz."

No trust issues there. Butch wanted to laugh, but he understood because he would have done the same thing. He shrugged into his pack, made sure he had spare magazines as well as his hunting knife and pistol at the ready, and covered his bald head with his shemagh. Maybe then he'd be mistaken for a local.

The trail sloped even more upward, and he felt the load on his heart as they gained altitude. He tried not to breathe too loudly through this mouth. The only noise was the crunch of gravel under their boots. Hardly audible in the valley on the other side of the ridge. Butch kept his rifle ready to fire if needed. One quick glance behind assured that Jibril did too.

As they neared the top, the angle eased off. Butch slowed and listened. A low hum, almost like bees in a hive. He froze and held his hand in a fist. The others stopped, and Jibril crept up so he stood near his shoulder. Butch murmured, "Ridge ahead. We go low and slow now."

He eased to his knees, then to his front to reduce his profile. The others did the same. Like a snake, he wormed between blackened husks of trees and boulders strewn along the rim of the valley. Ever so carefully, he made his way to the edge. Turned out the valley was shallower than he'd anticipated, maybe two hundred or so vertical feet. Where they lay on the western side dropped off in a sheer wall to the valley's floor. The other sides were shaped almost like a bowl, with steep slopes leading to the rim. A road ran out of the valley from the northeast. One way in. One way out. Probably intensely guarded.

The hum had increased from beehive volume to like a well-tuned fan.

Operation Silver Star

The setting sun cast a golden light across what seemed to be a sea of men that shifted and twisted with few clear spots of ground visible. Campfires littered the landscape. Butch reached into his vest and pulled out a pair of binoculars. He dialed in as he surveyed the scene. Soldiers, all of them. And all armed. Also, personnel carriers. Other vehicles. Especially pickups with mortars in the back and stacked with shells. A veritable mobile mortar unit. And rocket-propelled grenades. No good militia left home without them. All of that troubled him. But what worried him the most was the sheer numbers. When training for Special Forces, he'd taken a class on recon work, and one of those was estimating numbers of enemy troops.

Beside him, Jibril also had his binoculars out. He whispered, "What do you think?"

"Five hundred, my butt. Probably more like a fifteen hundred to two thousand in a valley that's maybe two kilometers by two kilometers."

Jibril dropped his head. Farsi words escaped him.

Butch studied the Turk's men again. They milled about as if they were waiting for orders. "Did your men have anything on them that would reveal them as *Quds*?"

"No. My worry is they were taken into camp and interrogated. Or their attackers took their packs. Our radios have Farsi on them."

A huge worry.

Butch refocused on the scene before them. Then a voice distracted him, one amplified by a microphone. The hum ceased as the man began yammering away.

"The Turk," Jibril whispered.

Butch studied the man more closely. Dressed in all black robes, including a black turban, the man gestured and shouted as he called to his faithful. Butch didn't understand what he said, but the hatred behind it conveyed all he needed to know. They did not, repeat, did not want to fall into his hands.

Ever so carefully, he inched away from the edge. Where were Diana and Parviz? They hadn't joined them. For a brief, terrifying moment, he feared they'd met the same fate as the scouts.

Then came a soft owl call. Diana.

Once he was sure he was out of sight of anyone in the valley, Butch climbed to his knees, then winced as he stood.

Diana and Parviz crouched near a jumble of rocks. Her eyes wide, Diana frantically gestured. Come here. His stomach sank. She pressed her fist to her mouth, and tears pooled in the corners of her eyes. Gaze drifting downward, she straightened and swiped at a tear on her cheek. "They're butchers."

"Oh, man, oh, man, oh, man." Butch winced as he stared at Makmoud's two scouts—or what was left of them.

One body lay on its front. He found the man's head against one of the rocks. The other stared sightlessly at them. They'd ripped his shirt off and gutted him. Butch's stomach twisted.

Jibril winced, hung his head, and muttered several words in Farsi.

"I'm sorry." Butch stopped short of saying, "my friend," which he would have done had they been on the same side.

Jibril walked a few paces away as he keyed his headset and made a rapid report in low Farsi, undoubtedly to Makmoud.

Parviz stared at the bodies, his eyes wide. "Their packs are gone."

"Meaning those jokers down there probably know someone's keeping tabs on them." Butch took a knee. "I don't think we can get the bodies down, not without exposing our—Ooomph!"

A man rammed into him, and he tumbled off his feet. After skidding a few feet on the rocky soil, he rolled to a crouch with his pistol up and ready.

Crap.

Two of the Turk's goons had guns pointed at them, and a lanky third one wrapped his arm around Diana's chest with a pistol to her head. Thanks to their discovery, they'd lost situational awareness, and it would cost them if they weren't careful.

Adrenaline pumping through his system, Butch raised his hands, as did Jibril and Parviz.

"Drop your guns," the tall radical growled at them in Arabic. "Now, or she dies."

Diana met Butch's gaze. She winked, then slammed the back of her head into her guard's face. His hold loosened, and he stumbled backward. She followed with a quick kick to his gut that doubled him over. He staggered farther back. With a cry, he toppled over the edge of the cliff.

Butch charged another, bigger one and hit him like he would anyone he'd wrestled against in high school. The man landed hard on his rear. He grabbed Butch's throat. Not this time. Butch delivered a jab to the man's nose. He sagged against Butch's grip just as two guns discharged with loud reports.

Butch whipped around. Jibril rose and kicked his guard, who writhed on the ground from a chest shot. He finished him off. "He shot Parviz." With that he stalked to the other attacker and delivered a double tap to his forehead. The two pops echoed across the valley. Game totally over. The Turk now knew trouble brewed.

Butch crouched beside Diana, who'd already begun assessing the young man. Parviz groaned and thrashed. Blood tinged the white T-shirt he wore a dark red. "He got hit in the stomach. We've got to get him out of here."

In the valley, the Turk had ceased his speech. Sweat broke out on Butch's hands. "If they didn't see that body fall, you know they heard the shots."

Shoulders heaving, Jibril stood above them, his gaze smoldering as he glared at the bodies of the two scouts.

Men shouted. Butch didn't doubt that someone pointed toward their hideout.

Man, they were in trouble now. Time to abandon ship. Past time. If those goons caught them, they'd be shredded within an hour.

Diana ripped her shemagh from her neck and stuffed it into the wound. She wrapped gauze around the medic's middle to hold it in place. "We've got to get out of here so I can take care of Parviz. Butch, you carry him."

More frenzied cries.

Butch swooped the moaning man into a fireman's carry. "Jibril, lead the way."

This time, no argument from their captor.

Dusk rapidly drained the daylight from the area. Dang it! They had to slow their steps to avoid falling off the path.

"Hold up, Butch." Diana fished around in her pack and came up with a headlamp. She placed it around his head. "Get going. I'll be fine."

"Thanks," he huffed. Ahead of him, Jibril turned on his headlamp, and they made their way down the trail as fast as safely possible. He could only hope Diana stepped where he stepped and didn't fall off the narrow path. A rock skidded under his boot, and he almost went down. Her hand on his back stabilized him and reassured him she was there. A flashlight's red beam bobbed. She'd pulled out her Maglite and turned it to the red setting.

Butch's muscles began aching under Parviz's weight. He sounded like a freight train as he sucked in precious oxygen through his mouth. His head began hurting again.

They hit the bottom.

As he laid Parviz in the back seat, Butch barely heard Jibril's rapid report back to base. In the red light of his headlamp, the blood that had seeped onto Diana's black and white shemagh turned black. "Diana, he's still bleeding."

Jibril jumped into the driver's seat.

"I've got him," Diana said. "Get up front and go!"

Butch swung into the front seat, and Jibril gunned the engine. They shot onto the road and toward safety.

Just how long would it take those jokers to mobilize? Despite the chilly air rushing through the open Jeep, Butch grabbed the map and studied it. He found the valley, then its exit on the northeast side. The army would come onto the main highway east of the turnoff to the hideout, which would cut them off from Iran. He didn't know whether to be terrified or happy. "Jibril, you know they're going to mobilize, and if they've sent out scouts, they'll find your location."

"I realize that." Jibril kept his eyes on the road and the Wrangler under perfect control.

Butch's heart lifted a little. "Their access to the east-west road is east of here."

At that, Jibril swore long and loud.

Point in their favor. Maybe.

"We need to reassess when we get back."

"Tell me something I don't know. Diana," Jibril glanced into the rear-view mirror. "How is he?"

Parviz's cries reached them over the wind. He thrashed, his boots hitting the back door. Diana had her stethoscope pressed to his chest. "Still bleeding heavily. Blood's dark red, and I'm worried a major vein got hit. Pulse and breathing are rapid. Skin's clammy. He's going into shock."

That increased Jibril's speed.

They swung a hard right onto the east-west road, then a hard left that would have thrown Butch out had he not buckled himself in.

Diana grabbed the roll bar as Parviz's flailing fist caught her in the face. "Youch!"

Jibril slowed to a stop and faced her. "Are you okay?"

She rubbed her cheek. "Just drive. Butch, give me your shemagh and help me hold him down."

Butch ripped the material from his neck and passed it back. Turning in his seat, he leaned over and held the young man's legs.

In the now-white glow of Diana's headlamp, Parviz's olive coloring paled to a sickly yellow. He trembled, and low groans escaped him.

The Jeep roared up the valley road and skidded to a stop in front of the villa.

Butch wasted no time in getting the medic out, cradling him in his arms.

"Get him inside. Stat!" Diana ordered. In her haste, her foot caught on the lip of the door frame. She tumbled onto the rocky ground and grunted.

Jibril lifted her to her feet.

Despite the blood now pouring from her split lip, she brushed the gravel off her palms and ordered, "Jibril, get my bigger kit out of the first Humvee."

He raced to the back and opened the cargo door. He lifted a big pack with a red cross on it.

Mustapa sagged in Butch's arms, and his head rolled back. Butch shouted, "We've got a trauma patient! Get ready!"

16

When the Jeep screeched to a halt outside the courtyard, Makmoud ceased wearing a groove in front of the wall. He opened the gate and allowed for Butch to pass him. "To the kitchen."

Makmoud followed him through the swinging door. Never had he imagined needing an operating table. He shoved away the chairs from the large table and turned on the overhead light. "Lay him here."

Butch gently deposited him on the wood.

The swinging door banged open, and Diana swooped through. Blood ran down her chin and dribbled onto the floor. Dark red going to brown covered her front, as did dust. It was almost like she didn't notice as she barked orders that made clear who was boss now, at least temporarily. Jibril set a large pack on the table and immediately began pulling equipment from it.

He ripped open Parviz's shirt and attached leads that ran from his chest to an EKG machine. Butch held an IV bag as Diana quickly inserted a line. "Makmoud, he's in shock. He's lost a ton of blood."

The heart rate monitor began chirping in rapid sequence.

He moved closer. "What can I do?"

"Pray." She pulled on gloves and examined an ugly wound in the young

135

man's middle. "He took one to the gut. I'm worried he's torn up inside."

Makmoud backed away. With his hands still bound behind him, Victor joined him in silent vigil. Together, they watched as Diana worked and murmured to both Butch and Jibril in low, urgent tones. They were as compliant as nurses. Parviz's limbs spasmed, and Makmoud cringed at the guttural cry that escaped him. Despite their efforts, dark red blood seeped from the wound and ran down his side. The young man convulsed, then sagged to the table.

The beep turned to a low tone. Blood began dripping onto the floor.

Makmoud clenched his jaw. He knew what it meant. The bullet had hit either a vital blood vessel or organ, and he'd bled out.

"Get back!" Diana ordered as she grasped a pair of AED paddles.

Parviz's back arched, then crashed onto the table.

Nothing. The machine continued blaring.

Again, she applied the paddles. The machine sparked. A trail of acrid smoke coiled into the air.

Diana tossed them aside, jumped onto the table, and began chest compressions. "No. No. No!"

A resounding crack echoed through the room, and the table collapsed under the combined weight of her and her patient.

Jibril pulled her away.

She struggled. "No, no!"

The heart rate monitor continued its screech until Butch knelt and lowered the volume.

She stared at the flat line, then sagged into Jibril's arms as Butch powered down the machine. Her shoulders shook, and tears ran down her face. Jibril bent and murmured into her ear, "You did your best."

Still not releasing her, he rose. She pulled away and faced the wall as she yanked off her gloves and swiped at her face.

Butch touched her on the shoulder. "I'm sorry, Diana. I don't think there was anything you could do."

Drawing in a shaky breath, she nodded, then faced her patient and gently closed his eyes. She touched the young man's hair. "I'm sorry, Parviz. I'm so sorry."

Makmoud's heart ached at the loss of his man. He shoved it down. Maybe later, he'd think about what had just occurred. Now, he needed to know what had happened. "Butch, Jibril, Victor, with me."

He slammed through the door into the living room, where several of his men paused from packing the equipment they'd brought. He glared at them. "Who said to stop? Continue!" He led the way to the pool table and flipped on the light as he jammed his reading glasses onto his face. "Tell me exactly what happened."

In terse sentences of English, Jibril reported out. Bad news all the way around. Makmoud stared at the map. He located the egress road from the Turk's valley. A quick escape to Iran was definitely too risky, especially at night, and most especially with the Turk now agitated. He focused on their location and found the back route. A risky move that would lead them either to their alternative escape to Iran or to the east-west highway at Harifi al-Hafa. A rock slide the day after they'd taken Libby had blocked their alternative escape, and they didn't have enough provisions to head farther south. They would have to retreat to Amal, then reassess. "We need to make our escape sooner rather than later via this route."

"How long will that take?" Victor asked.

"Probably a good hour to hour and a half. Perhaps two hours. It is a tough drive along a narrow valley and then over this ridge to a north-south road that leads to Harifi al-Hafa." He traced the route as he spoke.

"They have the scouts' packs," Jibril said. "For sure they will be arriving."

Makmoud cursed his bad luck. "They must be stopped." No matter how much it grated against his original objective, he needed Victor's team to fully engage. He turned to his foe and undid his cuffs. "Your turn to help. Just remember."

Victor nodded. "An escape attempt means we'll be shot."

"Exactly."

"Trust me, we're with you on this one," Victor said. "What do you need us to do?"

"Help us load. Then fight if need be. We'll leave Libby upstairs until we're ready to pull out. Jibril, you and Butch prepare something—

anything—to stop them." Light flashed through the window, and he jumped. Nothing except the predicted storm front drawing closer. "Go now. We'll have to leave Parviz."

Jibril muttered under his breath, but he pushed into the night with Butch on his heels. Makmoud led the way into the holding room where the rest of Victor's team awaited. Methodically, he undid their chains. Fiona smirked, as did Skylar. Suleiman wouldn't meet his gaze, and both Sana and Shelly merely looked confused.

Victor stepped forward. "It's okay, team. We're needed. The Turk is on the way here, and if we don't get a move on it, we're all going to be toast. Let's go."

Makmoud turned on his heel. Time to move before unwelcome company showed up.

Friday, July 12, 2019, 2050 hours local time, northeastern Iraq

Butch followed Jibril to a small outbuilding. "What's your plan?"

Jibril flipped on his headlamp and spun a combination lock. "I don't have one."

Butch's headache was making a major comeback. He ground his teeth and winced at the grit in his mouth. He spat on the ground. Rubbing his temples helped a little, and he took a deep breath to stave off his growing frustration. "C'mon. We've got potentially a lot of bad guys headed our way who are plenty mad now."

Jibril ignored him and flipped on a light.

Butch stared. The small building was stuffed to the gills with guns on racks and several crates with Farsi written all over them. "Should I ask if this is a safe house rather than a temporary abode for you guys? What did Yado say your cover story was? Something about hunting wild boar. Nope, y'all were hunting something else. Us."

Again, no response as Jibril studied what they had. With a grunt, he snagged a sledgehammer, shovel, and mattock and tossed them to his unwilling comrade. "Put those outside and help me with this crate."

"What's in it?"

"What we need."

Butch knelt and caught one end while Jibril got the other. They carefully set it on the ground outside. Jibril dumped a small duffel bag and the tools on top. "Let's go."

"How far?"

"One kilometer."

"What? The road didn't—"

"We drove up here in a Jeep, remember?"

Grrr. This was getting worse and worse. No shared plan. With his luck, the crate was full of spiders, the only creature on earth that would send him running and screaming like a girl.

"Get your end and let's go." Jibril squatted. "I have the back."

Butch shifted his rifle to his front and made sure the muzzle pointed downward. Backing up against the crate, he got the front edges. As they walked, he felt the rough wood pushing against him. "Hey, slow down there, why don't you?"

"We have no time!"

"You keep pushing me, I'm going to fall on my face, and I ain't interested in breaking my nose again."

At least the man slowed a little as they trundled their cargo down the road. The almost full moon provided plenty of silvery light to keep them on the dark ribbon of macadam as it gently curved to the left and right. After ten or so minutes, the valley narrowed to where the almost vertical slopes came nearly to the edge of the one-lane road. A perfect pinch point for a trap. "Our spot?"

"Our spot."

Butch eased his load to the ground, then turned. "Okay. I'm asking again. What's your plan? And don't tell me you have none. Because then I have to think, and in my condition, any kind of deep thinking makes my head hurt."

"We dig two shallow trenches, lay five mines in each, staggered. I will arm each row when they are in place."

"What's the range?"

"A good twenty meters or more."

Butch eyed the landscape around them. Where the valley widened toward the villa, he noted a couple of large boulders. Just in case Jibril went boom when arming them. Of course, he too would probably be shredded. "Let's not die tonight."

"Not by our hand, for sure not." Jibril turned on his headlamp. "Get that sledgehammer and start breaking up the road."

No problem there. Butch flipped the switch on his headlamp, took the sledgehammer, and began pounding away. The soft pavement easily broke apart. As he worked up a good sweat, the effort energized him and chased away the headache. The freshening breeze cooled him. He ignored the flickers of lightning and low rumbles of an approaching storm. Behind him, Jibril shoved away the debris until they'd sufficiently widened the trench. Then, with mattock and shovel, they dug down.

How much time had passed? Butch didn't want to stop long enough to find out. Probably a good half hour, including their walk. No way would he think about what the Turk's men were doing.

"Enough," Jibril grunted. Using a crowbar from the duffel, he pried off the top of the crate. "Lift those out carefully. They are not armed, but I'm not taking any chances."

"Not if we want to live."

"Exactly. We will set the first row, then fill in around them with debris."

"What's the sensitivity?"

"A man has to step on it."

Butch folded his arms across his chest. "I ain't taking any chances."

Jibril paused from where he placed the first mine. "If they see the mine, they will step over it."

"And I don't want to go boom."

"You will not." Jibril huffed out a hard breath. "Just do as I say. A light coating of debris should be enough."

Muttering, Butch watched as Jibril armed the first row, then nodded for him to do his task.

"Like putting sprinkles on cupcakes," he muttered.

Jibril stared. "What? You bake?"

"No, my wife does, and she makes great cupcakes." Butch lightly placed small chunks of macadam over the plates. He sucked in a breath. No boom. Praise God. He finished his task.

Jibril began laying the second row. "You help her cook?"

"Not usually. Just on the grill. But man, I love watching her."

Jibril shook his head.

"Hey, you oughta get married one day. Might change how you think about some things. Like acting like a jerk." Yeah, he couldn't resist that little dig.

Once more, his comrade ignored him and finished arming the remaining mines.

Whatever. Butch finished his task, then tossed the tools and duffel into the empty crate. "That's it. We've got to—"

Jibril held up his hand in a closed fist.

Stop. Butch got that signal all too well. He froze, and goosebumps popped up on his arms. In a whisper, he asked, "What is it?"

"Behind that boulder. Now!" Jibril hefted the crate, and they scurried behind one of the boulders at the edge of the blast zone. He crouched and peered at Butch. "Do you smell that?"

"Smell what?" Butch glared at him and pointed to his face. "Broken nose, remember? Thanks to one of your pals."

Jibril muttered low in Farsi, then whispered, "Cigarette smoke."

Dang it. Butch unslung his rifle and made sure a round was chambered. He listened. Shelly had always said he had dog ears as well as a dog nose. Now he heard the noise. Shuffling feet. Murmurs. Someone was coming. Probably a forward scouting party of the Turk's men. Didn't seem like they were schooled in the art of moving silently.

Oh so carefully, he peeked around the rock.

Sure enough, the shadowy forms of four men approached the line of mines.

"If they cross safely, we are in trouble." Jibril raised his radio to his lips and murmured in barely audible Farsi. He reclipped it to his belt and lifted his rifle.

The men weren't slowing. Butch's eyes widened. "Get down!"

He grabbed Jibril and pressed both of them tightly to the rock.

A deafening blast assaulted the quiet night, and a blinding flash pierced the darkness. Butch winced at the sizzling sound of smoking hot shrapnel hitting the rock. More flew over them, along with softer fragments he didn't want to name. The carnage was over in seconds. When he was sure it was safe, he popped upright. No one remained alive. He cringed, then helped Jibril to his feet. "We've got to get out of here. Now!"

Jibril blinked as if stunned. He reached for the crate.

"Forget the crate. C'mon!" Butch took off up the road toward the villa. If his guess was correct, there was a whole squad behind those four scouts. And once they figured out their pals were dead, they'd come at them with a vengeance.

In the floodlights of the villa, the others had lined up all eight vehicles in a staggered formation. The crew had mounted fifty-cal guns to the Humvees as well as the lead and chase Jeep Wranglers. People carried boxes and packs to the vehicles.

Butch shouted, "We've been blown! Gotta get going now!"

That froze everyone to the spot.

Then Makmoud came out of the shadows. He snarled what must have been the Farsi equivalent of "get moving" because everyone sprang into action. He yelled at Jibril, who replied back. Drivers ran to each of the eight vehicles. None were his team. Not surprising.

Butch whipped around. "Where's Libby?"

"Upstairs." Jibril veered toward the Jeep at the end of the convoy. "Get her and join us in the last Wrangler."

"Roger that."

Machine gun fire destroyed any remnant of peace. He barely heard Makmoud and Victor urging the others to get into the vehicles. He saw only a blur of curls as Shelly climbed into a Toyota SUV alongside Sana. The other team members were split between Makmoud's guys, effectively destroying any chance of breaking away from the *Quds* men.

Butch darted to the gate in the villa's wall.

Gunfire from their teams answered. Engines revved, and the first vehicles began a slow roll up the slope toward their escape route.

Butch ducked inside the courtyard. An explosion blazed outside the wall. Crap. Mortar. He cringed as the round fell short of the villa. It wouldn't take them long to dial it in. He burst into the main room, which had been stripped bare save for the television and pool table. "Libby!"

He barely heard her voice above the rising sound of the battle outside. A rocket-propelled grenade hissed from the team. Then came an explosion down the road. Makmoud's guys battled back.

He raced up the stairs as a mortar round landed in the courtyard. The ground shook, and windows blew inward. He turned his face to the wall and crouched as glass tinkled against the plaster. A shard buried itself in his back. Knocked off balance, Butch tumbled to the landing. He sucked in a frantic breath as he reached behind him and yanked it out. His head began spinning. "Libby!"

"Up here!"

Praise God, she'd bolted into the hallway.

He grabbed her hand as a roar filled the air. Another rocket-propelled grenade.

Their feet hit the first set of steps downward.

The wall of the living room exploded. The force of it threw him into her, and they crashed into the wall. Butch kept her shielded with his body. Points of fire opened up on his back. He winced. They had to keep moving.

The deep chir of Makmoud's fifty-cal guns filled the air. They stumbled onto the landing, took a left, and sprinted down the remaining steps. Just as his feet hit bottom, another mortar round scored a direct hit on the roof. Tile, timber, nails, and plaster blasted downward. He pushed her to the floor and landed on top of her at the base of the stairs.

A glancing blow knocked the breath out of him.

"Butch?"

He wheezed and tried to rise. Debris covered them.

A beam had caught on the steps and floor, effectively pinning them. He tried to push upward. Nothing. "I'm okay. You?"

"Okay."

Time to get out of there. Otherwise, they'd die for sure. He pushed up again. A little give. "Help me, Libby."

She joined him, and together, they shoved aside the beam enough to worm through a hole in the mess. He pushed her out first. "Go to the last Jeep. Now!"

He leveraged himself through and stared. No roof anymore over the great room. Just a gaping hole. Flames had kicked up and began licking at the timber. Then he saw it. The propane tank. If that blew...

Libby seemed stuck in place. She swayed a little like she might pass out.

Heaving himself to his feet, he grabbed her hand. "C'mon!"

Another mortar whistled inward.

He saw the gunner in the last Jeep with a driver and Jibril up front. Barely heard their shouts. He lengthened his stride.

The round found the propane tank. With an earth-quaking blast, flames shot outward.

The explosion sent Butch into the side of the Wrangler. Libby collapsed beside him. He lifted her to her feet. The gunner helped her inside, and Butch threw himself into the backseat.

The Jeep began moving even before the door closed.

As they made their way upslope, Butch could only pray they wouldn't die during their escape.

17

Butch twisted in his seat as they bumped up the rutted road of their escape route. An orange glow from the flames of the blazing villa flickered against the stone slopes. Smoke obscured their attackers. As they crested the ridge, he cast one last glance at the villa. An engine roared, and he gripped his pistol. Not that it would do any good if someone came after them. *Lord, keep them so focused on searching the villa that they don't look toward us as we get out of here.* The night's darkness draped its mantle over them and concealed them as they angled downward.

Facing forward, he grimaced as he eased onto the seat on the Jeep's right side. *Lord, hide us from our pursuers.* His mind swung to all of the psalms of David when the young Israelite king-to-be had hidden from a king who wanted him dead. *Hide us under Your wings.*

Adrenaline began seeping from his system. His hands trembled, and he balled them into fists to keep them from shaking. Burning began in his back. Diana would probably have fun picking stuff out of him. His ears rang from the attack, and once more, his head throbbed. Fatigue washed over him. He needed sleep. Badly.

They descended on a rutted road that narrowed as they lost altitude.

145

The caravan had doused their lights, and they had only the moonlight to guide them. The road evened out with a river on the left that tumbled over rocks as it rushed southward, probably toward the Tigris. Thanks to the unpaved road, their progress slowed to a crawl.

They bounced over a particularly hard bump, one that sent both him and Libby out of their seats. Butch grabbed the roll bar, and only his arm around her shoulders kept her from flying out of the Wrangler. He reached around and found a seatbelt. "Libby, get your belt on."

She stared at him dumbly, and her lips trembled.

He pulled the belt across her and latched it. "So you won't go flying into the river."

Her trembling smile answered him. She quivered from the earlier trauma of their escape. He leaned forward and tapped Jibril on the shoulder. "Where's Shelly?"

He barely heard the man's answer over the rumble of the Jeep's engine. "In the Land Cruiser ahead of us with Sana."

Butch didn't dare ask where Suleiman was. Probably with Makmoud. For some reason, the man had it out for their sniper/observer. Had he been in Makmoud's *Quds* cell in South America? He couldn't remember what the young man had told him as the team was getting to know one another years before. "Where does this road lead?"

Jibril said something to the driver in Farsi. The man sped up slightly and kept close to the Land Cruiser. "Harifi al-Hafa, which, as you know, sits on the east-west highway."

Yeah, much to his regret did he know. His impulsivity had gotten them into this mess. Just how would he get them out of it? Hard to know right now. He parsed through what he knew. The turnoff for the *Quds* safe house had been farther east, much closer—too close—to the Iranian border. The road leading from the Turk's valley lay between them and the border. Twenty miles west of Harifi al-Hafa was Amal, which provided a conduit. It clicked. "The Turk and his crew probably are massing for an invasion."

Jibril kept his eyes on the road. "They would be fools to go against Iran."

"You'll get no argument from me. But what about Amal?"

Silence.

"The Iraqis are letting the Kurds pretty much run things, save for the border. The Kurds obviously don't have a standing army save for their militia, which I don't think is that big and certainly not heavily armed. What's to stop the Turk and his pals from moving in and setting up shop?" The implications of it stung as he thought about Jace and the town that had only just begun recovering from the brutality of ISIS years before. "And if they do that? How long will it take them to move reinforcements into the area from Turkey? If they gather enough forces, all of Kurdistan could be in danger, including Mosul. It'd be like ISIS all over again, and it could threaten Iran."

He didn't expect an answer, and Jibril obliged him with stony silence. Maybe he'd planted a seed in the man's mind. Hopefully, Victor was doing the same thing with Makmoud.

The driver made an abrupt right, and the road steepened. The rush of water fell away. To the right, the angled mountain slope gleamed a faint silver in the moonlight. To the left, mountain peaks far across the valley almost glowed. And nothing to his immediate left but darkness. They ascended the side of a mountain, and to fall off the road meant certain death.

Resting his elbows on his knees, Butch slowly rubbed his temples, which eased his headache a little. Not much farther to safe haven. Then maybe he could rest. At least physically. His mind remained stuck in overdrive with too many questions racing through it. Like, how his team could escape Makmoud's clutches. Nothing came to mind, and that's what worried him. And how could they warn Jace and the others? No answers. None.

A rock pinged off his side of the Jeep. He gazed up the slope. Almost sheer faces, like what he remembered in the Rockies. He cringed at the sight of boulders. Hopefully their passage wouldn't break any loose. Despite the danger, the caravan kept pressing upward. "You sure we're going to Harifi al-Hafa?"

Jibril huffed out a sigh as if Butch were a little kid asking way too many questions. "We're heading to a high pass. We cross through that, go down the other side, and that leads right to it, about a two-hour drive."

Butch checked his watch. 2100 hours. He could do that.

"At this speed?"

"Perhaps longer."

What was an extra hour? A lot, according to his back. Each time he leaned against the seat, pain flared. He needed Diana to look at it. But he kept his mouth shut since complaining wouldn't do any good. Libby huddled against the left side of the Wrangler. She hadn't said a word. Hadn't moved, really. A tear trickled down her cheek, but she didn't seem to notice. Her fingers found his, and she gripped his hand.

Butch jumped but didn't pull back. He studied her. She'd endured so much over the past several years. First losing her husband in a brutal way. Then not knowing the fate of her children. Fighting with the militia despite her traumatic brain injury. Enduring a long recovery. Seeking answers in the very place that had nearly destroyed her. Throw in being kidnapped and spending ten days as Makmoud's hostage, and she was probably undone. She needed his comfort right then, and he wasn't going to shun her.

Lord, we need to rest and regroup. Please? He rested his head against the door frame as fatigue threatened to overwhelm him. The engine noise soothed him, and he dozed.

A sharp crack penetrated his haze. The Jeep ground to a halt and listed hard to the left. Thrown off balance, the gunner cried out and pitched from the cargo area. Only a harness and safety line kept him from certain death.

Jibril whipped around in his seat. "Ehsan!"

The Jeep creaked and began listing farther to the left as gravity threatened to draw it into the valley.

"No one move!" Jibril shouted. "Stay absolutely still."

Libby whimpered.

Jibril passed back a Maglite. "Butch, here's a light. Tell me what you see."

Oh so carefully, Butch shifted so he faced backward. He shivered. No gunner in the back and no view of the road behind them. "I gotta climb over the seat."

"Butch?" Fear colored his name as it flew from Libby's lips.

"Libby, when I climb over, slowly move to where I was sitting. The more weight there, the better." Careful to stay as close to the right side of the vehicle as he could, Butch eased over the headrest and into the cargo area. He shone the light behind the Wrangler. A shudder rippled through him as he stared at absolute blackness where the outer half of the road should have been. "Jibril, a problem. The road collapsed under the left rear wheel and is starting to crack toward the right. We've got to put it into four-wheel drive. If we can get out of the hole, we'll be good."

The engine revved.

Ehsan's pleas were faint, panicked. Well, Butch would be panicked too, if he were dangling over nothingness.

"Ehsan, buddy, listen to me," Butch called in Arabic. "Can you do that?"

"What…" The Wrangler rocked as the gunner struggled.

"Stop moving because you're knocking us off balance. We're going to get onto solid ground soon." He could only hope. "When we get there, we'll get you back in."

Those words seemed to reassure the young man, and he relaxed.

"Okay. Try it now."

The driver pressed the accelerator. The back right wheel spun against the soil. Cracks leading to the right side of the Jeep began widening.

Sweat broke out on Butch's brow despite a freshening breeze generated by the approaching storm front. His head began spinning. "Easy there. Nice and slow does the trick."

The driver eased off the accelerator and kept a steady pressure on it.

The wheels gained purchase. Too slowly, the Jeep moved forward until all wheels were on solid ground.

With a resounding crack, the remaining road behind them gave way and tumbled into the gorge, leaving a huge gap. No time for a breath of relief. Not yet. Not until they were safely away from this part of the road because chances were really good the cracks could chase them all the way up the gorge. "Keep slowly moving forward, and I'll pull in Ehsan."

Jibril murmured into his radio. The convoy resumed, moving at a snail's pace toward the peak.

Butch crept to the other side of the cargo area and peered over the left side. Still nothingness. Ehsan gripped his safety line, and below him lay only blackness. If that line frayed, he'd fall to his death.

Butch pulled on it. "Get the edges when you can, Ehsan."

Once the young man had a secure grip, Butch grabbed him under the arms and heaved into the Jeep. Pain blazed across his back, and he fell into the cargo area with the gunner on top. Oh, man. He released a groan. The sooner they got out of this mess, the better. He tapped Ehsan on the arm. "You good there?"

"Yes, yes." The young man pushed himself upright. In the glow of the flashlight, he placed his hand over his heart. "Thank you."

Bless him, he clambered to his feet and resumed his position at the gun. Yeah, Makmoud had trained his men well.

Butch climbed into the back seat and settled where Libby had been a few minutes before. She immediately attached herself to his side.

The driver stopped the Jeep. Jibril undid his seatbelt, and twisted around so he faced them. His eyes shifted between them, then landed on Butch. "Thank you, friend. You saved my comrade, and we're in your debt."

"Anytime." Butch tucked it away for future reference. "So with the road busted like it is, I don't think anyone can follow us now. Best we get a move on it as fast as possible."

"I could not agree more." Jibril faced forward as the driver put the Jeep into gear again. The convoy resumed its trek. "And when we get to Harifi al-Hafa, we need to regroup."

18

"Brother, we need to return to Iran as soon as we can."

Jibril's statement pulled Makmoud from his weariness. Thanks to the treacherous nature of the roads and the waves of rain from the storm that caught up with them, the two-hour trip had turned to four. They arrived at the The Falafel Restaurant in Harifi al-Hafa a bedraggled mess. Those who'd ridden in open vehicles now huddled under blankets supplied by Yado's men and women. They sipped on cups of chai and coffee to warm up and keep them awake. That included Butch, who hunched in a corner of the restaurant as Diana examined him under the watchful eyes of two of Makmoud's men.

"Makmoud." Both his brother's voice and a light punch on the arm now held an impatient push to them.

How could he disagree? He couldn't. Except that now, the Turk's army stood in the way. "What do you propose we do? Just waltz up to the Turk and ask him for safe passage?"

"Well, yes."

"Are you out of your mind?" Makmoud began pacing around the corner dining area of The Falafel they'd claimed as their space. "Do you think they would let us through? Not after we killed their men."

Jibril's nose flared. "Just as they killed ours. It was fair retrib—"

"We came within a hairsbreadth of dying." Fatigue edged Makmoud's voice. "We barely escaped with our lives. And we are out of provisions, correct?"

Jibril stared at Victor's team. The men and women remained separated, sitting in different parts of the restaurant. Only Diana and Butch were allowed to be together as she gave him a cursory examination. His brother returned his attention to the conversation at hand. "Perhaps Yado will give us safe passage into Turkey. We can go eastward from there, cross into Iran."

A good idea.

Yado, who sat with them and smoked on a hookah while listening to their conversation, straightened. He shook his head and replied in his own version of rough Farsi, "No. My men have been lucky that we have not been captured or killed by the Turk's men. It is foolishness to head in that direction. Do you understand?"

"But you move goods and services there all of the time," Jibril protested.

"I *used* to do that. They have robbed our convoys, so I focus more of my efforts northwest of here. I am no fool, Jibril Hidari." Yado lifted the hookah pipe to his lips, inhaled, and blew a stream of smoke out the corners of his mouth.

Makmoud hated hookah smoke with a passion. Scowling, he resumed his pacing as he considered his options. Trying to force Yado and his men to take them through eastern Turkey would never work. He'd draw his gun, aim it at the man, and the rest of the traffickers occupying the restaurant would shoot them in a heartbeat. He cut his gaze toward the far side where the men of the former Shadow Box team sprawled. Butch now eased onto one of the divans beside Victor, who'd not taken his eyes off the men discussing his team's fate.

Makmoud rubbed his chin. On the ride over, Victor had spoken of teaming together. He saw it as the only way to survive. Makmoud resumed his seat as he considered his larger foe lurking in the mountains east of their location. "Yado, what do you now know of the Turk?"

"What your men saw today," Yado shook his head, "maybe a fraction of their forces, probably amassing to move west."

"How many do you estimate?"

"We don't know. You said two thousand?"

"Yes. And if they move out in full force, it will be right along the east-west highway." Makmoud shook his head. No more discussion of heading east. Not in his mind.

"What do you think is their final destination?" Jibril asked.

"Amal." That word flew from Yado's lips without question.

A chill rippled through Makmoud, and he fought a shiver. "I see."

He focused on Victor. The man met his gaze without fear, something that both irritated and pleased him at the same time. He called, "Victor, come over here."

Slowly, the leader of the captured team rose. Butch did as well, but with a small wave of his friend's hand, he resumed his seat. When Victor joined them, Makmoud pointed to one of the divans. "Sit."

His eyes never leaving his face, Victor eased onto the seat. "What do you want, Makmoud?"

"Surprisingly, your input."

"I find that hard to believe, seeing that we're your captives and all."

Makmoud ignored his sarcasm. "Tell me something. What are your thoughts on The Turk?"

"He took your villa, didn't he? Blew it up. He's probably figured Iranians are in his neighborhood, which is bad news for you. My gut says he's going to push all the way through to Amal. And the Kurds don't have a standing army, just the militia. Yado, what is their size?"

Yado shifted. "Maybe ten thousand, but that is spread over Iraq and Syria."

"They may not see the Turk as enough of a problem right now," Makmoud hedged.

Victor eyed the hookah with disdain. He switched his gaze to his captor. "I assume the Iraqi army claims to protect their part of Kurdistan as well. I doubt they'll be much protection against the Turk's army, meaning he and his men will do what ISIS did five or so years ago when they overran Amal."

What could Makmoud do? Disagree? He'd seen the photos Jibril had taken of his two dead scouts. And seen with his own eyes what they had done to Parviz.

Yado snorted and in his heavily accented English said, "All the Iraqi army wants to do in this area is protect the border. You see what a good job they have done with keeping them out of their country."

Makmoud closed his eyes. When would this stop? "You are right. If Amal falls, it falls without a sound due to its isolation. Then the Turk will bring in many more men, take everything north of Mosul and wend his way back to Syria to gather other ISIS followers before moving east toward Iran. Then we have a repeat of just a few years ago."

"Makmoud," Victor's voice penetrated his rampaging thoughts, "it's like I told you coming over here. With the combined skills of our teams, we may have a chance at saving Amal."

"My mission is to get you back to Iran."

"I get that, but there's no way you can get there now."

Too true. He ground his teeth. "Then we temporarily join forces together—and with you, Yado. And with those in Amal."

Victor nodded. "Agreed. We need to get to Amal safely as well as keep tabs on the Turk."

The trafficker gazed at the map Jibril had slapped onto a table, then sprang into action. He volunteered his men as scouts to place surveillance on the Turk. The rest of the village would retreat to Amal. Yado set down his hookah pipe and left them alone so he could dispatch his men.

That left Makmoud with Victor. Silence fell, and Makmoud checked his SAT phone. The voice mail icon glowed. Due to their escape, he hadn't heard it ring. He entered his access code and lifted his phone to his ear.

Tank Russell, Roo's right-hand man, had left a message. "Makmoud, Tank here. I've arrived in Mosul and would like a status update on your mission. Call me as soon as you get this message."

Not going to happen. Makmoud deleted it and swung his gaze to Victor. His thoughts drifted to their conversation just after he'd captured the man and his team.

Victor grimaced as he sniffed his jacket. "I hate hookah smoke. I'm going to stink to high heaven now."

That brought an unwilling smile to Makmoud's face. "You and me both. Victor, you said there is a price on my head. Twenty million, yes?"

"Has been for seven years, ever since you attempted to kidnap former President Badin's daughter and killed Rachel. How can you argue with that amount of reward?" Victor cocked his head. "How much was this client of yours willing to pay you?"

The bounty on his head was twice the amount Roo had been willing to pay to smooth away his "problem" in the form of Libby Mansour and the team. Would his client betray him?

"Ten million, right?" Victor's lip curled slightly as if challenging him to deny it. "Something tells me you wouldn't have gone after us, wouldn't have known we were in-country, save for this client of yours. Sure, you hold the upper hand now, but things could go south real quick like. Then he might say something to our guys in Washington and make his money back, all without getting his hands dirty. Or he might decide to take care of the problem himself."

Would LaRue do such a thing? The gubernatorial candidate wasn't beyond that. Makmoud very well knew what LaRue International Transport did beyond the legitimate side of the business. Gunrunning. Ever since the American Civil War, that side of the house had made far more money than any kind of legitimate transport company would. He easily had the means to wipe out Makmoud so he could collect the bounty.

LaRue had made it clear that Libby Mansour was a liability to his political future, as were Butch and his team, simply by association. Makmoud had proposed a bullet in Libby's head. So easy in this area, especially since few would ask questions. But certain people like Butch and her parents would ask, and LaRue said he couldn't afford that. Hence why he'd hired Makmoud to take down Victor and his team. Or had he hired the team to take down his squad?

Was he being double-crossed? Was going to Amal walking into a trap? "You are not here to take me."

"Not at all." Victor sat forward with his elbows on his knees. "I promise you, I had no idea you were here, and I would never, ever use my team as bait to lure you out. That's simple foolishness." He stared at the map on the table. "But if this client finds out about your 'unfortunate' demise, he can crow about it and say he hired us to do it, even if we died in the process. All he would need would be solid evidence that someone could collect. Look. That's back-burnered for now. We work with others in Amal to fortify it and get rid of the Turk. We'll sort things out later."

"Later, you will go with us to Iran."

Victor let that one pass by in silence.

"Until then, your team will not be together. Understood?"

"Yes."

"Then we go to Amal and regroup so we can defeat The Turk." And only then would Makmoud deal with the issue of Tank Russell and his potentially not-trustworthy client.

19

By the time the convoy of thirty or so vehicles arrived in Amal, dawn lit the area with a soft pink glow. Butch's body now let him know loud and clear it needed a break. His head throbbed to the point where nausea tinged his gut, even with the aspirin he popped shortly after their arrival in Harifi al-Hafa. His back burned, and he worried an infection had already started from the many wounds he'd received.

Libby dozed with her head on his shoulder. Strange that Jibril had let her stay with them in the Wrangler, but maybe he assumed she'd go more quietly if she were with someone she knew. No way would he let Jibril take her back to Iran to be his wife.

She was returning to her home in Amal, what had once been Butch's home away from home. Worries about worming their way out of their predicament with Makmoud preyed on his weary mind. But Victor was right. Face the immediate threat of the Turk first. Then worry with the larger, looming threat of being shipped to Iran.

When they arrived, first things first. He'd get Diana to take care of his back, maybe give him something so he could sleep. Then get that rack time he so badly needed—everyone needed, Makmoud's guys included.

Since they led the convoy, Jibril slowed as members of the local militia waved them to a stop with rifles held at a relaxed ready.

Colonel Farhad stepped to the front of the group, and Butch straightened. After extricating himself from Libby, he grasped the roll bar and pulled himself to a standing position. "Colonel!"

The militia commander's eyes widened, and his jaw dropped as he pressed a hand over his heart. "Mr. Addison! When you didn't return last night, we thought for sure you had perished, at least until Yado contacted us and let us know you are safe. Praise God for your return."

"Where do you want us to go?"

"You to the compound. We have a place for those from Harifi al-Hafa."

Jibril glanced at Butch in the rear view mirror. "Where is this compound?"

Butch eased downward. "South side of town. It's a bunch of warehouses behind the wire. Has plenty of space for us and you guys. It also has a great kitchen, 'cause I know you boys like to eat as much as we did—and do."

A smile briefly flashed across Jibril's normally serious features. "You sound very familiar with it."

"I was here during my time in the Army." Butch didn't feel like elaborating. Not then, and certainly not to a man who would look down upon his fall from glory.

His temporary ally let that one pass in silence. "And did you meet Libby here?"

"No." Jibril didn't need to know about his hot romance with her during high school.

Libby blinked in the brightening morning. "Butch, where are we?"

"Amal."

She sat up straighter. "What? Amal?"

"The Turk's coming this way, and we've got to get ready to defend it."

A shudder rippled through her thin frame.

"We're going to stop them, Libby. Promise." One bad bump, and his back roared with all sorts of complaints. "But first, we've got to rest before our bodies make that decision for us." He leaned forward as they came to a T-intersection. "Turn left. Then the compound will be on your left."

Jibril's driver obeyed, and within a few minutes, they pulled up to the gates and ground to a stop.

"Let me get the gates unlocked." Butch eased open his door. He hopped down. Yow! Wrong move. His back protested, and he braced his hands on his knees until the flames of agony settled to a low burn. His head spun, and he didn't move until he steadied. He hobbled to the gate and punched in the code Colonel Farhad had given him.

The convoy of eight vehicles rumbled into the dusty yard. Taking deep breaths to stave off the pain, Butch relocked the padlock and swiveled. Jace wouldn't be there for a bit, so—

"Butch?" Jace stood on the porch of the medical clinic.

"Hey, man." Butch winced as his back flared. "Sorry we're late. Shouldn't you be in bed?"

"Not when a mom and dad brought their sick kid into the clinic at three this morning." His gaze darted to the other vehicles in the convoy as they began shutting down their engines. "You want to tell me what's going on? I mean, I didn't expect you to bring friends with you. When you didn't return, we feared—"

"Long story. We're here. And we've got a problem." Butch risked a glance at Jibril, who opened his door.

Jace's eyes clouded. "What happened? Who are these guys?"

"Butch? Jace?" Libby's thin, ethereal voice caught them both up short. She stood at the back left door of the Jeep and swayed, then slumped forward.

Butch caught her in his arms. "Libby!"

The dizzies really got ahold of him, and he fell to his knees. From afar, Jace said, "I've got her. I think you need to get checked out."

Diana knelt beside him. A man joined her and introduced himself as Ali, another one of Makmoud's medics. He crouched next to Butch. "Sir, if I must say, he is right. We need to examine you."

"You ain't gonna get no argument from me." Butch got one foot underneath him. Whoo, the ground began shifting, and he toppled over. He briefly sank into blackness.

"Butch." Diana leaned over him and lightly slapped his cheeks. "C'mon, wake up."

He opened his eyes. "Sorry, I…"

"You passed out. Ali, help me here."

They lifted him to his feet and walked him into the medical building.

"Libby…" Fire consumed his back. "Man, I'm hurting."

Diana's hand on his arm became firmer. "Jace is taking care of her." They arrived at an exam room. "Get that T-shirt off and lie on your stomach. We'll take a look."

Ali helped him remove his tattered T-shirt.

Diana shoved a pillow to him and tucked one under his middle. A low whistle escaped her. "I've seen porch screens with fewer holes than this."

At her touch, Butch hissed in a breath. "You're quite the comedian."

"It's pretty bad. I've got to stitch up a few."

The soft pillow felt so good against his battered face. "Wake me up when you're finished."

"No worries there. I think I may be keeping you awake."

"How many pieces of stuff in me?"

"A lot. Think about a dog getting into porcupine quills."

"What is a porcupine?" Ali asked.

Butch groaned and listened as Diana explained. A light warmed his back, and they began the long, hard work of removing debris from his skin. "Diana, talk to me, girl."

"Lots of glass." Which stung as they began removing it. The pieces clinked as they dropped them into a metal basin.

Butch lost count of the stuff they pulled out.

"You've got some nails. Small splinters of wood." She murmured to Ali, who began sanitizing the wounds.

Butch grunted when she removed something large. "I'm scared to ask."

"Big splinter of wood. It left a good, two-inch gash. I'll need to stitch three of these closed, and the rest can take Band-Aids. After I stitch these up and put waterproof bandages on them, I want you to grab a shower before we put the Band-Aids on. Ali, while I do that, could you locate a set of fresh clothing for him? His bag should be in his and Shelly's room. Second floor of the warehouse on the end."

The medic left them alone.

"I've got to give you a few doses of lidocaine. Just a few stings."

He grunted. He didn't even want to know what he looked like. Probably some morbid fantasy of an abstract artist. "What's a few more stitches?"

"You tell me. They'll go nicely with your tattoos. I like how they come together to form a dragon."

At that, he tried a chuckle. It came out more like a squeak as she began injecting the local anesthetic.

"Tell me about them."

"About what?"

"Your tattoos. I mean, some of these look old. Like really old."

"Thanks, I think."

She chuckled. "Not like that. I've seen my share of tattoos over the years, and whoever did these did a good job. The dragon seems to be about ten years old. I mean, I see the Iraqi flag in here. And also what may be a mountain peak around here."

Memories of joking it up with his team members while deployed wormed their way to the surface. Then came his early days of Basic Training and losing his hair due to stress. Back then he always joked about not having to worry about shaving his head. "The cue ball is for when I lost my hair during basic. You know, *bald as a cue ball* and everything."

"I get it. I see the Green Beret seal."

"Yeah. When I got tabbed."

"And the airborne parachute."

"Jump school."

"A beer mug?" She chuckled.

"For my buddies. We loved to have a good time." He closed his eyes. "I guess not all of my Army memories are bad."

"They don't have to be."

He really wanted to believe her, and it had been true—until the betrayal in 2009. "When I got out, I wanted to erase them. Or at least not to see them individually. One of my neighbors at the apartment complex where I lived was a tattoo artist and a good one at that. He helped me with the dragon design to pull everything together, then did it. I have to say it turned out great." Thanks to exhaustion, he slurred his words. *Time to get some rack time.* More pinches brought him back to reality. "More lidocaine?"

"I'm done with that. Give me ten. Then I'll put some waterproof bandages on these bad boys so that you can get showered. Just don't linger under the water."

"Yes, ma'am." As she worked, Butch's mind wandered to his past. Deep down, he knew he'd made the right decision to join the Army. It'd impacted his life in so many ways. His thoughts drifted toward the land of what-ifs. What if he'd gotten saved when he was in high school rather than just turned twenty-one? Would he and Libby have stayed together? God had put them on totally different paths, he into the Army, she to college and then teaching in Iraq. Would she have avoided all of that pain? *And why does it matter? Dude, why are you wondering? It's not like you can go back and change the past. And why the heck did I suddenly sound just like Skylar?* He muffled a groan.

Diana ceased her work. "You okay? That didn't sound too good."

"Just thinking."

"You tell me the second you start feeling any pain. I got two of the three stitched. This last one's a bit of a doozy. A screw embedded itself."

He winced. "Like how long is the cut?"

"An inch. Long but not too long."

One inch too long. He could feel her working. Not pain, just the pressure of the needle penetrating his skin and thread running through it. He needed to distract himself. "How's Libby?"

The exam room's door closed, and Ali sat down at his head. "I have your clothing, Mr. Addison, and I have checked with Jace Choi about Libby. She will be fine. She was weak and dehydrated, but that is not surprising. I looked after her at the villa, and she refused to eat or drink a lot. She is resting in the infirmary right now. Makmoud has decreed that she stay here at the compound."

Oh, great. *No chance of Jace shuttling her to safety. At least not now.*

Essentially, they'd gotten a stay of execution.

Finally, Diana finished and wiped down his back before applying waterproof bandages over the three places she'd stitched. "Two pokes. Then I'll let you go shower. One for pain and anti-inflammatory, one for tetanus. I've got some oral antibiotics that you'll need to take. And some Doxylamine so you can sleep well. Take a tablet. That should help you get to sleep and stay asleep."

He sat up, and sure enough, each of his arms got a poke. Four needles in one day. Pretty much a record for him.

She held up his T-shirt. A small grin crossed her face. "You want to wear this after your shower?"

He scowled at the tattered, blood-stained gray fabric that now resembled a T-shirt in name only. "Please tell me you're kidding."

She tossed it into a nearby trashcan. "I am. Go clean up. If you linger, I may be asleep when you get back. Jace said there's a bathroom with a shower on this hall."

With a grunt, he slid off the table and found it just as he'd anticipated. The hot water felt so good except when it hit his wounds. They stung, and he hissed through his teeth. Once he'd pulled on a fresh pair of boxers and cargo pants, he left his old ones in the trash and shuffled in flip-flops back to the exam room. Diana was now alone as she cleaned up from the procedure. "Hey, girl. I'm ready for the Band-Aids."

"Lie down."

"If I lie down, I'm going to fall asleep." He sat on the exam table, and she began applying bandages. A small sigh escaped her.

"What's going on?"

She gathered up the packaging, then faced him with a sea-green gaze that would have been alluring had he not been married. Some guys would have probably called it fascinating. More than once he'd caught some of Makmoud's pals gazing at her. "May I ask you a question?"

He shrugged into his new T-shirt. "Of course."

"What's up with you and Libby?"

Where had that come from? Left field, for sure. He frowned. "What do you mean, what's up? Nothing."

"You've virtually ignored your wife and paid all the attention in the world to Libby."

His gut tightened. "In case you didn't realize it, Libby's been kidnapped, knocked around, threatened, maybe even starved. What am I supposed to do? Ignore her?"

"Did I say that?"

"Sounds like it," he muttered.

She huffed out a breath. "Butch, honestly. Do you know Shelly got smacked around when we were kidnapped? Did you see her black eye? Did you check on her when we got to Makmoud's hideout?"

Ouch. Her questions, though gentle, drove daggers into his heart. "Just when did I have time to do that? We were there for maybe six hours. If I remember correctly, you and I were recruited to go and find Makmoud's dead scouts. And to try and save Parviz, which didn't work." He hardly noticed her flinch. "And then, oh, yeah, that's right, I had to help save our skins before we barely made it out alive, and then—"

"I get it, okay?" Diana held up her hands to fend off his verbal grenades, then turned away with her hands on her hips and stared out at the bright summer day. "I also get that Shelly was looking at you earlier this morning at Harifi al-Hafa. I know we were separated, but I don't think you looked her way once. She's devastated, Butch. She thinks you're shifting your affections back to Libby. Did you two date at some point?"

"High school." He ground out those words. "But I've barely seen her since, okay? And a lot of that was with *her husband*."

"Who died years ago."

Say what? Was he hearing what he thought he was hearing? "Really, Diana?"

"I get it." She closed her eyes for a moment. When she opened them, the sadness in them pierced his soul. "I know you've only been married for about eight weeks or so. You're just putting down roots. Don't take her for granted, okay?"

"I don't." He couldn't keep a touch of anger from his voice. "I'm not going to discuss this any further."

Doubt filled her eyes. So did something else. Pain? She busied herself with her instruments, placing them in her kit and stowing the clinic's in various drawers. "You're right. We won't. We're both so tired neither of us are making sense. Get some sleep. Vic wants to meet up with the group tonight, okay? At six."

"Whatever," he grunted. His back now stiff, he shuffled down the hall, from the building, and through the blinding daylight to the warehouse. At the sight of one of Makmoud's men walking sentry duty, his heart sank, even more so when he saw another one inside. No way could they steal away.

He crept up the stairs to the bedroom he and Shelly shared. Diana's words echoed in his ears. Shelly was strong. She could take care of herself. Libby, on the other hand, needed him. He'd be there for her no matter what.

He quietly shut the door. Shelly already slept curled into a ball on her side of the bed. Oh, so carefully to avoid pulling out his stitches, he eased from his shirt and pants. In the daylight sifting around the blackout curtains, he gazed at her. Wetness streaked her cheeks. Tear stains? Looked that way. She was beyond exhausted. So was he.

After popping his sleeping pill, he eased onto the bed and pulled the covers up over them. Then, with his nose buried in Shelly's curls, he fell into the hard darkness of sleep.

20

Butch's eyes snapped open. Dreams had dogged him in his sleep. Ones of having each wrist chained to two sides of a hot, stinking shipping crate. Of whips. Chains shredding skin off his back. Starvation. And freezing cold water thrown on him. A victim of his nightmares, the sheets hung half off the bed. He lay on his side and blinked as reality slowly returned.

From the footlocker, a fan cooled the hot sweat on his skin. A light shiver coursed through him. He reached a hand behind him to where Shelly slept. "Shel?"

Nothing but sheets. He pushed himself upright. More pull than pain. He carefully twisted to avoid tearing his stitches. No Shelly. She must have risen earlier. Bracing his hands on the edge of the mattress, he took inventory. No headache for a change. His back ached, but this time, in a good way, like maybe healing had begun.

Time to stand. He put one foot on the floor, then another. All systems on green. Sure, he could use more rest, but he could function now. He shambled from the room to the latrine. Once inside, he turned and stared over his shoulder at his back in the mirror. The humming fluorescent light sallowed his olive skin. Three waterproof bandages stood out in stark white contrast. Probably two dozen Band-Aids turned his dragon sad. And yeah,

167

Butch sure felt the way his dragon looked. Beat up. All of the band-aids had characters from Paw Patrol on them, which caused him to smile. Marie, Vic and Deborah's youngest daughter, must have helped Diana restock her medical kit.

After pulling on a T-shirt, he headed down the stairs. At the table closest to the kitchen's pass-through window, Jibril hunched with a large mug of coffee. The man liked his java as much as Butch did. At least they had that in common. Butch approached him. "Where did you get that?"

"Over there." Jibril nodded in the direction of a large urn with an orange light glowing. More mugs sat beside it. "Your friend, Jace, said the women knew we have a need of coffee. I must say this is some of the best I have tasted."

"And we'll need lots of it." Butch poured himself a mug. "I'm going to take a walk and will be back in time for our meeting at 1800 hours."

Jibril's hand shot to a pistol sitting on the table beside the mug. "You are not going anywhere."

Really? Like Butch would endanger the rest of his team? He battled the urge to tell him off and cradled the mug between his hands instead. "Look. I get it. You don't want us to escape. And I'm not going to try, okay? Why would I when my wife's whereabouts are unknown to me? And by the way, have you seen her?"

"She went into the locker room." Jibril nodded toward the locker room on the bottom floor that held the showers. The sound of water splattering on tile easily reached them. "You may go, but do not leave the compound."

"I'm not going to. Promise on that one."

He pushed through the door of the warehouse and headed across the dusty courtyard toward the clinic. A hot wind puffed across his face, and dust surrounded the nearby peaks. Mindful of his back, he allowed himself a cautious stretch as he peered around him. One of Makmoud's men walked patrol with his rifle slung over his shoulder. It irked him that they still had no sure way of breaking free of the *Quds* men. *Not now. Not until we deal with the Turk.*

Inside, Jace sat behind a desk in the reception area, squinting at his laptop screen. A sentry stood guard next to the front door. Butch ignored him and leaned against the counter. "Hey, Jace. How's it hanging?"

"No rest for the weary." Jace didn't meet his friend's gaze. "While you guys rested, I had a full day of work, so bedtime can't come soon enough." He scrubbed a hand across his face and muffled a yawn. "Eighteen days and counting until I'm finished."

Butch studied his friend. Why wouldn't he look at him? He shoved it aside for later. Like after he checked on Libby. "Hey, is Libby still here?"

Only then did Jace gaze at him with exhausted, reddened eyes before glancing away. "Yeah. After supper, I'll discharge her so she can sleep in something more comfortable than a hospital bed. Down that hall there." He nodded toward his right. "Last room on the right. Figured having a quiet room was better than anything else."

"Thanks, man." Butch angled in for a fist bump, but Jace turned and grabbed a sheaf of papers off the printer.

What was that all about? He didn't need anyone else going weird on him.

Libby curled up on a love seat and stared out the open window to the right of her bed. A book lay on her lap, and she absentmindedly ran her finger down the page. Jace had probably brought it to her to help her wile away the long hours of being stuck under medical observation. Though her face remained pale, the bruises had begun fading in earnest. Her almost-black hair hung past her shoulders, free of any headscarf but in clumps that signaled an overdue need for a washing. The sunlight streaming through the partially open window silhouetted her profile.

He tapped on the door frame. "Knock. Knock."

She smiled. "Butch! Come on in."

Across from her, he eased onto the edge of the mattress. "Jace said you're doing better. Feeling stronger."

"I am. That's what happens when I don't fear getting beaten, have some decent rest, and get good food in me." She nodded toward a tray on a rolling table at the head of the bed. "Though I have to say I'm getting really tired of chicken noodle soup since that's what they fed me at the villa."

That earned a chuckle from him. "I hear ya. Vic said something about meeting up to grab some chow and brief out at 1800 hours, so I won't keep you."

"I'm glad for the company. Jace and Diana have been wonderful, and even the medics, Hassan and Ali, checked on me." She flipped the book face down, then smiled at him again. "It's good to see your face."

"Same here. I'm just glad we got you out."

Her brow wrinkled, and she bit her lip. "Earlier today, I walked with Jace to the lobby. A guard's there. One with a rifle. Butch, what's going on? Just who *are* these guys?"

"Makmoud, that's the ringleader, has had a bone to pick with us for over five years. He saw his chance to get even, and he took it." Again, he forced away his worries. "Darned if I'm going to let him win this one."

"The night they took me, it was totally dark, so I didn't see anyone. But I do remember their leader. What did you say his name is?"

"Makmoud."

"He triggered a memory from three years ago. I remember him because he speaks English like an American but with a nice accent. I think he fought with our militia then. Or at least he was in Amal when some of the Green Berets were here."

"The enemy of my enemy is my friend."

Her eyes grave, she gazed at him a moment before taking a deep breath. "Butch, why do they want you?"

"Payback. It's a long story."

Her finger moved faster and faster until she spread her hand on the cover. Only the sound of someone calling to the guard filtered through the open window. "How... how did you find out about me? I mean, about my kidnapping."

"Roo told us."

"That's what you said yesterday, right? Everything was such a blur for me, but I do remember that."

Butch nodded. "He called me up, said he'd gotten intel that you'd been kidnapped. He asked us to come and find you."

"But how would he know?"

Butch's back began aching from his awkward position. He eyed the love seat. "You mind if I take a seat there?"

She shook her head and pulled a pillow from beside her onto her lap.

Butch settled on the worn upholstery that had probably seen its heyday in the early nineties. "I don't know. I just know that Roo has connections that are kind of spooky. Then, I guess the night of the Fourth of July, your folks got a video."

Tears filled Libby's eyes. "Their leader… what did you say his name is?"

"Makmoud."

"He beat me up. Made me do the video. It mystified me. I knew they weren't ISIS." He jumped at her short bark of laughter. "I mean, I wasn't dead or raped, and I still had all of my body parts."

Butch closed his eyes. He'd forgotten the way her beautiful Cajun accent rolled off those full lips. Lips he'd kissed so long ago. It conjured up memories of what could have been. Back to the land of what-ifs. *Live in the present, Addison, 'cause living in the past isn't healthy for the here and now.* "Your parents were frantic. Vic was hesitant at first since we had no real evidence. But once I got that video from your folks, he was all in."

"In for a trap."

Sadly too true. But he couldn't solve that problem right then, not when Makmoud and his merry band of men ensured the team remained separated so they had no chance of escape. Any remote chance they'd had faded when Libby came under the man's thumb.

Once more, a comfortable silence filled the room. It reminded him of their days in junior and senior high school when they would study together in silence for hours on end. Two men held a conversation outside the window. A bass voice he recognized and another one. Jibril chatted with the guard walking sentry. Wouldn't the man leave him alone?

He couldn't focus on that. Not now. "You came back because you didn't know about your children, right?"

Outside, Jibril ceased his conversation. The sound of children's voices playing just beyond the wire overtook them. So did giggles. With a sigh, she closed her book and covered it with her pillow. "What did I tell you way back when, in 2017?"

He remembered the couple of days when Libby had come to spend time with him, Shelly and the others at Last Chance Ranch. "You were more Kurdish than American. But you clammed up when I asked you about what happened, just like you did when I visited your folks for Thanksgiving in 2016."

She drew her knees up to her chest. "I know. And I'm sorry for that. I arrived in Birmingham in October of that year. Honestly, I don't remember much of the rest of the year, even when you visited. It was one appointment after the other. Dental visits. Psychologists. Physicians. Physical therapy. Counseling. I was in a lot worse shape than anyone realized. My TBI caused all sorts of issues. Emotional ones. Memory issues. Issues with relating to people." Her lips drew down at the corners. "I'm sorry. It's hard for me. It's a struggle to remember what happened, to vocalize it."

Butch wanted to pull her away from her ruminations. "I know you were happy here at first, you and Samir. You made a life for yourselves right here in Amal."

Her eyes briefly lit up. "We did. We married in 2002, shortly before Gulf II started."

"Which brought me back here. I still can't believe the way our paths crossed."

"Right." A brief smile crossed her face. "We had three children. Rachel was the oldest, then Miriam, then baby Elijah." She paused and picked up the picture of her family that Jace must have brought to her to ease her stay in the clinic. She caressed the glass as tenderly as she probably had Samir's face. "Things were really good. We got into a rhythm here with teaching and our family. And with trips back home to see Mom and Dad when the kids were born. Things began changing in 2011. We'd heard the rumors just like everyone else. ISIS was gaining strength in Syria. The Yazidis were being persecuted there. Killed. We thought there was no way they would move into this area of the Zagros Mountains. Denial." She bit her lip and began kneading the pillow. "Why were we so unwilling to see the handwriting on the wall?"

Butch shrugged. "Human nature, I guess. What does your mama say?"

"Don't invite trouble," they chorused.

She began blinking as she drew in a deep, shaky breath. "No one wanted to admit ISIS was strong, too strong for the Kurds. In 2013, ISIS began their move into the Kurdish area of Iraq. By the spring of 2014, Mosul fell, and along with it, Amal. The Iraqi army did nothing. Nothing!" She drove her fist into the pillow and began trembling. "I still remember that day they marched into town."

Butch faced her and draped his arm along the back of the love seat.

She crinkled the pillow's fabric. "Arrogant as conquerors, they marched into town, that black ISIS flag flying. At first, they assured us they meant no harm." A harsh laugh escaped her. "We knew better, and within a day, they shut down all of the schools. All of them! And the three churches we had, plus the mosque. Not even the Muslim members of our town were acceptable to their brand of Islam. We women had to wear black chadors and veils." With a shaky breath, she closed her eyes and brought her fingers to her lips. "Then three days later, the bloodletting began."

At the tear trickling down her cheek, Butch scooched closer.

Her voice trembled as she continued, "We tried to fight back, and miraculously, some of our men and women escaped. But overall, they were too much for us. Samir…" Tears began dripping down her cheeks in earnest. "He and some of the men created a distraction that allowed the others to escape. They caught him and beat him before dragging him to the town square along with the other men and boys over the age of twelve. It didn't matter if they were Christian or Muslim. All of them were sentenced to death for insurrection. He was terrified. He knew what would happen, had seen what was happening in other places. But he stood firm." She wiped at her eyes with the sleeve of her caftan. "They lined the rest of us up, made us watch. Samir met my gaze. I saw… peace." She sniffled and took a deep, jerky breath. "They brought that sword down on his neck and beheaded him."

With that, she drew her knees to her chest and wept into her arms.

Butch drew her close and rocked her like he had years ago when they were in high school and she'd found out her grandpa had passed away from cancer. Nothing he could say or do would bring comfort. The proverb about not singing songs over a heavy heart raced through his mind.

She leaned into him. "I miss him, Butch. Every day. Even now."

A lump filled his throat. Since he'd lost his kid sister to an overdose years before, he knew the ache of losing someone who was precious.

Libby pulled back and wiped her cheeks again. "I started screaming. So did the children. They bludgeoned me across the head to shut me up. The blow knocked me out. When I came to, they were raping and executing the women. I remember the wailing." A shudder rippled through her thin frame. "It was the women. And the children. I hurt so much." She dropped her head into her hands. "They... started searching for anyone still alive. I stayed so still and kept my breathing shallow because they ran anyone who appeared to be still alive through with swords and bayonets."

Butch muttered under his breath.

Libby pulled back and hunched. She quivered. "I... passed out again. When I came to, it was so quiet. They were gone on their push to the east. Only bodies were left in the town square. Thanks to my head injury, I had a hard time grasping that I needed to leave. Finally, I got myself together enough to stagger toward the edge of town. I wound up collapsing just inside the walls of a courtyard."

One massive lump in his throat nearly choked him. "Who rescued you?"

"The men and women who escaped. They hid in animal caves in the mountains that no human should feasibly be able to find. They crept in and searched the town. Only fourteen of us women were still living. Our town was reduced from two thousand to three hundred."

Eighty-five percent. Butch shook his head as he thought about the people lost.

"It took me a year to recover enough to be able to walk. During that time, they took such good care of me. Never was I alone." She stared off into the distance. "When I was well enough, I begged them to let me fight against ISIS. We fought so hard for survival and lost many more along the way." She swiped at her tears. "Throughout it all, I kept asking about the children because there were none with us." She peered out the window for a few moments. "There was no time to search. It was all we could do to survive."

Butch handed her a tissue box. "Then our guys showed up."

She took one out and dabbed her eyes. "Yes. And some of *Quds*, it seemed. At first, I had a hard time convincing the Special Forces that I was American because I look Kurdish and speak the language like a native. I hadn't spoken English in so long that it was hard, along with the TBI, to get enough English words together to tell them who I was. I guess they shared word with the State Department because they convinced me to let them evacuate me. Two of them stayed with me all the way to Birmingham. I guess they realized I'd never make it home on my own." She snatched a tissue and dabbed at her nose. "2017 was a healing year for me. The impacts of the TBI have receded, but I do get dizzy when under stress. I struggle with memory issues. Both short term and long term. The way my doctor described it, my brain is gradually rewiring itself."

Butch remained still.

"I guess you know about Project Peace."

"Jace told us." He struggled to change the subject. "He said he met you when you arrived."

"I remembered him from when you all deployed here. 2003, 2004, 2006 and 2008, right?"

He nodded.

She traced circles on the book's cover. "He's my best friend now. I know he cares for me. As more than just friends. Being with him has helped me to piece together some of the memories I lost in 2014. I joke with him that he's a great therapist."

"Do you think you'll get your answer?"

Her gaze flicked to him, then dropped to her hands, which traced a random pattern on the pillow. "I need to know."

Butch studied her. "But what if it's inconclusive? What if no DNA matches? Is that the last mass grave? That's what the email intimated."

The trembling returned.

"Seriously. I know you're scheduled to fly out with Jace on the second of August. Are you going to honor that, even if you don't find out?"

She wrung her hands. "If there's no sign, then they're in the hands of ISIS. Then who knows? They could be indoctrinated. Or dead without my knowledge. And I can't live with that."

She wept. Butch drew her close and rested his chin on her hair. *Lord, this has got to end for her. The uncertainty. The worry. The sadness. She needs to put this behind her, and she needs to leave here. I'm afraid she won't if she doesn't have closure. Can You help here? Somehow? Bring her the peace she needs regardless of the outcome about the upcoming meeting.* Without thinking, he kissed her on the forehead.

A gasp exploded across the room. Time slowed like it did when he was in combat. Then reality jerked into place. Shelly stood there, her hazel eyes wide, a hand to her mouth. The color drained from her cheeks. From behind her right shoulder, Diana glared at him.

It clicked. Jace's avoidance. Diana's questioning. Shelly's tears.

Libby's eyes flew open. She shoved him away. "Butch!"

He jumped to his feet. "Shelly, it's okay. It's..."

Tears began trickling down her cheeks.

"I told you so," Diana mouthed as she wrapped an arm around his wife's shoulders. They vanished from view.

He bolted into the hall, then pushed through the hallway door and into the lobby. "Shel—"

Bright daylight spilled into the lobby as Diana rounded on him. "Leave her alone, Butch." With that, she slammed the door in his face.

Once more, he barely avoided having his nose broken again. He glanced at the guard, who smirked at him.

Butch blasted into the evening air. Too late. The darkness of the warehouse's pedestrian door swallowed up the two women. He had no idea of how to mend things with Shelly.

21

"Dude, what is going on between you and Shelly?"

That question, asked in low tones by Skylar James, their intelligence and procurement specialist, broke into Butch's misery as he stared at the lamb on his plate. He couldn't eat the potatoes. Or the fresh cucumbers and tomatoes mixed with yogurt, which was normally a favorite of his. Tonight, he, who lived by the motto "No food, no fuel, no go" and ate almost anything under all circumstances, picked at his food. He finally shoved his plate aside and gazed at Shelly, who sat at the table the women occupied and pushed her food around on her plate. He badly wanted to run his hands down those curls and beg her forgiveness. One scathing glare from Fiona convinced him to not to approach their table.

"It's a long story." He rose and carried his food to the kitchen, where some of the women from Amal had begun cleaning up. One of the older ones babbled at him in Kurdish and gestured to his mostly untouched food. She probably said what any good mama would say. "You're wasting good food, and growing men like you need to eat."

No, right then, he needed to apologize rather than eat.

The woman's face broke into a smile as she patted Skylar's cheek, a sure reward for being a member of the clean plate club. Skylar stuffed his hands into the pockets of his khaki cargo pants and smiled what Butch called his "aw, shucks" smile. As they meandered toward the counter where the coffee urns sat, Skylar pierced him with a look. "It's starting to feel like some sort of teen drama or something. You don't think Vic or Makmoud haven't noticed? Or Jibril? Not everyone's clueless like you've apparently been, even our fearless leader, who's normally the most clueless of them all when it comes to relational stuff."

Butch risked a glance toward the table where some of the men sat. True that. With narrowed eyes, Victor studied him like he was a strange species that had just crawled out of the swamp. "So I realized."

Skylar took a pomegranate from a bowl and wandered toward their table. In a low voice, he continued, "Word on the street is Shelly thinks you've got the hots for Libby. And word on the street, too, is that Jace thinks you're moving in on her."

Butch's cheeks flamed. "I'm married, all right?"

Skylar snorted. "Didn't seem that way to Shelly or Diana. And Libby apparently realized how it looked because she's already apologized to Shelly. Profusely."

Butch rounded on him. "Just how on earth do you know all of this? You never struck me as the town gossip."

His friend didn't back down. "'Cause believe it or not, I've been able to talk with Fiona some. I'd best avoid her if I were you. She wants nothing more than to pound you to a pulp."

No doubt she'd win. She could be formidable when angered, and anyone who hurt any of the Shadow Box ladies fell into that corner, even one of the Shadow Box men.

"You see why Fi and I aren't getting married? Too many complications." With that, Skylar harumphed and walked away, leaving Butch standing there like an idiot.

Once more, he risked a glance around. Jibril glared at him and shook his head before returning to an animated conversation with Victor and Makmoud.

Shelly fled toward the stairs and dashed upward.

Get moving! That one command from his brain broke him from his trance. He charged after her. "Shelly, wait!"

He leapt the railing as he swung onto the treads just a few steps behind her. "We need to talk."

At the top, she whipped around, and he nearly bowled her over. He steadied her, but her red-hot glare told him to take his hands off her and back away. Immediately. He did so. "What is there to talk about?"

"A lot. It's not—"

"What? What it looked like?" Though she kept her words quiet, they still cut into him like last night's shrapnel. "I remember what you said about Libby. You two were quite an item in high school. What about now? I mean, she's single again. What's to stop you?"

He clenched his jaw until pain shot through it. "Maybe the fact that I'm married? To you?"

Had he been made of wax, her glare would have melted him to the floor. "That's never stopped men before."

Ow. Talk about a knife to the heart. And his pride. Heat flashed through him, and he huffed out a noisy breath. "Shel, that's uncalled for, and you know it."

"Do I?" Tears pooled in those hazel eyes he loved. "Do I, Butch Addison? I thought you cared about me."

Back down, boy, before you hurt her more than she's already hurt. "I do!"

"I'm not so sure about that." She began trembling. The tears streamed down her cheeks, and her voice quavered. "I thought I was so fortunate in marrying you, like the luckiest girl in the world. And I thought you felt the same way. I should have realized even two years of dating didn't tell me enough."

With that, she shoved past him. The stairs shook as she ran down them.

"Shelly, wait!" Butch tore after her—at least until she fled into the locker room. Makmoud had decreed that the women would shower directly after supper. He moved to follow.

Victor caught him and slammed him into the wall. Yow! He flinched as his back protested. His team commander speared him with a scathing look that almost matched Shelly's. He was in trouble. Could be in more trouble if he wasn't careful. "Stand down, will you? I don't think you want to go in there with our *Quds* pals watching. Or when you know Fi's in there showering. I don't think Shelly's in a thinking mood. And we need you right now."

Victor was right. Butch wanted to hit something but settled for several deep breaths. He'd figure things out later, but he needed to turn off his desire to set things right with Shelly. Compartmentalization. He'd excelled at it in the Army. He needed to do the same now. "Okay. Okay. I get it."

Yeah, he sounded like a petulant toddler.

"Then come on over and take a seat. Yado's scouts just came back, and they have a report." Victor led him to the table where some of the *Quds* men gathered. He pointed to a bench that put his back to the locker room. No way could Butch draw a bead on Shelly, not when he couldn't turn his head like an owl.

Time to focus on work. The rugged Kurdish trafficker sat with Jibril and Makmoud as well as two other men who led the team of scouts. The news coming from northeast of Harifi al-Hafa confirmed their fears. The original army of two thousand men had swollen to twenty-five hundred. Horrible news for a town of only five hundred, not all of them able-bodied enough to fight.

"Yado, even with your men, we don't have enough fighters," Makmoud said. "Especially if they come more heavily armed, which it sounds like they may."

Victor scrubbed his hands across his face. His fingers slid under the backup pair of reading glasses he always carried, and he caught them before they fell to the table. "Yeah. We need more intel. But what do we know now?"

"An army of that size takes time to mobilize," Makmoud said.

Yado bobbed his head. "Agreed. I have posted men near the egress point. People are still arriving. We will know as soon as they begin leaving."

"We can't wait long," Jibril said. "How long do you think we have?"

"Our scouts have eavesdropped on the Turk's sermons. It sounds like Friday, the holy day of the week, is when they plan to strike."

"We have a few days, but I refuse to take any chances. We act sooner rather than later with a Plan B." Makmoud slapped his hands onto the table as he stood. "Gentlemen, we break until five tomorrow morning, and then we will formulate that Plan B."

No way was Butch going to take orders from their captors, even if they had a temporary truce. "Boss?"

Victor rose as well and scratched his head as he studied the map. "Five it is. Until then."

Butch stalked toward the stairs to wait until the guys could shower. His mind switched to the mess he'd made with Shelly. He needed to fix it and fast. Sana joined him and carried her toiletries in a small bag. Her black hair hung just past her chin in damp strands. He nodded for her to precede him.

She only gazed at him with deep, dark eyes that told him one thing. He'd saddened her. Disappointed her. That hurt almost as much as the agony radiating from Shelly. When they reached the top of the stairs, she faced him. "Butch, I love you like my own brother. Well, you are my brother in Christ. But you messed up. Please make things right with Shelly."

"I know," he whispered.

A quivering smile answered him, and she slipped into the room she and Suleiman shared. Since their capture, Butch had barely seen her husband, but he knew the young man inevitably thought about the fate he would suffer at the hands of half brothers who hated him. Nope. It wouldn't come to that. Somehow, some way, they wouldn't go to Iran. *Lord, I know that's been back-burnered, but don't let it fall from our minds. For all of our sakes.*

He came to his and Shelly's room on the far end of the walkway. The door was closed. No surprise there—until he tried the knob. It wouldn't move. She'd locked him out. Dang it! He raised his hand to knock. The sound on the other side of the door penetrated his racing thoughts.

Crying. Deep sobs that tore at his heart like vultures.

He pressed his palm against the metal, then leaned his forehead against it as the full impact of his words and actions from earlier that evening slammed into him. He might as well have taken a bayonet and run her through. Sure, his intentions had been pure. He cared for Libby and wanted to be there for her. But he'd done so without regard for how it came across to anyone, especially a wife who loved him and trusted him with her heart. He'd abused that trust. Big time. Abused it and hurt her. Hurt his team too. Probably lost their respect. And Libby's. She'd been impacted since she'd been viewed as the Other Woman, at least until she apologized. *Shel, I'm sorry. I've been a fool. I'm sorry. I'm sorry. And Libby, I'm sorry to you as well. I should have thought about this some more. I didn't. And I hurt you and probably ticked off Jace.*

Ouch. He hadn't even thought of that. Time to call a retreat before anyone else became collateral damage. His back began aching, and his head joined in the dance. Sure, he could camp out on the sectional sofa downstairs in the recreational area, but he needed a real bed tonight because a good night's rest would spur his healing and give him enough strength for the fight bound to come. Maybe after an apology, Jace would take him in.

A man cleared his throat. Jibril stood on the landing. His gaze now smoldered in disappointment rather than smoked in anger. Even that hurt. His counterpart didn't move, only said, "Tomorrow, set things right with her because we will need every able-bodied person fully available."

"I'll do my best."

"Yes, you had better." With that, he brushed by him and turned into the room next to his and Shelly's—well, Shelly's, at least for tonight.

Way to go, Butch. Now what? He poked his head into Jibril's room. "Hey, just FYI, I'm going to go and take a walk into town. So don't kill my team members if I wind up bunking somewhere else tonight."

"Where?"

"With Jace. And if he turns me out, I'll be downstairs."

Without a word, Jibril shut the door in his face.

Whatever. Butch headed into the light of a full moon. Yeah, he'd stepped in it with Shelly. *Lord, show me how to mend this. Please. With Shel. With Jace, even with Diana.* He slipped through the gate and began walking into town. One of Makmoud's guards followed him. Not that Jibril trusted him or anything. He bit back a sigh.

"Fancy meeting you here," a familiar voice remarked in the dark.

In the silvery glow of the moon, Butch easily recognized Jace. "Hey. Yeah, I, um, well, Shelly kicked me out. For good reason."

Now dressed in jeans and a fleece pullover, Jace shoved his hands into his pockets. "You humiliated Libby, you know."

Would this ever end? "I'm sorry. I realize that now. And I hurt you too. Abused your trust."

Jace sighed and lightly kicked the cinder block wall of his courtyard. "No. It just looked like it. Libby explained. And I know about your history with her. The way you grew up together and dated for a few months in high school. Then the way you two got into trouble and you beat up her dad after he called you two out for sleeping together."

Butch hung his head.

"But her dad forgave you. And she finally admitted her part in it when she was in college. She said it took her a few years, that you were better than she in that regard."

"We both messed up."

Jace took a step closer and jabbed his finger into Butch's shoulder. Though he had a good six inches on him, he knew Jace was skilled in tae kwon do and could take him down any day of the week. And he knew that protective anger as well. Jace loved Libby fiercely, just as fiercely as Butch loved Shelly. "I see you as my brother in Christ, but if you ever do something like that to Libby again, you'll be dealing with me."

Point taken. "Copy that."

Jace backed off a few steps. "You want to bunk here? The other PA, who's also my roommate, isn't due back in-country until next week. You can crash in his rack."

"Thanks, man." Butch preceded his friend through the gate.

Jace locked it. "I love her, Butch. We've been friends ever since she arrived, but for me, at least, it's grown stronger."

Butch nodded. If he hadn't been so blind, he would have caught on to Jace's reticence that afternoon. And the way his friend cared for Libby. Not just doctor to patient but as a man who loved her. "What does she think?"

"I think she feels the same way. Not that we've said those three words, mind you, but I've invited her to join me in Colorado after the first of the year."

Unexpected joy coursed through Butch. "What did she say?"

Jace's smile stretched to his eyes. "She said yes. She wants to spend time with her parents, get reacclimated to being back in the States. But she said she would. And don't worry. Since we're flying home on the same flight, I'll make sure she gets on that plane."

"I wish you the best." Butch's gaze switched to Libby's house. "And I sure hope things between you two will grow and thrive—if we get out of here alive, that is."

"Me too, buddy." Jace followed his gaze. "Me too."

22

"This brings back so many memories," Butch remarked the next morning as he brought his travel mug to the kitchen's large pass-through window where Libby and a couple of other women cleaned up from serving breakfast.

Libby ignored him as she stacked plates on an open shelf.

0500 hours had come early, and Makmoud hadn't wasted any time in launching into his plan to keep them from having to face The Turk and his army. Problem was, people were tired, cranky, and hungry, even with coffee. Hangry took over sensible, and at 0600 hours Makmoud wisely called for a break, to resume at 0800 hours, after everyone ate and stocked up on caffeine. Fine by him.

Right then, he wasn't sure they could save Amal. Bad news all the way around.

Libby refilled his mug in silence, then shoved it across the counter without a smile.

He glanced around. None of his team or the *Quds* men remained near the tables. The guys most likely sought showers while the women also got ready for the day. Libby's friends chattered away in the kitchen. Resting his elbows on the metal, he leaned closer. "Can we talk?"

Her lips pinched as she stepped back a little. "Why should I?"

"I'd like to apologize."

She opened her mouth to say something, then snapped her jaw shut. "The last time we talked, your *wife* barely spoke to me until this morning. I'm not doing that because, believe it or not, I care about Shelly and respect her."

She wasn't making this easy. "Please?"

"Okay. Fine. We sit there." She pointed to the row of long tables, "Or we don't talk at all."

Roger that. Loud and clear. Without another word, he retreated to one of the tables. With a sigh, he eased onto it so he sat on the top with his feet on the bench.

Libby joined him from the kitchen and settled on the bench at a table across from him. She crossed her legs, rested her elbows on the tabletop, and surveyed him through narrowed eyes. Even with her *shalwar kameez* and headscarf, she intimidated him. The indignation and anger from the night before wafted from her like perfume. Could he have messed things up any more?

Much as he wanted to, he didn't break his gaze as he leaned forward with his elbows on his knees and his mug in his hands. "I'm sorry about yesterday. I put you in a bad spot."

She folded her arms across her chest and jiggled one foot. Why didn't she make this easy for him? She snorted. "Darned straight you did. I've never been so humiliated in my life."

Heat began climbing in his cheeks. "I'll apologize to Shel as soon as I'm able."

She stared him down. "You haven't apologized to her?"

"I haven't had a chance. She locked me out of the room. I wound up bunking with Jace."

"Please tell me you *did* apologize to him."

"I did, okay?"

A terse nod answered him. At least her taut features relaxed a fraction. She blew out a breath. "Thank you. And yes, I do forgive you. I still feel bad, because of the way it looked, and I've apologized profusely to Shelly.

And to Diana and the other women. They view her like a sister."

"Yeah, they do. Especially Fiona."

Libby's sherry eyes widened slightly. "She's not going to kill me?"

"No, but she may pound *me* to a pulp."

That garnered a small smile. Then it faded as she glanced upstairs where Makmoud emerged from his and Jibril's room. A shudder rippled through her. "They scare me."

"Me too, to be honest." Butch tried to keep his concern about what would eventually happen at bay. He couldn't worry about that when neutralizing the Turk stayed at the forefront.

She shifted her gaze before the *Quds* leader met it. Quietly, she said, "I've been thinking about what you told me about Roo, that he was the instigator behind y'all coming over here to find me. When I couldn't sleep last night, I began praying. And thinking about it. And about what happened in 2009."

Kerplunk! There went his cautiously up mood that had come with Libby's forgiveness. "What about it?"

"What happened that night when you came under attack. What do you remember?"

"It was butt cold."

That earned a weary laugh. "Strange how I remember that it was. Yes. It was very cold."

"I drew guard duty along with Cowboy and a couple of militia members." Butch's jaw twitched. They'd shared supper that night before his shift started. His team's joshing echoed in his mind. Cowboy had guffawed in his typical way, which set off some more laughter. "We knew the insurgents were nearby, so we were keeping close watch. I'd gotten some really good rack time, so I was stoked."

"I was here cleaning up." She drew in a breath as if mulling over how to phrase her next few words. "Roo came in that night. I remember you two talking."

"Yeah, he always liked to check on us before we began our shifts."

"You went to the restroom before going out on patrol."

"Standard practice. Peeing while on duty could get you killed." His mind swung to that night. His conversation with Roo and hitting the latrine, then grabbing his rifle and taking up his post at the ordnance shed. "Someone slipped Ketamine into my mug. I got so sleepy I passed out."

"Roo did it."

He blinked. Cowboy with his slit throat flashed before him. Had he heard her right? "Come again?"

"I saw him do it."

Shocked at the venom in her voice, Butch stared at her. "You sure?"

"I saw him do it, Butch." She cut her eyes toward where Makmoud called to Jibril. At the far end of the tables, he laid out a map. She leaned closer and lowered her voice. "At first he didn't know I saw him. I was in the kitchen putting away the last dishes. I'd said hi to him, but I guess he thought I was out of sight. He had it in a syringe. Then when you headed to the bathroom, he dumped it into your coffee."

"But you say he didn't see you."

"You know I can't hide my emotions." She fingered a corner of her headscarf. "He immediately noticed my face, my shock. That's when he threatened me, told me if I said a word, tried to warn you or tell anyone, he'd make sure harm came to my family. Not just here but in Louisiana. And to you."

Butch's chest tightened. "You're sure of that?"

"Sure as I am that there are over two thousand men out there preparing to take down this town."

Butch focused on the floor and ran a hand over his bald head. "This isn't making sense. Seriously. What does that have to do with our being here today?"

"Roo hired you to come and find me. Why did he finger me to Makmoud? Why have me kidnapped? Didn't you say he's running for governor?"

"I did."

Red seeped into her tawny features. "He knew I was here. How, I don't know. Not that it's a great secret or anything. I guess he worried I was a liability to his campaign because I'd witnessed him doping your coffee, which resulted in your friend dying and an entire ordnance warehouse getting emptied. That's probably why he had me kidnapped."

Butch jumped up and began pacing. "Why call us? He could have easily made you disappear, and that was the end of it. Except…" His heart dropped as a memory rolled into his brain, one that sent shivers through him. "This so stinks."

Libby rose, but she didn't approach him. "What? I'm not following."

"Shelly and I got married in May, and Roo was one of the groomsmen."

"What does that have to do with—"

"Roo didn't get there until Thursday, and he missed the bachelor party. When he did arrive, we four vets: me, Vic, Roo, and Old Man, Henry Nakamura, went to a bar to catch up. Roo had replaced Vic as my team's CO in 2005, and Old Man had gotten out when Vic did. So it was good to catch up. We had a grand time too. Probably drank a bit too much, if you want the honest truth. Somehow, it came around to you. I guess we got to talking about ISIS and how you'd gotten overrun here in Amal in 2014. And how our guys had found you in 2016. And the way I saw you for Thanksgiving in 2016 and you came and visited in 2017."

Her eyes flashed. "He thought I told you about what had happened."

Could this get any worse? "Maybe so."

"And maybe he worried you'd told Vic and the rest of your team."

All of the pieces began dropping into place, and he didn't like the picture they formed. One of a man who would do anything to ensure no one squealed about his past. "Looks like it."

Her fists clenched. "That man. I can't believe it."

"He's got the money to get it done. You know he's COO for LaRue International Transport."

"I do." Though quiet, those two words came across like a clap of thunder. This was a Libby he didn't remember, one who had survived one of the greatest losses ever and lived to tell about it. "This is unconscionable. Truly." She kicked the table, and Makmoud glanced up. She lowered her head as he returned to studying the map.

She stepped closer to the kitchen and gestured for Butch to follow. In a hushed voice, she continued, "The man has no scruples. He's called you a friend. Led you to trust him, and… Words fail me." She focused on him, her eyes suddenly bright. "This is the first time I remembered all of that. After they questioned me those years ago, I let it go because I was too scared. Then I couldn't remember after my TBI. But now? I'm not going to let this go. Not when he's put all of you as well as me in incredible danger."

"Me neither."

A door on the first floor shut, and Victor strode toward them, purpose written all across his face.

Butch waved him aside, and the three of them retreated into the kitchen. In a low voice, he said, "Hey, boss, we need to talk."

Victor snatched a mug from the counter. "About what? We've got a mission to plan, and the rest of the crew will be here in half an hour."

"That's enough time." Butch glanced at Libby. "We'd got a problem to discuss. Seems our client was a lot less than forthcoming about his intentions."

23

As Butch wound down his story in quiet tones, Victor stared at his deputy. They'd seated themselves at the table where Butch had sat. Thankfully, no one else joined them, because if they had, the three of them probably wouldn't be talking right now. "Wow. And Libby, you're sure?"

She bobbed her head. "Without a doubt."

Butch dropped his face onto his hands and groaned. "I can't believe I fell for it hook, line, and sinker. I should have known about Roo."

"How could you know he'd sell you out? The man you served with and the man who's running for the governor of Louisiana are not the same people. Power's changed him." Victor's mind scrambled on how best to use this information. It was critical at that point. Use it right, and they had the potential to walk away relatively unscathed. Use it wrong, and he'd obliterate any trust between him and Makmoud.

"But," he leaned forward, "that helps us. Maybe we can talk some sense into Makmoud. If he knows we know who his client is, maybe we can convince him the enemy isn't us. It's Roo."

Butch cracked his knuckles. "Yeah, when I get my hands on him— when, not if—it ain't going to be pretty."

"I hear you." Victor bumped fists with him. "Let me do the talking on

191

this, okay?"

"Wilco."

Libby abruptly rose.

It didn't take Victor long to understand why. Jibril came their way, and he would tell her the women shouldn't be consorting with the men until absolutely necessary. Fine by him because Victor now had enough intel to act when the proper time arose.

He had to wait because the rest of his team, ladies included, joined them. Time to share the idea he'd come up with during their break. If it worked, they'd never have to engage in a battle at Amal that they would most likely lose. "One shot."

Makmoud nodded. "I agree. We have one shot at this."

Victor shook his head. "Literally. I mean one shot from Suleiman can end all of this."

The *Quds* leader studied him, no surprise, nothing on his face. "How so?"

"You said it yourself. The Turk centers power on himself. Chop the head off the snake, the rest of the body dies."

Shelly ran her fingers along the edge of her laptop. In a hoarse voice, she asked, "How so? Won't his followers come after Amal for revenge?"

Jibril fixed her in his gaze. In his low rumble, he replied, "No. The man is an egomaniac. Our sources place his army's formation at the middle of last year. We kill him, and his movement will fall apart because there are no deep loyalties."

"I can take the shot." Suleiman briefly met his half brother's gaze. "I can do it. But due to it being at night, I need an infrared laser to determine exactly where to aim the range finder."

Jibril smirked. "It will be like 2012 all over again because I will be your spotter." He stood and studied the map for a moment. He jabbed a beefy finger at a spot. "We will do it from here. From where we found the scouts. It is on the western edge of the valley and has plenty of cover. And the winds prevail out of the west."

The remark about 2012 rattled Victor and fanned old flames of anger. That fateful shot had stolen the life of his then-fiancée. *I will not react. I will not react. I need to focus.* He shoved the thought away. "But can you lase the target from there?"

Suleiman shook his head. "Not from there. It appears to be a kilometer away from where he stands to make his speeches, if he does so in the middle of the valley. We do not have a laser with that much power."

"And how are we going to get up close?" Butch asked.

An idea spun into Victor's head. He peered at his friend. "Your Silver Star mission."

Butch cocked his head. "What?"

"2005. Remember? I recommended you for a Silver Star afterward. And if memory serves me right, you indeed were awarded it."

"But I don't have me Old Man here."

"No, but you've got me, like last time." Victor shifted his attention to Makmoud. "And Makmoud. One of the best at blending in." Maybe the compliment would lower the *Quds* leader's guard.

Butch refocused on the map. "Alrighty, then. Sounds like we have to plan."

They did, and it would take every member of his team, split up among Makmoud's squad, of course. Again, he and Butch could rub out Makmoud, but to do so would mean the rest of the team would die. And if they escaped after doing the dirty deed, Amal would still fall. They still had to stick with the *Quds* men because only together could they secure Amal's future, and then hopefully their own, if they could outwit Makmoud and his crew. But boy, if something happened while they were downrange, it wouldn't be a pretty death for the trio.

He couldn't think that way. They were skilled at blending in. All of them. And between Makmoud, Butch, Jibril, and him, they'd plan this one to perfection.

Just as they began discussing time frames, the pedestrian door leading to the outside banged open. One of Yado's scouts, dressed in desert camouflage and covered in dirt and dust, approached the trafficker. He whispered into his ear.

Yado's features tightened, and he nodded before clapping the man on the shoulder and sending him away. "Gentlemen, I am not sure of your time to launch this mission, but our scouts got close enough to get more information. The Turk plans to move out at dawn tomorrow toward Amal."

Victor's stomach dropped to the soles of his hiking boots. Four days sooner than anticipated. That didn't bode well. They were now officially out of time to perfect things, from contingency plans to escape plans. He met Makmoud's gaze. A new urgency filled them both. Victor broke his gaze and stared at the map. "I guess we need to leave at dusk, then."

Makmoud nodded. "We will. It is now noon. Let's break for lunch and finish planning before we take a rest so we are refreshed for tonight."

Everyone rose and began gathering coffee mugs and empty plates from breakfast. Shelly snatched up her computer and bolted toward the stairs. Butch started to follow, then stopped and turned toward Suleiman. Victor needed both of them to be professional, and he hoped Shelly worked things out within herself to be so. Any apology would now have to wait until after their return.

Jibril wandered toward the stairs. Once he was out of earshot, Victor softly called, "Makmoud, you got a minute?"

The *Quds* leader paused. "What is it?"

"First, good job back there. I think we have a solid plan."

"That is so long as nothing untoward happens."

"Agreed."

Makmoud stared at the map. "What did you want to discuss?"

Here went nothing. "We need to talk."

Makmoud tossed his pen down and put his hands on his hips. "About what?"

"Paul LaRue is your client, isn't he?"

Oh, he would have paid lots of money to record for all time the the way Makmoud stiffened and widened his eyes. He quickly smoothed his features into disinterest as he gazed at the map. "Paul LaRue. I haven't heard that name."

"A decorated Green Beret. Put in time here in the sandbox. He's running for the governor of Louisiana. I know you have because he fingered Libby to you."

Makmoud gazed at him for a long moment. With a sigh, he gestured for him to sit down. "And how did you find out?"

"Libby put it together. Don't underestimate her."

"Obviously."

"And I'm here to restate the obvious as well." Victor took a deep breath to calm thoughts trying to race all over the place like wild horses. "All I'm doing is asking you to think about it. If he sold Butch, who's one of his best friends, down the river, you think he's above doing the same to you?"

With a huff, Makmoud rose and paced with his hands in his back pockets. "This is troubling."

"I agree. To be honest, he's never been my favorite person, and I sure as heck don't trust him now. You let us go, and I promise we'll ensure he won't be a threat to you because you'd better believe I have a bone to pick with him now."

Makmoud froze at the far end of his pacing. He lifted his face to the ceiling, then pulled a phone off his belt. His fingers flicked the screen as he wandered toward him. "Yesterday, I received a voice mail message from Tank Russell, who manages LIT's gunrunning business."

"Why am I not surprised?"

"You shouldn't be. That family is very dirty, Victor Chavez. Very. First slave running before your country's Civil War. Then gunrunning afterward. Tank is also Paul LaRue's chief of security for the campaign, and he has connections all over the underworld." His lips thinned. "He was the one who initiated contact."

"How did he find you?"

"That is only for me to know." Makmoud studied him. "How much did he offer you to come and find Libby?"

"Five million. And that's just in fee."

Victor could almost see the thoughts running through his mind as Makmoud muttered in Farsi. He had five million already in his account as a down payment for bringing down Victor and the team. He'd get five million more upon proof of success. Thing was, Tank Russell could collect twenty million for his boss if he killed or captured Makmoud. "Not only did Tank leave a voice mail, but he also texted me and asked to meet and bring proof that I have killed you."

"Which you can't do if you intend to take us to Iran."

"I sense this is a trap." He gripped his hair and, muttering in Farsi. He paled.

"What's bothering you?"

Makmoud lowered his hands. "It's not that I worry about Tank Russell. I am fully prepared to handle him. It is more the man who is my boss. General Soleimani."

Victor stilled. He knew the name of the *Quds* commander too well.

"If I don't bring you all to Iran, then my wife and two children may perish, and I will most certainly be punished." He peered at Victor. "That is not a chance I'm willing to take. I will deal with Tank Russell after to-morrow night."

Victor felt like he'd been plunged into ice water. He knew the drive a man had for his family since he felt it too for Deborah and the kids. And if Makmoud didn't change his mind, he and his team would never breathe free air again.

24

A full moon. Too bad Butch wasn't still in Amal, trying to get back into Shelly's good graces beneath its silvery beams. Instead, he was out here in the middle of who-knew-where, Iraq, literally about to walk into danger.

During final preparations, whenever Shelly met his gaze, a sadness so deep he wanted to bellow permeated his soul. He'd hurt her almost as surely as if he'd indeed strayed. He should have been apologizing to her in person instead of with a hastily scrawled note he'd tucked under her pillow while she was out of their room.

He couldn't worry about that now, not when the mission stared him in the face. *Lord, just let me live long enough to make it up to my best friend, to tell her how much I love her and that I won't ever, ever let her go.* Done. He'd said his prayer. Laid his plea before the cross. Time to focus. He stuffed his marital worries into a compartment in his mind labeled For Later.

He, Victor, and Makmoud crept up another goat trail on the southeastern side of the valley where The Turk had his lair. Again, that low hum, except it seemed stronger than he remembered from a couple of days before. Meaning more soldiers had gathered, just as Yado's scouts had said.

The trio arrived at the top and crouched just below the rim. Butch kept his head on a swivel and his finger on the trigger guard as he surveyed the area for sentries. None at the moment.

"Over there." Victor pointed toward a massive jumble of rocks.

Butch darted toward it. Once safely concealed, he peered between two of the boulders, which afforded a view of the valley and the opposite side. The wind blew into his face, meaning it came from the northwest. His eyes watered a little from the smoke of campfires. With his binoculars, he easily picked out the sheer cliff, then the rocks where Diana had found Makmoud's men murdered. Now, Jibril, Suleiman, Fiona, and one other of Makmoud's men occupied the position. No way would anyone sneak up on them.

"Wolf Den, One, Five, and Wolverine are here." Victor's soft report crackled in Butch's ears.

"Roger that." Not a shake in Shelly's voice. No hoarseness now. Pride surged through him. Professional to the core, that Shelly of his. Yet playful when off duty. He loved her all the more for it. She wouldn't let the events of the past two days impact her work.

Jibril's bass voice penetrated his thoughts. "Two and Gray Wolf are in place with Seven and Wild Dog."

"Go time," Victor whispered.

Butch jettisoned all extraneous thoughts and switched into combat mode.

From Yado's scouts, they knew The Turk's men patrolled the rim of the valley with a light layer of four three-man teams. That was all. A chink in their flank, for sure. Regular fifteen-minute intervals. Enough time for them to slip an arrow through.

Butch listened. Voices rose and fell on the evening breeze. A squad of three chattered as if they were high school girls gossiping about the hunky new football player on the team. Someone laughed. No discipline whatsoever, it seemed. Maybe they thought they were secure. Mistake number one. Never assume you're a hundred percent secure. Chatter meant attention diverted from the task at hand, which was patrolling the perimeter. Mistake number two.

A match flared, meaning one of them had lit a cigarette, a dead giveaway to Victor and Makmoud, both who had functioning noses and a sharp sense of smell. The tobacco odor would broadcast their presence to any lurking intruders like Butch and his crew. Mistake number three.

With his chin, Butch gestured toward the group. Time to get some guards. Thing was, they couldn't kill them, lest they get blood on their robes. And they needed to wear them.

One of the three lagged behind and called out in Arabic to his buddies. Butch easily understood his words. Time to use the restroom, and he'd decided their hiding place made the perfect wilderness toilet. The guard slung his rifle over his shoulder and moved toward their rocks as he hummed softly under his breath. Mistake number four and a fatal one. He was distracted by the call to nature.

Makmoud and Victor drew back out of sight.

As the guard relieved himself, Butch crept around the front of the rocks with one eye on his victim's buddies, who meandered on at a leisurely pace. He raised his tranquilizer gun. Click, whoosh. Butch rushed forward, covered the man's mouth, and dragged his collapsing form behind the rocks.

Makmoud began disrobing him and handed the clothing to Victor, who slid it on as Butch reloaded his tranquilizer gun.

"Jamal?" one of the men called in Arabic with a Syrian accent. "Jamal, where are you?"

Crap. His buddies missed him.

Victor, who had just wrapped his own shemagh around his head, stepped onto the path. He gestured for his pals to join him as if he'd found something amiss.

"Jamal, what is it? What did you find?" the taller of the two asked.

With the hand tucked behind him. Victor counted down from three. Butch and Makmoud sprang from their hiding places. Both darts scored, and the two remaining men collapsed without a sound. They dragged them behind the rocks, and Butch immediately disrobed the taller one. He slipped cable ties onto his wrists and ankles and slapped a piece of tape over his mouth just in case the tranquilizer wore off before the end of the prescribed four-hour time period. He wrapped his shemagh around his head. Maybe he could pass for one of them long enough to accomplish their mission. He hid his rifle beneath his robes and shouldered his victim's.

"One, Five, and Wolverine are inbound," Victor softly reported. He glanced at his two comrades. "Check the infrared laser one more time."

Butch retrieved it from Makmoud's backpack. They'd loaded fresh batteries into it, guaranteeing it would run until they finished their mission. The indicator light glowed green, and Makmoud hid it in his robes.

Butch glanced at Victor. His commander, the only clean-shaven one of the group, had covered his mouth and nose with his shemagh so only his eyes were visible. Good point. Butch did the same, as did Makmoud, so no one would recognize them as outsiders.

Time to do the best acting of his life. Just like in 2005 when he'd penetrated a fully armed camp of insurgents and taken out the guards one by one during his Silver Star mission. He squared his shoulders. Best not to give the enemy any excuse to gut them.

Swaggering seemed to work. But then again, no one paid them any mind. Most huddled around campfires in groups of twenty or so as if The Turk had organized everyone by squad. He noted a nearby pickup truck loaded with a mortar and crates of shells in the bed. One of the mobile mortar units. And open crates of RPGs. People laughed. Smoke from the fires and cigarettes drifted away in the breeze.

Too bad he wasn't with his team from his SF days. They would have stayed up on the rim and used a powerful laser to focus an AC-130 Spectre gunship on these jokers and end it once and for all. Just the three of them now with a laser running on twenty-four AA batteries that would last for fifteen minutes before conking out. *You've done this before. Keep it calm. Amp that swagger. No eye contact with anyone.* Each step took them toward the heart of the enemy camp. His hand tightened around the grip of his rifle. Every functioning sense sharpened.

Jibril murmured, "We see you, Wolfpack. You are not too far from the hub where The Turk resides. Just a hundred or so meters."

Slightly over the length of a football field. Each step brought them closer to a small stage. The Turk stood high and proud above his men as he strutted about. Man, oh, man. The guy didn't know how to keep a low profile. Not in his black robes. This time, he didn't wear a turban but instead let his long, black hair flow past his shoulders. A black headband covered his forehead and ran down in a long tail the length of his hair. White Arabic festooned it, the same writing Butch had seen on ISIS flags. Kohl lined his eyes, just like it did the eyes of the Taliban in Afghanistan, who were notoriously radical.

Boy, we mess this up, it's going to be a long, slow, painful death. Or we might as well just kill ourselves and get it over with fast.

The Turk took a microphone from one of his cronies. He tapped on it. It squelched and screeched for a moment. Everyone quieted. The trio drew close to the back of a cluster of men. That was a mere hundred or so feet from the stage. A perfect range for the laser. They'd have to get Makmoud toward the front of the group.

The Turk began his speech in Arabic for the benefit of those from other countries besides Turkey. His words turned Butch's stomach to lead. He described certain victory. Annihilation of the Kurdish population, beginning with those in Amal. He painted the Kurds, then others living in northern Iraq and eastern Syria, as traitors to their brand of Islam, ones who should be exterminated by all means possible. Throughout it all, he punctuated his speech with a raised fists and chants.

Then he threw the Shia Muslims into the mix. Makmoud stiffened, then began shifting around the group.

Butch knew what was on his mind.

Stopping this maniac from whipping his boys into a full-fledged, rip-intruders-apart frenzy.

"Wolverine, you are within range now." Suleiman's voice was almost drowned out by the shouting around them.

Makmoud looked quickly at Butch. He winked, a sign to lase their target so they could beat feet out of there.

Trick was, they had one shot and one shot only at this. Or Suleiman did. Paint the dude's forehead. Wait for the shots to happen, then scram. As he and Victor raised their fists in the same chants as the men who wanted them dead, Makmoud remained in the middle of the trio. He slipped his hands inside his robe as if he were cold. The folds parted slightly.

"Wolverine, we have the marker," Jibril reported.

Butch knew what was happening in the sniper's nest. Suleiman would have his eye pressed to the big gun's night scope as he focused on the target. Jibril would run calculations related to wind speed and direction, gravity, humidity, and other factors, and would instruct Suleiman on how to adjust his aim. Suleiman would slow his breathing and heart rate to steady his hands even further. Jibril was watching through his own scope and softly guiding his half brother as well as Makmoud.

"Hold steady, Wolverine."

Bless him. With one hand, Makmoud held the marker motionless. With his other hand, he raised his fist as if one with the masses. Butch shouted all the louder to make up for his comrade's lack of enthusiasm.

"Down a click... Steady... Fire," Jibril added in a hushed voice as if he were in a library rather than on the battlefield.

One, one thous—

The Turk's head exploded.

The man crumpled as the rifle's loud report echoed off the sides of the valley. Two more shots tore through his center mass, ensuring he collapsed into a lifeless heap on the platform.

Silence fell.

Then, like waves rising to crest as they hit the shore, the volume of noise increased to a fever pitch. Chaos followed. People rushed toward the middle.

They had to get out of there. Dang it! Complete mayhem.

Time for a distraction.

Butch dropped the rifle he carried. He withdrew a grenade from his robes. One quick yank of the pin armed it, and he rolled it toward the man's remains. Time to hustle.

He led the way away, against the tide. Makmoud grabbed his robes so they wouldn't get separated, and hopefully Victor did the same to Makmoud's.

Strangely, no one seemed to notice.

An explosion ripped through the camp.

Screams. Cries. The mass surged toward the middle like one big blob.

Butch elbowed people aside. Oh, no. They were beginning to draw attention to themselves.

Still almost a thousand feet to the base of the hill that would lead to their freedom.

People began shouting. Pointing toward them. "Two, some help here. Create chaos somewhere else."

Suleiman's reply came clipped, precise, just like his aim a few moments earlier. "On it, Five."

More rifle reports. Incendiary bullets blazed into the camp and slammed into stockpiles of ammunition. Echoing explosions from the mobile mortar units battered the walls, turning the night as bright as day. But they revealed the location of the sniper's nest. The crowd shifted in that direction.

"Wolf Pack Two, all of you get out of there." Urgency bled into Victor's voice. "You've got company coming fast."

Butch wasted no time. Moving like an icebreaker, he cut a line through the crowd with Victor and Makmoud just off his shoulders. He quickened his pace to a fast walk. Five hundred feet. More gunfire echoed.

He drew in a sharp breath as one of the Turk's men lifted an RPG to his shoulder. "Gray Wolf, they've got an RPG. Get out of there. Now!"

A rocket streaked toward the cliff.

Lord, protect them. He broke into a run toward the hill. Time to put his heart to the test.

Fire obliterated the rock formation atop the cliff. More and more RPGs hammered the other side of the gorge. The former hideout of his comrades collapsed into the valley.

They hit the toe of the slope leading upward. In a defensive position, Butch faced the crowd and forced his feet to move in a fast, backward march. Victor and Makmoud flanked him in the same manner. Butch's quads burned. His knees cried out for relief. At least the Turk's men streamed toward the cliff.

Butch glanced over his shoulder. Three quarters of the way there.

Heads began turning their way.

A man pointed. Shouted.

Dang it! "You two, go. They're a'coming. You've got fifty meters. Go!"

Puffs of rock and sand kicked up as bullets stitched around him. His quads went numb. He couldn't stop. Not now.

"Get going, Five!" Victor shouted. "We've got you."

Butch turned and fled as both Makmoud and Victor hurled smoke grenades toward the advancing attackers to obscure their escape. They had maybe a minute before the troops figured things out enough to push through the haze. Above him, both of his comrades let loose with their rifles. Screams rewarded them as the bullets found their marks.

Then came the chanting he never wanted to hear again, had thought he never would after leaving Iraq in 2009. "Jihad! Jihad! Jihad!"

He passed Victor on his right and Makmoud on his left. "C'mon!"

In quick succession, he lobbed two more grenades as Victor said into the radio, "Eight, we're outbound."

"Markers on," Skylar replied.

"Roger that." At a run, Butch yanked off his robe. He hit a switch on his belt, which activated the infrared markers each man wore on the front and back of their tactical vests.

Just a couple of hundred yards to the goat path.

Victor vanished from view as he escaped downward.

Butch's lungs really began burning. His quads began spasming, and he staggered.

"I see you, One. Waiting on the rest of you."

"Right behind you," Butch reported.

Makmoud's breath huffed in their ears. "Wolverine is—oof!"

Butch skidded to a stop and whipped around. His heart sank.

Makmoud hit the ground shoulder first with a guttural cry. He tumbled a few feet down the slope, then jammed his feet into the dirt and slid to a stop. He moaned and grasped his right shoulder.

His attacker loomed over him and lowered his gun for a kill shot.

Butch raised his rifle and delivered three shots into the man.

Another one charged upward. Three more shots, and the second man fell face down.

Makmoud tried to rise on one elbow and failed. "Leave me here, Butch."

Not going to happen. Butch snagged a loop at the top of Makmoud's tactical vest and hauled upward. His comrade's moans meant only one thing. Pretty serious injury. "Sorry, buddy. Hold on!"

More men followed the first two.

Butch fired his rifle three more times and took out a few more as he and Makmoud crested the hill. He pulled the trigger again for another triple shot at one who tried to rise. Click. Empty. He tossed the useless gun away. "Can you stand?"

"Y-Yes." Makmoud gritted his teeth and rose to his feet with Butch's help. He wobbled, then steadied. "Dislocated shoulder."

"Goat path is at your ten o'clock. Give me your grenades, and I've got you covered. Go!"

Makmoud tossed them to him. After pulling the pins, Butch hurled them downward along with his last smoke grenade and two flash bangs. He drew his pistol.

Bullets began whizzing by him. Time to retreat.

"We see you, Wolverine," Skylar reported. "Five, get your butt down here."

"On the way." Butch blanched at the swarm of very angry men charging upward. He emptied his pistol and rammed home a new magazine.

A bullet whizzed by his ear, too close for comfort.

A line of hot, burning agony opened up on the inside of his right arm. Somehow, he held on to the pistol.

He ran as fast as his aching legs could carry him and then some.

Hand clamped over his right arm, he charged downward. Immediately, the angle of the trail steepened.

Pressure. Keep pressure on it. He holstered the gun and flexed his right hand. At least it still worked. Maybe a muscle wound, maybe a graze. Blood seeped through his fingers and ran down his arm. He could die from even a graze if it had nicked an artery. "Five's on the way down. And hit. And we've got company."

"We see you, Five." Skylar's voice reassured him.

Butch staggered and slid down the trail. The dizzies hit, and the trail tilted back and forth as if he'd stumbled into a fun house. He tipped over the side. *Dear Lord, save me now!* That prayer shot through his mind as he tumbled down the steep slope, skidded across the switchback, then rolled some more. He could only hang on and pray he didn't hit a rock head first.

"Five! Five!" Skylar's voice got lost in a jumble of pain.

Finally, he landed on his back on the lowest run of the trail, right in front of Makmoud as he dashed toward safety.

The *Quds* leader tripped over him and collapsed onto his dislocated shoulder. He yowled, then turned onto his back. Both men moaned.

The terrain tilted before Butch as his head spun. He tried to sit up, only to collapse onto his back again.

The deep burr of gunfire blasted from the fifty-cal guns on the small convoy that waited at the base of the slope.

"Five!" Skylar helped Butch sit up. "Where do you hurt?"

"Everywhere" he muttered through gritted teeth. "And I kinda took a tumble. Haven't done that in a long time. Wolverine…"

Makmoud pushed himself upright with a groan. His right arm hung uselessly. His face twisted in pain, he allowed one of his men to help him to his feet.

"We need to get out of here." Skylar looped Butch's good arm over his shoulder. "C'mon, big guy. Stay with me."

Now, every bit of Butch ached, and he could only pray he'd not broken anything. Hey, he could walk, and he could move his fingers, though it did hurt a little to breathe. And his arm. Blood ran down it in a thick stream and dripped from his fingers. His knees began trembling. Probably from his tumble.

Skylar's grip on him tightened. "Five, stay with me. I don't want to have to carry you."

"Hard to do, Eight. Guess my… poor imitation of Westley from *The Princess… Bride…*"

Sana came alongside his other side and wrapped her arm around his waist to steady him. "Don't you dare, Five."

His knees gave way just as they reached the Humvee.

Breath whooshed from Sana as he knocked her to the ground.

"Sorry…"

Skylar's voice blurred above him. Everything spun. Matter of fact, he felt like he was floating. Doors slammed. Then a big engine growled to life. Tires chirped. Slowly, reality returned. He lay on his back, still breathing through his mouth, hoping and praying he hadn't damaged his broken nose even further. He risked opening his eyes.

Their gunner loomed over him, his gaze on the road.

Sana sat in the back against the tailgate, the wind whipping her chin-length black hair about her face, a streak of his blood on her cheek. She kept one hand on her rifle. With her free hand, she held a tourniquet taut on his arm, then briefly released it. More blood flowed.

Weakness surged over him as he turned his head. Makmoud, his arm now in a makeshift splint, managed a smile. "Thank you, my friend. You saved my life."

"No prob…" Butch sagged into darkness.

25

Makmoud came awake to a dull throbbing. It pulsed in time with his heart. For a moment, he didn't want to open his eyes, didn't even want to acknowledge he lived. Of course, the alternative would have been much, much worse.

His eyes snapped open, and he took stock. Bare chested. His right arm in a sling. Ice packs surrounded it and secured it so much that he felt like he wore the shoulder pads of an American football player. He gazed at the IV line running out of his left forearm.

A nasty taste filled his mouth, like that of his last meal and not having brushed his teeth in a few days. Like sticky tar paper. Right then, the two things he wanted most were a toothbrush and toothpaste.

Rough fit him perfectly. At least he lived, and Yado's scouts reported that the Turk's army had already begun dispersing. They'd receive reports throughout the rest of the day. The team had screeched into town shortly before midnight. During the rough ride back, Sana monitored Butch's tourniquet as well as his blood pressure. He remained passed out, and once they arrived at the compound, the doctor—Jace?—had met them with a stretcher and another man.

Diana brought him to the present when she pushed open his partially closed door. "Hey, tiger."

Thanks to feeling dopey, he offered a lazy smile. When he realized he wore only a pair of pajama pants, he flushed and pulled the sheet tighter across his waist. "Hi, yourself. What do you Americans say? You're a sight for sore eyes?"

"Something like that." She came all the way inside and left the door open. As a yawn broke loose, she pulled a tie from her hair, letting her tight curls spill across her shoulders. "I'm not sitting down because I'm afraid if I do, I'll fall asleep. A trick I learned during my residency days."

"How is Butch?"

Her smile vanished as she yawned again. "Sorry about that. I've been up for thirty-six hours now. We operated on him for six hours."

"Did you save his arm?"

She nodded. "Thankfully. Dr. Rogers, who's the doctor stationed with Jace's organization in Mosul, came up and was waiting on us. He's an orthopedic surgeon, and the two of us together were able to save it. The bullet got a vein. If it had been an artery..."

Makmoud understood. They would have lost him before they got back to Amal, or he would have lost his arm.

She resecured her hair, and a stray curl escaped to tease her cheek. He could see why Ali had taken a strong interest in her. She was a beautiful woman, even in her exhausted, disheveled state and wearing scrubs. "Ali's a good medic. I saw the x-rays, and he did a good job resetting your shoulder."

"And making a grown man cry."

That earned a weary laugh. "So he said. Dislocated shoulders are no fun for anyone. Also, Hassan was able to get Jibril's blood donation. It saved Butch's life. But for that, he would have bled out. He'll be weak for a while. A long while. But he'll make a full recovery."

"I am in Butch's debt. He almost lost his life saving mine." At the thought, he sat up straighter and grimaced.

She studied his face. "You okay? I can order up some more painkiller for you."

As if agreeing, his shoulder throbbed even more. He flinched. "That might be good."

"Will do. I'm going to head out and do one last check on Butch before I get some rest. Jace is going to be here on duty along with Hassan, so if you need either one of them, that button on your bed rail will send them in. Amal is so small that there are no nurses here save for when Dr. Rogers brings one with him from Mosul." She rested a light hand on his uninjured shoulder. "You know the drill. Sling for a while. Then a few weeks of physical therapy. Jace will explain more. And he'll be by in a bit to give you another dose of painkiller."

"Diana, thank you again."

With a small nod, she slipped through the door. Her voice receded down the corridor, then faded.

Makmoud stared at the ceiling as his mind circled through the events of the past twenty-four hours. He closed his eyes and thought about Diana. She'd served well along with the others. Fearlessly, like any of his own men. She cared deeply about all of them. After all, she'd been the one to show emotion when she couldn't save Parviz, and she'd given her all to do so. He grimaced at the notion.

Rest. He needed to rest and hoped Jace would be along shortly with his painkiller.

"Brother."

At the sound of Jibril's bass voice, Makmoud's eyes flickered open. Had he been dozing? Hard to tell. "Hi, brother. Please, come inside and sit."

Jibril still wore his night camo pants and a black T-shirt. At the edges of his hairline, smudges of camouflage paint remained.

Makmoud shifted and hissed through his teeth as another bolt of pain shot up his arm. "I still cannot believe you survived those RPGs last night."

"Our half brother called it a miracle," Jibril replied. "We had just descended below the lip of the rim when the first one hit."

Miracle. Makmoud let that word roll around in his head for a bit. He'd ceased believing in miracles long ago, probably about the time he'd ceased believing in Islam. He noted the bandage at the crook of his brother's left arm. "Diana told me you donated blood for Butch."

"All they could take. Hassan said it saved his life."

"So I heard. He will remain weak for several weeks, apparently."

Jibril sprawled in a visitor chair. "Then we cannot break them as soon as we planned."

Off the back burner and to the forefront. His sudden predicament caused another hiss of pain. "You are correct."

"But we need to get them to Iran. The sooner the better."

Makmoud's pulse sped up, as did the flick of the line on the heart rate monitor. "Not if Butch is not well enough to travel."

Jibril leaned forward and rested his elbows on his knees. His penetrating gaze hardened. "The general will want an update. I can do it if you—"

"I will contact him later this afternoon."

"But—"

"Let me handle it." He didn't miss the edge in his voice. His mind darted in all sorts of directions, none good. "We are safe here in Amal." So long as they didn't try to take the team to Iran. He'd seen the hard looks of some of the townspeople. Kidnapping Libby had cast him and his team in a bad light, and if... He shut down that line of thought and stowed it for later. He also had to deal with another problem. "Tank Russell contacted me. And I discovered something."

He shared Victor's revelation about LaRue.

"All the more reason to take Victor and his team to Iran sooner rather than later."

"That's off the table for now."

Jibril jumped to his feet. "We have a mission, brother."

"Do you not think I realize that? We also have a man who demands proof that we have killed nine people. He is demanding we meet soon. Very soon. Just what do you propose we do?"

Jibril opened his mouth, but no sound came out. He muttered a Farsi cuss word and shook his head.

"That is what I thought." Makmoud's shoulders didn't relax, and his injured one began burning. "We are both exhausted. Get some sleep, and I will do the same. I will contact General Soleimani later this evening."

Jibril glared at him, but he headed toward the door. He bumped shoulders with Jace, who stared at him.

Makmoud shook his head. "My brother can be rude when he is upset."

"As can we all." Jace did a quick check of his vitals and scribbled the results in a folder. "Diana said you needed some painkiller."

"That would be nice."

"Coming up." He held up a syringe. "This is it for you. Tylenol only after this one."

Makmoud nodded and watched as he injected the liquid into the IV.

Warmth surged into his veins. Then came that fuzzy feeling. He barely heard what Jace said. As his vision blurred, he realized one thing. He stood at a crossroads. Then nothing mattered.

26

"Butch, can you hear me?"

A voice from a long way off penetrated the gray haze that had surrounded Butch ever since he'd passed out in the back of the Humvee. A woman. She tapped him on the shoulder. Firm. Almost like a shove.

He slowly shook his head from side to side. "Hey, stop it, would ya?"

Or at least that's what he thought he said. Whatever actually crossed his lips resulted in a chuckle from the woman. More gently, she touched his left shoulder. "C'mon, Butch. Wake up."

Ugh. His body began coming back online. His throat hurt. So did his right bicep. Which seemed to be immobilized. And his side. And his nose. And everywhere else. Just what the heck had happened? He cracked his eyes open and blinked a few times.

The fuzzy image of a woman cleared with the effort. Diana leaned over him. "Hey, Butch. It's good to see you open your eyes."

"I hurt all over."

"Well, you took quite a tumble, plus a bullet."

"But I'm alive."

"That, you are. Thanks to Jibril. We had to do a transfusion, and he's the only one here who had a compatible blood type with yours."

215

"O negative," he slurred. His world began spinning. "Duzzat make us blood brothers?"

Her lips twitched upward as she scribbled on a clipboard. "Something like that."

Whooeee. Had she put him on a Tilt-a-Whirl or something? "Aw, man I gotta make him Cajun... somehow."

Diana smiled. Or at least he thought she did. His eyelids began drooping closed. He slurred, "Wha time izzit?"

"Nine in the morning. Rest easy. You'll be okay." She bent and kissed him on the forehead. "Welcome back to the land of the living. I'll let Shelly and the others know you're awake. Everyone refused to leave the lobby, even some of Makmoud's guys."

The mist surrounded him again. Who knew how much time had passed? Slowly, he opened his eyes. He caught a glimpse of a clock on the wall across from him. The short hand pointed to seven. Golden light beamed through the window of his room. Evening or morning? What was that warm sensation encompassing his hand? He turned his head to the left. Ow. Even that hurt.

A mass of blond curls dark at the roots rested on the mattress beside him. Curls that looked a lot like Shelly's. She cradled his left hand in her right one. His heart filled.

"Shel," he tried, but nothing came out. He swallowed. Man, his throat hurt. He licked his dry lips, then tried again. It came out as a croak. "Shel."

She stirred, lifted her head. The earpiece of her glasses created a crease along her face, and he didn't miss the dried tearstains on her cheeks. "You're awake."

"Finally. Diana..." He still couldn't string together enough words for a sentence. "How long... am I... have I been out?"

"You came out from recovery at nine this morning. It's seven in the evening now."

"Dang." He closed his eyes and felt himself drifting again.

She tightened her grip on his hand, wakening him further. "She said it was touch and go for a while. The bullet nicked a vein, and you lost a ton of blood."

216

"She said Jibril was the one who gave me the blood for the transfusion."

"Without him…" Another tear trickled down her cheek. Her shoulders shook, and she bit down hard on her lip.

His heart ached to see how worn and exhausted she looked. "Does that make us blood brothers?"

Her giggle turned to a sob, and more tears began rolling down her cheeks. Her chair scraped along linoleum as she scooted closer to him. Her grip on his hand tightened even further.

That infernal lump in his throat increased, making it hurt even more. "I love you."

"I was so scared." She sniffled. "If it had hit an artery—"

"It didn't. I'll be okay. At least I think I will be." He cupped her cheek and wiped at her tears.

She laid her head on his shoulder. "I started thinking, and my mind went places I didn't want it to go, and—"

"I'm here, babe. I promise. I won't leave you." He nuzzled her curls. So soft. She must have showered earlier that day because her hair remained damp. Oh, he'd missed that feeling. "I'm sorry, Shel. I'm so sorry for all that happened."

"Forgiven," she whispered. She gently laid her arm across his chest and cried out the emotions that had dogged her for the past several days.

His eyes filled. He hated the tear that seeped out of the corner of his eye. He'd cried maybe three times in his life, once when his kid sister had died, then when he'd proposed to Shelly, then when he'd wed her a few weeks before their misadventures. With effort, he stroked those blond strands. "I love you, Shelly. I love you so much!"

She raised her face.

Careful of the IV in his arm, he ran his fingers through her curls, then kissed her gently. It rocked him to his core. "I love you, my beloved, and I will never, ever leave you."

27

Freedom. At least from the infirmary. In the ten days since the combined efforts of the Shadow Box and *Quds* teams saved Amal, Butch had remained hospitalized, first due to his injuries and blood loss, then because he remained too weak to stand for more than a few minutes. Diana reported that his body was spending most of its energy replacing the blood he'd lost. Shelly remained by his side his entire waking time, save for when others came to sit with him when she needed a break. Bless her, she even helped him bathe.

Diana released him that morning. She and Fiona willingly swapped rooms with him and Shelly so he wouldn't have to climb stairs. One long, hot shower and a nap later, and he finally began feeling like a normal guy, albeit with his arm in a sling. When he awakened, Shelly wasn't in the room. Not that he blamed her, not when there was nowhere to sit but on the twin bed across from his.

He rose and flexed his arm. Still sore, but once Diana took the stitches out in a few days, he could dispense with the sling he still wore when awake. Carefully, he slid into a T-shirt, then his sling. Even that effort sent a wave of tiredness through him. He found Shelly at one of the tables in the eating area. She squinted and tapped away at her laptop.

He placed his good hand on her shoulder and kissed her temple. He couldn't wait until he could smell again because he loved the scent of her shampoo. "Hey, babe."

She covered his hand with her right one. "Hey, yourself."

"Whatcha doing?"

She minimized the window she'd opened. "Digging up dirt on Paul LaRue."

"Roger that." He peered across the warehouse toward the rec area where a recliner, sectional sofa, wall-mounted big-screen television, pool table, and ping-pong table awaited him. Not that he had the energy to play pool or slap a ball around. He'd have to settle for watching others do that. "I'm going to go and sit down for a minute or two."

She acknowledged him with a nod. He bit back his smile, then shuffled across the wide space. With a deep sigh, he eased into the recliner and closed his eyes. It'd be so easy to sleep. Maybe he would.

"Hey, man." Victor flopped onto the part of the sectional closest to Butch. "I heard you broke out of jail this morning. How are you doing?"

"Weak as a kitten." He patted the tattered leather on the arm of the recliner. "I can't believe they still have this around. It was old when we were here ten years ago. I always joked it'd be good for a bachelor apartment but not much else."

Victor chuckled and swung his feet onto a coffee table. "Jace said the community pooled their money for the big screen television and that hanging it was more stressful than some of the surgeries he's worked on. The town uses this as a movie theater. Apparently, Bollywood is a really big deal here."

Butch laughed—until his rib protested. "Diana said I only cracked my rib, but it feels like a break."

"You sure you didn't shout 'As you wish' as you rolled down the slope? You know. Like the Dread Pirate Roberts in *The Princess Bride*?"

Butch laughed again, then groaned. "Boss, stop. You're going to make me blow another rib."

Victor peered around as if looking for any eavesdroppers. "You have a minute?"

"For you? Always. What's up?" With effort, Butch leaned forward on the elbow of his good arm.

"First off, where are Libby and Jace?"

"At their meeting. She asked me to go with them. I said no. JC is with her, as he needs to be."

"Good move." Once more, Victor peered around them.

"Something worrying you?"

"Eh, you could say that."

Strangely enough, everyone except Shelly seemed to be outside, probably enjoying the cooler weather a recent cold front had brought. Butch returned his attention to his team commander. "Guess we can't walk away from this situation with the *Quds* guys."

"No, except Amal is made up of fiercely independent and loyal Kurds. Jace reported that the way Makmoud and his guys kidnapped Libby has set them on edge. They're stockpiling arms and are willing to fight the *Quds* guys to save us."

Butch winced. "It'd be a bloodbath, and not all of us would walk away."

"Let's hope it doesn't come to that." Victor glanced toward the far end of the open area where Shelly sat. She rested her chin on her hand, then typed. "What's she doing?"

"You know Shel. When she's not physically in action, her brain is in action. She said she's working on stuff related to Roo."

On the walkway leading to the second-story rooms, Makmoud's footsteps sent metallic echoes across the cavernous space. He, too, wore his arm in a sling. Physical therapy was helping, though, and he was confident he'd be free of the sling in a couple of weeks. Shelly stopped her typing. She shot a questioning look Butch's way.

"It's okay," he mouthed.

A faint smile answered him. She returned to her work, but he could tell she kept one ear out for anything of note. She reached into her backpack.

As he made his way to the rec area, Makmoud barely acknowledged her. He seated himself on the other part of the sectional. "It's good to see you're feeling better, Butch Addison."

"How's the shoulder?" Butch asked.

"Ali said I am progressing well with the physical therapy. In a couple of weeks, I will no longer have need of the sling."

Butch tried not to think about what a couple of weeks might entail. His injuries had prevented the team from being taken to Iran. But now that he was out of the infirmary, no excuse remained. He peered around him. "Where's Jibril? You two are like Mutt and Jeff, always together."

"He does not need to be a part of this discussion."

Butch glanced at Victor. The smallest of shrugs. "Okay. I'll bite. What's going on?"

Makmoud leaned back, crossed his ankle over his knee, and rested his good arm on the sofa. "He's not here because he disagrees with me, though he trusts my judgment in this matter and agreed to obey my order regarding this. It did take quite a bit of persuasion, though."

Butch drew in a quick breath. "About what?"

"You saved my life."

"And you're welcome." The *Quds* team leader had visited him in the infirmary at least once a day. They'd come to an understanding of sorts. Or maybe a friendship. It was hard to tell at times. "I'm never going to be the one to leave anyone to die. We had a motto in SF. No man left behind. I take that very seriously."

"So I realize. And yes, I understand." Makmoud cast a glance upward, like Victor, searching for eavesdroppers. He rubbed his good hand on his pants leg and leaned forward as he switched his gaze from Butch to Victor. "I'm letting all of you go."

Butch's mouth dropped open. Say what?

A smile flickered across the man's face. "Don't look so surprised, Butch Addison. As I said, I'm in your debt, and I do intend to fulfill my end of it. But," he raised a finger, "it's on one condition."

He tensed. *He wants Suleiman. Nope. Not going to happen. Either we all go home together, or we all go to Iran together. No way am I giving up my adopted little brother.*

Victor raised his hand in the smallest of motions. Butch got it. Stay put. Hard to do right then. "What is your condition?"

"Leave Paul LaRue to me."

Wait. Huh? No way. Uh-uh. Not going to happen. Roo was his. Butch had a bone to pick with the man. "Do you know what he did to me? The way his actions ended my career? And caused the deaths of men I fought with?"

"And how he wanted to get you out of the way so you would never be able to tarnish his supposedly spotless record? Yes, I'm very well aware." Makmoud smiled, bearing his fangs in a prominent display of dominance. "And I'm also very aware he was willing to send you to your deaths at my hand. Only he didn't know the plans I had for you. I only said I would *take care of* you. Not kill you."

"Ain't no kind of care to break us like you planned."

Makmoud ignored his comment. "Apparently, that was not enough for him, if Tank Russell's presence in Mosul is any indication." He focused on Victor. "I've thought a lot about your words regarding Paul LaRue. Tank is still in Mosul, and I'm inclined to believe you, Victor Chavez. I like living and so will be taking care of him tomorrow."

Butch cocked his head. "But—"

"What do you want from us in return?" Victor asked as if he knew where that conversation was heading, which was precisely nowhere.

Makmoud sat back again. "Let Paul LaRue see your arrival in the States. Make him squirm. Then you provide the intelligence I need to put the man in the ground." That wolfish smile returned. "That way, your hands won't be dirty. You see, I have absolutely no issue with getting my own hands dirty. Paul LaRue is a dead man walking even now." He stared Butch down. "If you so much as try to do the deed for me, you might as well look over your shoulder for the rest of your life because I will hunt down each and every member of your team and kill them. Understand?"

Like a good soldier, Butch wanted to stand, salute, and shout, "Yes, sir!"

"And trust me when I say there is no rush. I take my time in planning." With that, he rose. "Thank you again, both of you. Tonight, our two teams together celebrate saving Amal. We will be leaving in the morning to return to Iran. And after that, may our paths never cross again.'"

He headed toward the pedestrian door. Once it slapped shut behind him, Butch blew out a long sigh. "You got that right."

He carefully twisted and risked a glance at Shelly, who smiled and pointed to her computer. Only then did he notice the small but very powerful microphone sitting half-hidden by her phone. She must have recorded the conversation.

His cheeks puffed out in a sigh, and he leaned back as he gazed at the ceiling. "Praise God he didn't ask to keep Suleiman."

Victor rubbed a hand across his face. "Amen to that."

Victor's look from a few days ago flitted before Butch's eyes. "Boss, you mind if I ask something?"

"Sure. Weariness laced Victor's question. He probably knew what was coming.

Butch cast another look around, this time to make sure Sana or Suleiman weren't within earshot. "Is Suleiman's real name Ibrahim Hidari?"

"Yeah. He's Makmoud's half brother." Victor scrubbed his hands across his face. "He's the one who, years ago, fingered the South American *Quds* compound. That's what led to his entry into the States and the name change to Suleiman al-Ibrahim."

Butch pushed back on the recliner. Oh, yeah. The chair still worked. "Dang. What was Makmoud insinuating when he said Suleiman and Jibril had done that shot before?"

Victor's expression darkened. "I'd rather not talk about it."

"Fair enough." Butch's gaze flicked to the closed door to Makmoud and Jibril's room. "But to be honest, Suleiman is in no way like his brothers. No way."

"Agreed." Victor hadn't moved a bit from his position on the couch. He closed his eyes, and a few minutes of silence passed. Had he fallen asleep? Then came a quiet, "You know something, Butch?"

"What's that?"

"I've known Jesus as my Lord and Savior for five years now. My testimony isn't exactly stellar in terms of where I was before, so I know what it's like to be forgiven of my sins. But I don't think I have the appreciation for it like Suleiman does."

Butch closed his eyes and digested that one in silence. Gradually, it became clear to him. Suleiman was a sniper by training. Most likely before he'd been saved, when he'd been with the _Quds_ cell in South America, he'd killed someone who meant a lot to Victor. Six years ago when the team met for the first time. Suleiman insisted on not killing if at all possible. It hadn't turned out that way, unfortunately, and he had talked occasionally about the agony of taking a life, even if that life would have taken theirs. Soldier to soldier, Butch understood because he'd done the same thing while in the Army and even a few days before. He'd feel the fallout for days and weeks to come. "Oh, but for the grace of God go I."

"I hear ya." That sleepy remark came from Victor.

Butch let loose a Wookie-like yawn and settled more comfortably in the recliner. Yeah, his body must have once again put manufacturing red blood cells at the top of the list because the sleepies overtook him.

The outer door to the warehouse closed. Huh? Had he been asleep? Thanks to smashing his watch during his tumble down the mountain, he had no idea of what time it was. But the square of light streaming through the high windows had shifted and lengthened. On the sectional, Victor still slouched, but now he slept.

Carefully, Butch came upright.

Jace and Libby slipped through. Jace had his arm around her shoulders, and she leaned into him. Her headscarf had come partway down, revealing strands of her dark hair clinging to tears. Uh-oh. What had they learned? Either way Butch turned it, the news wouldn't be good. Either her children were alive in the hands of ISIS or dead in a mass grave.

He struggled to his feet. Shelly was suddenly right there, and he tucked her under his arm to avoid falling over since his head really swam from the change in blood pressure. He whispered into her ear, "I'm yours, babe. Always remember that." Louder, he asked, "Libby, what is it?"

The couple stopped at the sectional.

"They found their remains," Libby whispered. With that, she turned her face into Jace's shoulder and wept. He held her close. Her wails echoed off the corrugated metal walls. And they were loud. Butch hurt for her, especially as the rest of the team gathered around at the sound of her cries.

Finally, Jace drew her down to the couch. Her eyes were red, and tears streaked her cheeks. Diana handed her a tissue, and she dabbed her face and blew her nose. Fiona brought a damp washcloth from the locker room, and she held it to her face for a few seconds as her shoulders heaved. Finally she lowered it. "Thank you. Thank you for not being embarrassed by my tears."

Diana now sat on the other side of her. "That was a hard bit of news to take in."

Jace took her hand, and Libby surveyed all of the team. "Thank you for rescuing me. And now supporting me. It means the world to me. It brought me closure."

Jace rubbed her shoulder.

That seemed to strengthen her. "And yes, I'm leaving and not returning. No need now, but it hurts to finish this chapter of my life." She closed her eyes and took a deep breath. When she opened them, peace radiated. And sadness. Butch wondered if it would ever leave her eyes. "The UN will bring them home to Alabama. And Samir as well since his parents and siblings were killed when ISIS invaded."

Man, oh, man. Who knew grief and joy could coexist? Butch now saw it for real.

"When do you fly out?" Fiona asked.

"The second of August," Jace replied.

Victor straightened. "I have some news."

Sana squirmed between Suleiman and Victor. "I'm afraid to ask."

"We're not letting them take you," Jace said. "Not without a fight. I think the town and Yado made that quite clear."

"They have. And Makmoud's no dummy. He said he's in Butch's debt. He's releasing us."

Sana took her husband's hand. "All of us? Including Suleiman, right?"

Victor nodded. "Yes, all of us."

Libby shivered. "When are you all leaving?"

Fiona looked at Butch. "Depends on if my copilot thinks he can help out. It's a long way home."

"Day after tomorrow?" Butch asked. "Maybe, now that we've been officially released, I can sleep better."

Libby rose and took Jace's hand. "Thank you all. I'm going back to my house. I guess I have some cleaning up to do. And some packing."

Butch watched them go, then gazed around him. For the first time since their initial run-in with the *Quds* squad, the entire team was together alone. Well, save for Suleiman. That boy had slipped away without anyone's knowledge.

"Speaking of packing," Skylar said. "Where are Makmoud and his pals?"

Sana popped to her feet. "I saw them outside doing that very thing. And some of them are preparing some sort of meat to be roasted over a fire pit."

Butch's stomach growled at the notion, and he patted it. "Looks like we're going to have ourselves a party."

Diana shook her head. "This is so strange. Are you sure we're not in an alternative universe?"

"They're leaving in the morning." Butch caught Victor's gaze. A small shake of the head. Best not to mention Makmoud's condition for their release.

"Ahem." Sana cleared her throat. "Butch, Shelly took the liberty of filling us in on what went down between you, Libby, and Roo years ago. And the way you almost died saving your guys. When we planned this last op, you referenced getting a Silver Star for your mission in 2005 right here. We felt that by saving Makmoud's skin and all of ours, you deserve something similar."

Confused, Butch stared at her. "I'm not sure where you're going with this."

"Suleiman, if you would," Sana called.

In a stately walk, Suleiman headed toward him. A white towel covered a book. And on top of the white towel lay a star wrapped in, of all things, aluminum foil. Paper clips joined together formed a lanyard. Suleiman came to stop before the recliner and formally bowed.

In her most serious tone, Sana pronounced. "Butch Addison, though we were not able to pawn enough items to create a Silver Star for your bravery in battle, as the Shadow Box team, we present to you the Order of the Aluminum Star." She lifted it from the towel and draped it over his neck.

He burst out laughing.

That did it. The team began guffawing as a way to relieve the stress of the past several days. Butch fingered the star. "Man, what would I do without you guys?"

"Probably shrivel up and die," Skylar drawled in his finest Southern accent. That sent them into howls of laughter again.

Butch rose. "Y'all, it's been too long. I think we need a group hug."

All eight members pressed together. A collective sigh released as they hugged. It was good to be with the team. And with Shelly. He took her hand and mouthed, "I love you."

They were going home. No, he *was* home. With the team. And with Shelly. No matter where he was, so long as Shelly was with him, he was home.

28

Makmoud heaved his ruck into the back of his quad cab pickup truck and surveyed the small convey as his team climbed into the vehicles for the trip to Tehran. He wouldn't be joining them. Not today or ever. In just a few hours, his life would change and not for the better.

Jibril's low rumble drew him out of his contemplation. "We should be at the border by early afternoon and will wait for your arrival."

"I will not be joining you." Makmoud braced himself for the fallout from his news.

"What?" Jibril's gaze hardened. "Are you out of your mind? Why?"

Makmoud ignored his question. "When you arrive, delay in contacting the general until early afternoon."

"Why are you doing this?"

"Because the general will see my decision as treason."

"It is."

Makmoud's face heated. "Do you not understand? I'm in debt to Butch Addison for saving my life. My fulfillment of that debt is releasing them."

"You are a fool, Makmoud."

His brother would never comprehend the disquiet in his spirit that had haunted him ever since their battle with the Turk. "So be it."

Jibril stared toward the east as the sun began its march across the sky. "What of Susanna and the girls? You know the general will take them. Torture them to ensure you return."

His question seared Makmoud's heart. Again, another thing he'd contemplated as he'd lain on his bed and stared at the ceiling over several sleepless nights. His daughters, Mihrab and Rana, had given him great joy. Their innocence had made him question his own life. And Susanna. He winced as he thought about the woman he'd grown to love over the past seven years. He closed his eyes, then faced the same rising sun his family saw. "Marry her."

Jibril cocked his head. "Excuse me?"

He faced his brother. "You know the general will annul our marriage when he finds out I have deserted *Quds*."

Jibril's jaw twitched.

"I know you love them very much. Your nieces adore you. And Susanna? She will learn to love you in time."

His brother didn't say anything for a few moments, instead kicked at the ground and put his hands on his hips.

"I love you, Jibril. I know that is hard for you to say. But I do."

Jibril huffed, then met his gaze. "I will delay the general only long enough for you to accomplish this last mission. And I promise to love and protect Susanna and the girls."

That was all Makmoud could ask for. He gripped him in a tight hug. "Take care, brother."

Jibril released him and walked away.

Makmoud bit back his emotion. He didn't have time for that now. Without a goodbye to his team, he retreated to the pickup and headed south. A couple of hours later, he arrived in Mosul.

In this city of almost four million souls, he found all sorts of people, from traffickers like Yado to those like himself, city dwellers. He climbed from the vehicle. At this time of morning, the hot sun beat down on the city, and he sought shelter in the shadow of a wall. He peered across the way at an elegant five-story hotel where Tank Russell had taken up residence. Makmoud's shemagh and sunglasses hid him from instant recognition by his adversary. Tank had no idea about what had happened with the Turk, so a sling wouldn't draw undue attention.

Makmoud glanced at his phone. Tank's text conveyed it all. Makmoud, we must meet today, as I'm flying out tonight. If we do not meet, then I will be unable to authorize payment without POD. Makmoud didn't have to imagine what POD meant. Not Proof of Delivery. Proof of Death. Not going to happen since Victor and his team would leave the next day.

The night before had been a somewhat relaxed, celebratory time that confirmed his decision. Even Jibril finally warmed up to the people who were supposed to be his captives. They dined together, played some games as well. He'd watched as Jibril and Skylar went head to head in a ping-pong match that Butch called epic. Laughter. That's what he'd remember from that night and what would carry him through the difficult days ahead. His attachment to them had become emotionally dangerous but necessary to keep them alive during their battle to save Amal. Jibril wouldn't take the fall for his decision the day before. He would.

The thought made Makmoud slightly nauseous. He wouldn't worry about that now. He couldn't when staying alive took precedence.

The door to the lobby kept opening and closing. People left, mostly business people. Then came Tank with a blond man beside him. Makmoud removed a small listening device from his pocket. It transmitted their conversation to him via the earbud he wore. He began recording.

"You know what to do, then." Tank peered around. The hot summer sun gleamed off the man's bald head.

Makmoud kept his gaze on his phone as if completely disinterested in the conversation going on across the street.

"I do. I've found the perfect place," the man said with a German accent. "He's arriving when?"

"Noon." Tank's gaze didn't stop on Makmoud. The man smirked. "He's not to walk away."

"He won't." With that, the blond man strode down the sidewalk with a backpack slung over his shoulders. Makmoud didn't doubt what it contained.

Tank walked the other way toward their meeting place, a restaurant called the Exotic Café. Once he was out of sight, Makmoud removed his sling. He'd have to go without it today lest it hinder him. He carefully rotated his shoulder. It hurt, but it worked. That was all that mattered. He followed the blond man, who didn't bother checking behind him for tails. He probably assumed Makmoud was hiding somewhere. He nearly laughed. What better place to hide than in plain sight?

Makmoud followed the blond man down the main thoroughfare with a knife he'd strapped across his chest and a gun in its holster at the small of his back under his denim jacket. No matter that the hot sun threatened to bake his brains. In a roundabout way, the blond man led Makmoud close to the Exotic Café. It all became clear. The man was assigned to assassinate him at some point during his meeting with Tank. Not at all uncommon in a city barely emerging from the iron grip of ISIS. Once the initial fuss calmed down, no one would think anything of it.

Not going to happen. He liked living.

The assassin turned down an alley. Makmoud passed it, then doubled back. He peered into the semi-dark space just in time to see a door shut. A dead giveaway. With his hand on the butt of his pistol for a quick draw, he stole into the alley. He waited a precious second to ensure no one had followed him, then tried the door. Open. What sort of fool left a door unlocked?

Makmoud found himself in a dark stairwell. He stood still for a few minutes to let his eyes adjust, then carefully placed his feet at the edge of the treads as he crept up the stairs. Sunlight streamed through the windows of whatever room the door opened onto. He peeked through the door.

The citizens of Mosul were gradually rebuilding their city, and this building was a new one, maybe some sort of store since the third floor seemed to be one big room. The half-finished interior only lacked electrical work and windows. Wires hung from the ceiling. Exposed pipes gave it an industrial feel. Overall, it would most likely be a cheery, modern space, maybe a catalyst for the creation of the new, improved Mosul.

Tank's cohort had taken a knee in front of a large opening where a window would be once the contractor installed one. He assembled a rifle.

Clearly, he expected no visitors.

Makmoud carefully rotated his right shoulder again. No doubt his task would make it hurt more. He'd have to work it out later. He slipped his knife, a stiletto blade made for quick, quiet kills, from under his shirt. Knife at the ready, he stole toward the man.

He delivered a brutal kick to him that drove him into the wall in front of him. Stunned, the would-be assassin sagged to the floor, then flipped over. A punch to his jaw stunned him, then Makmoud drove the blade hard and upward just beneath his ribcage so it pierced his heart. His body stiffened, then stilled. Chest heaving, Makmoud straightened. The man stared up at him with sightless eyes.

No pulse. After wiping his blade on the man's pants, he snapped a picture of his victim's wound and blood on his shirt as well as his face. Proof of death. Just not what Tank expected.

Makmoud checked his watch. Time to go. After removing his she-magh, he made his way downstairs. Checking for any other assailants, he strolled to the Exotic Café like he hadn't killed a man moments before.

Like most cafés in his part of the world, several tables and chairs sat outside under an awning. Men lounged and either sipped coffee or dined on hummus, pita, and other foods from around the region. Tank sat along the railing next to the street. The perfect position for his assassin to kill his guest.

Without preamble, Makmoud pulled out a chair and sat across from him. "So very good to see you, Tank Russell."

Per Iraqi culture, they made useless small talk throughout the meal. Makmoud stretched it out even further. With each passing minute, Tank grew a little more agitated. So American. So impatient and wanting to get on with his business, even when his plane didn't leave until after midnight. Makmoud smirked inwardly. He ordered another round of tea and baklava just to irritate him some more. The man finally had to go to the restroom.

Once alone, Makmoud shifted the gun from its holster to his lap and covered it with his napkin. From an interior pocket of his jacket, he withdrew a silencer and carefully screwed it on. A last resort, but he wanted to be ready just in case Tank needed to be taken care of.

Finally, Tank returned. He leaned forward and rested his elbows on the table. "Makmoud, it's past time that we discuss our business. You know we paid you five million as a down payment for taking out Victor Chavez and his team. We promised you another five million upon POD. You remember, of course?"

His patronizing tone irritated Makmoud. Just who did he think he was? His hand slid to the grip of his gun. "Of course I do. And I did indeed take Victor Chavez and his team."

"As we agreed."

"Yes, as we agreed." He lazily ran a finger along the rim of his teacup. "I have your POD."

"Show me."

Makmoud pulled out his phone and located the pictures he'd taken of Tank's accomplice. Resting his elbow on the table, he held it up. "Perhaps you should select better assassins to take me out."

Tank froze. His tanned face drained of color, leaving it a sickly yellow. He cleared his throat and ran a hand along the collar of his shirt. "I didn't—"

"I recorded your conversation with him as you left the hotel earlier today." Beneath the table, his finger slid to the trigger guard. "Paul LaRue should know better than to try and double-cross me. I said I would take care of them. And I did."

"How so?" Tank squeaked.

"I let them go."

Tank began spluttering.

"Situations on the ground changed dramatically." Makmoud didn't bother to explain because it didn't matter. All Tank cared about was that Victor and his team wouldn't draw another breath. "This is how it will go. Give me your phone."

Tank stared. "What?"

"Give me your phone."

He handed it over. Makmoud glanced up. A large truck rumbled toward them. Without hesitation, he flipped it into the street, where the truck's tires promptly ground it into oblivion.

Tank jumped to his feet. "Hey! What the— I need that!"

"No you don't. Sit down, Tank Russell. Because right now, I have a silenced gun pointed at your knees. You keep protesting or try to attack me, and I will shoot you. Then you will greatly extend your stay here and be disabled for the rest of your life."

With a groan, Tank collapsed on his chair.

"Good. At least you see the value in following directions. Now listen to me and listen to me carefully because I'm only going to say this once."

"What?"

Insolence. Had they not been in a public place, he would have slapped him for it. He settled for delivering his directive. "I know the motives of your boss, Paul LaRue. When I figured out his reason hiring me, I decided it was not good to follow through. Paul LaRue, and by extension, you, are to leave Libby Mansour and her family alone. All of them, including her boyfriend. And you are to leave Victor Chavez and his team alone as well. And their families. Am I clear?"

Like a stone, Tank sat there.

"Am. I. Clear?"

A nod.

"And if you or Paul LaRue or anyone you hire tries to go against my directive, I will come and kill you and your family very slowly. All of them, even your grandchildren. Don't think I can't get to you in Texas. I can, and I will. Do you understand?"

Another nod.

"Then repeat everything back to me."

In a monotone, Tank did.

"At least you were paying attention. Now leave Iraq. Leave and don't come back." Makmoud tossed a few Iraqi dinars onto the table. No way would he allow the man to pay for his meal. "May I never see your face again."

With that, he rose. Keeping an eye on the man, he crossed the street, returned to the pickup near the hotel, and pulled away. He could only hope Tank would be wise enough to obey his orders.

Ten minutes later, he crossed the Tigris River, then pulled into a nearby park as he considered his next move. Now that the immediate danger was past, his shoulder began throbbing. Grimacing, he dry-swallowed an anti-inflammatory and nearly gagged. As he resecured his sling, he considered his options. Jibril and the others were on their way to Iran. He should be too.

General Soleimani's words before he left on his ill-fated mission echoed in his ears. *"Don't fail me this time, Colonel Hidari. If you do, it will not go well for you at all. Do you understand?"*

He had, and he did now. For letting Victor and his team go, he'd face charges of dereliction of duty, maybe even treason. Those charges carried with them execution, never mind the torture and interrogation beforehand. As he thought about his wife and two daughters, his throat tightened. If he returned, he would never see them again anyway. If he stayed away, Jibril would take care of them, would ensure they weren't killed. His brother's promise echoed in his ears.

Makmoud knew what he had to do.

He texted his brother. Thank you, brother, for loving me and my family. Take care of the girls. They love their Uncle Jibril dearly. Susanna will learn to love you.

He rested his head against the seat and fought the sadness that threatened to overwhelm him before dialing a number. Susanna answered on the first ring. "Makmoud! I'm so glad to hear from you."

A lump rose in his throat.

"Makmoud?"

"So sorry," he managed. "It's good to hear your voice."

"We're eager to see you tomorrow."

How could he tell her? No easy way. Just the pure, unvarnished truth. "I'm not coming back."

Silence. Then, "What? I don't understand."

"Things changed on the ground. I had to make a decision the general will view as treason."

"No, Makmoud. No!" A low sob escaped her.

"I need you to be strong for me, Susanna. Take care of the girls." He clenched his jaw as he remembered Jibril's promise to him. "They will come for you, *eshgam*. You and the girls."

"Who?"

"The general's men."

A sharp intake of breath answered.

"General Soleimani will annul our marriage. Jibril is on his way back. He will ask to marry you. Let him."

"But I love *you*, Makmoud."

"I know. But marrying Jibril will ensure your future. Yours, Mihrab's, and Rana's. Please, Susanna."

Her mewls broke his heart.

His eyes burned, and he whispered, "Be strong for me. I beg you. I love you, beloved. I'm so sorry it came to this. Know that you will be always in my heart."

He broke the connection and fought the lump in his throat for several minutes.

Then he dialed another number. Within half an hour, he'd transferred the five million in deposit he had collected as well as other funds into one of the secret Swiss bank accounts he'd set up years ago when he'd first gone into the field as a *Quds* officer and made regular deposits. Not that his superiors knew about it. Add that to his growing list of troubles with his own government. At least he could live for several years on it if he were thrifty and stayed in backwater countries. And he'd find something to do to bring in an income.

Then there was the matter of getting out of Iraq. He had a secret cache in Baghdad full of money and passports. He could buy a burner phone later.

He picked up his phone and whispered, "Forgive me, Susanna. Forgive me, Jibril. Take care of the girls for me." Then he tapped out a message to his now-former commanding officer. It was my decision to let them go. Jibril argued that we bring them to Iran. I owe them my life. Please let your punishment focus on me. His thumb hovered over the Send button. He pressed it.

And changed his life forever.

He went from rising *Quds* star to fallen angel within seconds.

Makmoud Hidari would simply cease to exist.

He powered down the phone, took out the battery and the SIM card, and dumped everything into separate trash cans.

With a deep breath, he turned his wheels southward toward Baghdad.

29

Never in his life had Makmoud thought he'd be a man on the run from his own government. That time had come. He needed to hide. Fast. Before General Soleimani sent squads to search for him. Thankfully, the general didn't know about a safe house he and Jibril had purchased long ago with their own funds.

Once he arrived in Baghdad, he parked several kilometers away since any searchers would start from there and fan out across the city. He stowed his gun underneath his denim jacket, then slid his ruck onto his back. As he drifted toward his hideout, counter-surveillance revealed no one interested in his movements. By the time he had arrived at a street surrounded by stone row houses, darkness had completely fallen. Very few people walked along the street.

A loose stone on the ground at the base of the row house's wall hid his key. He unlocked the door and slipped inside. Exhaustion surged over him. With his back to the door, he slid to the floor and rested his wrists on his knees. Susanna. Her name crept into his mind, and he forced the thought away. He couldn't think about her. Not now when Baghdad was radioactive for him.

With a grunt, Makmoud climbed to his feet. He headed upstairs and to the back bedroom. Once there, he collapsed on the unmade bed. He'd rest. Just for a few minutes.

The call to prayer awakened him. What time was it? Fatigue had stunned him unconscious. He raised his head and squinted out the window. His room faced east, and dawn's light had begun on the horizon. The call to prayer began. His stomach growled, then cramped. If he didn't get food soon, he'd rapidly weaken. He pushed himself upright and shambled down the stairs.

In the living area, he rolled the carpet back, then counted ten tiles from the eastern wall and twelve tiles from the northern wall. With his fingernails, he lifted one loose to reveal a cache of identities. He sorted through the passports. He had five, one Iraqi, one Egyptian, one Argentinian, one Panamanian, and one American. An idea began formulating. He pulled out the one for the Iraqi cleric. He grinned. Adnan al-Rafiq, meet Makmoud Hidari.

Over coffee, he formulated his plan. It would work. It had to. Panama would be his final destination. He had the Network there, a group of *Quds* agents in Central and South America who weren't as loyal to Iran as General Soleimani thought. They'd protect him. He knew they would. Getting there would require great care.

A good breakfast at a café, where he kept his back to the wall, refueled him. A visit to a phone store and computer store provided his new identity with what he needed. Once back at the safe house, he painstakingly transferred the contacts from his old phone to his new phone by hand. Rafael Cortez, the *Quds* officer in Panama City, picked up on the first ring. "*Hola?*"

Makmoud stared at the Panamanian passport. "Rafael, Jose Marino."

Rafael was no dummy. He'd caught that Makmoud was on the other end of the line. "*Comó estás, amigo?* So good to hear your voice!"

"Likewise." Makmoud stared at his personal phone. Its SIM card lay beside it. "I need your help."

"What happened?"

"I've had to walk away and need to disappear."

"I will work things out on my end. Book a ticket for Jose Marino from

Madrid to Panama City. I will also contact someone in Madrid to set up a safe house for you. I assume you already have a plan to get there?"

"Of course."

"Safe travels, then, *amigo*. I'll text you the address to this number. Let me know your arrival time."

Makmoud carefully placed the phone on the coffee table. He huffed out a hard breath as he began ticking through what he had to do. He flipped open the passport for Adnan al-Rafiq. A scowling man, just like Father had been when he'd been an imam.

He scheduled his flight for the thirty-first from Baghdad to Casablanca in Morocco as Imam Adnan al-Rafiq. He'd cross the Strait of Gibraltar on a ferry, then head to the safe house Madrid. Once there, the imam would cease to exist, and Jose Marino would fly from Madrid to Panama City. He spent the next four days gathering the supplies for his disguise.

The evening before his departure, Makmoud returned to the row house with a satchel and beat-up hard-sided suitcase an imam would use. Only one task remained, that of sewing the cash, credit cards, and other documents into the lining of the satchel.

He unlocked the door. Darkness filled most of the room. A lone streak of sunlight poured through the transom's window and illuminated the jewel tones of a vase sitting on a credenza across the room. He closed the door behind him and engaged all three locks. Setting his burdens down, he frowned. No lights. Hadn't he turned on the small lamp beside the vase before he'd left?

A heavy weight slammed into his back. Makmoud fell to the floor and landed on all fours. He reared up. His attacker bumped into the door.

Makmoud scrambled to his feet and staggered off balance into the credenza. The lamp wobbled, as the vase, and both fell to the ground. The vase shattered as his attacker raised a gun.

Click. Click.

A dart impaled Makmoud's thigh, and another hit him in the shoulder.

He pushed off toward the man, but the floor tilted underneath him. He staggered and regained his footing, then crashed onto the hard tile. His attacker reached for him.

Makmoud fell into a pit of blackness.

Tuesday, July 30, 2019, 2000 hours local time, Baghdad, Iraq

"Get up." Those harsh words and a blow to Makmoud's legs brought him back to reality.

His eyes snapped open. His cheek rested on a pillow. He lay on his side on the hard tile with his hands bound behind him. No getting around it now. He was a dead man walking. Maybe it was that realization or the drugs, but bile rose inside of him. Nausea roiled his insides. He grunted, "I'm going to be sick."

With a sigh, his captor grabbed the collar of his denim jacket as well as his belt and hauled him into the bathroom. He dropped him onto the tile and held his collar while Makmoud vomited over and over until his stomach finally gave up cramping. The man released him, and he collapsed to the tile against the wall.

Above him, the toilet flushed. A burly man in black from head to toe held a glass to his lips. Cool water hit Makmoud's tongue and cleansed his mouth. His captor lifted him to his feet and marched him into the living area. He shoved him onto the couch. Once he seated himself on a chair across from him and pulled off his balaclava.

Makmoud gasped. "Ji-Jibril!"

No show of emotion from his brother.

Makmoud snapped his eyes closed. "If you're going to kill me, do it now and be quick about it. Or are you going to take me back to Tehran and kill me slowly?"

Jibril held his silence for several seconds. He tsked and shook his head. "You should know better than to come to a place I know of."

He was right. Makmoud had been a fool to come here. Or to trust his brother.

Jibril snorted. "If I were going to kill you, wouldn't I have done so already? And why would I send my brother to a very slow, agonizing death?"

Makmoud's jaw dropped. "You're not going to kill me?"

"If you promise you will not kill me, I will remove those." He nodded toward Makmoud's hands, which were still tied behind his back.

"I won't. Promise on that."

Jibril rose. He drew his hunting knife. Makmoud tried not to stare at the serrated edges as he approached. Within seconds, his hands came free. His brother resumed his seat but kept his pistol resting on his knee with the muzzle pointed at him. A few more seconds ticked by. "Baghdad, the whole region, is too dangerous for you."

"I know. I have plans to leave completely." Makmoud swallowed hard and took several deep breaths. The nausea began receding, and he steadied. "The general sent you."

Jibril glared at him, and his insides clenched. Then he leaned forward with his elbows on his knees. "When I arrived with the rest of the team, he was furious. He immediately ordered Susanna, Mihrab, and Rana to be brought to headquarters. He planned to adopt out the girls to other families in *Quds* and torture Susanna to make you return."

Makmoud flinched.

"I could not let him do that. Brother, I did as you said and offered to take her as my wife, the girls as my daughters."

Pain shot through Makmoud's chest. Was this what a broken heart felt like? He groaned and put his head in his hands. His shoulders heaved.

When he dared look at him, Jibril gazed at him with sadness pooling in his eyes. For a brief moment, he was the brother from their youth, not a hardened soldier. "I will take care of them. I promise, Makmoud. They will be safe with me. Mihrab and Rana adore me. I will protect them and Susanna. I took them away that night, returned them to Mama's house. General Soleimani contacted the Ayatollah, and immediately, your marriage to her was annulled."

In the eyes of Iran, he and Susanna had never been married. He suddenly found it hard to breathe. Had his brother shot him?

Jibril continued in his bass rumble, "The girls were glad to be back with their grandmother. After we put them to bed, I assured Susanna that she was safe. I will take care of all three. I promise."

Even with him present, waves of loneliness washed over Makmoud. He was on his own, at least until he could get to the safe haven of Panama. Jibril rose and paced around the living area. He picked up the passport for Adnan al-Rafiq. "I took a look around while you were out."

Makmoud drew in a sharp breath. He'd stowed Jose Marino's passport after he'd made the plane reservation for his Madrid-to-Panama flight. Had Jibril found his cache? He hoped not. He made every effort not to let his gaze drop to the floor under the table between the two chairs.

Jibril grinned. "Adnan al-Rafiq, eh? Looks like Father to me. How clever in becoming the type of man you despise."

"Or what I'll look like when I get old."

"Where are you going?" Then he held up a hand. "I will not ask. The best so that I can plead ignorance when the general questions me. Flee as far from here as you can. The Americas are a big place."

"You didn't bring anyone with you?"

"I only told them I had a lead and would return by midnight. No one followed me. I made sure of that. I have two squads scouring the city. We found the pickup, but then we lost your trail. I thought about faking your death, but it wasn't to be."

Why hadn't he thought of that? It would have been so simple. "Why not?"

"He wants your head on a plate, literally."

Makmoud shivered. He had to run, had to be out there on the wind, which meant he'd always look over his shoulder.

Jibril peered at the door and huffed out a hard breath. Brother turned to soldier. "I must go now. I'll report to the general that we lost your trail in Bagdad and will head to Basra. When do you leave?"

"Nine tomorrow."

"Then be safe." He nodded to Makmoud's pistol, which now sat on the credenza. "Keep that with you until security at the airport." He gripped his brother in a tight hug. "I will miss you, brother."

Unmanly tears gathered in Makmoud's eyes, and for a second, he couldn't speak. Then he choked out, "Thank you for taking care of Su-sanna. I'll never forget that."

Jibril clapped him on the shoulder, then slipped into the night.

Makmoud made sure to turn all three locks. Once more, he slid to the floor with his back against the wood. He released a bellow and could only hope no one heard him. He sat there—breathing hard, trembling—as he stuffed his emotions back to where they belonged. Right then, he couldn't grieve, not when he had to get ready.

He took a long, hot shower, probably the last one he'd take for quite a while. Then came food. He forced down enough to get him to the airport and on the plane to Istanbul where he'd connect to Casablanca. He used an hour to sew his documents and cash into his satchel, then added four Korans to it to mask the extra weight. He packed robes and toiletries in the battered suitcase.

Then, behind the closed curtains of the bedroom, he began working on his face. Gradually, Makmoud Hidari disappeared. In his place came Adnan al-Rafiq. He peered into the mirror. Wrinkles. A few age spots. Gray beard, and gray hair peeking from underneath his *taqiyah*, the skull cap many Muslim men wore. Of course, the old face didn't go well with the jeans and button-down shirt he'd worn that day. A grin crossed his face, and he changed into the cleric robes he'd bought. He practiced his stern imam look and walk.

In the pre-dawn darkness, he called for a taxi, then slipped on thin leather gloves and wiped his pistol clean of prints. He stowed the gun in a holster that he secured underneath his robes for a quick draw. The driver collected him shortly after morning prayers, and they headed toward the airport.

"I hope you're going somewhere fun," the driver said, each word coming out with a bounce, like he'd downed too many energy drinks. "Life isn't any good without fun. Like when I go to nightclubs, I have fun. I like to listen to the music. Dancing's good too."

Not now. Makmoud gave his stern imam stare.

"The girls are pretty, and..." The driver caught the look from his passenger. He blanched, then hastily changed the subject to the Koran. Good boy. He knew better than to cross an imam.

Once at the airport, Makmoud tipped him well but not so well that he would be remembered. He headed into the cavernous building and checked in for his flight. Soldiers were everywhere, their eyes alert for any signs of trouble. Time to lose the gun. Once in a family a restroom, he locked the door. He shoved the gun and holster as far as he could into the trashcan. Hopefully, he'd be long gone before anyone discovered it.

One more hurdle. Security. He waited in line and practiced his haughty look. No worries there. Everyone met his gaze once, then stayed away. Even through security. No one questioned his satchel. All the soldiers cared about were guns. He strolled along the concourse toward the gate. One more step. Getting onto that plane. Thirty minutes until boarding. He took a walk, then returned just as a squad of soldiers poured into the area.

Adrenaline spiked. Had they found him? Time to play it cool. He watched as they began questioning every male in the boarding area. One soldier approached. "Passport and boarding pass, please."

Makmoud handed the document over, then fixed the young man in his sternest glare yet. The soldier studied his face before returning the documents. "Have a good flight, sir."

Gradually, Makmoud's thundering pulse eased off. From down the concourse came shouts. The soldiers rushed in that direction. As if nothing had happened, the gate agent announced boarding.

Makmoud found his seat in the front of the plane. He stowed his suitcase, then shoved his satchel underneath the seat in front of him. A portly man settled in the middle seat. He scowled at him. Almost there.

The door closed and sealed as the flight attendants began their safety briefing.

A bump, and the plane began push back.

They taxied to the runway.

The forward roll began. The plane lifted free of the ground, and they soared into the sky.

Makmoud relaxed only a fraction as he flew toward safe haven.

30

"This is ridiculous! Just where is he? He knows better to drop off the face of the earth for twenty-four hours, let alone a week." Roo demanded as he paced the length of his top-floor office at LaRue International Transport. He needed Tank here in New Orleans, not missing in action somewhere in the boonies.

The Swamp Rat slouched against the sofa cushions on the other side of the large room and stared at his phone as if already bored with the conversation. "You know he made it to Germany. He texted you using the pilot's phone."

"But he could have called. How do I know it was him? He could have—"

"And you called his wife in Texas, right? She said he arrived." The Swamp Rat lowered his phone and gazed at him from behind his glasses, which magnified his eyes and exaggerated his owl-like appearance.

"But he was unavailable." Roo dropped into his plush leather desk chair and stared at his phone. "And he'd better show up today in time for the function."

The Swamp Rat checked his watch. "We have to leave in half an hour. He'd better be here by then."

"You think I don't know that?" Roo's phone pinged with a new text message. He opened it, then gawked at a picture from none other than Libby Holt Mansour. She stood between her parents at Atlanta's airport. Two large suitcases and a carry-on surrounded her. Her message cut him to the heart. Roo, thank you for sending Butch and his team to find me. Because of them, I'm now safe and sound back in the States. Your concern for me is touching. He easily detected sarcasm behind that last remark. She remembered, and it scared him. "She's home."

The Swamp Rat blew out an impatient breath. "Who?"

Roo tossed his phone onto the blotter and ground his teeth. "Libby. That's who."

"Shouldn't you be happy about that? You can tell your voters you went out of your way to save a daughter of Louisiana from the clutches of ISIS."

Roo bit his tongue lest he say anything that would insinuate his intentions had been much less than honorable. The Swamp Rat didn't know the truth. Not at all.

The outer door to his suite opened, and Tank strode into the room.

Roo jumped to his feet. "Where have you been?"

One glare from his enforcer cowed him. The man broke his gaze and faced the Swamp Rat. "Give us a few minutes, would you? The car's already waiting downstairs with Tina in it. We'll meet you when we're done here."

"Will do." The Swamp Rat rose and headed into the hall.

Tank called into the receptionist's area, "Jerry, shut and lock the door to the suite, will you? And keep watch. We'll be out in a few." With that, he closed the door.

Roo sat on the edge of his desk and tapped a pen against the leg of his tuxedo pants. "Just what happened? You were to ensure Makmoud Hidari killed them, and then you were to take him out. When I got an invoice from Victor Chavez's Sentry Securities company, I knew something was wrong. Then you go dark and—"

"Makmoud figured it out." Once more on the job in his typical uniform of black denim jacket, cargo pants, and T-shirt, Tank folded his arms across his chest. "He killed my assassin, then threw my phone in front of a truck. I'm lucky I escaped with my life."

"So, they can still finger me." A string of words he'd learned during his time in the Army flew from Roo's mouth. He kicked his desk chair, and it skittered across the polished hardwood and slammed into a curio cabinet displaying his military memorabilia. The glass cracked, but he didn't care.

"Does it matter?"

"You better believe it matters." His shout echoed off the twelve-foot ceiling. "They talk to the wrong people, I'm looking at jail time. You got that? Jail! Not to mention losing the governor's race. Now, that's the least of my problems." He snatched up Victor's invoice and rattled it. "And have you forgotten the ten mil I'm out?"

Tank's jaw clenched. "You don't know who you're dealing with when it comes to Makmoud."

"Yeah, someone who can't follow orders."

"He followed orders, Roo. He took down the team."

"Then what happened? He just let them go?"

Tank studied a painting from a Civil War battle that hung above the couch. Which one, Roo never bothered finding out. "Yeah, he did. Apparently, things changed on the ground for him. He didn't say how but felt it warranted letting them go."

"What about your guy? The one who was supposed to take him out?"

Tank faced him. "Makmoud got to him first."

Roo's jaw dropped. Like a beautiful but poisonous flower, the slightest bit of fear began unfurling within him. "What? How?"

"I don't know." Sweat broke out on Tank's bald pate. "He got to the table, and his version of POD was my guy dead from a stab wound he delivered. He told me we should cease and desist from Libby, her family, her boyfriend, Butch, his pals, and their families."

"We can't."

"Oh, yes we can, and we will." Tank huffed out a hard breath. "My family's lives depend on it. I'm not interested in pursuing anything. And besides, it's a dead issue in my mind."

Roo stalked toward him. "She can still finger me. And you know she had to tell Cajun Man at some point."

"Really? Roo, they were friends in high school, not people who are in regular contact with each other."

"But she knows. That's the problem. She knows too much, and now Cajun Man probably does too. They've got to be wiped out. Otherwise I'm toast."

Before Roo could take a breath, Tank snagged his tuxedo lapels and slammed him against the wall hard enough to rattle his teeth. He'd never been on the business side of Tank's anger before, and the man's bestial snarl assured him he never wanted to again.

"Did you not hear a word I said?" he growled. "Did you?" He slammed him again, and his head bounced against the wall. "Makmoud will hunt down my family!"

Struggling to remain calm, Roo tried to placate him. "There's no way Makmoud could get to you in Tex—"

"In that sieve of a place they call a border?" He barked out a laugh, then gave him a shake. "Pull your head out of your butt, LaRue! Makmoud is one of the most dangerous men out there. And I will not do anything to put my family on his radar." Another shake. "You got that? We're backing off!"

"But—"

"Am I clear?"

What could he do? Argue? Not when his security chief really held the upper hand. "Okay. Okay. I get it."

"Good." Tank released hin, straightened his lapels, and smoothed the satin fabric. "I'm glad we understand each other. You have three months left in your campaign. I'll keep an eye on Libby Mansour and her family as well as the others." He nodded toward the invoice that had fluttered to the floor. "You pay that like you do any other business transaction, understand? If you don't, people will get suspicious. And tonight, you go and you do your little song and dance. And then you go home to your wife and kids and thank God they aren't under a virtual death sentence like my family is. Then you hit the campaign trail again. Got it?"

"Okay," Roo whispered.

Tank picked up the invoice and tossed it onto the desk. "Good. I'm glad we have an understanding. I have a new phone now."

Roo blew out a breath. He squared his shoulders. *Put it behind you. Tank's right. Just a few more weeks, then it'll all be over with.* His phone pinged with a summons from the Swamp Rat. He needed to get down to the car so they could go to the hotel. He shoved the incident with his security chief out of his mind.

Two hours later, the speech went off without a hitch. So did the mingling, though by the end of the evening, he became vaguely aware that he'd downed a few too many mixed drinks from the open bar. Tina looked stunning as usual, this time in a black-sequined cocktail dress that turned more than a few heads. He found his hands wandering where they shouldn't, and finally, Tank suggested they leave before he really embarrassed himself. Rather than take his wife to the bedroom, he wandered into his study. He pulled out his burner phone and dialed Makmoud's number. Nothing. No answer. Not even voice mail. The traitor. He stumbled to the door and up the stairs, only smacking into a wall once.

Tina lay curled on her side with her hand next to her face on the pillow. Roo fell into bed and instantly slept. He dreamed, and once more, the old hag shook her finger at him. Then came images of what he'd read about his family's involvement in blowing the levee of the Mississippi River downstream of New Orleans in the spring of 1927 during the great flood. They'd refused to compensate those who had lost everything in an unneeded effort to save the city. The woman returned, shaking her finger again. "Your family will pay, Paul LaRue. *You* will pay. Your life will be required of you." She morphed into a skeleton as she began laughing.

"No!" Roo cried. "No, no, no!"

"Roo?"

His eyes snapped open. Tina leaned over him, her blond hair brushing his bare shoulder. His breath shuddered out of him. "Sorry. I'm…"

"You were having a dream," she murmured in a voice thick with sleep. "You had too much to drink tonight, and that's when you have bad dreams. Go back to sleep."

With that, she turned over and returned to la-la land.

Roo lay there, eyes wide open as he stared at the tray ceiling and the fan as it spun lazily and whispered cool air onto his sweaty body. The hag had vanished. But he still worried. Would Libby hold her peace? Would Cajun Man? Hard to know. But he had to trust Tank on this one. That's all he could do right then.

31

A coyote howled in the predawn darkness. Butch's eyes snapped open, and he listened. Another howl, this one coming from closer to their window, almost like it was on the grounds of the apartment complex. Good thing Shelly's cat, Gizmo, hadn't decided to go wandering tonight. Small pets disappeared on a regular basis around here.

He closed his eyes, willing the howls, which sounded like music to him, to lull him back into the lion's sleep that loving Shelly had brought upon him.

Now she lay snuggled against his side.

He thought about their conversation earlier that afternoon. Cathartic. That's the word she had used in the afterglow of their time together. He'd smiled and teased her about using big words, which earned a giggle and a kiss that led to many more.

Forgiveness.

In some ways, he took it for granted. Shelly had extended it to him, and he'd readily grasped it like a freezing man did a warm blanket. Maybe he finally got what Victor was saying about the way Suleiman lived. Of course, rarely did apologies precede forgiveness. He thought about Lydia, his baby sister, who'd died of an overdose. Myra, his other sister, had accused him of not caring even though it'd taken him three days to get from where he'd been deployed in Iraq to New Orleans. She'd been drunk, but her words still smarted to the point they hadn't spoken in years, not even a word of apology. And let's not even talk about Mama and Daddy.

That thought drove him from the bed. With sweats and a fleece blanket to keep him warm, Butch crept from the bedroom onto the balcony. He eased into a rocker and lit a cigarette as he thought about that one. How could he forgive the people who were supposed to nurture and protect their children? How could he forgive Leroy, his younger brother, who'd freely molested his sisters and driven Lydia to her death?

Lord, I can't!

You can. That still, small voice spoke almost as if Jesus sat in the other rocker. *You must. As I forgave you.*

Butch took a drag as he squeezed his eyes shut. *How, Lord? How much?*

Seventy times seven.

His conversation with Libby's daddy about forgiveness came to mind. Gerald Holt said he knew Butch had needed to hear those words. Every day as he'd healed from the assault, Gerald stood in front of the mirror and practiced them. Over and over again. And even afterward. His remark? Try seven hundred times seven. He'd said that with a wry laugh when they'd talked. Point taken.

Butch's breath shuddered out as he considered what Jesus had spoken so long ago. His conversation with Shelly earlier that night echoed in his ears. Like an onion. Many layers. More anger. More betrayal. Some layers came without a problem. Many didn't.

He stubbed out his smoke, leaned forward with his elbows on his knees, and put his head in his hands. His shoulders shook as emotion pent up from years of abuse and neglect bubbled to the surface. He'd come so far, literally and figuratively, since those growing-up years. Slowly, he ticked through those he needed to forgive. Myra. Leroy. Mama and Daddy. Makmoud. Roo...

His old CO's name slid unbidden into his mind.

This time, anger churned within his gut.

He'd nearly died because of Roo. Twice. Ten years ago and in July. The man's actions had definitely cost him a career he loved. *No. Sorry, Lord. Not ready to let go of that one. Not at all. Maybe one day.*

He set his jaw.

"But not this day, Lord," he whispered. "Not this day."

No way could he go back to sleep, and he'd promised his crew he'd be at the shop by eight. Too much coursed through his mind. Since he was up, he might as well head out to Last Chance Ranch to get in a workout at the on-site gym. Then maybe he could come back and treat Shelly to breakfast, one of the few meals he did well, before heading into work. But first, he scrawled a quick note for Shelly. He tiptoed into the bedroom.

His beloved still slept curled on her side, her knees drawn up, one hand tucked underneath her cheek. He kissed her on the hairline. She sighed and snuggled deeper under the blankets. Butch left the note on his pillow and let himself out into the chilly morning.

When he arrived at the gate, dawn was beginning to brighten the area to the point where the Last Chance Ranch logo was silhouetted against a pale blue sky. He rumbled up the drive and parked in the gravel lot next to the Tool Barn where Shelly had her lab on the second floor and he maintained the ranch's machinery. A light was on in the horse barn toward the back of the ranch. He veered in that direction and found Victor leading two of the dozen horses from the barn. Thanks to the fencing around the property, they freely roamed and would be back by the corral fence by sunset. A rooster crowed.

"Hey, boss."

"Aren't you up a little early for still being in recovery?"

"Shouldn't I be asking you the same question?"

Victor laughed. "I've learned that getting up at the same time each day is helpful. Gives me some time to myself before the day starts."

"I hear ya. Need some help?"

"Sure."

Butch headed to the tack room and grabbed a halter. As they set the horses loose for the day, they worked in silence. Butch considered everything that had raged through his mind several minutes before. He needed to deal with the anger related to Roo. Years ago, it would have gone unchecked, like when he'd assaulted Gerald Holt. And then there was the time when Leroy had goaded him after he'd confronted him about Lydia's overdose. Back then, Roo had talked him down.

Butch fought a lip curl. The very man who had saved him then later betrayed him, not just once but twice.

"Something on your mind?" Victor asked as they let the last one go. "Normally, you, the morning person, are a little chatty."

"Well, you know the proverb about talking too much in the morning and having your neighbor curse you."

That earned a chuckle. "I get it. C'mon. Let's get some coffee in the studio so we won't wake Deb and the kids."

On one of the window sills of the studio, Butch found his favorite mug. Victor had gotten it for him shortly after they did the *Peacemaker* gig in 2015. It was huge and had a rat on it, which brought back memories of when they'd planned that mission. One of Victor's daughters let loose a pet rat inside the Big House. Said rat wreaked havoc and wound up falling into his coffee.

His friend had always been a good leader, be it when he'd been his CO way back in their Army days or when he'd joined the team for Operation Shadow Box in 2014. He'd always been steady, loyal, and capable. And a good friend.

With a sigh, Victor eased into one of the chairs in the conversation area of the studio. "What's up?"

Butch took the other chair. "Shel and I finally cleared the air."

"Good. I was getting worried, you know. I could tell things were off with you two, even after we got back."

"I learned a hard lesson."

"Oh?"

"She nailed it. Forgiveness is like the layers of onion. Peel one off, another's there. You just have to keep going at it until all the layers are peeled away."

"You married a wise woman."

"Did I ever." Butch sipped his coffee and stared through the window at the pinion pine trees between the studio and the barn, which had begun swaying in a morning breeze. His thoughts turned toward his time on the balcony. Tough stuff to consider. "Storms today?"

"From what I read, yeah." Victor rested his foot on the edge of the glass coffee tale. He studied his friend. "That's all?"

"Huh?"

"You seem to have a lot on your mind."

"I can't believe it took only eight or so weeks to take Shelly for granted. I guess I learned the hard way that forgiveness isn't something given without effort and cost. Effort and cost to give it. Effort and cost to accept it. It takes real work to build up that trust again."

Victor shifted. "Truth."

"I spent a lot of time on the balcony this morning as I finally forgave several people in my life. It cost me my pride to forgive Myra for accusing me of not caring when it took me three days to get from Iraq to New Orleans when Lydia died. My anger to forgive Leroy when he molested Lydia and Myra. Mama, and Daddy for the way they raised me. And Makmoud? Heck, it cost almost nothing. Is it weird to think a friendship might have sprung up between me and him?"

"I'm not sure I'd go that far, but I can see your point." Victor rested his elbows on his knees and stared at the table. "What he did for us cost him dearly. I'm sure of it."

"I hear ya." Butch's thoughts turned to the betrayal. "I'm having a hard time with Roo."

"Yeah, me too." Victor's gaze lifted toward the worktable. "I've sent him my invoice, and he has yet to pay up. Or even send questions about the summary I sent. Which I find to be terribly strange."

"But you send the summary as standard operating procedure, right?"

"Oh, yeah. Everyone gets that from me at the end along with an invoice. And I almost always get some sort of questions before they pay. From him, no questions and no payment."

"I don't think he expected us to come back."

"He didn't, and from what I'm gathering, he thought he'd make his money back and then some by collecting on the reward offered for Makmoud. Crossing Makmoud is going to be costly to him."

"I thought about going after Roo myself."

Victor began shaking his head. "Not a good idea, and you know it. You heard what Makmoud said."

"Yeah, I did. Shel's started digging into Roo's life."

"Part of our 'condition' for being let go." Victor jabbed his fingers in air quotes.

"I know. Security's so tight on Roo anyway since he's almost to the home stretch of his campaign." His thoughts flashed to Shelly. "Not to mention, I've got me a woman who loves me dearly, so yeah, I've got too much to lose now." He drained the rest of his coffee. "Can we let this go, boss?"

"For kicks, I did check with an old Army buddy of mine to see who the officer was who investigated what happened to you in 2009."

"An Abigail Ward-Bocelli."

"Now that's a good memory. She did her job the right way and followed the facts instead of drawing foregone conclusions. The case is now considered closed. I asked in a roundabout way if there would be any benefit to asking Libby to testify. He said it was a big lift, especially since Ward-Bocelli left the Army in 2017."

"But—"

"But if Libby is willing to testify, they might reopen it. There's no statute of limitations on the likes of what happened."

"I think she wants to let it go. She's like Shelly in that regard, a mercy-before-justice kind of person. And honestly, it would be so hard to prove, even with the evidence of Ketamine in my blood when everything went down."

"God's justice is always best."

"You think he'll get justice?"

Victor ran his finger along the armrest of the chair. "If not in this world, than certainly in the next."

A thought clicked in Butch's mind as he gazed at his friend. "Boss, may I ask you a question?"

"Of course."

"I've been thinking about what you said about Suleiman. And what

Jibril said. Did Suleiman… Did he kill your fiancée way back when?"

"Yeah. He did." Sadness filled his gaze. He refocused on the coffee table. "And that's why I know how hard it is to extend forgiveness. It's costly. I so badly wanted to hold on to that anger, that hatred."

"I can't imagine you hating anyone."

"Oh, don't imagine too hard, then." Victor studied his Secret Service mug. "But I knew what would happen. You've heard the saying 'Not forgiving is like drinking poison and expecting the other person to die,' right?"

"Can't say I have."

"Not forgiving turns the person who doesn't forgive bitter and eats them up. Deb convinced me of it, and you know something? She's right. But that didn't mean it wasn't hard."

"Amen. I'm sorry I brought that up."

"No, no. Just don't go asking Suleiman about it."

"Nope. Not going to happen."

A shiver rippled through Victor. "Back to Roo. He's bothering me. He's a desperate man. Since we're getting closer to the election, I took the liberty of advising Libby's family to take precautions until it's over. Gerald said Jace's family offered them use of their mountain cabin in Colorado for as long as they need. Sounds like they're going to take some R&R there as Libby re-acclimates."

"A good idea."

"And as a precaution, I want us to start carrying, at least until the election is over."

Butch's mug clunked as he set it on the side table. "Will do." He set his jaw. "But if he comes after us, the gloves come off."

"I couldn't agree more."

32

If people could see him now. At the Diablo Canyon trailhead outside
of Flagstaff, Roo hunched behind the wheel of a beat-up black Chevy
Blazer with a thin coating of red dust on it, a product of a two-grand cash
purchase at a cheap motel near the Dallas-Fort Worth airport where he'd
left his Cayenne in long-term parking. Outside a small town in New Mexico, he'd camped at a mom-and-pop campground that welcomed his cash.
No flicker of recognition had crossed the old man's face as he took his
twenty bucks and pointed him to a site at the far end of the property.

He scowled as he thought about Tank. The man had warned him—
again—to stay away. He couldn't. Not with Cajun Man and Libby able to
finger him. At least he knew where his former gunny lived. To avoid suspicion, he'd finally authorized payment of Ghost's invoice. Then all it took
was a little lie to Tina about heading to Tank's ranch for a retreat before
the final push on the campaign. Since Tank had retreated to Texas, he
didn't know about Roo's side venture.

Now he scraped his hand down his unshaven jaw and studied the
USGS topographic map spread out before him on the steering wheel. Earlier that afternoon, he had followed Cajun Man from his apartment to the
ranch. He had a gym bag slung over his shoulder, probably intending to

pump iron at the ranch's gym. With the end of a pen, Roo traced the route from Last Chance Ranch to the trailhead where he'd parked. About two miles or so away from the ranch, close to the end of the highway. A place where Cajun Man might go to hike, leaving his truck at the ranch. The trail led into the narrow, steep Diablo Canyon.

Roo had also checked out information about it. A tough hike, labeled very strenuous. So, no recreational hikers on a day with rain in the forecast, only those willing to take on the harsh wilderness around them, including the mountain lions, bears, and coyotes that lurked within its confines. Not to mention the flash floods that would pop up in the slot canyon.

Would Shelly buy Roo's little lie?

She would. She trusted her man, even to the point of helping him based on a few text messages.

He extracted one of two burner phones from a small duffel. To hide his true destination from any prying eyes, he'd turned off his current phone when he passed Tank's ranch. He'd bought the burner phones from a convenience store in Flagstaff so a northern Arizona area code would pop up when he made his call.

He laughed. Here he was, gubernatorial candidate Paul LaRue, Junior, morphed into former Special Forces Captain Paul LaRue, Junior, man bent on keeping secrets where they belonged—buried. He had all of the chops needed to do so.

He texted a message to Shelly, using her number from when he'd contracted with her to put into place cybersecurity for his campaign. Hey, Shel. It's Butch. Can you come and pick me up at the Diablo Canyon trailhead?

He raked his hand through his hair, which was badly in need of a wash. His own body odor tweaked his nose and brought back memories of being deployed in the sandbox, where showers had been a luxury. *C'mon, Shelly. You know the drill. Answer me.*

A message flashed up. Butch? Why are you at a different number?

Roo closed his eyes as he remembered Cajun Man's speech patterns and cadence. His fingers flew across the keypad as he answered the way his friend would. I was hiking where the trail gets really narrow. I fell, got me a twisted ankle, and lost my pack and phone.

Three dots pulsed. Her reply flashed up. Are you hurt?

Roo thumbed out another answer. Banged up. A hiker helped me out and lent me his phone 'cause I can't hike back to the ranch.

I'll be there in half an hour.

Roo smirked at how fast her reply came, then tapped out a response. She trusted Cajun Man was at the other end. Thanks. I'll be here. Love you, babe. He cackled. "And I'll be the one waiting on you, *babe*."

He checked his watch. She'd be there at four-thirty. Time for a quick energy bar, which he scarfed down and followed up with a swig of cold coffee. He'd get a fresh mug on his way back to Texas. As he waited, he eyed the trailhead and the wide sky where the mouth of the canyon rose up. Farther in the distance, red rock mesas created the narrow, twisting slot canyon that had been carved out by a stream that could grow wild when rain fell. Clouds had overtaken the sun and begun dipping lower.

Arizona's monsoon season was in full swing, and the weatherman had called for storms later in the evening. Earthy wet rode upon the breeze whispering through the open windows of his Blazer. For a moment, he closed his eyes and let it cool his cheeks. His breathing roared in his ears. Just like he had so many years before when entering combat, he tingled all over as every sense came on high alert. Only this time, it was him and him alone.

Against a woman. One who would be getting the surprise of her life and one who could strike back if he let his guard down.

Where to hide? The trailhead's parking lot held few places. A small stand with a box where hikers completed permits and dropped them into the slot. Way too small. He'd be like an elephant trying to hide behind a telephone pole. A waterless toilet concealed by a clapboard shanty. Another potential, until he realized he could lose the advantage of surprise if she didn't approach the building. Those were about his only options. What about the boulders across the parking lot from his truck? He could climb on top and have the advantage of height. Perfect for his purposes.

After closing the Blazer's windows, he set a rolled-up balaclava on his head, and concealed himself behind the rocks. Most excellent. They afforded him a view of the parking lot's entrance as well as the trailhead. He checked his watch again. Almost time.

A low rumble distracted him. Thunder? Could be. Or rocks tumbling into the canyon, one of the hazards he'd noted during his research. Many a hiker had been injured by those rocks.

The gritty sound of tires on gravel signaled the approach of a vehicle. Hopefully Shelly. He crouched and pressed his eye against the cracks between the boulders, which afforded him a view of the entrance.

Shelly's practical Honda Accord pulled into the gravel lot. The engine shut off. A moment later, she climbed from the car. She wore jeans shorts, a tank top, and sandals. He must have pulled her away from painting, judging by the streak of vibrant brown across her cheek. She'd piled her hair on the top of her head in a messy bun. As she walked toward the outbuilding and then away from it, her feet crunched on pebbles and dirt. "Butch? Where are you? Did you hike up here? Where's your truck?"

No answer. Roo pulled the balaclava over his face and shifted so he peered between two of the boulders. One last check. She had her back to him as she gazed toward the trail. Her keys dangled from the fingers of one hand smeared with light blue, and she held her phone in the other. A drop of rain hit his neck. Time to move before he got caught in a downpour.

He climbed atop the boulder and crouched.

She must have seen him out of the corner of her eye because she swiveled.

He threw himself toward her and caught her on the left side.

"No!"

Roo knocked the cry from her, and she crashed onto her side. Her keys went flying, as did her phone and glasses. She wheezed and thrashed, then caught him on the face with a weak open palm.

More drops peppered him on the back as he drove a hard right into her cheek.

Stunned, she sagged to the ground and didn't move.

The rain thickened to a downpour.

Operation Silver Star

Cursing under his breath, Roo grabbed her under the arms and dragged her across the lot to the Blazer. He yanked his duffel from the front. After popping the back window and gate to the cargo area, he shoved her inside and hopped up beside her. He lashed her wrists and ankles together with duct tape. A fast moment later, he slapped a piece of tape over her mouth and covered her eyes with a strip torn from a T-shirt he'd purchased in Albuquerque. He climbed from the cargo area and secured her inside. Now rain pelted him, and within seconds, it soaked him to the bone. He smirked. "Sorry, Shelly. But you're going to be of great help to me."

He peered at her car as well as her keys, glasses, and phone. Should he get rid of them? No time. It wouldn't matter anyway. Once he swung into the driver's seat, he ripped the balaclava from his face. Wet sprayed from his hair and splattered the interior with droplets. He muttered under his breath.

Time to go to Harper's Cave. He remembered the place well from earlier that year. Cajun Man had told him about its isolation and dangerous hikes. Uninformed hikers usually met with some sort of calamity due to the sheer darkness of the maze of tunnels and the way shafts led into the depths of the earth where underground rivers could spring up unexpectedly during the monsoon season. Too difficult to get out if you didn't mark your way in. In no way did he intend to become a corpse. Now Cajun Man and his wife? A different kind of story.

A forty-five-minute drive took him deep into the Coconino National Forest. He pulled into the cave's parking lot. No one around. Expected since locals knew better than to venture into Harper's Cave at this time of year. He'd park somewhere else and walk in. He found another, more remote parking area a quarter mile away near another trailhead that would make it look like someone was hiking there rather than in the cave.

Though the rain had faded to a few random drops, the sky remained a leaden gray, signaling the approach of more bad weather. Could be good or bad. For Shelly, that is. Cajun Man wouldn't live to see another day.

Roo shrugged into a heavier jacket, then opened the tailgate and lowered it. Shelly squirmed as she tried to work loose the tape around her wrists and ankles. He grabbed her, dragged her backward and hauled her to a sitting position so her feet dangled off the tailgate. With a deft slash of his knife, he cut the bonds around her feet. When he spoke, he changed his accent to the bland one of someone from the Midwest. "Sorry, but you're walking under your own power now."

Noise emanated from behind the tape. Probably pleas to let her go already. Nope. Not to happen. He once more donned his balaclava, then released her blindfold. He slung his duffel over his shoulder, then drew his pistol. "You walk ahead of me, understand? Don't try to run because if you do, I'll kill you right here and now. Move it."

Shelly stared at the cave, and a shudder coursed through her.

He jabbed her between the shoulder blades with his gun. "Move, I say!"

Only then did she begin walking.

When they reached the entrance, he pointed to the wall next to the cave's entrance. "Sit."

She crouched.

"All the way down."

Her brow knitted as she tried to figure out how he knew her.

Roo tied a line of cord around a post at the entrance. He secured the spindle to the duffel's handle. Two thousand feet of line should do it. Do aplenty. He donned a headlamp, then nudged her. "Get up."

With her in front of him, they stepped into the darkness of the cave. His headlamp lit the way as they headed deeper and deeper into the bowels of the mountain. Several twists and turns later and feet downward, they arrived at a chamber he deemed satisfactory for his needs. He pulled out a powerful flashlight and examined the space. Ceilings a good thirty feet high. A shelf ten feet up that seemed to have handholds he could use to climb up. Two tunnels led away from the shelf and two more from the level where he stood.

With his hand firmly around Shelly's bicep, he headed toward the tunnel that appeared to have a drop-off in front of it. He shone his light downward, then listened. Water. Like a subterranean stream. Ten feet down in the chasm was a ledge with no handholds leading upward. So perfect. This was going to be good. He pointed to his left where the wall rose up from the floor. "Sit there. Now."

Shelly crouched.

"Again, all the way down on your rear. I know better than to trust you where you can get me."

Only when she obeyed did he tie off the guideline. He removed another length of cord. Brandishing his hunting knife, he tilted it so the bright light of his headlamp flashed off the blade and into her eyes. That should serve as a good warning. Mess with him, and she'd pay with her life. He sliced the tape around her wrists. "You can take the tape off your mouth and scream all you want. No one's around."

Slowly, she obeyed. He tossed her the end of his line. "Tie this around your waist."

She stared at him. "What?"

He raised his gun. "Do it now."

She did so.

"Now get up and go over there." He gestured toward the black hole.

Shelly began shaking her head. "No, please. Don't. I don't understand. What did I do to deserve this?"

"It's not what you did, *babe*. It's what your man did. There's a ledge ten feet below, and I'm going to lower you to that."

"But what if it's not strong enough to hold me?"

"You'd better hope it is. Now get going." He backed away. "You try and strike me, you're dead, so don't even bother."

She cast him a long look, obviously wondering who he was and why he wanted her husband. Who cared? He was past that. She hesitated.

"Now, or do you want your man to find you dead? Or maybe the rats will get you before he arrives." He snickered at his own statement.

She cast him one last look, then tied the rope around her waist. She extended her hand in a silent request for his assistance to get to her feet.

"Nice try, but that's not going to work. You're perfectly capable of getting up yourself."

Shelly squinted at him. "You knocked my glasses off at the trailhead. I'm having a really hard time seeing. I'm surprised I didn't run into a wall."

Roo wasn't going to fall for that either. "If you can make it this far, you can walk toward that chasm over there."

She climbed to her feet, then stopped when she stared downward at the ledge that was maybe five feet wide. "This is insane."

"No, it's perfectly sane. I'm going to lower you down."

Again, she began shaking her head.

"Would you rather I push you? You don't know how far down it is or where that water goes. I promise I won't let you fall."

"Yeah, right." Her sarcasm bounced off the rock walls.

"You're no good to me dead. Now get going."

She let him lower her.

"Untie the rope."

She obeyed, and he pulled it up, leaving her trapped with nowhere to go. He snapped a picture of her. "Enjoy yourself, Shelly. I'll leave a lantern on for you and will be back in a few minutes."

With that, Roo checked reception. As expected, no bars. Leaving an electric lantern on the floor near the chasm, he verified he could use a remote to turn it on. Then he returned outside. No one around. He checked reception again. Five bars now. Plenty for what he needed. "Now, time to see what Cajun Man will do."

33

What a storm. Butch stood in the open doorway of the gym at Last Chance Ranch and stared at the soaking wet ground. While weightlifting, the noise of the rain grew so loud it almost drowned out the heavy metal playing on the Bluetooth speakers Victor had installed a couple of years before. Earlier today, he and his family went out riding in the nearby Coconino National Forest. Butch could only hope they'd found shelter and hadn't gotten caught in a flash flood. Skylar was in town opening Regions Café, and Fiona was flying cargo across the country. Sana and Suleiman had taken a long weekend away. Just him and Diana at the ranch right now, and when he arrived, she'd said something about taking a nap before exercising.

Time to go. He'd promised Shelly, he'd be back by six, and here he was, already running late. That's what happened when he got totally into lifting like he had today. It'd felt so good after not having done it for so long, even though he'd cut way back on the weight. He picked up his duffel containing the gear he'd brought and located his weight belt.

His phone pinged. Probably Shelly wondering where the heck he was, especially since they'd planned to go out to supper in town tonight. Maybe they could dress up and go to Regions. Skylar always had a table open for

269

any of the former Shadow Box crew. He picked up his phone and thumbed through the lock screen to the text messages.

Unknown phone number with a northern Arizona area code and the following message: You need to see this to believe it.

Huh. Sounded like a smishing message to him. His thumb hovered over it to dismiss the conversation. Heck. Those things usually had a link in them, and as long as he didn't click on it, it was okay to look. Curiosity got the better of him. He tapped it.

His blood ran cold.

Shelly stared up at the camera with total darkness behind her.

From deep within, his composure unmoored. He began shaking so hard he eased onto the bench beside his bag. *Shel, no. No! Who… Breathe, man. You're not going to help her if you're panicking.*

His phone began trilling. Not Harry Connick Jr.'s "It Had to be You", Shelly's ringtone. An unknown number with a bland ringtone. The same number as the text. He slowly lifted the phone to his ear.

"I was wondering when you would pick up." An electronically modulated voice rippled across the airwaves. "Shelly's counting on you to be prompt."

Butch gripped his knee. "Who are you, and what do you want? Obviously, you have my wife."

"Who I am doesn't matter. What matters is that she is now on a ledge in a cave wondering when you're going to save her. If you show up at Harper's Cave by six-thirty, maybe you can."

Pain blossomed in five hot spots on his knee. "Why don't I believe that?"

"Believe what you want. But you get yourself here. Time's ticking, Butch. If you're not here by six-thirty, I'll kill her and leave her for the cave critters to eat. Got it? When you arrive, you come in nicely, or she doesn't live to see tomorrow."

"How do I find you? Harper's Cave is big."

"You'll figure it out." With that, silence ruled.

Snatching up his duffel, Butch raced outside as the clock began its countdown in his mind. Harper's Cave. He hadn't hiked there in ages, maybe a few years ago when he went with Victor and Suleiman. It'd creeped him out. Too many ways to get lost and die. As a volunteer with the Coconino County search-and-rescue team, he'd been there that spring when they found the body of a kid who'd gotten lost and died from exposure.

He cringed as he thought about that one. Bad juju for him. The notion of Shelly stuck there terrified him. How long would it take him? If he floored it, less than forty-five minutes. Thanks to his SAR volunteer work, he knew some of the back roads around this area pretty well.

People died all of the time in the caves around northern Arizona. He didn't want Shelly to be one of them. Or him either. Meaning he needed to go in with the proper equipment. He tossed his duffel into the back of the truck's cab, then headed to the Weapons Building, where the team kept everything for the more dangerous jobs Sentry Securities did. He also stored his SAR gear there.

Butch grabbed his backpack from its peg. What would he need? He studied the image on his phone. Shelly seemed to be on some sort of a ledge that had a width of maybe five feet. He needed a coil of rope. Her kidnapper would probably try to take the guideline out, so he'd need some spray paint that wouldn't be visible to the naked eye but would fluoresce in black light. He tossed two cans into the pack and added two black lights with backup batteries. And headlamps with backup batteries. Night vision goggles would be useless in a cave since there was no ambient light. He threw in a couple of harnesses and other climbing gear. And helmets.

Since he faced a kidnapper, he added a pistol. Not his trusty Beretta since it was at the apartment. Nope. A Sig Sauer he'd shot many times. He filled a magazine with rounds and chambered one. He added bullets to another magazine, then snagged a hunting knife from its peg on the wall. Pack in hand, he headed to his truck.

"Butch, hey!"

He barely slowed at Diana's cheery voice.

Dressed in running gear, she must have been headed out for a workout between storms. Her brow knitted as she gazed at him. "What's going on? You look like you're about to kill someone."

"Someone got Shelly."

She cocked her head. "What do you mean?"

"Kidnapped her." He bit off the words. "They want me. Probably want me dead. I've got to get her back."

"Wait for Vic—"

"No time. She dies at 1830 hours. I'll be at Harper's Cave. Tell Vic and bring backup."

Her eyes widened. "Let me go with you."

He shook his head. "Negative. I can't wait. Vic should be back soon. You know where to find me." *And hopefully Shelly as well and not our bodies.* He shook that off. He had to think positive. *Lord, I need Your wisdom here.* "And if you want to do something, you can be in prayer for me."

With that, he swung into the driver's seat and cranked the big engine. His last view of Diana was her standing there, her jaw slack.

He couldn't worry about that. Not now. Not when Shelly's life depended on him.

Saturday, August 31, 2019, 1800 hours MST, Flagstaff, AZ

"Vic! Thank goodness you're back!"

At Diana's frantic call, Victor dismounted from his dripping wet horse and tried not to shiver in the cooler temperature left behind by the storm. "We're fine, Diana. Just got caught—"

"Shelly's in trouble."

That stopped him midsentence. "What do you mean?"

"Someone kidnapped her."

At that, Deborah, who'd ridden with him along with their son and two youngest daughters, gasped. "What happened?"

"I don't know. I don't." The doctor chewed her lower lip. "I saw him bolt out of the Weapons Building with a pack and a coil of rope over his shoulders. Something about Harper's Cave and having to be there by six-thirty or she'd die. Vic, he's going there by himself."

Victor's mind flashed to Harper's Cave. He served with Butch on the volunteer SAR team, had been with him that spring when they'd found the boy. Not good. Not good at all. He turned to his son. "DJ, can you and the girls get the horses taken care of? Rub them down and put our tack in the tack room to dry. Deb, can you get me some dry clothing?"

"On it. DJ, I'll be there in a few minutes." Deborah handed him the reins of her horse and dashed toward the house.

"Diana, get changed," Victor ordered. "I'll do the same."

He rushed to the Weapons Building and began loading his pack. Just as Deborah arrived with a dry pair of cargo pants, T-shirt, and jacket, his phone chimed. He glanced at the number. Unknown. He hesitated. Could be a spam caller. *Answer it.* That command came across so strongly that he looked at Deborah as if she'd spoken. He snatched the phone off a crate where he'd placed it. "Victor Chavez."

"Tank Russell here." An unfamiliar, gravelly voice blared in his ear. "I'm Paul LaRue's security chief."

Victor straightened. "What's going on?"

"We have a situation."

Yeah, you'd better believe we do. "And what is that?"

"I think Roo's headed your way. He told his wife he was coming to my ranch in east Texas for a personal retreat over the weekend. His last phone location shows him near the ranch, but no one who works here has seen him. I thought he was in Destin with his family until his wife called me up frantic because their son broke his arm and she couldn't get ahold of him."

Victor put the phone on speaker and began changing. "In short, he lied to his wife and to you."

"Yeah. He's been all hot under the collar ever since you guys rescued Libby and got back to the States." A low cuss word escaped him. "I should have known he'd pull a stunt like this. I should have! I think hearing that Libby went into hiding sent him over the edge."

"I told her to do that because I figured something like this might happen." Victor ground out his words as his ire rose. "Roo may already be here."

"Why am I not surprised?"

273

Victor told him what little he knew. "You'd best hope I don't get my hands on him."

"You and me both. Mr. Chavez, I'm sorry. This is terrible. My family's dead if certain people find out."

Victor shucked his dripping wet T-shirt and pulled on the dry one. "Makmoud, right?"

"How did you know?"

"An educated guess since he told me you were in Iraq."

"What can I do?"

"Hang tight. I'll keep you posted." Victor disconnected and snatched up his pack.

"I love you." Deborah. He'd completely forgotten she'd been standing there.

He skimmed his fingers down her cheek. "I'm sorry you had to hear that."

She shook her head. "No, no. It was good that I hear. I'll be praying for you."

"Thanks. I'm going to need it." He kissed her and dashed from the building.

He found Diana waiting at his Tundra pickup. She wore a similar outfit and sported her Sig Sauer in a holster at her hip. He swung into the driver's seat. "Let's go. We'll call the sheriff on the way over."

34

Butch's pickup ate up the highway at a steady clip. Thankfully, he knew the area like the back of his hand, which chopped off several minutes. With a hard right, he swung onto a back road that tracked northeast toward Harper's Cave.

One final turn. His truck fishtailed, and he fought to keep it on the road. As he neared the parking lot, the clouds lowered, and the weak light dimmed even further. More storms were moving in. Hopefully none would be severe with torrential downpours because flash flooding could happen. Streams in the area went underground on a regular basis, and they could flood the cave.

He slowed and passed an old Chevy Blazer parked at one of the trailheads. Probably someone hiking in the woods. A fat drop of rain hit his windshield, followed by another. And another. The sporadic drizzle turned into one big, massive downpour. He pulled into the deserted parking lot of Harper's Cave. Not a soul around.

After shrugging into a sweatshirt and a rain jacket, Butch grabbed his pack and rope coil. A quick dash through the downpour. He pressed himself against the wall next to the cave's entrance and listened. Darned rain. It was so heavy he couldn't hear a thing.

He slipped into the cave and crouched to remove his dripping rain jacket. After putting on his headlamp for use later, he placed his gun and hunting knife on his belt and pulled out a can of paint and a black light. Still in a crouch, he shouldered his pack and rope and peered around him. A line of cord led into the blackness ahead of him. At least now, he had a way to get to his destination without turning on his light. With one hand, he grasped it lightly and let it run through his fingers. Occasionally, he paused and sprayed a blotch of paint on the side of the cave. He checked it with his black light. The blotch fluoresced. Good to go if he needed it.

As he made a series of twists and turns, the tunnel shifted slightly downward, and the temperature dropped. An earthy smell filled his freshly healed nose as rain seeped into the cave system with drips that sounded loud in the dead quiet of the passage. Here and there, water echoed as if the subterranean streams that wound through the cave system were already rising. A chill permeated his sweatshirt, and he shivered. The ceiling had to be close to his head, maybe seven or eight feet. He stretched his arm upward. Yep. Best to get there and get Shelly out. And face whoever had taken her.

The line eased downward, and he crouched as he came to the end. Total, absolute, disorienting darkness. He forced himself to take deep, slow breaths as he got a read on where he was. His experience of fighting blind-folded under Sana's tutelage came back to him. He had no sight, but he had every other sense, even smell. He let them all tell him what was going on. Water running, echoing, like where he stood had a high ceiling. His hard breathing in and out, meaning his foe could probably hear him. He quieted it. The temperature remained cold, most likely a consistent mid-forties. He drew in a deep breath through his nose. Earth, for sure. Water over dry dirt creating that organic smell he loved. And another scent. Like a dog, he sampled the air. Sweat and body odor.

The enemy lurked nearby.

Oh so carefully, he slid the coil of rope and his backpack from his shoulders. A few steps to the left revealed a wall. He set the pack down, then drew his gun and listened again. He didn't dare call out for Shelly, didn't want to reveal his position to any ambushers in case her kidnapper had a pal working with him.

He stepped forward.

An electric lantern blazed from across the chamber at the base of the far wall.

Shelf. That's all he had time to think before he spotted the green light from a laser pointed in his direction. He dove to the side, and a bullet gouged the hard rock just behind where he'd stood.

The gun's blast nearly deafened him.

A woman screamed.

Shelly.

"I'm okay," Butch called. His voice bounced against the ceiling. He dashed below the shelf where his attacker held the high ground and pressed himself against the rock at the base . He had to get up there, had to stop him.

The man poked his head over the ledge.

Butch took the shot before his enemy could. Another deafening blast. Another cry from Shelly that faded to whimpers.

No dice for either shooter.

At least he lived.

Like a ghost, he flitted along the base and kept his gun pointed upward. Shadows in the dim light indicated handholds. Probably the way the kidnapper had gone. Butch needed a distraction. Small rocks lay scattered along the floor. Holstering his gun, he grabbed one and hurled it against the far wall with all of his strength.

Scuffling gave away the kidnapper's position. Butch leaped up and grabbed the lip of the shelf ten feet above him. His feet found purchase on the handholds, and he powered himself over the edge.

The masked kidnapper charged him, colliding into him like a linebacker. Even with a shorter and more slender frame than Butch's burly six-four, the force made him stagger. A foot sweep knocked his feet from underneath him. He hit the ground hard. The man pounced and drew back a fist.

Butch jerked to the side.

A cry rewarded him as fist bit into rock.

He rolled to his feet.

The masked man brought up his gun. Butch whipped out a kick that sent it flying to parts unknown. He drew his pistol.

His attacker charged again and drove him against the rock wall behind him. His gun fell to the earth below. Grappling, they spun around. The man dove toward the weapon.

Butch swept off the shelf. It clattered somewhere below.

His opponent grabbed his ankle and yanked. Butch slammed onto the hard earth. Pain shot up his hip. Gritting his teeth, he rolled to his feet and swung a hard right. His attacker ducked, then charged. They collided and spun around.

The man pushed Butch.

He stumbled backward. Nothing but air.

His headlamp went flying as he landed feet first. He heard the crunch, and pain blasted up his leg.

Broken ankle, for sure.

No time to stop. He struggled to stand on his good leg.

Like a big cat, the man landed beside him and rolled to dissipate the energy. He bounced to his feet, then aimed a haymaker at his head.

Butch blocked it and jabbed a hard one at his face. His fist connected with flesh, and the motion sent him to the ground as the man staggered back.

Even with a bum ankle, Butch came to his feet. He leapt at him, this time sending his foe onto his back. Butch landed on top of him. Pain exploded in his jaw, and stars sparked across his vision.

"You're a fool, Cajun Man."

His refined Louisiana accent and Army moniker stunned Butch as effectively as any punch. "Roo? What the…"

A knife blade flashed in the lantern's light. Butch jerked to the side, and the blade bit into the rocky ground. He rolled to the right. "I can't stop you, Roo, but I know someone who can. And will."

Roo grabbed his gun and pulled the trigger. Click.

Jammed.

With a growl, he hurled it at the lantern. Bulls eye. It shattered, throwing everyone into total darkness.

Scuffling feet retreated up the passage and faded to silence. Shelly whimpered. "Butch! Butch!"

"Y-yeah. Oohhhh." Thanks to dwindling adrenaline, his ankle began throbbing. He didn't even want to look at it, didn't want to contemplate that Roo had left them to die in the chamber's darkness. "Busted ankle."

"Help me. Please!"

"Hold on, Shel." The darkness was quickly disorienting him. A roaring noise began filling the room. He shut it out and tried to reorient himself. He'd been facing the room's entrance when Roo destroyed the lantern. His pack would be to his two o'clock.

He attempted to stand. Raging pain shot up his leg. Blast it. No good. He lowered himself to his knees and crawled toward the wall. His hands found his pack, and by touch he located the cold, hard barrel of one of the flashlights he'd brought. He turned it on and set it on its end.

Roo had taken the guideline with him. Smart on his part. Butch began shivering as his body registered just how cold it really was. He located his pistol and shoved it into its holster.

"Butch, help me. Get me out of here!" Shelly's voice trembled. Reality slammed into him. Flagstaff had been warm that day, and when he'd left her that morning, she'd only been wearing shorts, a tank top, and sandals.

"I'm coming, babe." Dragging the pack with him, he crawled closer and found his headlamp. He stuffed it on his head. "Where are you?"

"Here!" It sounded like her voice came from his eleven o'clock. With his headlamp burning, he headed toward a gaping hole between the room and a tunnel. Shelly huddled ten feet below on a ledge five feet wide. Blackness yawned as if she could fall to the center of the earth. Water thundered as one of the subterranean rivers began rising from the storm. He had maybe minutes before it flooded the entire room. Already, the ground trembled beneath him from its force. Cracks began appearing at the edges of the ledge. Not much time before it sheared off and fell, taking her with it.

Butch located his coil of climbing rope, grabbed a carabiner, and tied a knot around it. After securing a harness to it, he eased to the chasm's edge. "I'm dropping you a rope with a harness. Get into it, and I'll pull you up."

Small rocks tinkled. Then a larger one.

"Butch, it's breaking." Panic edged her voice.

"I know, babe. Here." He tossed the harness over. "Get into it. You remember how, right?"

"Y-yeah."

He peered around him. No place to tie it off. He'd have to use his own weight as a base. "Hold on. I've got to back up to anchor you."

He wormed his way backward.

"Butch!" She cried out again. "It's breaking off!"

He wrapped the cord several times around his hips. "I'm going to start pulling you—"

"The ledge!" She screamed, and the rope jerked tight.

As he took her full weight, he slid several feet toward the lip.

He jammed both feet into the ground and dug his heels in enough to stop. Pain exploded in his injured ankle. He gritted his teeth against the agony. "I... I got you, Shel. I need your help. Find any handhold and foothold you can 'cause I can't pull you up like this."

He lay as flat as he could to keep his center of gravity low. The tension lessened a little. "Shel?"

"I-I found something."

"I'm gonna start pulling." Hand over hand he pulled and took on her one hundred-forty-five-pound frame. "Help me, babe."

"I'm trying." That came out with a sob.

Groans escaped him as the pain amped up. He began panting to relieve it. Five feet. Six. Seven. He couldn't count on his injured ankle lasting. "Shel... try to... grab the edge."

His ankle gave way. He began sliding closer.

"Got it."

Just a little more. He pulled enough for her to get her arms over.

With one last, superhuman effort, he grasped her right hand and yanked backward as hard as he could.

Shelly came all the way up and scrambled on top of him, away from the ledge. Her leg hit his ankle. She rolled off him.

Butch roared to release the pain. Using his elbows, he crawled to her, then collapsed completely as his chest heaved. "I… my ankle."

She rested her head on his chest, and for a few seconds, they lay there quietly and listened to the river. "Butch, what happened?"

"Busted my ankle," he replied through gritted teeth. He sat up, then made his way to the chasm. Already, the water consumed the remains of the shelf where Shelly had stood. "We've got to get out of here 'cause this room's going to flood. Can you stand?"

"Y-yeah."

"My pack. Against the wall." Butch climbed to his knees.

She scrambled to her feet. "Found it."

"Get out the black light." He yelped when he tried to put weight on his injured leg. No way could he get to his feet without her. "Help me up."

She slung his pack over her shoulders, then helped him stand. She stumbled under his weight but steadied.

"He took the guideline." Butch grunted. For the first time, he noticed she didn't wear her glasses. "I'm not even going to ask what happened."

"Later. First, let's get out of here. Take the light because I can hardly see anything." At least her voice steadied, and some confidence returned. They hobbled into the cave's passages. The paint marks glowed green in the purple light. "You're such a smart man, Butch."

"I try." He focused on finding the next mark. And the next. Mark by mark, they made their way toward the entrance. Good thing too because the pain had gone DEFCON 1 on him. He wanted to yowl to relieve it. He settled for loud groans that sounded like a Wookie. Beneath his fingers, Shelly shivered uncontrollably.

"There!" she cried.

A faint point of light up ahead. The entrance. More pinpricks shone.

"Butch?" Victor called.

"Praise God, boss." Rescue was near, and Butch began shaking.

"S-s-stay with me," Shelly begged through chattering teeth.

Feet ran toward them, and moments later, Victor, Diana, and members of the sheriff's SAR team gathered around him.

Shelly eased him to a sitting position against one of the walls. She crouched in front of him, and her teeth chattered. "Boss, Shel's hypothermic."

"We've got the both of you."

Diana took off her sweatshirt. "Put this on, Shelly."

"Litter's here," one of the SAR guys called.

"Just a few minutes more, Butch. Hang in there." Victor helped him roll onto the litter.

As it lifted, Butch raised a hand. "Lemme kiss my bride."

She bent toward him. Cupping her face in his hands, he slowly kissed her, which drew relieved laughter and some applause from the SAR team. "I love you, babe. Forever and ever, amen."

35

"I can't believe it! I just can't believe it!" Roo swore aloud as he roared down the highway at close to a hundred in the Chevy Blazer. Heavy metal blasted from the speakers, and he pounded out his frustration against the steering wheel. He had to get out of the area. Boost another car and keep pushing toward the Dallas-Fort Worth airport.

Things had started out so well. Shelly went down easily. He just hadn't counted on Cajun Man's tenacity. Roo's jaw hurt. His hand throbbed where he'd made hard contact with the rock of the shelf in Harper's Cave. Thankfully, nothing seemed broken. Cajun Man's words rang in his ears like an out-of-control gong. *"I can't stop you, Roo. But I know someone who can and will."*

No way could Cajun Man identify his attacker. At least not positively. All Cajun Man had was one sentence to go on and a whole lot of pain from his busted ankle to blur any certainty. Roo hadn't meant to blurt anything in his own Louisiana accent. He cussed again. Time to get back to New Orleans. And find some way to spin this so people could indeed place him at the ranch.

Tank would take care of that. Using the other burner phone, he dialed the number of his enforcer. When he answered, Roo spent the next ten minutes describing everything. He had to hand it to Tank. The man chewed him out like he'd done during his Army days, but he didn't threaten him, didn't question him. He'd probably grown used to Roo's requests over the past few years, no matter how ludicrous. Like killing the other skeleton in Roo's closet. Tank's voice remained deadly calm, even through the butt chewing. But Roo knew he'd stretched his friend's generosity to the limit, maybe even gone beyond.

Tank growled, "You'd best get your butt back to the ranch so at least some people can have an eyewitness sighting of you. Understand?"

"I'll be there first thing tomorrow morning."

"We'll talk more then."

"See you then."

Silence answered him.

Roo tossed his phone into the slot beneath the stereo and gripped the wheel tighter. His foolishness had nearly cost him everything. Darkness was complete, and he squinted through the windshield as he focused on his driving. Sixteen hours to go in a miserable drive. If he were lucky, he'd be there by mid morning.

Eight turned over to nine, and dark became as dark is it could be in the desert on a rainy night. Roo stopped for gas, then pressed onward. Energy drinks wired him. Coffee fired him. But exhaustion pressed so close he feared he was losing his mind. It took him just a few minutes at a truck stop to steal a Toyota Tacoma, switch the license plates a few times to slow any investigation, and get back on the road. Somewhere in there, he crossed from Arizona into New Mexico and made it past Albuquerque.

His encounter with the old hag the year before replayed itself in his mind like it was stuck in an endless do-loop. In the inky darkness, she stood in the middle of the highway and stared at him as she raised a bony finger and shook it. *"I know who you are, Paul LaRue. Who your family is. A curse be upon you for what your ancestors did! And you will pay the price for that and your own sins."* He jerked the wheel to the right to avoid hitting her.

A loud noise brought him back to the present. He was going off the road. Immediately he came wide awake and took his foot off the accelerator. He stopped, jumped out, and ran around the truck, looking frantically for the old woman or at least her body. No one there. No one at all. Just him and the coyotes. Bracing his hands against the side of the Tacoma, he groaned.

He was too close to losing it.

Roo turned with his back to the passenger door and rested his head against the window. Gradually, he calmed. He couldn't lose his mind. Not now. He was too close.

Time to finish his drive. Somehow, he made it through the rest of the night. As the sun rose, he pulled into a gas station around the New Mexico/Texas border and gassed up with the engine still running. More energy bars and drinks fueled him. That got him to Dallas, where he made the exchange with the Cayenne, then to Tank's ranch. He punched in the gate code and rumbled down the road to the expansive ranch house where Tank and his wife lived.

Though it was Sunday morning, guards armed in flak jackets and rifles walked the property. In the years he'd visited the ranch, he'd never seen patrols like that. Makmoud Hidari's threat must have put a scare in Tank. Roo swallowed and dragged his palms along the fabric of his pants. Chills shimmied up and down his spine. Was Tank going to kill him? When they'd talked on the phone the night before, he'd sensed the rage building in the man's carefully controlled words.

Tank, dressed in khaki cargo pants, black T-shirt, and bullet-proof vest, stepped from the open garage. His face remained expressionless.

Hope rose inside of Roo. Maybe things would be okay.

Tank yanked open the driver's door. "Get out. Now."

Or not.

Adrenaline electrified Roo as he climbed from the SUV. "I can explain."

"And I'm done listening." Tank clipped him on the jaw and sent him into the dust. Roo tried to rise, but he pushed him back into the dirt with his foot. "You lied to me. Lied to your wife. And put the heads of me and my family on the chopping block. Right now, my wife, kids, and grandkids are on their way to an all-expense-paid trip to Hawaii to get them out of harm's way. And guess what? You're going to pay for it. Was it worth it?

Was it really worth it?"

Roo laid his head against the ground. No. He hadn't succeeded. Not by a long shot.

Tank clasped his hands behind his back and paced. "Get up."

"I'm sorry, Tank. I erred."

"Severely so. You broke my trust. Lord knows what you did to your marriage. That's not for me to say." He paused at the end of his track and narrowed his eyes. "You can work that one out. I let Tina know you were coming here first. And I've already contacted the Swamp Rat. He'll spin this that you indeed needed some downtime. You tried bull riding here and it didn't go well for you and resulted in that nice shiner you have. But guess what? I'm done. I'll see you through this election and to the end of the year, but as of the New Year, you need to find yourself a new security chief." He bit those words off in a gruff tone he'd never used with Roo. "Of course, if you get your way, it won't matter because the State of Louisiana will have things in hand."

"Th-thank you." Roo stuck out his hand.

Tank ignored it. "Go get some sleep. And in the meantime, I've got to figure out how to tell Makmoud I never encouraged you to go awry with your harebrained scheme."

36

Friday, September 10, 2019, 1900 hours MST, Flagstaff, AZ

Home. Nothing like it. At least in Butch's mind. Especially since he
was down to taking only one painkiller at night to help him sleep. The doc
had inserted some plates and screws to repair his ankle. The pills held him
in a fog, and during his more lucid moments, he wondered if he'd ever
walk again, let alone run. For the first time in a long time, depression tried
to wrap its tentacles around him, despite the doc's hopeful words and
Shelly's comforting presence. He could only hope things would look up
soon.

"Probably in the spring," his doc had told him the week before as he
drafted the release orders from the hospital. "You stick to the physical
therapy I've prescribed, and I promise you'll get there."

He would. Ten years in the Army had taught him the discipline he'd
use to make a comeback. Then discouragement slammed into him. He'd
just recovered from being shot when he busted his ankle. *Lord, You've got
this. I need to leave it in Your hands where it belongs.*

Now, from his position on the couch, he stared at CNN as the news
rolled out of Louisiana. Far from damaging his campaign, Roo had taken
on a new persona, that of the rugged former Special Forces officer. Including leaving stubble on his face and discarding the tie that had been the

hallmark of his campaign before. The spin worked because the shift had thrown his opponent off balance. Now the other man seemed stuffy, out of touch, compared to Roo. But something was off. Tina LaRue hadn't been seen since before Labor Day. He barely spoke of her. Roo used the excuse that one of their kids had wound up in the hospital with a broken arm. Could be true, but there had to be more to it. Butch noticed a wild-eyed look too, one that most people didn't seem to care about, if he'd read the poll results right. Roo had pulled ahead by ten percent. Pundits proclaimed him the winner of the election one month ahead of time. But things could change, and maybe his opponent could stage a comeback.

No one knew the truth. Would it matter even if they did? *Things can change. They can really change. Justice will prevail. Somehow.* Butch rubbed a hand over his face. Constantly watching the news was so not good for his mental health. He muted the television, laid his head against the cushion, and listened.

Fingers tapped on a keyboard as Shelly worked in her study. She hummed softly, a trait he found endearing. She'd been working almost nonstop for the past week. At first, he hadn't cared since he'd been dosed up on painkillers after his surgery. Now, he missed his wife. "Shel?"

The noise ceased. Footsteps padded down the hall. "Do you need anything?"

He tried what he hoped was a beguiling grin. "You?"

Pink tinged her cheeks where only faint traces of a bruise remained. "I'm sorry. I'm just"—her gaze shot to the study— "trying to finish up something for Vic. Give me half an hour?"

"Sure." Not really, but hey, he'd cope, just like he always did. Again, the dark tendrils of sadness crept into the edges of his psyche. Until he remembered the way Shelly had stayed so close to him when they slept. And when she wasn't working, she curled up on the couch beside him. She wasn't angry with him, for sure. "Since you're here, can you grab me a water?"

"Coming right up." Water swished into a glass, and she set it within his reach on the coffee table. She leaned down and kissed him, lingering on his lips.

He wrapped his hand behind her neck and murmured against her mouth, "Don't stop."

Giggling, she pulled back. "I love you. I'll be there in a few."

Once she resumed her work, he bit back his sigh and shifted from DirecTV to Roku. He found the YouTube channel, then a set of fail videos. Good enough for now. He yawned. Thanks to his surgery and meds, his sleep schedule was off. It was only 1930 hours, and he already wanted the warmth of bed with Shelly beside him. Again, he yawned like a lion and closed his eyes, then dozed.

The doorbell rang. He cracked his eyes open. Outside, nothing but dark, like the sun had set hours ago. A lamp glowed on the side table at the far end of the sofa. He glanced at his phone. 2000 hours, so he hadn't been out for long. Not wanting to be fully awake, he pulled a fleece blanket over his face.

"Vic, hey!"

Huh? Victor was here? He pushed up on his elbows, then swung upright so his ankle in its hard cast rested on the coffee table.

"Boss, hey," he said as Victor strolled into the living room and shucked his fleece pullover. He left it on a bar stool and flopped into one of their comfy chairs.

"I thought I'd come by and visit before Deb and I head out tomorrow. You're looking better."

"Hah. I'm down to one painkiller. Doc said no weight on the foot for six weeks, so I got me a knee scooter." He nodded toward the scooter in the corner. "Then I can put weight on it. Then comes PT for who knows how long. He did say by spring I can probably run again." Butch's mind finally registered what his friend had said. "Where are you going?"

Shelly joined them and curled up in a circular chair.

"Cabo San Lucas. Deb's been wanting to go down there, and I scored a good long-weekend deal. Down tomorrow, back on Tuesday. Sana and Suleiman have the kids."

"I don't blame you." Butch rubbed his eyes. "Sorry. My days and nights are kind of messed up right now."

"Understandable." With his brow furrowed, Victor studied the floor before lifting his gaze. "Have you been following the election in Louisiana?"

Butch turned the television off. "Roo's gonna win. But I tell you. Something's off with him. And it may not be any good."

"Yeah, probably." Victor fixed him in his dark gaze. "I'm still trying to figure out why you declined to file a criminal complaint against him."

Butch shrugged. "With what evidence? Neither Shel nor I saw his face. He spoke only once in an accent I would recognize. And I was in agony at the time. She couldn't say for sure he was the guy who kidnapped her. How's that for an eye witness statement? Not to mention, there wasn't any forensic evidence. Not much of a case, if I remember the prosecutor correctly."

"What about the bruising he showed after getting back onto the campaign trail?"

"What did he say? Something like he'd gotten thrown by a bull on his supposed 'retreat.'" Butch jabbed his fingers in air quotes. "The press ate it up. But it does seem strange that his wife hasn't been seen in like ten days." He tossed the remote onto the coffee table. It clattered and slid off the edge. "According to the DA, if I tried it in the media by calling in tips about what happened in 2009, I'd have my life taken apart. Libby's too. I don't want to go through that, and I wouldn't put her through it either."

Victor leaned down and placed the remote on the dark wood. "You hear from her?"

"Shel called her to let her know what happened. She and her family are staying in Colorado until Thanksgiving, then returning to Birmingham. I guess they're scared. I would be too. But the good news is she and Jace are getting some good time together. She's moving to Colorado Springs in January."

"Amen." Victor nodded his approval. "I hope this ends well for the both of them."

"Me too." Butch cleared his throat. "But yeah, I've thought about calling the cops on him. Prayed about it. God's saying have mercy." He glanced Shelly's way. "I guess my bride is rubbing off on me."

"Or you on me," she replied with a small smile. It dimmed as she held out a thumb drive. "Vic, here's what you requested. Goodness knows, there's nothing admissible on it."

He took it and turned it over and over in his hands. He stared at it as if it held the secret to world peace. "Doesn't have to be."

"Boss, what's going on?"

Victor stared into the darkness beyond the balcony, then sighed as he refocused on his friends. "I haven't forgotten what happened in Iraq. It was a conditional release, remember?"

A coyote howled, followed by another of its buddies answering somewhere farther away. A lost, lonely sound. At points in his life, Butch had empathized. He shivered as he remembered Makmoud's words. "This is going to our friend?"

"Exactly. All I'm going to do is turn it over to him while we're away. What happens after that," Victor held up his hands, "is not up to me."

"Let me put it this way. What do you hope to happen?"

A grim smile crossed his face. "Justice."

37

Sunset Resort in Cabo San Lucas, Mexico. A good deal on a long week-end away for him and Deborah. Too bad it came with a task Victor had to complete if he didn't want to look over his shoulder for the rest of his life. The thumb drive he'd taken from Shelly two nights before sat in the suite's safe beside Deborah's diamond wedding set, where it would remain until he made contact with Makmoud. What was stored on it could, at best, get him into hot water with the CIA. At worst, it could get him killed.

He and Deborah had spent the afternoon sunning themselves on the beach and eating lunch at the resort's beachside restaurant. Now, he yawned long and loud as they walked hand in hand toward their suite.

Deborah shot him a look, one of those reproachful yet teasing ones that made him dream of time with her before a long nap. Of course, he could sleep in tomorrow since they weren't flying back until Tuesday.

They strolled into the open-air lobby toward the stairs that would lead to their suite.

"Señor Chavez!" the man at the front desk called.

Victor angled toward him. "That's me. What's up?"

The clerk held up a business envelope with Victor's name on it in block letters. "A gentleman left this message for you. He said to give it directly to you."

Victor went on high alert. With what he was sure was a fake smile, he took it. "Thanks. I appreciate it."

Time to get to his room before he revealed just how stressed he'd become in the span of a few seconds. He ushered Deborah inside, then locked the door and activated the security lock.

"What is it?" Deborah asked.

"A message from our friend." Only then did he open it and pull out the paper. Plain old copy paper. Scrawled handwriting, as if the man had been in a hurry.

Sunset Bar tonight at 5:30. I will find you. Send your wife shopping during that time. MH.

Finally time. Could he trust Makmoud on this? He had to. The man had set them free with the one condition that he hand over intelligence on Roo. The thought made Victor almost sick.

"Makmoud?" Deborah's voice was barely above a whisper.

"Yeah." He ripped the note to tiny pieces, then flushed them down the toilet. He'd swept for bugs when they'd first arrived, and for paranoia's sake, he did another fast one. Nothing. His attempt at a smile failed. "Want to do some shopping?"

She stared. "Tonight?"

"He wants to meet me at the bar alone. Besides, I don't think you'd react well if you met the man who nearly killed you five years ago and threatened to take the kids into bondage."

She harumphed and lifted her chin. "I think I'll do some retail therapy, then."

While under the hot stream of a shower, Victor considered the man who'd nearly spelled their end just weeks ago. He was cool. Calculating. Pragmatic to the nth degree. He'd been in their debt because Butch had saved his life. But that had come with one condition—providing information that would surely sign Roo's death warrant.

At the thought, nausea tinged Victor's gut. *But remember, too, that you have your freedom. If you'd refused to turn over information about Roo, where would that leave you?* Too well he knew where. Somewhere in a cell in Iran as he and the team were slowly but surely broken and probably executed or turned into traitors. If he backed out now, Makmoud would pick off his team and family one by one. Of that, he had no doubt. Maybe he'd made a deal with the devil.

Until he remembered a devil of a different variety.

"Lord, I don't like this," Victor whispered as the hot stream of the water poured over him. He turned off the taps, dried, and dressed in a pair of khakis and a white linen shirt, leaving the tails out. He knelt in front of the safe and paused. Just above a whisper, he continued his prayer from the shower. "I struggle. He set us free, but I know what will happen. I know You're a God of mercy, but You're also a God of justice. Give me peace about this." With that, he pulled the thumb drive from the safe. He slid it into his shirt pocket and made sure it didn't leave an outline. His credit card for the evening concealed it. He tucked his phone into his front pants pocket.

"Are we doing the right thing?" Deborah's question came from the doorway.

"I'm not sure," Victor took her in his arms and ran his hands down her back. His fingertips caressed skin left bare by the sundress she wore. He inhaled her scent, something he'd worried weeks before he would never smell again. Gardenia mixed with lavender. In the past few weeks, he'd learned to treasure it. From beyond the balcony, the sun's rays nearly blinded him. "We honestly have no choice."

He'd read her fully into what had happened, which left her pale and shaken when she fully understood just how close she'd come to losing her husband. She pulled back and ran her fingers down his jaw. "So we're doing the wrong thing?"

He nuzzled her hair. "I don't know. I've struggled so much with this. Then I remember Butch and Shelly. And that Butch may or may not be able to walk without a limp, let alone run. Roo ordered Libby's kidnapping and sold us out to Makmoud. We nearly lost everything, and I can't abide by a man like him potentially being in a position of significant power. I just can't."

She rested her head on his shoulder, and her arms tightened around him. "So really, we're doing 'the thing'."

He smiled against her hair, then tipped her chin and kissed her. "I guess that's a way to look at it. I've prayed hard about this. I'm still not sure of the right answer, and it bothers me. Let the chips fall where they may, I guess. Let's go."

He held tightly to her hand as they strolled from their suite to the courtyard of the sprawling resort. It had its own shopping area with stores ringing a plaza containing several fountains and a large restaurant with outdoor seating for patrons of the resort.

Most people around them were buying drinks and taking them onto the beach to watch the sun set. Deborah kissed him. He slid onto a stool at the end of the oval bar so he had a view of both the beach and the courtyard, then waved the bartender over and ordered a margarita. Would he recognize Makmoud? Probably not. The man was an expert in disguises. And he was high on the most-wanted list of the CIA. Mexico bordered the United States and was rife with drug problems. CIA, DEA, and a host of other federal agencies had a tight eye on Cabo. But then again, so did the cartels. That worried him. What if Makmoud had other plans for him? At least they were in a public place. Not a dark alley, thank goodness.

The sun began its final drop toward the ocean. More people arrived at the bar, and the remaining chairs filled up. A woman and her boyfriend sat to his right so they faced the ocean. They flirted so much he wanted to shout at them to get a room. To his left, a man in khaki cargo pants and a Hawaiian shirt of bright blues and yellows slid onto a chair. His hair was long, gray, and thick, like his beard, and wrinkles adorned his eyes and brow. Clearly, he'd lived his life in the sun. A bush hat sat on his head. He ordered a drink, chips, and salsa in a crackly voice. Victor had seen him earlier that day while he and Deborah sunned themselves on the beach. The guy had strolled up and down the sand with a metal detector. Occasionally, he'd dug for metal trinkets and come up with nothing. A few minutes later, the bartender delivered the man's piña colada, a basket of chips, and bowls of salsa and guacamole. He munched on the chips, every few seconds dipping one one of the bowls.

More people pressed themselves between the two men to buy drinks.

Victor fiddled with his phone on the bar. A text flashed up from Anna, his oldest daughter and a sophomore in college in North Carolina, regarding his upcoming trip to the region for work. He thumbed out his answer, telling her he and her mom were flying back to Flagstaff from Cabo on Tuesday. A green smiley emoticon flashed up. He chuckled, then raised his gaze.

No more sun. As dusk rapidly filled the air, people wandered toward the restaurant and shopping area. Over half an hour had passed, and he began fidgeting. He was used to this game, had played it here and there in his work with the Secret Service and Special Forces. That didn't make the waiting any easier. He texted Deborah. Having fun yet?

Her answer came seconds later. Of course. Let me loose to shop, and I do. Getting a table for supper. You coming soon? He thought he caught a glimpse of her coming out of a women's clothing store with a couple of bags looped over her arms.

"Cha-ching," the beachcomber beside him commented. "I see your wife took my suggestion to heart."

It took all of Victor's self-control not to react. He shifted. The man faced him. He lowered the black-framed glasses he wore. Intelligent brown eyes peered at him. Makmoud slid the glasses back in place. "Good to see you, my friend. And no worries. I've had this area under surveillance almost all day. No CIA. No *Quds* either. You have what I need, I hope."

"I do."

Makmoud glanced toward his napkin, which lay crumpled by the basket of chips. "Slide it under there, if you would."

As he raised his hand for the check, Victor slipped both thumb drive and credit card from his shirt pocket. Once the bartender had turned his back to ring it up, he laid the card on the teak and deftly slid the drive under the napkin.

"It's good to see you still have your tradecraft," Makmoud murmured.

Like he'd forget it? Victor smarted at that remark and tamped down his reaction. "I do have one thing to tell you. It's important because you probably heard about what happened to Butch and Shelly."

"I did." The man made a tsking sound. "I warned Tank."

297

"Call off your dogs."

Makmoud's eyes narrowed.

"Tank called me and warned me that Roo was on the way to Flagstaff. Thing was, Roo got there faster than anyone thought possible. Tank was terrified you would take out him and his family."

"I see."

"Please, spare them. He did his part."

"If you wish, then I will do so."

It clicked in Victor's mind. He cocked his head as he took another sip of margarita. "You said there were no *Quds* here. Normally, you'd have at least one person watching you to ensure I didn't harm you. Has something happened?"

"Jibril is hard to hide, no? Like a camel behind a palm." That came in an even tone. Then he shifted his piña colada on the bar so it left a trail of wetness behind. "But I jest when I shouldn't. I am no longer an agent with them. It's hard for a *persona non grata* to be so."

Victor gave up and stared at him.

Makmoud nodded toward his drink. "Drink your margarita before all of the ice melts."

Victor forced himself to focus on it. He took more of a gulp than a sip. "Care to share?"

"General Soleimani did not take kindly to my decision to set you free." Only then did Makmoud's lips turn downward. "It was costly."

Victor's heart clenched. "Your wife."

"The general had our marriage annulled, and Jibril took her as his wife. And yes, there is now a price on my head."

Dizziness assailed Victor. The drink he'd almost sucked down or a reaction to the news? "I'm sorry to hear that."

Could he say anything dumber?

"It was worth it, my friend."

Victor shot him a sideways glance. "You'll be okay?"

A shrug answered him. "Perhaps. Perhaps not. I have funds. And," then came a small smile, "Central America isn't so bad. I still have some contacts I trust within *Quds*. But yes, there is a bounty on my head now from my government as well as yours." Makmoud dabbed his lips with his napkin and tossed a wad of pesos onto the bar. No doubt he stashed the thumb drive somewhere. "Enough of that. Your wife is waiting on you. Hug her and kiss her and treasure her."

"Always."

Makmoud gazed at him for a long moment. "Never take her for granted."

Not now. "I won't. Godspeed, friend. Take care of yourself."

"You do the same." With that, Makmoud slipped into the crowds now spilling onto the plaza.

Victor watched him for a long moment, his heart heavy and light at the same time.

38

The motorboat Makmoud piloted eased from a throaty roar to a purr as he puttered through the No Wake Zone of Hurricane Bay on St. John. To ordinary passersby watching from the docks, he looked like a man arriving at the luxurious island to spend the night with a friend. Fine by him. Let everyone believe the lie. It made his job that night all the easier.

Though he'd become a pariah among *Quds*, he still had contacts he trusted in the Western Hemisphere, those who had believed in him for the past fifteen years and stood by him even when things in Venezuela went disastrously wrong in 2014, after his failed attempt to capture the Shadow Box team. He called them the Network. One of them had been glad to provide everything he needed for tonight's venture, including an agent, at no charge.

Loyal contacts. A man of his lowly stature needed those, and he would reward his man well, if and when he made it back to his hideout in Panama. He eased into a vacant birth. No one paid him any mind, and if they did, his dyed black hair, clean-shaven face, and contacts tinting his eyes a deep blue wouldn't paint him as Makmoud Hidari, man on the run, but as a Brit named Devin Miles, who had motored from the British Virgin Islands for an evening of dining with a lady friend.

Said lady friend was really a *Quds* agent with the Network who his contact trusted. She spent her time on the Grand Cayman Island masquerading as a jeweler. Her job allowed her to travel freely among the Caribbean Islands and Central America, and she did so with great pleasure, sometimes for her covert capacity but much of the time as a woman who loved sunning herself on some of the most beautiful beaches in the world.

As he tied up to the dock at the marina in Coral Bay on the eastern side of St. John, she waved from one of the docks and approached. "I was told to expect you, Mr. Miles. I'm Ariana," she called in a perfect British accent. "You are well regarded by my friend, even though you have somewhat of a rakish reputation among your peers."

"I'm simply misunderstood."

That garnered a laugh. "He also said you had quite a sense of humor." She lowered her chin and softly added, "Not all of us are fans of the general. Do keep that in mind. The Network is willing to help you as we can." Glancing upward, she added in a louder voice, "Toss me that stern line. I'll tie you up."

A US Customs officer approached, and Makmoud handed over his passport to match his cover identity. The man handed it back after inspecting it. "Enjoy your evening, sir."

Once he'd walked away, Ariana quietly asked, "What can I do to help?"

"Dine with me?" he asked with a charming smile. "I have someone I want to investigate. And be my eyes and ears later."

"I wish I could, but I have a date."

He stiffened and clenched his jaw. She was here to work, not play.

She added, "With one Paul LaRue, who's now calling himself James Shore."

Annoyance shifted to pleasure. She was already on the job. Makmoud lifted a black backpack from the boat, paid the attendant a night's rent for the slip, and laced his fingers through hers as if he were indeed here for a date.

Ariana led him to a Toyota 4Runner. "I got this on St. Thomas as my rental. Far easier, though slower, to rent from there than wrangle with getting from the airport to the ferry terminal via taxi."

"How long have you been on-island?" Makmoud asked.

"Since Saturday. A long weekend in the sun was nice and much needed. I'll leave tomorrow evening for St. Thomas."

He nodded. Good tactics. Use a vacation as a cover for her other job. She knew what she was doing. "So, you've been tracking my target?"

The smile drained from her tanned face. "It seems without his wife, he's quite the player, as if in his alternate reality, he's single. I spent Saturday night flirting with him."

Not surprising. Once more, the pollsters and pundits got it wrong. Paul LaRue hadn't won his election in October with the expected wide margin because his opponent rallied at the last minute. Instead, he'd narrowly squeaked by as a winner. That forced a runoff the week before, which he won with a higher percentage. Once he declared he needed some downtime on his own to decompress after winning the election on the sixteenth, Governor-elect LaRue had left on Thursday, the twenty-first, for another supposed retreat at Tank Russell's ranch before he and his family headed to St. John for ten days at a luxury villa. Thanks to Shelly's information, Makmoud knew better. He also knew all about his target, including a critical fact: he had a tell that would confirm his identity despite his poor attempt to change his appearance. It also seemed like the governor-elect had begun looking at other women a little too much.

He fought a lip curl at the thought.

"Devin?"

"So sorry. I was thinking. Do you know where he will be?"

She offered a devilish smile and a small eye roll as if he'd forgotten her earlier statement. "I'm having supper with him, remember? I'll be wearing a wire, so no worries. You'll hear everything."

"Too bad we never could have worked together."

Her smile turned daring. "Oh, but we are. Now let's head into Cruz Bay. Hold on because we have a bit of a drive."

On the trip to the other side of the island, she filled him in on what she'd learned from her time flirting with Governor-elect LaRue, also known as James Shore. He wasn't stable. Not really. Full of himself. Thinking of himself as a man of great prowess. He'd even tried to coax her to his villa, something that was a new characteristic of the man. Reckless. Her instinct had told her no, not to go. At least not yet.

They were meeting at an outdoor restaurant in one of the shopping districts of Cruz Bay that overlooked the sea and the sunset that would happen within minutes. Makmoud did a coms check with Ariana. Then she sashayed ahead of him.

He drank in her figure in khaki linen slacks, high heels, and sleeveless white blouse. Combine that with her flawless olive skin, dancing dark eyes, and straight black hair cut to just beneath her chin, and she painted a pretty picture, one he would have wanted to pursue if his heart weren't so raw from the untimely demise of his marriage. He shook himself. Time to focus solely on work.

He wandered into the restaurant and found her sitting at a table for two with the other chair empty. Had Roo gotten wise to him and turned her? Most likely not. Ariana gave away no tells that her intentions were less than honorable. Instead, the man was probably running late, another recent characteristic that had appeared in him since the end of August. As if his newly found power allowed him to be so imperious. Makmoud sneered at the notion.

He ordered a mojito and waited.

A few minutes later, Roo strutted through the gate.

Makmoud fought the urge to laugh. The man screamed tourist in the worst way, what with his loud Hawaiian shirt, Bermuda shorts, and baseball cap. His hair had grown out and showed a bit of curl bleached nearly white from a bad peroxide job, and his feet sported Birkenstocks. Like he feared someone would spot him. No one paid him a bit of attention. Makmoud noted Tank Russell a few paces behind.

When the security chief settled beside him at the bar, Makmoud carefully waited for any signs of recognition. None. Makmoud's disguise worked well. And he was out of context because Tank wouldn't expect him to stalk his target so closely. Perfect for his warning.

Ariana greeted Roo with a smile and a kiss on the cheek. As they settled in to chat and order their drinks and food, Makmoud received his tuna steak. He studied Tank in the mirror below the televisions. Over the next few minutes, he showed no interest. Makmoud finished off his plate and gathered his knife in his hand in case he needed it.

Here went nothing.

Makmoud took a deep breath. "We meet again, Tank Russell."

Tank started. He stared.

"Not so obvious, my friend. I mean no harm," Makmoud added quietly.

"Why should I believe you?"

"Victor Chavez told me what happened. I mean you no harm. Now your principal there…"

"He was reckless. I had no way to control him."

"I understand." Makmoud carefully listened through his earpiece to the patter of conversation at the table. It seemed that once more, Roo invited Ariana back to his villa. This time, she seemed interested. His curiosity piqued. She had something planned. He shoved his clean plate away. "And I will give you a chance to show you are genuine in your intent. How many of your men are with you?"

"Three others for a total detail of four. They're scattered around the restaurant."

Makmoud called to the bartender for a rum and Coke. "Then this is what you do. When you return to the villa, you will quietly pull your detail back because Roo told all of you to stand down and to take a night on the town. You do that, and I will know you were honest regarding your warning to Victor Chavez. If you don't, I have a contact in place who will take care of you. Am I clear?"

A sharp nod answered him.

"Then good."

They said not a word as Tank finished off his meal. Or tried to. He left half of the eight-ounce steak. At the table for two, Ariana thanked Roo for the meal. He leaned forward and whispered something in her ear before dropping a quick kiss on her cheek. He paid in cash, most likely to protect his credit card from any untoward charges—like a meal for two when his wife wasn't there. The man dabbed his lips, then folded his cloth napkin first into a larger triangle, then a smaller one, before laying it on his plate.

Confirmation since Shelly had noted that quirk in the information she'd provided.

Makmoud paid his bill in cash, then peered at Tank one last time. "Just until midnight. Give your men the night off. They deserve it, after all, because they've worked so hard during the campaign. Tell them the governor-elect will be safe since he's at the villa. Then leave him to me."

Tank nodded.

Makmoud slipped into the shadows. Ariana had given him the keys to the SUV. Once behind the darkened windows in the back of the 4Runner, he quickly changed from the trousers and white shirt he'd worn to the island to night camo. He used a mirror and applied camouflage makeup to his face, then tapped out a message to her. Time for the next phase, my friend.

A few minutes later, the front door opened. "Devin?"

"In the backseat. Just so I don't scare you."

She slid into the front seat. "I have a surprise for you."

Maybe he'd misread her. His hand curled around the grip of his pistol. "And that would be?"

Paper ripped off a pad. She handed it back. "Something you may need later."

He briefly turned on his flashlight, then smiled when he noted the four numbers. "A gate code, I take it."

"He's expecting me at ten."

"Most excellent. I've asked Tank to tell his men to take the evening off."

"Perfect."

"You are a genius, my dear Ariana."

She smiled at him in the mirror. "So, to the villa?"

"Drop me off there. Then wait for my text to pick me up."

They drove into the mountains and rode along the spine for a few minutes. At a driveway, she pulled to the side of the road. "Your villa, kind sir. You can hide in the trees here, then wait."

Makmoud slipped from the SUV. His location offered cover and provided a good view of the gate. He checked his watch. Getting on toward half past eight. He hoped Tank didn't renege on his word. Otherwise, Makmoud would have more work to do before he seriously contemplated putting his blown-apart life back together. From where he sat, he had a straight view down the driveway to the villa where a Range Rover and Ford Escape were parked.

Laughter caught his attention. Gravel crunched as the silhouettes of three men appeared in the dim porch light. Car doors slammed, and a moment later, the headlights of the Range Rover flashed across him. He ducked low and hoped no one had seen him.

Not to worry. Their guard was down because the boss had given them the night off. The gate opened and closed, and within seconds, the engine noise faded to the hum of the nighttime insects. Most likely, Tank's men wouldn't return for a while.

Makmoud checked his watch. Gradually, his eyes reoriented to the total darkness brought on by a new moon, and he discerned all he needed to see. He carefully made his way to the gate. A keypad stuck out from the side of the driveway. He entered the four-digit code. A moment later, the gate whirred open. He strolled through and listened. Low conversation. More like arguing that had been going on for a bit.

Tank huffed out a breath. "I'm done discussing your problems with my security. I'm wiped out, okay? I'm headed inside," Tank said. "Don't stay out here too long because even St. John isn't the safest."

"You're treating me like a toddler," Roo whined.

"'Cause you're acting like one. Good night, Roo. And remember to at least dye your hair back to its normal color, and maybe a good night's rest will help you act like a decent human being when your family gets here tomorrow night." Footsteps receded into the house. Upstairs, a light clicked on in a room.

Makmoud crept closer so he had a view of the patio with its beautiful pool and covered bar. Lights glowed dimly from the bar's ceiling. Behind it, Roo poured himself some sort of a drink in a very tall glass. He retreated to a chaise lounge in the shadows at the far end of the pool.

All the more perfect for the job Makmoud needed to do. He watched a few more minutes as Roo downed most of his drink, then belched before yawning long and loud. So disgusting. Any lady friend would be appalled.

Makmoud checked his watch again. Ten. Exactly when the man expected the woman of his dreams. He'd get the man of his nightmares instead.

He strolled onto the patio and made sure the light was to his back to block out his features.

"Ariana? Zat you?" Roo slurred.

Good. His reflexes would be slower now. He struggled to a sitting position and pushed to his feet. "Ariana?"

It finally registered that the silhouette he saw wasn't a woman. Roo froze. "Who… who are you?"

"Someone who has a bit of payback for you," Makmoud replied and let his accent bleed through. His hand slid to the stiletto blade he'd strapped across his chest.

"What…"

Makmoud jabbed him in the face with his fist. It wasn't a heavy hit, just one to knock him off balance and infuriate him.

Roo staggered. With a growl, he charged.

Makmoud ducked under the sloppy swing.

Roo spun around and swayed. He came at Makmoud again.

Makmoud drew the blade and drove it hard up underneath his ribcage. The man's eyes widened. He opened his mouth to scream, but no sound came out as the blood instantly drained from a vital artery. Makmoud withdrew the knife and gently pushed him toward the pool. With a mighty splash, he toppled into the water, his blood staining the azure water a dark red.

Makmoud knelt and dipped his blade into the pool. As he wiped it on his pants leg and slid it back into its sheath, he gazed toward the house.

Tank stood on a balcony, his hands in the pockets of his pants.

With a small salute, Makmoud retreated the same way he came. One brief text ensured that Ariana picked him up. She drove him to her small rental in the lower level of another nearby villa.

While she steeped some tea, he showered under as hot a stream as he could manage. They said nothing as they shared a cup of tea on the veranda. She retreated to bed, and he lay on the veranda's couch the rest of the night and contemplated how empty his life now was without Susana and his daughters.

As the sun rose, he spent a silent breakfast with Ariana, then she took him to the marina. He dropped his bag into the motorboat and faced her. This time he spoke in Farsi rather than English. "Thank you for your help."

"The pleasure was mine," she replied in the same language, her dark gaze sleepy and solemn at the same time. "If you're going to stay in this hemisphere, don't be a stranger. Come and visit me on Grand Cayman. I own a villa there. It will be nice to see a familiar face."

He offered only a brief smile as an answer.

She stood on tiptoes and kissed him. Her lips were soft and full and reminded him of Susanna. His heart skidded, and he pulled away.

She stepped back. "Take care, Makmoud Hidari. I will see you again, I'm sure."

Maybe. He flipped her a small salute and unloosed the lines. Then he headed toward the British Virgin Islands and his very uncertain future.

39

"Birthday, schmirthday," Butch muttered as he stood behind the counter at his shop and rang up the receipts for the night. He'd been open today for the auto emergencies that always seemed to happen Thanksgiving weekend. It'd been a skeleton crew of him and one other guy. He stuffed the deposit bag full of the day's proceeds.

Time to call it and head home, then out to the ranch. They were going to pick up Suleiman, then head for a soiree at Regions Café. Read, celebrate the milestone birthday he'd always dreaded. He felt his age now more than ever thanks to his bum ankle. At least it was healing on schedule. He'd shed the crutches and scooter a month ago and now wore a space boot that allowed him to put weight on it. PT would begin in earnest in a couple of weeks.

His phone pinged. Shelly. Are you coming? You need to get ready.

Outta here. Running by the bank, and I'll be home. With that, he shut off the lights, locked up, and hobbled to his truck. After popping the locks, he tossed the deposit bag onto the front passenger seat and grasped the handle to haul himself inside. A piece of paper sat on the driver's seat. He froze. "Hello. What's this?"

Butch whipped around and surveyed his surroundings. Not a soul around. With one eye on the parking lot, he unfolded it and scanned the writing. Not English, for sure. Arabic? Nope. Farsi? A shiver worked its way up his spine as he considered the ramifications of that. Someone had broken into his truck during the workday and left it. He fought the notion of running back inside and looking at the security cams. They probably would show nothing but a person skilled at staying off camera. And doing so would make him impossibly late.

With a growl, he stuffed the paper into his leather jacket pocket, hopped inside, and completed his errand before heading to the apartment. Shelly greeted him at the door. Oh, man. His mouth watered as he drank in the elegant black dress she'd worn to their rehearsal dinner. Her curls piled on her head. Two teased her cheeks and dared him to wrap them around his fingers. And that perfume. Made him want to shout, "Sorry, guys, we won't be there 'cause I've got to romance my wife."

"Babe, you're gorgeous." He drew her into a kiss and savored it until she giggled. Against her mouth, he murmured, "Do we have to go?"

She gently pushed him back a little. "Yes. Not going won't prevent you from turning forty."

He laughed and headed to the shower. With the water running to warm up, he took off his space boot and stared. So pitiful. Thanks to atrophy, his calf had shrunk to half its size. The doc promised he'd regain his muscle tone. He could only hope. Once showered, he carefully trimmed his beard and checked the hoops in his ears. Nice and polished. He pulled on a pair of black jeans and a sailcloth shirt. On his good foot, he added his silver-tipped boot. On his bad foot, he added a thick wool sock and the space boot. Then came his silver-trimmed belt. Yeah, he'd match Shelly in the looks department.

"Butch, we're running late," Shelly called, then whistled when he emerged. Conformation he looked as good as he'd hoped.

He walked her outside and helped her into his truck. Once they were on their way to Last Chance Ranch, he asked, "Why couldn't Suleiman ride with some of the others?"

"Because Sana's going directly from Pause. She had to work late, and she saw no need for him to drive all the way into town since she'll drive him home. And Diana had to go to the hospital for an emergency and is meeting us there. And Fi's already in town. And Vic's got Deborah."

"Gotcha. Point taken. Well, let's go get the boy, then." As he drove, Shelly's thumbs flew across the screen of her phone. "Who ya texting?"

"Mom. She's wanting to know when we're arriving for Christmas." She dimmed her screen and slid the phone into her purse. Twenty minutes later, they passed through the gates of Last Chance Ranch. No lights were on in the al-Ibrahim house. Hopefully, Suleiman was waiting just inside the door.

Butch knocked, and the it cracked open. Suleiman peered around it. "Come, in."

"We're late," Butch grumped.

"So sorry. I forgot the gift. It is back in the bedroom. Come inside."

Butch cast a look at Shelly. "You're rubbing off on him."

She shut the door behind her. "Very funny, dear husband."

"Surprise!" voices shouted in the sudden glare of light.

Butch nearly jumped out of his skin. "What the—"

"Happy fortieth!" Shelly sang out as the team crowded around him.

His smile spread across his face. "Wow, this is so cool!" He gazed around at the decorations. No Over-the-Hill black decorations like he'd feared. Instead, happy ones, ones that made him realize that forty was just a number and nothing else. Unexpectedly, tears filled his eyes. He fought them back and grinned. "This is great guys."

"Let's eat!" Sana sang out.

"Boy, y'all got me good. All of your excuses?"

"Just excuses." Victor winked. "Now is forty so bad?"

"Not with you guys at the helm." Butch filled his plate until it heaped with food. "This is so wonderful. Thanks, y'all."

They all settled around the dining room table. He gazed at his eight closest friends in the world. His heart filled as he remembered just how close he'd come to losing them all that summer. That reminded him. "Be back in a sec."

He rose and retrieved the note from his jacket pocket. "I was leaving work and found this in my truck."

Sana frowned. "Inside?"

"Yep. Someone put it there. It ain't English, of course. Or Arabic. Maybe Farsi?"

Suleiman took it from him and studied it. In a quiet voice, he announced, "It is."

A shiver that had nothing to do with the first snow of the season that had begun falling outside worked its way up Butch's spine. "What does it say?"

"'You have no need to fear now. Justice has been done. Makmoud.'" Suleiman raised his gaze. "That is what it says."

For better or worse. Butch stared at his plate. He'd seen the news reports, had watched the television just about all day as every network reported on Roo's murder. The man had died from a single, expertly placed stab wound. Tank Russell, his security head, had been in bed and seen no one slip on and off the property. Butch doubted that. His heart ached for Tina and the kids, now collateral damage thanks to Roo's foolish actions. Until a new election could be held, the current lieutenant governor would take the helm of the state.

"Sorry. Didn't mean to put a damper on things."

Victor took a deep breath. "Roo gambled and lost. That's all I can say."

"Amen."

The silence grew thick. Awkward. Finally, Sana rose and asked, "Anyone want cake?"

At her suggestion, the mood lightened, and with laughter and some seriously bad singing, the team pronounced Butch to be officially forty. More laughter followed as they began a massive round of Uno, his favorite game, that would last well into the night. Throughout it all, he noted Diana had gone quiet. Diana of the ready wit and laugh that always brought a smile to his face. When she headed into the kitchen, he followed her. "You doing okay?"

"Working on it," she replied as she poured herself a Coke. "You know how this time of year is for me."

Her struggles with depression in the winter had been the subject of many of his prayers. "I'm sorry."

"We lost another patient today. It's harder during this time of year." She sipped her drink and sighed. "I'm actually taking a six-month leave of absence next year. Well, three months volunteer work, some travel, then another month of volunteer work."

Butch nodded. "I think that'll do you some good."

"I hope. C'mon." She nodded toward the others, who laughed and chatted. "Let's go play some Uno."

Later that night, much later, Butch helped Shelly into her coat. He wasn't ready to go to bed. Not by a long shot. They walked outside. He wrapped his arm around her shoulders and kissed her temple. "That was the best, babe."

She faced him. "You liked it?"

"Of course! Who knew you could dress up for a party in a home?" He gazed at her as the snowflakes created a delicate netting on her hair, like God Himself had adorned her. He wanted that moment to last forever—until he remembered their warm bed at home. "I love you, babe. And I will always cherish you." With that he tipped her chin and kissed her lips.

At last, deep in his heart, true healing had come.

ACKNOWLEDGEMENTS

It's hard to believe that I'm now more than halfway through the Last Chance series. It's been a journey, for sure. And many thanks to those who have accompanied me through this journey. Many thanks to God for blessing me with the ability to write. And thanks to my family, especially Steve, for being an encouragement to me over the years. Many thanks to my beta readers, who didn't let me get away with anything. Rich, Pam, Jenny, Robin, and Steve, thank you. Your suggestions and ideas made this book what it is. Linda, thank you so much for your edits. They were spot-on, as always. And many thanks to my new cover designer, Hanna Linder of Hannah Linder Designs. I'm so thankful to have her on the team. And many thanks to my prayer group. Matt, Lisa, Randy, Cathy, Nathan, Viviane, Andrea, Garrett, Cindy, Bill, Chris, Terri, Kate, Jonathan, Craig, Christine, Mark, and Elizabeth, thank you for praying me through this. Your prayer cover is invaluable. Blessings to all of you who are my readers too. Without you, none of this would be possible.